Aristophanes

Eight Comedies of Aristophanes

Aristophanes

Eight Comedies of Aristophanes

ISBN/EAN: 9783744777025

Printed in Europe, USA, Canada, Australia, Japan

Cover: Foto ©Andreas Hilbeck / pixelio.de

More available books at **www.hansebooks.com**

EIGHT ·COMEDIES ·

OF

ARISTOPHANES

TRANSLATED INTO RHYMED METRES

BY

LEONARD-HAMPSON RUDD, M.A.

LONDON

LONGMANS, GREEN, AND CO.

1867

CONTENTS.

GENERAL INTRODUCTION.

THE OBJECT of the Translator has been to offer a readable version of the Comedies of Aristophanes to the English general reader; an engraving from a picture to which he has no access. At the same time he must own the hope that his rendering may not be unacceptable to scholars, who have not mastered all the comedies of his author, and even to some who have done so; inasmuch as the careful engraver, while studying his original, may bring out features in the composition not noticed by every eye. But, wishing to say and profess as little of himself as possible, he disclaims the ambition of having primarily addressed himself to scholars.

Whether the object which has been avowed was in any way feasible, seems to depend on the answers which may be found to several questions. 1. How far any comedy of Aristophanes could be presented as a readable whole, after every stain of grossness has been thoroughly discharged from the page? 2. Seeing that these productions are in the nature of photographs from the political and social life of the place and period, how far their abounding wit and humour could be made appreciable by those who are not already instructed and interested in the men and events of the time? 3. How much of pure wit would remain after the most part of that kind of humour which depends upon parody or play of words had been evaporated in the process of translation?

If the Translator had not hoped that his versions would give a reasonably satisfactory answer to these questions, of course he would not now be venturing to offer them to the public.

Whatever might be the result, he undertook with himself that his pages should be as free, not only from every expression, but from every hint or suggestion of license as is happily the best light literature of this day. This requirement has, in his judgment, necessitated in two or three cases the excision of scenes, the point of which seemed to depend on an exceptionable idea, though that might not be absolutely expressed.

In consideration of the second difficulty also the Translator has allowed himself occasional curtailment of his original. Those to whom smaller features of personal or political allusion will be interesting, will have command of them from the Author's text.

It is an evil that a poem, serious or comic, should require notes at all. But for the first reading of Aristophanes they are indispensable. Aiming, however, always at being sparing, the Translator hopes that he has given sufficient to assist the mere English reader who would be likely to find interest or amusement in these Comedies. They may stimulate some who read to ask further information on the events or customs referred to. In these days one may feel confidence that books of reference for such matter will be easily within the reach of such a class of readers.

These Comedies not only contain lively pictures of Athenian life, but are remarkable as having been produced for the amusement of the very people who are caricatured. The Wit and Poet, whose productions have won for him a world-wide and enduring name, submitted his work to the judgment of the whole indiscriminate mass of Athenian citizens gathered in the public theatres. These Comedies, a mere specimen of their kind, remain to us a monument of the high quality of wit, thought, and expression which this People could appreciate and enjoy. The case is so remarkable, nay, so unique in the world's history, that it may excuse a few suggestive observations on the social and intellectual training of this democracy of art-critics. The more, as the same will illustrate generally some of those special characteristics of the Athenian citizen with which Aristophanes is constantly making merry.

The Day of MARATHON, it will be seen, is again and again touched as if it were the beginning of Athenian history, the Birthday of the State. It was not indeed quite that, but it was the day on which the State came of age. The People who were the life and soul of the Anti-Persian Confederacy had been formed in the silence of many generations; but from that day forth they felt their own life and rights and power: they took their own place, and began to push their way to preeminence among the independent communities, known to us collectively as *Greece*. For a long time their political constitution had been that of a limited aristocracy. Political power had originally been apportioned to classes in the ratio of their means of contributing to State-burdens. But as the rich must always be the few, and as in a State not yet commercial, wealth will generally be hereditary, the aristocracy of wealth would naturally pass into one of birth. Magistracies and commands would come to be regarded as the right of men of family. But by the constitution of Solon the whole mass of the People in Common Assembly had at least a restraining share in government, ready to become very effective, whenever political power came to be valued. That time came. The Common Assembly in the Pnyx assumed and used its power legislative and executive. All free citizens were entitled to an equal vote in the Assembly. Many touches in these Comedies will show how the right of citizenship was jealously guarded against intrusion, and what pains were taken to establish the inherited right. Freedom then had a real meaning in relation to this right. It meant that the man was not a slave, but the master of slaves. In *Wasps* we shall see that the old man, who was so keen in earning the paltry daily fee of a dicast, was the master of at least two slaves. Household-service, farm-work, handiwork of all kinds, was done by slaves. So the citizen living in Athens had ample leisure to attend to business, and his business was self-government. There was no idea of being governed by Representation. The citizen living in the country acquiesced generally in the acts of his fellows in the city; but he might at any time come in and take his part with them. To make laws, then, was the business of every one. A People by nature very shrewd and energetic liked their business. Thus were they habituated to hearing arguments for and against measures, with the responsibility of decision lying upon them. The peculiar constitution of Athens opened to every citizen, not only the legislative Assembly, but the law courts too. They were free, and they were encouraged, to serve in them in great bodies, as dicasts, as something between our idea of a presiding judge of the law, and jurymen, whose province is the fact. A silent revolution was effected during the long State-management, or, so to say, ministry, of Pericles. Under his influence many matters were withdrawn from the more aristocratic court of Areopagus, to be submitted to the jurisdiction of the open popular courts: while he encouraged service in these courts by providing for the payment of a fee for every attendance.

In this way, again, a people was formed, accustomed daily to hear acute discussions of right and wrong, and to weigh arguments and evidence. It is a marked feature of every one of these Comedies that they are addressed to a people of such habits. It is curious to observe how Aristophanes, while he is reprobating the habit of mind so engendered, is constantly using it, and pandering to it. Such were some of the influences at work to train that peculiar people, to whose judgment Tragic and Comic Dramatists and Orators could submit works, which the intellect of all times since has accepted as masterpieces and models.

A few words more on the general political position of the Athenian Democracy in the early days of Aristophanes. When Pericles entered into public life he had all the title to power which the highest birth and connections could give him. But he did not represent the sentiments or interests of his class. The aristocratic party was in opposition to him. He crushed it; and by the banishment of its leader, Thucydides son of Milesias, obtained undisputed ascendency to the end of his life. So long, however, as Pericles was at the head of the democracy, the most fastidious aristocrat might feel himself under a government directed by a man of unquestionable genius, integrity, and refinement. Not so after his death. This was exactly the crisis when Aristophanes, as a very young man, appears upon the scene. Pericles had governed the People by the People. On his death they found the government in their own hands; and soon disposed themselves to follow the lead of men sprung from their own order, such as Cleon and Hyperbolus. Against this the very tastes, as well as the interests, of the old aristocratic party revolted. They cast about for the hope and means of recovering their old rights and influence. It seemed that they might be aided by the intervention of States where Aristocracy was still dominant, such as Corinth and Lacedæmon. Whereas the Democracy of Athens was, as such a polity usually is, propagandist. The collision between the two principles, long threatening, determined in the *Peloponnesian War*; wherein the parties were Athens and the democratic against Sparta and the oligocratic

interest.   Under such circumstances there was of course
a party within Athens whose hearts were really with *the*
enemy.   Of this party manifestly was Aristophanes.   Let
those who will approve and defend his political principles
and sagacity.   He is here presented only as wit, poet, and
painter of manners.

Subjoined is a brief Chronological Table, chiefly drawn
from Clinton's *Fasti Hellenici*.   It will tell not only the
order in which these Comedies were put upon the stage,
but may render some notes needless, or briefer, by indicating the date of historical events alluded to in the
Comedies, or of interest in connection with them.

CHRONOLOGICAL TABLE.

B.C.

490. Battle of Marathon. Æschylus a combatant.
480. Battle of Salamis. Euripides born.
472. Æschylus exhibits his Tragedy *Persians.*
471. Themistocles ostracised. Naxos reduced. *Wasps,* l. 186.
469. Great Earthquake at Sparta. Pericles enters public life.
468. Birth of Socrates.
456. Death of Æschylus, æt. 69.
446. Birth of Aristophanes (or within two years later).
     Birth of Eupolis.
445. Revolt of Eubœa. *Clouds,* l. 187.
     Attica invaded by Peloponnesians under Pleistoanax.
     Truce for thirty years.
444. Ostracism of Thucydides, son of Milesias.
431. Peloponnesian War. First Invasion of Attica. Alliance of Athens
     with Sitalces, King in Thrace.
430. Second Invasion of Attica. Plague at Athens.
429. Death of Pericles. Birth of Plato.
     Naval actions under Phormion. *Knights,* l. 562. *Peace,* l. 286.
428. Third Invasion of Attica.
427. Aristophanes gains second prize with *Daitaleis.*
     Fourth Invasion.
426. *Babylonians,* in which Aristophanes reflects severely upon his fellow-
     citizens in presence of Strangers.
425. ACHARNIANS, at the festival Lenæa.
     Fifth Invasion of Attica.
     Demosthenes occupies Pylos. Lacedæmonians cut off in the island
     Sphacteria.
     Expedition against Corinth in which Knights took part. Thucyd.
     iv. 42. *Knights,* l. 602.
     Lacedæmonians on Sphacteria surrender to Cleon.
     Overtures for accommodation from Sparta.
424. KNIGHTS, first prize. Cratinus, second prize.
     Amphipolis taken by Brasidas. Miscarriage of Thucydides, the
     Historian. Sitalces killed fighting against the Triballi.
423. Truce for a year. CLOUDS. Cratinus, first prize.
422. WASPS. Hostilities recommenced. Death of Cratinus, æt. 97.
     Death of Cleon and Brasidas in Thrace.

B.C.
421. Truce with Lacedæmonians for fifty years.
419. PEACE.
415. Athenian expedition of conquest to Sicily, under Nicias, Alcibiades, and Lamachus. Alcibiades recalled by the 'Salaminian.' *Birds,* l. 128. Escapes on his return.
414. BIRDS. Lamachus falls in Sicily.
413. Demosthenes takes reinforcements to Sicily. Utter destruction of Athenian fleet and forces in Sicily. Nicias and Demosthenes taken and put to death.
411. Oligarchic revolution effected in Athens under Pisander. Phrynicus joins the oligarchs. The 400. Phrynicus assassinated. Subversion of the 400. Pisander, Alexicles, Aristarchus, and others of the party quit Attica. Alcibiades recalled by the citizens in the fleet.
Lysistrata. Thesmophoriazusæ.
408. *First Plutus.*
406. Sea fight at Arginusæ.
Erasinides and other commanders put to death.
Death of Euripides.
405. Death of Sophocles, æt. 90. FROGS.
Athenian fleet destroyed at Ægospotami.
404. The Thirty Tyrants.
Athens surrenders to Lysander. End of Peloponnesian War.
399. Death of Socrates.
392. *Ecclesiazusæ.*
388. SECOND PLUTUS.

ACHARNIANS.

B

INTRODUCTION.

A SLIGHT KNOWLEDGE of the events of the Peloponnesian War in its first years is necessary in order to read this comedy with intelligence and appreciation.

CORRIGENDA

Page 21, line 10, *for* Shrew'd *read* Shrewd
„ 24, „ 14,' „ hearts „ heart's
„ 90, note 1, *after* in *supply* which
„ 133, „ 3, *for* scoliasts *read* scholiasts, *et passim*
„ 141, line 25, „ determined *read* determine
„ 191, „ 34, „ lay „ lie
„ 194, „ 22, „ sillus „ Sillus
„ 227, „ 16, „ supplied „ suppled
„ 254, „ 27, „ us „ our
„ 267, „ 24, „ you go „ go you
„ 294, note, *dele* index figure '4,' *and connect with preceding line.*
„ 313, line 21, *supply* Dram. Pers. *Text.*
„ 362, „ 21, *for* thy *read* the
„ 441, „ 20, *after* Giving *read* to

The Spartan trusted that such a body driven within the city walls, and having each man his even vote in the Popular Assembly, would influence the Athenians to come out and withstand him. He was disappointed. The smoke of the place went up in sight of the city walls—indeed, as it would seem by some lines in the opening of this comedy, in sight of the Pnyx, the very spot where the Popular Assembly was held : but no one came out. It did not consist either with the military art of the time to form the siege of large places, or with the habits of the Spartans to

B 2

INTRODUCTION.

A SLIGHT KNOWLEDGE of the events of the Peloponnesian War in its first years is necessary in order to read this comedy with intelligence and appreciation.

By reference to the Chronological Table it will be seen that in the previous six years there had been four invasions of Attica. In these efforts the Lacedæmonian energy had spent itself and was defeated by passive resistance. The Lacedæmonians were confident in their prowess as soldiers, and perhaps justly promised themselves superiority if the Athenians would meet them in the field. But the wisdom and moral influence of Pericles restrained them from being drawn to play the game of the enemy. He persuaded the country population of Attica to retire behind the city walls, and refuse battle. Archidamus, who led the Peloponnesian Confederates in the early invasions, could not believe that the Athenians would endure to see their country ravaged without striking a blow for it. For some days he held his troops only threatening the important district round ACHARNÆ. This was one of the largest boroughs of Attica, furnishing 4,000 able men and citizens.

The Spartan trusted that such a body driven within the city walls, and having each man his even vote in the Popular Assembly, would influence the Athenians to come out and withstand him. He was disappointed. The smoke of the place went up in sight of the city walls—indeed, as it would seem by some lines in the opening of this comedy, in sight of the Pnyx, the very spot where the Popular Assembly was held : but no one came out. It did not consist either with the military art of the time to form the siege of large places, or with the habits of the Spartans to

B 2

remain for any length of time in the field. Therefore having done as much damage as they could, after so many days' service, the confederated forces broke up, and each retired home. The operation was repeated in the following summer, and followed, in Athens, by the memorable and terrible plague. It is curious that Aristophanes nowhere refers to this scourge. Probably the fear of contact with it restrained the Peloponnesians from an invasion in the third year. At the end of six years, however, and though the master-mind of Pericles had passed away, the patriotic spirit of the Athenians remained unbroken.

There was, no doubt, a party in Athens opposed to the policy of the war from the beginning, and therefore ready at any time to seize an opportunity for promoting peace. To Aristophanes the sufferings of the last six years seemed to favour such a proposition. The play *Acharnians* is in fact such a suggestion made from the stage of Comedy. DICÆOPOLIS, the principal person, is a supposed yeoman of that very borough *Acharnæ*. Had the yeomen of all Attica been as short-sighted and selfish in their views as he is represented, Archidamus would not have been disappointed. Though Dicæopolis is nominally a countryman, he is not invested with any such characteristics as would give the impression that he really represented that class. On the contrary he is the same *citizen*, who will appear again and again under various names and circumstances; he is selfish, shrewd, ready of speech, thoroughly at home when he has got into an argument, and, confiding in his rhetorical powers, ready to risk everything on the certainty of making his points.

Aristophanes had the populace of Athens before him. He is evidently in earnest in his argument for disposing them towards the idea of peace with Sparta. The difficulty and the art with which he approaches this theme; first throwing it out playfully, then for a while diverting his audience with a witty quizzing of Euripides, all show how popular the war still was, how the ravages of the confederates had rather embittered the contest than disposed the sufferers to submit as the worsted party.

The comedy opens with some very lively sketches from

the PNYX, the court and presence-chamber of this royal people in General Assembly. In the second part the reader will make a first acquaintance with that pest of Athenian life, the Sycophant or Informer, and with Aristophanes's way of handling him. Though the name of Lamachus is historical, the character under that name in the comedy is so evidently a fancy picture, that it does not call for any vindication of a patriotic man and good soldier from the ridicule here cast upon him.

The comedy obtained the first prize or place : and it is only just to observe that it was the production of a man yet under twenty-one, or, as some suppose, only nineteen.

Dramatis Personæ.

DICÆOPOLIS *of Acharnæ.*

HERALD, *or Crier of the Court.*

AMPHITHEUS, *a crazy Citizen of Athens.*

Athenian AMBASSADORS *returned from the Court of Persia.*

SHAMARTABAS, *a pretended Envoy from the Persian King.*

Athenian ENVOY, *returned from the Court of Sitalces.*

CHORUS *of Acharnian Charcoal-burners.*

WIFE *and* DAUGHTER *of Dicæopolis.*

EURIPIDES, *the Tragic Poet.*

CEPHISOPHON, *Servant of Euripides.*

LAMACHUS, *a Soldier, and Partisan for War.*

A Megarian.

A Bœotian.

An Informer.

NICARCHUS, *another Informer.*

A Servant of Lamachus.

A Farmer.

A Bridegroom's-Man.

An Archer of the Town-Guard.

Messengers.

DICÆOPOLIS, *alone in the Pnyx.*

I'M sad and sick at heart : for few my satisfactions ;
They are but four poor things ; and then for my distrac-
tions,
They are sandmountain-fold. Come, let me count my
treasure.
What was it I enjoyed worthy the name of pleasure?
Ah ! yes, the sight of those five talents brought to light,
When Cleon threw them up ; that was a true delight.
I thank the Knights for it ; it was their doing, and
Done worthily of Greece.[1]   But on the other hand,
That was a tragic trouble—when my mouth was wide
Expecting Æschylus,[2] and then the herald cried—
' Theognis lead the Chorus in ; ' 'twill be believed
How very dreadful was the shock my heart received.
But then, I own, it cheered me up, and made me laugh
To see Dexitheus come in upon the calf
To sing Bœotian ; but when Chæris thrust his head
Upon the stage to pipe the Orthian I was dead !
But never since the day when first I knew the touch
Of soft soap on my eyelids did I smart so much
As now. This is their way ; the people should have met
This morning early, but there's not a soul come yet !
They're in the market-place to know what news is toward,
And shifting here and there to dodge the scarlet cord ;[3]

---

[1] Cleon was the reigning favourite of the people at this time, and the
principal object of Aristophanes's attack. It is unfortunate that we do
not know more of the circumstances here alluded to. It is alleged that
Cleon took a bribe of five talents from the islands to procure an alleviation
of their contributions to the anti-Persian confederacy, of which Athens
was the leading naval power, and further that he had in some way
insulted the order of Knights. No connection between the two facts
appears. But the Knights prosecuted him, and he was fined this
amount.

[2] Æschylus had been dead more than thirty years ; but dramas left by
him had been produced upon the stage.

[3] When no exciting business was toward, it was difficult to get a

Here are not even Presidents! Some hours too late
Will they rush in and set their elbows to debate
About the foremost bench. And what care they for Peace?
Oh! City, City, how shall our disorders cease?
Here, day by day, the first to come, I sit alone
And look about me, gape, I stretch my limbs and groan:
I don't know what to do; I scribble, pluck my hair,
I calculate. I let my eye rove here and there,
I see the fields afar, and let my heart go longing;
I hate the City ways; and thoughts of home come thronging!
Oh, for my borough home! where no one says, 'Come buy'
Coals, vinegar, or oil; we do not know the cry.
For who would buy the things which every farm produces?
But I have yet my plan to deal with these abuses.
Yes, they may try to speak; but no one shall be heard
For noise and jeering who shall dare to speak a word
Except about a Peace. But here they are with noon,
These Presidents! exactly as I said; and soon
Will follow, I predict, that hustle for a place.

[*Enter Presidents of the Assembly with a mixed crowd,
Heralds, Archers of the Guard,* AMPHITHEUS, *Ambassadors. Noise and hustling while they are taking
their places.*

Herald. Pass forward! pass to be within the lustral
        space.
Amphitheus (apart to Dicæopolis). Has anyone yet spoken?
Her.   Who desires to speak?
Amp. I do.
Her.   Your name?
Amp.   Amphitheus.
Her.   In simple Greek
'God on both sides;'[1]—but are you not a man?

---

sufficient number of people to attend the Assembly and transact ordinary
business; at such times two public officers were sent into the market-
place to fish it with a long line covered with ruddle or red paint. Whoever was touched by the cord was bound to attend the Assembly.

[1] That is the meaning of 'Amphitheus.' This is not expressed, but
necessarily implied in the question of the Herald.

Amp.   I'm not,
But an immortal. For Triptolemus begot,
Demeter bore to him, Amphitheus; and he
Keleos, who intermarried with Phœnareté,
My grandame; then of her Lucinus saw the light;
He was my sire; and therefore in my parents' right
I am immortal. Now unto my single care
It is committed by the Gods to you to bear
The overtures for Peace; I have not drawn my pay,
Nor, being an immortal, rations for the way;
In truth, the Prytanes will not—

Her.   Ho, archers there!

Amp. Oh my Triptolemus and Celeus, will ye bear [1]—

            [*Archers of the guard drag* AMP. *out of
the Pnyx.*

Dic. Ye wrong us, Prytanes, to oust a man who begs
To bring us peace and hang our shields upon their pegs.

Her. Sit down and hold your tongue.

Dic.   Not I, unless the question
Of Peace may be debated upon this suggestion.

Her. The Legates from the King—

Dic.   What king?—I can't abide
Legates and peacock's tails, and coxcombs with their pride!

Her. Silence!

          [*Ambassadors come forward in Persian
costume.*

Dic.   What figures!

Ambassadors.   You despatched us to the King
At two drachms daily for our pains and wayfaring.
Euthymenes was archon—

Dic.   Oh! the drachms! [2]

---

[1] Such was the popularity of the war at this period, that Aristophanes had undertaken a work of great personal risk in making a suggestion in behalf of peace; but this is obviously the aim of this drama. By way of preparing the minds of the audience for the line Dicæopolis is going to take, the dramatist begins by putting the proposal of peace in the mouth of a man *obviously crazy*. This, it appears to me, is the explanation of the part here given to Amphitheus.

[2] Euthymenes was archon eleven years before this time. So long had these ambassadors been on their mission, and so long had the pay been running.

Amb.   The pains
Of travel we endured on the Caÿstrian plains
Were hard to tell, the tented bivouac, the loads
Of cushions in the cars that bore us o'er their roads;
We'd nearly died of it.
    Dic. (aside)   I was in luck to sleep
Under the parapet upon a rubbish heap.
    Amb. There was no help for it where we entertained
But out of gold and crystal goblets must be drained
The richest wines untempered.
    Dic. (aside)   Simple citizen!
That you should bear to be bamboozled by such men!
    Amb. Three years and something more of this brought
        us at last
To the King's palace: there they brought for our repast
Whole oxen from the oven.
    Dic. (aside)   Home-baked bullocks! lies!
    Amb. Yes, and, by Jove, a bird of most enormous size,
At least three times the figure of Cleonymus,[1]
The name of it was Chetah.
    Dic. (aside)   You are cheating us,
With your two drachmas.
    Amb.   Now we bring you the 'King's eye'
Shamartabas.[2]
    Her.   The King's Eye.

    Enter SHAMARTABAS *and another as Persians.*

    Amb.   Vouchsafe, Sir, to say why
You come to Athens from the King, and what to say.
    Shamart. I artoman exarx ampissonai satray.
    Amb. You understand him?
    Dic.   By Apollo, not a word.

---

[1] Cleonymus, not otherwise known, is a perpetual butt for Aristophanes, as having two of the qualities of Falstaff upon which Shakespeare plays, superabundance of flesh and lack of valour. *Clouds,* 318. *Knights,* 1150. *Birds,* 272, 1307.

[2] The 'King's Eye' evidently a translation of the Persian name of office. For the stage he was dressed in character, with a mask having one huge eye.

Amb. He says the King will send us gold.
　　　　　　(*to Shamartabas*)　You are not heard,
Speak louder, Sir ; and lay a stress upon the gold.
Sham. Filthy Ionian sall never catch de cold.
Dic. That's plain !
Amb.　　　　　　　What does he say ?
Dic.　　　　　　　　　Without a compliment
To us, he says that Persian gold will not be sent.
Amb. No, no, he says it will be sent in Persian sacks.
Dic. Sacks, you impostor ! pooh ! give way and let me
　　tax
The man myself,—I'll paint your face with crimson dye,
Unless before this man you make distinct reply.—
Will the Great King your master send us any gold ?
　　　　　　[SHAMARTABAS *and his Colleague toss*
　　　　　　back their heads.
Are they mere lies which our Ambassadors have told ?
　　　　　　　　　　　. [*They nod assent.*
They nod their heads in such Greek fashion, that 'tis clear
The home of these impostors is not far from here.
Herald. Silence ! sit down. The Senate orders me to call
The King's Eye to their dinner in the public hall.
　　　　　　[*The Athenian and Persian Ambassadors*
　　　　　　retire to dinner.
Dic. There now ! A man might hang himself for less !
　　and I
Am left behind to cool my heels till by and bye.
The door of hospitality is never shut
When men like these may be invited in—
　　　　　　　　　　　But, tut,
I'll do a deed ! a deed which shall amaze the land.
Where is Amphitheus ?—
Amp.　　　　　　　I'm here.
Dic.　　　　　　　　　Take these in hand,
Eight drachmas. Go to Sparta and contract for me,
My children and my wife, a league of amity.
　　　　　　[*Exit* AMPHITHEUS *taking the drachmas.*
　　　　　　(*Spoken towards the audience.*)
For you, ye citizens, I leave you to your views,
To send your legates, and stand open-mouthed for news.

Herald. Let the States' Envoy to Sitalces [1] enter.

Enter ENVOY.

Envoy.   Here.

Dic. (*aside*) Another swaggerer is summoned to appear.

Envoy. In Thrace we should not have so much prolonged
    our stay—

Dic. (*aside*) No, that ye would not but to draw prodigi-
    ous pay.

Envoy. But that a heavy snow lay deep upon the ground
Over the whole of Thrace, and all the streams were bound,
Just when Theognis [2] set his drama on your stage.
That time Sitalces was so good as to engage
Our company to drink with him.   And truly he
On all occasions shows his partiality
For everything Athenian.   For his love of you
He writes upon his palace walls in public view
NOBLE ATHENIANS. His son [3] desires to try
His civic rights upon an Apaturian fry ;
And for his country pleads : the father, nothing loth,
Over his cups has sworn to God a solemn oath
To send us such a host that all of you shall say
'What wind has blown us such a cloud of gnats to day ? '

Dic. (*aside*) I don't believe a word ; no, hang me if I do,
Except about the gnats.

Envoy.   Now he has sent to you
The most pugnacious tribe that Thracia can boast.

Dic. Aye, that now is distinct.

Herald.   .   Admit the Thracian host.

Enter a starveling rabble of Thracians.

Dic. What pestilence is this ?

Envoy.   An Odomantine corps :

---

[1] King of Thrace.

[2] The tragic poet referred to by Dicæopolis (line 11).   It is suggested
that the frigidity of his poetry produced the unusual fall of snow in
Thrace.

[3] Sadocus.   On the first day of the feast Apaturia all the members of
the same tribe supped together.   Sadocus had been, honoris gratia,
admitted to the freedom of the city.

Two drachmas' pay will send this wasting flood to pour
O'er all Bœotia.

Dic.   What? such raff at such rate?
Hear it and groan, ye men, ye bulwarks of the state
Who man our gallant ships.

> [*Some of the Thracians find and appropriate*
> *the little bundle containing* DICÆOPOLIS'S
> *dinner.*

          —Oh, oh, my garlic store!
I'm being wasted by the Odomantine corps.
Put down the garlic, brutes.

Envoy.   Beware, you silly brains,
How you go near them with the garlic in their veins.

Dic. Is this my country, Sir? am I a citizen
To bear this usage? and from such outlandish men?
I claim it of you, Presidents, to interfere.
Nay, I forbid your holding the Assembly here.
The sign of God to-day precludes your entertaining
The question of the day: I tell you, it is raining.[1]

Herald. Then let the Thracians go till the third day from
          hence.
The meeting is adjourned, pronounce the Presidents.

> [*Exeunt all but* DICÆOPOLIS.

Dic. I've lost a pretty salad: but in happy time
Here comes Amphitheus from Lacedæmon. I'm
Rejoiced to welcome you.

Enter AMPHITHEUS *running.*

Amp.   Pray give me time to slack
A little from my race. They're hot upon my track,
Those fellows from Acharnæ.

Dic.   What is this about?

Amp. As I was running past they smelt the truces out,
Old gnarled and knotted bucks, as tough as heart of oak,
Men who at Marathon had struck their honest stroke;

---

[1] Dicæopolis is here exercising the ordinary power of a citizen to
demand the adjournment of the meeting, by declaring an inauspicious
'sign,' such as tempest, rain, or ill-omened words.

They set upon me yelling, 'Vagabond,' they said,
'You have got truces while the vines are lying dead,'[1]
And gathered stones to pelt me : but I left them, flying
As fast as I could run, and they came after crying.

    Dic. And let them cry. But have you really got the
        truces?

    Amp. Yes. Here you have the 'five years.' Taste
        how rich the juice is.[2]   [DICÆOPOLIS *tastes.*

    Dic. Ah, bah !   [*rejects it.*

    Amp.   Why, what is this?

    Dic.   They please me not at all ;
They smell of pitch and stores brought to the arsenal.

    Amp. Then try the 'ten years.'

    Dic.   No, they have too strong a smack
Of looking for new friends, and old ones holding back.

    Amp. Here are the truces then for 'thirty years' com-
        plete
By land and sea.

    Dic. (tasting).   Oh, Bacchic festival, how sweet !
Ambrosia their smell, and nectar in their taste :
And never buying rations,[3] for the march in haste.
It hangs about the tongue ! that, 'Go just where you please,'
I take ; I make libation ; aye, I drink up these.
Acharnians, to you I wish a pleasant morrow,
But for myself, from war delivered and from sorrow,
I'll seek the Bacchic feast and leave all care behind me,
And take myself away, before my friends can find me.

                              [*Exit.*

Enter CHORUS (*in search of* AMPHITHEUS).

In each nook and by each crook come
        follow up this jackanapes ;
Ask about and search him out, for
        ours the shame if he escapes.

---

[1] Destroyed by the Lacedæmonians in their invasion of Attica.

[2] Amphitheus produces the truces in some visible form, apparently
like 'sample bottles' of wine.

[3] The Athenian citizen summoned to active service was obliged to
provide and take food for so many days. This annoyance is illustrated
in the Comedy *Peace*, l. 960.

If you can, show me the man, do ;
        for I cannot understand
Where he went so impudently
        bringing truces through the land.
We're astray ; he's stole away ; ah,
        this it is to carry age !
Never would it, never should it
        so have happened I engage,
In the time when in my prime, and
        caring not about my pace,
With a sack upon my back, I
        dared Phaÿllus [1] to the race.
Now my thigh is shrunk and dry, and
        I am stiff about the knees ;
So the fellow thinks to tell how
        he can beat Lacratides.
Vain the brag : we will not flag, or
        lose the credit of our town ;
Though we're old, I will be bold that
        we will hunt the rascal down.
Zeus's nods, and all the Gods ! he's
        made a treaty with the foes,
Whom I feel a growing zeal to
        hammer with redoubled blows.
Let them go, eh ? will I ? no, a
        rush will pierce them to the heart;
Going right in, sharp and biting,
        they shall wriggle with the smart.
Such a lesson I'll impress on
        those who come with such designs
To do harm upon my farm and
        cut and trample down the vines.
On his track ; and never slack
        until this rogue we've safely got.
Haply he may barely be a
        stonesthrow from this very spot.
As to throwing, there's no knowing
        when I shall have had my fill—

---

[1] A famous runner, thrice victor in the Pythian Games. Herod. viii. 47.

(*Voice of* Dicæopolis *behind the scene.*)
  Keep ye silence, keep ye silence.[1]
Chorus. Hush ! ye heard the mystic word
                    repressing every sound of ill.
  He was speaking, whom we're seeking ;
                    and it seems some holy rite
  Is enacting ; so retracting
                    let us not come into sight.
                    [Chorus *retire, concealing themselves.*

Enter Dicæopolis *in procession with his* Wife, Daughter,
    and Slaves, as about to sacrifice to Bacchus.

Dic. Keep ye silence, keep ye silence.
A little onward, basket-bearer.[2]
  Wife.   Stay a minute,
Put down the basket, girl, and so let us begin it.
  Daughter. Then mother, let me have the ladle here to
              take
Some porridge from the pot to put upon the cake.
  Dic. Lord Bacchus ! it is well that now from service free,
I with my family should celebrate to thee
The service in the fields ; Oh, prosper to our use
For me, and all of mine, these Thirty years of truce !
  Wife. Fair daughter, fairly bear the basket, and be sure
That those who see may say, ' She's steady and demure ; '
And when you get among the crowd, pray have a care
That nobody shall filch the ornaments you wear.
  Dic. Now I will sing the hymn ; so, basket-bearer, lead,
And you, wife, from the roof will look at us.   Proceed.
              Phales, lover of delight,
              Phales, roamer of the night,
              Haunting Bacchus as his friend,
              At these weary six years' end [3]

---

  [1] Ritual words of one about to sacrifice, to repress or obviate any words or sounds of ill-omen.
  [2] The girl would be the ' Basket-bearer,' represented in the well-known figure the ' Caryatis.' The basket contained fruits, woollen fillet, knife, and other requisites for sacrifice.
  [3] The comedy was produced in the seventh year of the war.

Gladly do I chant to thee.
Gladly I my borough greet;
I have had the hap to treat;
Wars no more shall trouble us,
Politics, nor Lamachus,
  All is past and I am free.
Drink with us, and in the morning
  Draughts of Peace shall cool your tongue;
Then my buckler, service scorning,
  In the chimney shall be hung.

> [*As soon as* DICÆOPOLIS *has finished his hymn,*
> *the* CHORUS *rush out from their hiding-*
> *place and pelt him with a volley of stones.*

Chorus.	'Tis the very rogue at last!
	At him; hit him; knock him down;
	All together, straight and fast
	Volley him from shin to crown.
Dic.	Hercules! but what is this?
	You will crack the holy jar.[1]
Cho.	You at least we shall not miss,
	dirty rascal as you are.
Dic.	Wherefore? tell me what's the matter,
	ancients of Acharnæ borough?
Cho.	Shameless fellow, dare you chatter?
	Scoundrel utter, rank and thorough!
	When you've made a truce, you traitor,
	and your guilt is very plain,
	Can you dare to stand and prate, or
	look me in the face again?
Dic.	Hear me : for you do not know
	why I made that truce alone, Sir.
Cho.	Hear you? hang you! never! go,
	we will bury you with stones, Sir.
Dic.	Wait until you understand,
	worthy fellows, I beseech.

---

[1] In which was the porridge referred to by the Daughter.

C

Cho.   No, I will not hold my hand;
                    do not think to make a speech,
For I hate you altogether
                    more than I do Cleon, whose
Hide I mean to turn to leather,
                    which shall find the Knights in shoes.[1]
Do not think to make excuses;
                    it were only waste of breath.
With the Spartans you have truces,
                    therefore you shall die the death.

Dic.   Put the Spartans out of question;
                    take it in its proper light;
Only hear a slight suggestion,
                    you will say that I was right.

Cho.   You were right indeed! when you
                    ventured upon entertaining
Commerce with a people who
                    have nor faith nor truth remaining.

Dic.   Spartans—yes, no doubt—are double-
                    minded fellows; all the same,
Though we hate them, for our trouble
                    they are not alone to blame.

Cho.   Not alone to blame! and dare you
                    say so much before my face,
And suppose that I will spare you,
                    speaking out your own disgrace?

Dic.   Not to blame for *all*, I say.
                    I could show from the beginning
Certain matters in which they
                    were more sinned against than sinning.

Cho.   This is truly past endurance!
                    and our temper overflows
When we see such cool assurance;
                    you are pleading for our foes.

Dic.   I will plead my cause and get
                    verdict in my favour on it;
Let a chopping-block be set;
                    I will stake my head upon it.

---

[1] This threat against Cleon seems carried out in the Comedy *Knights*.

Cho.   Fellow burghers, tell me why
                    we should longer spare the varlet?
          We have stones; so let them fly;
                    dress the fellow up in scarlet.
Dic.   What a sudden flame and smother
                    from a black and sleeping brand!
          Won't you listen to a brother,
                    worthy sons of charcoal-land? [1]
Cho.   Cease so vain a hope to cherish.
Dic.   You will greatly injure us.
Cho.   If I listen may I perish.
Dic.   Neighbours, do not answer thus.
Cho.   Know that you are going to die.
Dic.   Then will I strike through and through you.
          I will slaughter in reply
                    those whom you hold dearest to you.
          Whom I have as hostages.
Cho.   What's the meaning of the man's
          Threatening? I cannot guess;
                    can you say, Acharnians?
          Has he any son or daughter
                    of this company in hold
          Whom he says that he will slaughter?
                    What can make the man so bold?
Dic.   Now then, if you like it, throw—
                    I will riddle *this* [2] with holes
          Till it's dead; and I shall know
                    who has any care for coals!
Cho.   'Tis our brother burgess! yes!
                    we are ruined! hear us ask it,
          Wring us not with this distress:
                    do not—do not hurt the basket.
Dic.   It must go; I care not whether
                    you may wring your hands and cry.

---

[1] The 'demos' or borough of Acharnæ lay under mount Parnes, on which grew woods, from which the main supply of charcoal was obtained. All Acharnians were more or less charcoal-burners or traders.

[2] Dicæopolis in one hand holds a knife, in the other *a charcoal-basket*, such as the Acharnians were daily in the habit of using in their business.

Cho.   We have lived and loved together
      Charcoal: no, it must not die.
Dic.   When I begged a word but now, you
      stiffly, utterly declined.
Cho.   Aye, but now we will allow you:
      say just what you have a mind.
 If indeed you are intent
      on your Spartan friendship, say it.
 As for that sweet innocent;
      no, I never will betray it.
Dic.   Throw away the stones.
Cho.   'Tis done:
    Put you, too, the knife away.
Dic.   Are you sure that you have none? ·
Cho.   Let me shake my apron: nay,
   Do not cheat me with a smile,
    Fairly put aside the steel,
    For I shook my pocket while
    I was turning on my heel.[1]
Dic. So, you at last could cease your clamour! what a
   fate
Hung over charcoal when ye were so obstinate!
See, like a cuttle-fish retreating in its fear,
The basket clouds me in a coal-dust atmosphere.
'Tis sad to see a man indulge a temper like
Sour grapes; and always want to clamour and to strike
Before he hears the other side. But I was willing
To lay my head upon a chopping-block for killing,
While showing how the Spartan trouble had begun:
And yet I love my life as well as anyone.
 Cho. Why then, unpack your precious burden for display:
For I should like to hear what you have got to say.

---

[1] The Chorus consisted of about twenty-four persons, of whom one was in general the leader and spokesman. Sometimes they divided themselves into two parties, each with its spokesman. They filled up breaks, or marked divisions in the drama by a figure dance on their portion of the stage, the orchestra. But it is obvious from this and many other places that they even continued their dance when engaged in earnest dialogue with a principal character. In the *Peace* the inopportune dancing of the Chorus is represented as irritating Trygæus, l. 257, *et seq.*

Agreed, that at your proper peril you must win.
So let the chopping-block be brought, and then begin.

> [*A large chopping-block and cleaver are
> brought.*

Dic. So be it. Here's the block; and I, that am to plead,
Am but a nobody.[1] What matter? and indeed
I throw my shield away. I'll speak just what I think
About the Spartans : yet I feel disposed to shrink.
I know so well the men who come in from their farms;
How easily a cunning lying coxcomb charms
Their ears by telling them that they are ' honest,' ' bold,'
' Shrew'd fellows ' too! 'Tis so the dupes are sold.
I know the humour of your ancients too. They like
Nothing so much as giving judgments[2] that will strike.
I know how much, myself, I suffered from the clutch
Of Cleon, whom last year my Play[3] was thought to touch.
He dragged me in with slanders, lied me through the
    Court;
He roared, he blustered, bucked and rinsed me out : in
    short,
The wonder is that any of my being lingers
After such busy mauling by his dirty fingers.
And so, before beginning, let me change my dress,
That I may move some pity for my squalidness.

Cho. Why do you try these tricks? But get, for aught
        I care,
Jerome's invisible pitch-darkness cap of hair;[4]
Get Sisyphus's shifts; but all in vain you try,
It will not be allowed to put this trial by.

---

[1] Under the humour and buffoonery which here follows, we have,
hardly disguised, Aristophanes, the keen politician of the unpopular peace-
party, addressing ' the People ' on the benches of the theatre, and trying
to win a hearing for the very idea of peace with Sparta.

[2] As ' Dicasts ' or judges for the day in the law courts.

[3] *The Babylonians*, not now extant. It was not Aristophanes himself, but the same actor who was now representing ' Dicæopolis,' who
suffered fine for the libellous words of the comedy referred to. Up to this
time Aristophanes had not put a play upon the stage in his own name,
as appears by the Parabasis of the *Knights*.

[4] Equivalent to the ' receipt of fern-seed,' that is Invisibility. The
allusion to Hieronymus is obscure.

Dic. Now for a daring stroke; for I am ill at ease!
So I will make a call upon Euripides.
Ho,´Slave.   [*calling at the door of* EURIPIDES'S *house.*

CEPHISOPHON (*looking out*).

Ceph.   Who's there?
Dic.   Pray is Euripides within?
Ceph. Within and not within,[1] if you can take that in.
Dic. 'Within and not within!' how's that?
Ceph.   'Tis true, old man,
His wits are not within, but gathering where they can
Word-delicacies: but his body is upstairs
Writing a tragedy.
Dic.   Thrice blest in his affairs,
Who has a slave can answer with such subtle wit.
But call him out.
Ceph.   I cannot.
Dic.   I insist on it.
I will not go away.   Nay, I'll beat down the door.
'Euripides,' 'my dearest 'Rippy'—I implore,
If ever prayer from man did favourably reach you,
I, Dicæopolis of Collidæ, beseech you.

EURIPIDES (*speaking from within*).

Eur. I have no leisure.
Dic.   Pray you; let them wheel you out.
Eur. Impossible.
Dic.   Nay, nay.
Eur.   Then, twirl the turnabout.
                    [*The upper story of* EURIPIDES'S *house, being
                        made to turn on a pivot, is turned half
                        round, and* EURIPIDES *is discovered to the
                        audience sitting in his composing-chair.*
I am too busy to descend.
Dic.   Euripides.
Eur. What sayest thou?

---

[1] This expression is in imitation and ridicule of a kind of verbal paradox not uncommon in Euripides.

Dic. Aloft you make your tragedies,
When on the earth below you might have done the same.
No wonder that your characters are often lame,[1]
But why have you collected all those ragged clothes?
' As pity properties ' for beggars, I suppose?
But, dear Euripides, give me to my relief,
From some old tragedy, a proper rag for grief.
For I before the Chorus have to plead my tale,
And nothing short of death awaits me if I fail.

    Eur. What sort of rags will suit you? Those I have in
        store
Which Œneus in his age and evil fortune wore?

    Dic. Not those of Œneus; no. There were some to my
        mind
More wretched still.

    Eur. What, those of Phœnix that was blind?

    Dic. Not Phœnix, no; a much more wretched man
        than he.

    Eur. What does the man require? What tatters can
        they be?
Eh! was it Philoctetes as a beggar seen?

    Dic. More beggarly by far the things were that I mean.

    Eur. You mean, perhaps, the garment which the man
        had on
Who acted in the part of lame Bellerophon?

    Dic. No, not Bellerophon. Though he indeed was lame,
And begged, and mouthed, and chattered, without stint or
        shame.

    Eur. I know the man; the Mysian Telephus?
    Dic.   Ah, yes.
Give me the things that stood for Telephus's dress.

    Eur. Slave, let him have the shreds; they lie between
        the bags

---

[1] It is suggested that they may have had a fall from the nurse's arms in infancy. This is one of Aristophanes's favourite points of attack upon Euripides. Here and elsewhere, especially in the *Frogs*, he is charged with degrading his art, by inviting the pity of his audience upon his characters by such adventitious means as representing them *lame, blind,* or *ill-clothed.* The instances suggested in this dialogue are all drawn from dramas of Euripides.

Of Ino and Thyestes.

Ceph.   Here, man, take the rags.

Dic. Oh Jupiter, whose eye can look through everywhere,
Most pitiable be the raiment that I bear.
Euripides, since you have kindly spared me these,
Pray let me be complete ; so, give me, if you please,
The Mysian felt upon my head : ' for I to-day
A very beggar's part must undertake to play;
To be just what I am, but other seem to be,' [1]
So that the audience may perfectly know me,
While I shall circumvent with subtle-worded art
The muddled wits of those who play the Chorus part.

Eur. Take it, you have a head nice matters to discuss.

Dic. ' God speed you and my hearts desire to Telephus.'
Bravo ! I feel the phrases coming on me thick.
But ah, to fit me out, I want a beggar's stick.

Eur. Then take this one and quit the ' stone-compacted
                port.' [2]

Dic. ' Soul, seest thou how I am driven from the court,'
Half furnished for my needs ? Now should I urge my pleas :
Stick close and be exacting.   So, Euripides,
Give me a basket which a candle has burnt through. [3]

Eur. How can the wicker be of any use to you ?

Dic. 'Tis not of any use : but yet I choose to ask it.

Eur. Go, you are troublesome : content you with the
                basket.

Dic. Bless you, as your good mother blessèd was before.

Eur. Do go away.

Dic.   I only ask a trifle more,
A little pitcher—broken at the lip were best.

Eur. Then take it and be hanged, and know yourself a
                pest.

Dic. And you, you do not know the wrong that you are
                doing.

---

[1] These lines in the original are said to be simply adapted from the
Telephus of Euripides.

[2] An affected expression for ' door,' probably borrowed also from
Euripides.

[3] Beggars carried a candle alight in a basket, as a substitute for a
lantern.

But once again, my sweetest, listen to my suing,
It is a sponge I want, and little basin.
    Eur.   Scamp,
He will have all my drama. Take it and decamp.
    Dic. Aye, aye, Sir, I am going : but what? there is but
        one,   ·
But one thing more, and failing that I am undone.
Dear, dear Euripides, supply the little lack,
And I will go away ; I will, and not come back :
Some greens [1] to put into my basket, just a few in.
    Eur. Take them : my tragedy is gone. You'll be my
        ruin.
    Dic. No more : I'm going—' I am too importunate ;
Too heedless of the ire of men in high estate.'
But, ah ! my evil stars ! I had forgotten quite
One thing the lack of which will ruin me outright.
This one, one only thing ; just this one if you please,
My very, very darling, my Euripides,
A pestilence upon me, if I ask another,
Give me some chervil—you can get it from your mother.
    Eur. The man insults me : bolt the doors.
               [*The turnabout is reversed;* EURIPIDES *and*
                  CEPHISOPHON *are shut in out of sight.*
  Dic.   My heart,
Alas ! without the chervil we must then depart :
Know you the work we have to do ? and what a theme on?
No less than pleading for the men of Lacedæmon.
Now forward, oh my soul ! This is the barrier,
Eh ? dost thou hesitate ? art thou afraid to stir,
Having imbibed Euripides ? I cannot blame
Your little confidence in him. But come, for shame,
Pluck up your spirit : proffer there your head ;
And what you deem is right, let it be boldly said.
Now forward for the cause and bravely do thy part.
Here's thy returning confidence. Well done, my heart !

---

[1] An honest woman of Athens, who sold garden stuff, has a son who
was an honour to his mother; Euripides was that son. Aristophanes
never loses an occasion of sneering at him about the trade of *his mother.*
This is the meaning of asking Euripides for ' greens.'

Chorus.　　　Now, Sir, what is your intent,
　　　　　　　Iron-cheeked and impudent?
　　　　　　　　One versus All.
　　　　　　　You have got your case to make:
　　　　　　　　So stand or fall,
　　　　　　　Since you put your neck at stake.
Semichorus.　Yet the vagabond is brisk!
　　　　　　　Speak: you chose yourself the risk.
Dic. Pray take it not amiss, if I, good audience,
Poor though I be, should offer you some words of sense
On matter of the State; albeit in Comedy.
For Comedy to see and aid the Right is free;
And Right, though sad to hear, is what I have to say.
Cleon shall not have room to slander me to-day;
Saying, I take ill opportunity to speak,
Wherein I think our policy is wrong or weak,
In presence of the strangers; at this time of year [1]
Our festal strife is private; strangers are not here.
No subject States are bringing in the year's supplies;
Nor from the cities do we see our good allies.
We are the bolted flour, wheat that has passed the fan;
I reckon sojourners to be the chaff and bran.
I hold Laconians all in rooted deep dislike.
I would that Neptune, God at Tænarus, should strike
The nether earth and bury all of them in ruins. [2]
I too have had my vines marred by their mischief doings.
And yet, (for none but friends will hear me say it) why
Should all the blame for this on Lacedæmon lie?
Certain of ours there were (the city it was not:
Mark that—'twas not the city) but a worthless lot,
Of an adulterate mint, light coins, which none would take,
Defaced, of more than questionable type and make,
These must be spying out and laying cunning plans
To catch the short coats of the poor Megarians:

---

[1] At the Lenæan or Spring festival of Bacchus, at which this drama was presented, visitors from the neighbour states were not usually present. The reference is to the poet's previous comedy *Babylonians.*

[2] Sparta was almost entirely destroyed by an earthquake rather more than forty years before.

And if they saw a water-melon or a hare,
Lump salt, a sucking pig or onion, would declare
These are 'Megarian goods,' and straightway they were
    sold.[1]
Small matters these, you say.   But presently more bold,
Some youths, wine-flustered, went to Megara one day
And brought by stealth a certain light-o-love away,
By name Simætha.   Sore and swelling at these raids,
The men of Megara requited on two jades
Who waited on Aspasia.[2]   For three harlots thus
Begun the war which is destroying us.
Olympian Pericles in fiery indignation
Launched lightning upon Greece, thunder and agitation :
And framed his ordinances to avenge these wrongs
(Apparently upon the type of drinking songs),[3]
Against Megarians; that they should not abide
On land, at sea, at market, or on earth beside.
What happened? when the march of hunger brought its
    grief
Upon the folks of Megara?   They sought relief
Of the Laconians; and begged that the decree
About the harlot-kind might be relaxed.   But we

---

[1] Protection to home producers, or other motive, led the Athenians to desire to exclude the produce of the little town and district of Megara from the Attic markets.   Smuggling in various ways followed the exclusion.   The smuggling gave employment to a class of people who at Athens became a public nuisance—the Sycophants or Informers : they made a living by detecting and declaring contraband articles ; or, it may be, by being bribed to shut their eyes and mouths.

[2] The world-famous mistress of Pericles.   This tale of the origin of the Peloponnesian War has no countenance from Thucydides.

[3] The 'scolion' or drinking song to which allusion is here made has come down to us.   It is by Timocreon of Rhodes, and is to this effect :—

> Blind Plutus, your abode should be
> Not on the land nor yet at sea,
>   Nor anywhere beside on earth :
> But you should live in Tartarus
> And Acheron : for unto us
>   Through thee all mischief has its birth.

The 'Megarian decree,' as related by Thucydides, restrained the Megarians from the use of any harbours under Athenian influence, and from the Attic markets.

Stiffly refused.   From this clatter of shields befell.
' It never should have been, say you: but prithee tell
What should have been?'[1]   To put a case: suppose
That some Laconians had got to sea (who knows!)
Landed upon Seriphus,[2] laid a felon hand
Upon a puppy-dog, declared it contraband
And sold it.   At our ease should we have eat our meals?
Far otherwise.   Three hundred ships had dipped their
        keels;
The city had been filled with every sort of noise;
Men quarrelling about their pay or their employs; ·
Wrangling of citizens unable to agree
Whose duty it should be to fit the ships for sea;
Gilding of figure-heads; serving out rations; throngs
About the meal-shops; buying barrels, bottles, thongs,
New olives, garlic, nets of onions for supplies,
Anchovies, chaplets, piping women and black eyes:
And in the arsenal a trimming up of oars,
A driving in of pins and taking in of stores,
Belaying, hauling, whistling, piping up of hands,
And everywhere a captain shouting his commands.
All this you would have done.—But, in his own defence,
' Not Telephus ' we think[3]?—then we are wanting sense. ✓
        1st Semichorus.   Is this to me, you pauper? dare you
                cast a slur
On some (if such there be) informer's character?
        2nd Semichorus.   By Neptune! but the man, for all that I
                have heard,
Is right in what he says; there's truth in every word.
        1st S. C.   What care I, right or not? Was it for him to
                say it?
No, no.   And with some broken bones the rogue shall
        pay it.
                [The Leader of this half-chorus rushes to-
                        wards DICÆOPOLIS.

---

[1] The words in commas are said to be from the *Telephus*.
[2] An insignificant island in the Athenian alliance.
[3] ' Not Telephus : ' by euphemism to avoid wounding the prejudices of
the audience, for ' not Lacedæmonians.' 'That which would be quite right
for Athenians in such cases, is *not* right for Lacedæmonians.'

2nd S. C. Where are you running? Stay: I warn you,
    have a câre;
Touch him and you shall find your legs are in the air.

> [*This Leader clips the other round the waist, as*
> *though to lift him off his legs, as an expert*
> *wrestler.*

1st S. C. Ho! lightning-looker, Lamachus,
    Ho! Gorgon-crested, succour us;
    My friend, my tribesman, hear me call,
    Or captain else, or general,
    Or rampart-scaler, hither; haste!
    For he has got me round the waist.

Enter LAMACHUS.

Lam. What battle-cry is this I hear about the place?
Who calls for help? who wakes the Gorgon [1] from its case?
2nd S. C. My hero Lamachus of crests and companies!
1st S. C. Here is, my Lamachus, this man of many lies,
Who troubles all the city with his foul aspersions.
Lam. You, beggar?—Have you dared to make some vile
    assertions?
Dic. My hero, Lamachus, I beg you to forgive,
Ĭf, for a beggar, I have been too talkative.
Lam. What did you say of us? Speak, Sir.
Dic.   Eh? what, Sir? Did I?
I quite forget; the aspect of your armour makes me giddy.
I do beseech you put the Mormon [2] out of sight.
Lam. I do.
Dic.   Nay, upside down.

> [LAMACHUS *laying the shield upon the ground,*
> *it looks like a large brazen basin.*

---

[1] The real Lamachus appears to have been a brave and energetic
soldier. No doubt as a zealot of the war-party he was obnoxious to
Aristophanes, who ridicules his disposition for fighting and his military
accoutrements; especially his floating triple crest, and shield, like
Minerva's, bearing the head of the Gorgon.   This shield he keeps in a
case, and, as will be presently seen, is very careful for its high polish.

[2] Mormon means a bugbear to frighten children; of course it is here
purposely misused for 'Gorgon.'

Lam.   Well, there it is.
Dic.   That's right.
And now the feather from your helmet.
Lam.   What you will.
> [LAMACHUS *takes a feather from his hel-*
> *met and gives it to* DICÆOPOLIS.

Dic. Then, pray you, hold my head : for I feel very—ill ;
I'm sick—of crests.
Lam.   Eh ? Sir, what do you think to do ?
You will not try to use the feather, Sir ?
Dic.   Aye, true :
A feather is it ?—Pray, of what bird ? may I know ?
Perhaps 'tis from the tail of Braggadocio ?
Lam. Ha ! villain, you shall die.
Dic.   No, no, my Lamachus,
It is not might but right which shall determine us.
Lam. Beggar ! this language to your General ? to me ?
Dic. Am I a beggar then ?
Lam.   If not, who may you be ?
Dic. An honest citizen, with no high place to boast ;
But, since the war began, a soldier at my post,
While you have been as long receiver of high pay.
Lam. They freely voted me.
Dic.   Three cuckoos make your ' they.'
To my disgust at things like this my Truce owes thanks.
I saw grey-headed men still marching in the ranks ;
While striplings, such as you, misliking toil and dust,
Found refuge in appointments of high pay and trust.
Some drew three drachmas for a Thracian embassy,
Ismeniophænippi, Roguehipparchidæ.[1]
Chaonia had—and Camarina had its share ;
Some Chares entertained ; to Gela some repair ;
Some went to—Scorn.[2]
Lam.   Freely elected all.
Dic.   But why ?
How falls it out that you, and you alone, supply

---

[1] The plain yeoman citizen means that men of high family connections got these commands, or ministries to various places, while men like himself bore the brunt of service.

[2] In the original there is here a play upon words ' Gela ' and ' Catagela.'

The city's needs ?—Marilades, your hair is grey,
Have ever you been legate, or received the pay ?—
He shakes his head : yet he's a shrewd hard-working man.
Dracyllus, have you ever been to Ecbatan ?
Did Prinides, or did Euphorides e'er go
To the Chaonians ? you see, they all say, No.
Aye, who are they that go but Cœsyra's wild son,
And Lamachus ?—whose credit with their friends has run
Beyond all bounds ; that, with their presence here annoyed,
Like folks who empt their slops at night, they say—Avoid !

   Lam. Democracy !—and are such words to be endured ?

   Dic. Yes, if to Lamachus good office is secured.

   Lam. Know all that dwell in Pelops' land that I engage
With them and theirs a never-ceasing war to wage ;
By sea and land, wherever boat can swim or man can fight,
Will I pursue and harry them with all my might.

   Dic. Know all that dwell in Pelops' land, and know the
      same,
Bœotians and Megarians, that I proclaim
Free market to them all, to buy and sell with us ;
From which free market I prohibit Lamachus.

                            [*Exeunt.*

PREFATORY NOTE ON PARABASIS.

The English dramatist may address his audience on any subject he pleases in Prologue or Epilogue. The custom of the Attic stage gave the author of Comedy the same license at any natural pause in the action of the piece. The Chorus leader was the author's mouthpiece.

The Monologue thus introduced was called 'Parabasis.' It is usually broken up into a number of parts more or less regulated in number and order, distinct in metrical construction and perhaps in the dance movements that may have accompanied them. The translator has followed the variations of the original, even to the general structure of the metre, where it seemed feasible to adapt it to the governing principle of rhyme. He would have been glad to give the English reader an adequate idea of one characteristic metre, so much used by Aristophanes as to have taken a name from him, namely the Anapestic Tetrameter. He owns himself, however, unable to surmount two practical difficulties. First, the comparatively rare occurrence of the anapest (two short syllables followed by one long) in natural English enunciation; for trisyllables, under the tendency of our accentuation, fall more generally into the form of the dactyl. Secondly, as would be almost necessary in order to secure a penultimate accent, the providing, under the rigour of translation, dissyllable rhymes at the end of every line, which shall not exhibit the perpetual recurrence of rhymes of the class 'ending,' 'mending,' 'action,' 'faction.'

The following is the scheme of the Aristophanic Tetrameter.

The three lines represent the alternative foot allowed in the several places of the line.

1	2	3	4	5	6	7	8
◡◡‒	◡◡‒	◡◡‒	◡◡‒	◡◡‒	◡◡‒	◡◡‒	◡
‒‒	‒‒	‒‒	‒‒	‒‒	‒‒		
‒◡◡	‒◡◡	‒◡◡		‒◡◡			

This scheme has been so far observed as to give a principle to the rhythm, in the opening of the following Parabasis, and in most other places where the anapestic tetrameter occurs: subject to the admission that the dactyl has beaten the anapest, and to the fact that the true spondee hardly ever appears in English. Our dissyllabic foot is either Iamb, or Trochee.

PARABASIS.

Chorus. Public opinion goes with the man, and
    thinks he has made a very good case
In behalf of his truce.—Therefore strip we :[1]
    this is a fitting anapest place.
Since this Author tutored the actors,
    he has never in his comedies
Offered himself upon the stage to
    tell the world how clever he is.[2]
Since, however, he is traduced by
    some who think they owe him a grudge,
In your ears, Athenians, who are
    quicker to hear than steady to judge ;
Now he appeals to your better judgment,
    confident you will acknowledge it true,
That he never insulted the people, or
    undertook to ridicule you.
Nay, but the City is his debtor :
    he it was who arrested the course
Of that fatal habit you had of
    yielding yourselves to flattery's force.
Heretofore when the States'[3] commissioners
    came with an eye to bamboozle the town,
Did they ever fail to address you
    as the men ' of the violet crown ' ?
Straight at the word you were up in your seats ; but
    if the cunning fellow should add
' Glistening Athens,' you would give him
    out of hand whatever you had.

---

[1] Metaphor drawn from the wrestling-ground ; equivalent to ' buckle to.'

[2] If the Author lost the occasion for doing so in his two first comedies, henceforth he is not chary of telling his particular merits ; and generally in his own practice illustrates the particular faults which he blames in his fellows.

[3] The cities or states in dependency called alliance with Athens.

All for the pleasure of the ' Glistening ! '
    very good word for the matter of that,
Happily chosen, very descriptive,
    when applied in the praise of a sprat.[1]
Thanks to the Poet, you in future
    will be freed from folly like this.
Has he not also taught the peoples
    out of the cities their infinite bliss
Being so thoroughly people-governed?
    Henceforth when the tribute is due,
They will come with a zeal to see that
    wonderful Poet who lives among you,
Who in the cause of justice ventured
    his very life in peril to bring.
Nay, so far the fame of his daring
    has already come, that the King [2]
Lately taxed the Spartan ambassador ;
    after asking which of us two [3]
Handled our ships best, tell me, quoth he,
    which of you harbours that witty man, who
Lashes his fellows right and left ? for
    that is the way to whip energy in,
And, by consequence, his is the side which
    in your war will assuredly win.
Therefore it is that Lacedæmonians
    offering us the plan of a peace,
Make the demand that in Ægina
    all our rights and interests cease ;
Not that they care at all for the island,
    but they indulge their cunning and hate,
Well aware that, in that event, your
    Poet will certainly lose his estate.

---

[1] In spite of this ridicule of the epithet, Aristophanes freely uses the word whenever he wishes to coax his audience ; as *Knights,* 1326 (Gr.) 1101 (Trans.), where it is combined with the other favourite ' violet-crowned,' and *Clouds,* 290.

[2] ' The King' in the mouth of a Greek means of course ' of Persia.'

[3] Sc. Athens or Sparta. The very suggestion of embassy to ' The King' shows how the simple anti-l'ersian feeling, which had combined the Greek communities, had passed or was passing away in the interest of home rivalry.

Yield it not, but trust that he will
      ever his powers of comedy use
Only to foster the city's welfare,
      only to teach, correct, and amuse.
Do not look that he should flatter, or
      cheat your ears with any pretence,
Tickle your whims, or buy off enemies;
      only look for thorough good sense.
Cunning [1] as Cleon is, he shall not match me;
Not all his artifice ever shall catch me.
I shall have honour in trusty alliance;
True to the State, I set him at defiance.
Me at the least you never shall find
Braggart in front and coward behind.[2]

1st Semichorus. Oh, for a muse of fiery flashes,
      Impetuous, Acharnian!
As the spark leaps up from the oakwood ashes,
      Stirred by the breath of the fan:
When the little fish for frying
Are beside the embers lying,
When the Phasian sauce is making,
When the girdle cakes are baking.
      Such a stirring melody,
Loud and strong, and free as the breeze
That whistles through our native trees,
      Hither, Muse, and bring to me.

Chorus. Listen, City: we thy ancients
      charge thee with a heavy blame.[3]
All unworthy of the men who
      fought thy ships and won thy name,

---

[1] This small division of the 'Parabasis' was called the 'long piece'; the actor was expected to say it without drawing breath.

[2] Like this Cleon—he would say.

[3] Athenian citizens of the younger generation, perpetually haunting the law-courts, were perfectly at home in the management of an action, for the prosecution or defence. No doubt it was great sport to them to prosecute some old fellow for an offence he had never heard of, and get him into Court to answer for himself. This is the grievance of the 'Old men' who form this 'Chorus.'

Are the grief and disrespect which
   overcloud our setting day.
Art thou not to blame in this for
   casting us uncared away?
Often vexed by informations,
   we are hurried into Court,
By some nimble-worded youngster
   loosely to be made a sport.
Think ye that we do not feel it?
   oh, but we are sorely tried!
Nay, but now the flute is broken;
   throw the tuneless thing aside!
We are nothing, we are nothing!
   let the witlings have their laugh.
We have no Protecting Neptune
   but our trusty walking staff.
There we stand before the Chairman
   mumbling out our words, and cowed,
Seeing not a glimpse of justice,
   nothing but a hazy cloud.
Comes my downy-bearded pleader,
   having spent his labour in it,
Strings his rounded words together,
   knocks me over in a minute!
Sets his scraps to bait his traps, and
   puts Tithonus [1] to the rack;
Draws him, rends him, turns him, bends him,
   proves that very white is black.
Who will hear his mumbled answers?
   So the poor old man is cast;
He must pay the fine and grumble
   while his tears are flowing fast:
And among his neighbours round him,
   fretting, you may hear him say,
What I had to bury me—ah!
   they have got, and I must pay.

---

[1] Meaning the poor 'old' man. Tithonus obtained from the Gods the gift of immortality; but his life became a burden to him; for he had omitted to ask perpetual vigour with it.

2nd Semichorus. Is it not shame to harry and spoil
   By clockrun [1] a man whose hair is white?
Who has wiped the sweat of his manly toil
   In the harvest-field and the fight?
Better soldier was there none
In the fight at Marathon.
  ' Then,' says he—nor wants it sense—
  ' Persians stood on their defence.
  But the fight has turned; for we
Are but defenders from the blows
Of native and ignoble foes.'
   Marpsias,[2] will you answer me?
Chorus. Shame to see Thucydides, when
    bent with years and fortune's stress,
 Overtaken, left to perish
    in that Scȳthian wilderness,[3]
Chatterpie Cephisodemus!
    Truth to say, my eye was wet
When I saw a man of worth by
    such a vagabond beset;
A townguard archer! yea, by Ceres,
    when he was Thucydides
He was one whom not Achæa
    would have ventured to displease.
Ten such as Euathlus would have
    known their length upon the ground
At his battle-cry; three thousand
    ' archers ' would have fled the sound.

---

[1] Referring to the clepsydra, or water-clocks, in the courts of justice, to limit the time allowed for speaking.

[2] Who was this Marpsias, and what the force of this appeal to him, it does not satisfactorily appear.

[3] Such would be a dreary place in which to be cast away, but it has a partially metaphorical sense here, meaning that Cephisodemus was of ' Scythian ' parentage. The 'archers,' town-guard or ' police ' of Athens, were commonly ' Scythians.' Theirs was black blood to be in the veins of a Greek. These lines suggest that Thucydides had lately suffered in some action, conducted by Cephisodemus, a low pleader. The Thucydides referred to, now old and fallen into poverty, was probably once the leader of the Aristocratic party, the son of Milesias, whose ostracism had left Pericles master of the position. See the Chronological Table.

Archer ! quotha : he had found the
        fellow's arrows better mark !
He had laid the archer's father
        and his kindred stiff and stark.
Nay, but if ye will not suffer
        aged men in peace to sleep,
Let them have a court where they may
        battle by themselves and creep.
If an old and toothless man must
        mumble in his petty cause,
Set a mumbling advocate to
        vindicate the city's laws.
Pit the young against the young, for
        they have muscle, teeth, and breath :
One of such in health may talk the
        son of Cleinias [1] to death.
If there must be prosecutor,
        criminated man and judge ;
If there must be banishment to
        satisfy a jealous grudge ;
Make a new decree about it,
        and in future let it hold,
That the young shall try the young men,
        and the old men try the old.

SCENE.—DICÆOPOLIS *in front of his house assigning the
bounds and order of his new Market-place.*

Dic. This is my market-place, and these its bounds : 'tis
    free
To enter and to leave; to buy and sell with me
To them of Megara, Bœotia, and all
Whose cities southward of the Gulf and Isthmus fall ;
But not to Lamachus.   Here are, assigned by lot,
Three thongs of knotted leather, WARDENS of the spot :

---

[1] Alcibiades, a young man at this time just rising into notice.

And let them understand it is their special charge,
That no informers here shall be allowed at large.
Now must I fetch the stone that bears upon its face
The Treaty terms, and set it in the market-place.

[Exit.

Enter MEGARIAN, carrying a sack.

Meg. A maukit-plaace in Authens ! does one good to see·
A' waunted of it sore ; and maany more nor me.
Lor' love you, but I'd liefer have this chance to sell
Than I 'ud see my mother !—so, I wish it well.[1]
But I must call the maister—' Dicæopolis '—

Re-enter DICÆOPOLIS.

Hey ! Sir : and may ye want to buy the like o' this ?
   Dic. Ha ! Megaric, what's this ?
   Meg.   These little pigs of mine.
   Dic. And how fare you ?
   Meg.   We sit before the fire and *whinê.*[2]
   Dic. Pleasant enough ! if you have got a piper too.
But otherwise, how do our worthy neighbours ?
   Meg.   Do ?
When I was setting out our councillors of state
Were at the business, with a very warm debate,
How they might bring us to the worst and quickest end.
   Dic. The sooner then will you be quit of troubles, friend.
   Meg. That's true.
   Dic.   What else at Megara ?—how's wheat ? the best—
   Meg. Quite equal to the Gods,—high and in great
      request.

---

[1] Usually the translator will not mark excisions ; but a considerable omission is made here which will not explain itself simply on the ground indicated in the Introduction. The Megarian, in default of other articles for exchange, brings, under the pretence of being pigs, his two little girls for sale. Though the incident powerfully represents the straits of the Megarians, surely the very idea is too revolting for comic treatment. The Megarian speaks in his characteristic dialect : it seems enough by a few touches to indicate this.

[2] Aristophanes has the advantage of a word here which signifies and ' are hungry '; but Dicæopolis pleasantly mistakes it for another word of nearly the same sound which signifies ' we drink.'

Dic. You've brought us salt perhaps?

Meg.   When you have got the pans![1]

Dic. Then garlic?

Meg.   Garlic! umph! when you Athenians
Like shoals of field mice through our gardens run,
Sniff at the precious bulbs and dig up every one.

Dic. What have you?

Meg.   Little pigs just fit for sacrifice.

Dic. Aye: that will do: let's see them.

Meg.   They'll be very nice.

Dic. Fair animals enough.   What do you set them at?

Meg. Aye, aye, they only want the food to make them
        fat,
A string of garlic for the one can't be a fault;
And for the other I will take a peck of salt.[2]

Dic. A bargain: I will go and fetch them.   [*Exit.*

Meg.   That will do;
So far, so well.

Enter an INFORMER.

Inf.   Good sir, what countryman are you?

Meg. A pig-dealer of Megara.

Inf.   Then you are prize,
You and your pigs: for you are goods of enemies.

Meg. Aye, here it is just where the trouble all began!

Inf. I'll teach you what it is to play Megarian:
Put down the sack.

Meg.   Hoi! Master Dicæopolis,
I'm forfeited by somebody.

Re-enter DICÆOPOLIS, *with garlic and salt.*

Dic.   Ah! what is this?
Here, wardens, do your duty; keep the market clear.
Inform him how we play the game of forfeits here.

---

[1] Megara had had some trade from the manufacture of salt, but since the war the Athenians had occupied the salt-pans.

[2] These articles were the ordinary produce *of* Megara.

Inf. What? Shall I not declare the goods of enemies?
Dic. Just anywhere you please but here, if you are wise.

> [*The* WARDENS *move towards the* IN-
> FORMER, *who runs off.*

Meg. The plagues!
Dic.   Pooh! Here's the price at which
you were to sell:
The garlic and the salt: take them and fare you well.
Meg. That's not a way with us.
Dic.   Then mend your education:
If you are surly, I recall the salutation.

> [*Exit* MEGARIAN.

Chorus.   'Tis a happy man! all of us agree
          Thriving in his plan.   If you go to see,
                    All about the place
                    Is in such good order,
                    That across the border   .
          No Informer dares to show his face.

. What though you should feel clean, and looking nice,;
What though you should deal, knowing not the price,
                    You need not to fear
                    You should ever meet
                    Dirty dog or cheat.
Men who go to law are not known here.

Dandies do not show; nor the men of taste,
Who are apt to go parti-washed in haste.
                    You shall never hear
                    Bitter jest or old,
                    Nor a story told
More than thirty days each month in the year.[1]

---

[1] The translator has taken for once great liberty with his author in rendering this description of the charms of Dicæopolis's market.   The original is little better than a tissue of scurrilous personalities.   In the market, say the Chorus, you will not meet this man who is a cheat; that man who is dirty; nor the other who is a pettifogger.   It will be seen that the translator, omitting the personalities, predicates the absence of the noxious qualities generally.

Enter a Bœotian *Dealer, followed by Pipers, and his Slave*
Ismenias, *carrying goods for the market.*

Bœo. Know Hercules! the weight has galled me, that
   it has.
Put down the flea-bane carefully, Ismenias.
You pipers, who from Thebes have followed all the way,
Now put some wind into your leather bags and play.
             [*Bagpipes play.*
 Dic. Confound ye, stop! Be off, ye drones! Whence
   have we these
Most dreary humble-bumble bees of Chærides?
 Bœo. By Iolas, my friend, and with my free consent,
For they have come from Thebes still blowing as they went,
And dropped me much good flea-bane. Please you, sir, to
   try:
I've brought a store of things; chicks, locusts; what d'ye
   buy?
 Dic. Ah, ah! my dumpling-eater, my Bœotian friend,
What have you?
 Bœo.   Some of all Bœotia can send.
Here's flea-bane, marjoram, here's wicks and mats of
   rushes,
Here's divers, dippers, daws, here's water-hens and
   thrushes;
Teal, landrail, field-fare, widgeon.
 Dic.   What a flight of words!
You've come into the market like a storm of birds.
 Bœo. I've geese besides, and hare, I've foxes, hedgehog,
   mole,
Rat, otter, beaver, weasel, and, to crown the whole,
Eels from Copäis.
 Dic.   Ha! man's choicest dainty! bless it!
Oh, if you have the eel, permit me to address it.
 Bœo. (*taking a fine eel from his basket*). Eldest of fifty
   daughters of Copaïs, deign
To smile upon the stranger and your name sustain.
 Dic. (*addressing the eel*). Much as I love and wish, thou,
   most desired of all,
Comest in welcome hour to this our festival!

Beloved of Morychus ! [1]   The frying-pan and bellows
Here, maids ; and look at it, the fairest of its fellows !
'Tis eight years since we saw the like ! eight weary years,
That we have longed for it with mingled hopes and fears.
Speak nicely to it, girls, and hark, let it be dressed,
For I will find the coals and entertain this guest.
But take her in.   For I confess I could not meet
My death composedly without thee—served in beet.

Bœo. But who will pay me for it?

Dic.   'Tis my market-due.
If you would sell the rest we can begin anew.

Bœo. All are for sale.

Dic.   Good then : what do you ask ahead?
Or will you take home other articles instead ?

Bœo. If there is anything which Athens has, and we
Have not.

Dic.   Phaleric sprats? or Attic pottery ?

Bœo. Pooh ! sprats and pottery ! we have them and to
          spare.
Find something which you have, and we have not got there.

Dic. I've hit it.   An Informer will be just the thing ;
Put up like pottery !

Bœo.   By the Gods ! he'll bring
A handsome profit for the show ; besides the fun in
Exhibiting my monkey, full of tricks and cunning.

Dic. Here comes Nicarchus, prowling for a prey no
          doubt.

Bœo. 'Tis but a little man.

Dic.   But solid rogue throughout.

Enter NICARCHUS.

Nic. Whose merchandise is this ?

Bœo.   I'd have you understand
'Tis mine ; from Thebes.

Nic.   Then I declare it contraband :
They're enemies.

---

[1] A well-known gourmand: *Peace,* 818.
[2] The approved way of dressing this delicacy.   See *Peace,* 781.

Dic.   What can the little birds have done
That you should rate them such?
Nic.   And I declare you one.
Bœo. What have I done?
Nic.   Before the standers round to fix
Your proper guilt; I say—You bring in candlewicks.
Bœo. And do the candlewicks so much inflame your ire?
Nic. Why! one of them might set the arsenal on fire.
Bœo. A wick can fire the arsenal?
Nic.   I say it can.
Bœo. How so?
Nic.   The thing is easy. Some Bœotian
Finds me an empty beanpod;—'tis a simple trick—
And in the bottom of it fixes me his wick:
He watches for a night when northern winds prevail;
Kindles his wick, and sets the little boat to sail
Down the main drain. If once the ships should catch the
      flame,
Then all would be ablaze—
Bœo.   And candlewick to blame!
Nic. That I attest.
Dic.   Gag him, and stop the fellow's ravings.
I'll pack him neatly; bring a flag mat and some shavings.
          [DICÆOPOLIS *and his servants seize* NICARCHUS,
            *and rapidly make him up like a parcel
            of pottery, and cord him.*
Cho. Aye, worthy fellow, do.   Assist the honest man
            To save his bargain if you can;
            There's danger of its breaking.
Dic. Don't be afraid: the thing shall be securely packed.
          [NICARCHUS *protests lustily during the packing
            process.*
            This earthenware is furnace-cracked,
            To hear the noise it's making!
Cho. How can one use the scamp?
Dic.   A hundred ways; he's at your need
            A cup of woes; a dish to feed
      Your appetite for suits; or a detective's lamp.
Cho.   But how can anybody wish
            To keep so very cracked a dish

That it will make a constant clatter?

Dic.   Pooh, pooh, there is not much the matter.

> [DICÆOPOLIS *and his Assistant toss their pack-
> age about roughly, and make it stand
> on the end where the Informer's head is
> known to be.*

You see, for all its jarring sound
It will not break when upside-downed.

Cho.   I see it is secure enough.

Bœo.   I'm going to gather up my stuff.

Cho.   Then, pray you, leave not *this* behind.

'Tis a man of information,
And fit for any situation;
So fling him where you have a mind.

Dic. The vagabond is packed : but it has made me hot.
So now, Bœotian, prithee carry off your pot.

Bœo. Ismenias, my lad, come stoop and give a back.
Be cautious how you go : and mind it does not crack.

Dic. 'Tis noisome stuff.   But if you can contrive to earn
A trifle by him, there are more for your return.

> [*Exeunt* BŒOTIAN *and Servants carrying
> off* NICARCHUS.

Enter a SERVANT *of* LAMACHUS.

Serv. Heigh ! Dicæopolis.

Dic.   Who calls me ?

Serv.   It is I,
Whom Lamachus has ordered with this drachm to buy
Some thrushes for the Pitchers' feast, and three to pay
For a Copaic eel.

Dic.   Eel ! Lamachus ?—but stay,
Who's Lamachus ?

Serv.   The shaker of the Gorgon shield ;
The terrible ; whose triple crests wave o'er the field.

Dic. Not for his shield, not I ! Go let your master shake
His triple crests, and make his pickled herring [1] quake.

---

[1] Constituting part of his supplies for the field.

Let him not think to vapour.   As some poet sings,
Will I go in 'On blackbirds' and on thrushes' wings.'
                    [*Exit* Dicæo. *carrying his Bœotian purchase.*

Chorus.   He was wise to make his peace :
              Now the city knows it.
         Wealth must in his house increase,
              Commerce overflows it.
         Articles of usefulness,
              Articles for eating,
         One upon another press,
              Happy at the meeting.

         I will never harbour WAR ;
              He shall not be guest of mine,
         Headstrong mischief-maker ; for,
              Say you, 'Take a cup of wine,'
         Roistering he comes to spoil,
         Mars the feasting with a broil ;
         Scatters, snatches, overturns,
         Takes your vine-stakes up and burns ;
         Yea, for all that you can say,
              Madly stabs the very vine,
         Lets its life-blood ebb away.—
              WAR shall not be guest of mine.

         Foster-sister to the Graces,
              RECONCILIATION !
         Hitherto how fair thy face is
              Passed my observation.
         Crowned with roses, would some youth
              (As we painted see LOVE),[1]
         Take you by the hand in truth
              And give you to me, love,—
         'Wedding winter unto spring,
              Laying snow-wreath on a flower '—
         Say you so ? but I will bring
              Three enhancements for thy dower :

---

[1] Said to refer to a well-known picture.

First, I'll trench a goodly line,
In it I will set the vine ;
Then a second I will dig
For young suckers of the fig ;
Wilder berries [1] have their charm,
    They shall have another row ;
And, encircling all the farm,
    Olives shall be set to grow.

SCENE.—DICÆOPOLIS *passing in and out of his house super-*
intending the cooking of a supper for the Festival of the
Pitchers.

Enter TOWN-CRIER.

Crier. Good people, hear. The statutes of the feast ordain
When as ye hear the trumpet sounding, ye shall drain
Your pitchers. He who first his pitcher shall have done
Shall have for his reward the skin—of Ctesiphon.[2]

 Dic. What are you doing, slaves ? wenches, where are
   your wits ?
Look to your business, take the leverets from the spits.
Do keep the pots a-boiling ; turn the fry ; and weave
Some garlands. I will spit the thrushes, with your leave.

 Cho. Good counsel you before had shown,
    Good living seems not less your own ;
     My envy is excited.
 Dic. Ah ! if you saw the thrushes roast,
    You would be quite delighted.
 Cho. You speak the truth without a boast.
 Dic. See, slave, that fire wants blowing.
 Cho. His orders are so like a cook's !
    How lordly, suppingly, he looks,
     And keeps the business going.

---

[1] Perhaps the parent-stock of our 'currants.'

[2] He should have said 'the skin of wine'; which would have been probably of goat-skin. But on this occasion the reward was unusually large, as Ctesiphon was known as *very* corpulent.

Enter à FARMER.

Far. Oh dear, Oh dear !

Dic.   Who's this ?

Far.   A man making a moan.

Dic. Then go your way.

Far.   Good Sir, the Truce is yours alone :
Give me a Peace, if 'tis a trifle of five years.

Dic. What is the matter ?

Far.   I have lost a yoke of steers.

Dic. Where from ?

Far.   From Phyle.[1] The Bœotians came across.

Dic. And you are not in mourning after such a loss ?

Far. And now I've lost my eyes, for crying in this
        fashion.

If Dercetes of Phyle can move your compassion,
Do drop some Peace into my eyes ; a little squeeze.

Dic. But I am not a parish doctor, Dercetes.

Far. It may be I may get the oxen back. Only a little.

Dic. Pooh ! go and carry your complaint to Doctor
        Pittal.

Far. The smallest drop of Peace. I do beseech you.
        Here's

A quill.

Dic.   No, not a whisper.

Far.   Oh, my yoke of steers !

                                        [*Exit.*

Chorus. The Truce he finds a dainty fare,
           Which he is indisposed to share,
                At anybody's wishes.

Dic.   Some honey on the sausages,
                And toast the jelly-fishes.

Cho.   The pompous air in all he says !

Dic.   See that the eels are frying.

Cho.   What with the noise and smell so good,
           And hunger, all the neighbourhood,
                And we, are almost dying.

Dic.   And brown them.

---

[1] A borough of Attica on the Bœotian border.

Enter a BRIDEGROOM'S-MAN.

B.'s M.   Dicæopolis.

Dic. Another comer! who is this?

B.'s M. A bridegroom from the breakfast sends this fricassee
For your acceptance.

Dic.   Thanks, whoever he may be.

B.'s M. And begs a vase of Peace; that military life
May not disturb the new enjoyment of his wife.

Dic. Off with the fricassee! I'll none. You need not
    stop;
Not for ten thousand drachmas shall he have a drop.
              [*Exit Bridegroom's-Man.*
Fetch me a wine-stoup here, that I at once may fill
The pitchers.

Cho.   Who comes here, like messenger of ill,
With knitted brows?

Enter FIRST MESSENGER *on one side.*

1st Mess.   Oh, toils and broils and Lamachus!

Enter LAMACHUS *on the opposite.*

Lam. Who thunders at the brazen gates? who calls on
    us?

1st Mess. It is the General's order that you go to-day,
Taking your companies and crests without delay,
To watch the passes in the snow: for it is told
That certain thieves from the Bœotian side, made bold
By reason of our feast, trouble the neighbourhood
With lifting prey.   [*Exit Messenger.*

Lam.   Oh, Generals far more than good!

Dic. To go and leave the feast! oh, terrible position!
Oh, lamentablelamachæan expedition!

Lam. Is it at me you dare to cast such scoffs as these?

Dic. Wouldst thou do battle with four-winged Geryones?[1]

---

[1] Perhaps Dicæopolis has picked up some of the birds' feathers there lying to make a mock at Lamachus.

E

Lam. Ah! ah! what heavy tidings did the herald bring
    me?

Dic. Hah! ha! what tidings will this coming fellow
    sing me?

Enter SECOND MESSENGER.

2nd Mess. Good Dicæopolis.

Dic.   What now?

2nd Mess.   Please you pack up
Your pitcher and provision-box,[1] and come to sup.
The Priest of Bacchus begs your company and waits.
The feast is all prepared from tables down to cates;
The cushions, couches, hangings, chaplets for the head,
The perfumes, sweetmeats, millet-cakes and wheaten bread,
And dancers: so make haste.

Lam.   My evil genius!

Dic. You chose the Gorgon. Why reproach your for-
    tune thus?
But peace; get ready.

Lam.   Boy, bring out my havresack.

Dic. Boy, bring out the provision-box for me to pack.

Lam. Some thyme-sauce and some onions for my service
    chest.

Dic. And me a slice of fish: for onions I detest.

Lam. Bring me a leaf[2] of saltfish; it is soldier's fare.

Dic. And me a leaf[2] of stuffing; I will dress it there.

Lam. Bring me the feathers, which upon my helmet sit.

Dic. And me the pigeons and the thrushes from the spit.

Lam. 'Tis full and white! the ostrich is a noble fellow .

Dic. The meat of wood-pigeon is very plump and yellow.

Lam. About my arms, my man, I'd have you cease your
    girds.

Dic. Can you refrain, my man, from looking at my
    birds?

---

[1] Social meetings were often arranged on the 'pic-nic' principle, so
that the provision-box was an ordinary article of furniture: we shall see
directly how it was stored.

[2] A fig-leaf, commonly used to wrap viands.

Lam. Now bring me out the mount that holds the triple
      crest.

Dic. And me the dish of hare so exquisitely dressed.

Lam. Alas! the moths have eat the long hair through
      and through.

Dic. Alas! I'm eating hare—and supper's yet to do!

Lam. Will you be pleased, my man, to cease addressing
      me?

Dic. Pooh! pooh! 'tis with my slave I venture to make
      free.

What? Locust yield a meat as sweet as thrushes? Nay,
I'll wager you it isn't; Lamachus shall say.

Lam. You're insolent.

Dic.   He says that locusts win the day.

Lam. Boy, boy, bring out my spear; it is above the
      shelf.

Dic. Boy, boy, bring out the string of sausage, stir your-
      self.

Lam. Come, let me get the spear out of its cover; lend
A hand to help me.

Dic. (*giving his slave an end of a spit on which are the
      Sausages.*) Aye, take you the other end.

Lam. Bring out the tressels to support my goodly
      shield.

Dic. To me bring out the rolls, their good support to
      yield.

Lam. And now the Gorgon-backed, the shield, sir, if
      you please.[1]

Dic. And now a pancake—broad and rounder than a
      cheese.

Lam. If men find *this* a joke, they'll own 'tis broad
      enough.

Dic. If men find *this* a pancake—why, 'tis toothsome
      stuff.

Lam. Now pour some oil upon the brass. I see reflected
An old man in the act of cowardice detected.

---

[1] The shield is here mounted on the tressels that it may be rubbed to
brightness; so that Lamachus sees reflections in it.

Dic. Now pour some honey on.   There is an old man
    here
Laughing at Lamachus Fitz-Gorgonus: that's clear.

Lam. Bring me the martial plate with which I arm my
    breast.

Dic. Bring me the pitcher wherewithal I warm my
    chest.

Lam. Against the enemies thus armed will I go out.

Dic. Thus armed am I prepared for any drinking-bout.

Lam. Now tie the blankets in the hollow of the shield,
And I myself will bear the wallet to the field.

Dic. Now shut the box; so shall the supper be concealed.

Lam. Now take you up the shield and we will go to-
    gether.

Dic. And I will take a wrap to go through any weather.

Lam. Bless me! it snows.   The night is very dark and
    stormy.

Dic. Pick up the box.   A pleasant evening is before me.

                                    [*Exeunt.*

Cho.   Go ye, each with cheery heart.
          But your ways lie wide apart:
          His to garlands and potation;
          Yours to shiver at your station.

1st Semichorus. Antimachus, the last Lenæa,[1]
          At getting up the Plays, played me a
          Scurvy trick; for he decreed
          That actors do not want to feed.
          May Jupiter reward the man,
          And do the worst on him he can.
          He will, if I should have my wish,
          Be one day cheated of his fish,
          Just when the dainty hissing hot
          Is coming to the table, not
          Upon it, let a dog astray
          Lay hold of it and get away.

---

[1] A feast of Bacchus, and chief occasion on which dramas were presented.   It had been customary for the wealthy citizen who undertook
the office of Choregus, while instructing the actors in their parts for a
new play, to give them their suppers.   Antimachus set himself to reform
this abuse.

2nd Semichorus. For one misfortune that may do.
   But I will find him number Two.
   With ague fevered, on his way
   Towards his house some evening, may
   Orestes [1] with a madman's force
   Surprise and knock him off his horse.
   Then blindly groping for a stone
   May he find out—what he has thrown
   Has left behind a dirty mark!
   And may it, flying in the dark,
   Escape the man at whom it sped
   But hit Cratinus [2] on the head.

SCENE.—*In front of the house of* LAMACHUS.

Enter SERVANT *of* LAMACHUS *running.*

Ser. Here women, get hot water, towels, lint and plaister,
And ankle bandages for Lamachus your master.
A ditch came in his way, which he must try to take;
But somehow in the dark he jumped upon a stake;
And got a dislocation of the ankle-bone.
Then in the fall he broke his head upon a stone.
Alas! the Gorgon's head has tumbled from the shield,
And, much I fear, is left for dead upon the field.
But when the Braggadocio fell among the stones
There burst from him a loud lament in tragic tones,
'Oh glorious eye, while thus on thee I look my last
I take my leave of light: for, I am dying fast.'
Thus having said, he fell into an open drain.
But then some thieves ran by and he rose up again.

---

[1] A noted footpad, the terror of citizens then, and many years after, to judge by the recurrence of his name in these plays.
[2] The father of Attic Comedy. On the principle of 'Sweets to the sweet,' the 'dirt' might not have gone far wrong if it had hit Aristophanes himself.

And followed with his spear, as they ran on before—
But here he comes himself.   So, pray undo the door.

Enter LAMACHUS, *wounded and lame.*

Lam.   Ahtattah! ahtattah!
Anguish thrills me, numbness chills me,
Constant bleeding—hope receding—
'Tis the foeman's spear that kills me.
But that which grieves me most is this,—
If that Dicæopolis
Should behold me,
He would mock my dismal plight,
He would say it served me right,
As he told me.

Enter DICÆOPOLIS, *reeling tipsily.*

Dic.   Ahtah-latattah, ahtahtay!
I drank the pitcher first to-day.
Lam. Oh, for the sorrow of my heart!
Oh, for my wounds! they throb, they smart.
Dic. (*recognising* LAMACHUS) My Lamachus! my jovial
lad!
Lam. I'm sorrowful—
Dic. (*falling on the neck of* LAMACHUS) I'm very sad!
Lam. Why kiss you me?
Dic.   Why do you bite?
Lam. I've lost my reckoning in the fight.
Dic. But who would call a guest to pay
His reckoning upon Pitcher-day?
Lam. Oh, bear me to the surgeon's,
let him take me in.
Dic. Oh, bear me to the judge's,
let me have the skin.
Lam. The spear has touched the bone;
I know it by the pains.
                               [LAMACHUS *is carried off.*
Dic. The pitcher was well filled,
and not a drop remains.
For victory! hurrah!

Cho.   And so say we, hurrah !

Dic.   The wine was neat, I did the feat
        Without a pause : hurrah !

Cho.   You justly win ; go, take the skin
        And our applause.   Hurrah !
           Hurrah

KNIGHTS.

INTRODUCTION.

It would seem that when Aristophanes put *Acharnians* upon the stage he.had already conceived the design of making an attack upon CLEON; and that, in connection with the Order of Knights. There he puts it into the mouth of his Chorus to say, ' I hate you more than I do Cleon, whom I will make into shoe-leather for the Knights.'

But in the autumn of that year an event had happened which not only established the power of Cleon beyond the force of any stroke delivered from the Comic Stage, but had a material influence on the course of the war.

Demosthenes, an enterprising officer, had, with a few men and ships, established himself in a hastily-built fort at Pylos, now Navarino, on the coast of Peloponnesus. Threatened thus at home, the Spartans hastily recalled their army, at the time invading Attica, and endeavoured to dislodge Demosthenes. In the course of their operations they landed a considerable body of men, with their attend-ant slaves, upon the island Sphacteria, which crossed the entrance of the harbour. Their attacks upon the fort failed. The Athenian fleet came up, and having obtained the mastery of the position, effectually cut off and block-aded the Spartans upon the island. Hereupon the Lace-dæmonians sent to Athens and made deliberate overtures for peace. Cleon induced the people to reject them. The Athenians believed that they were quite sure of taking the men upon the island, and that the actual possession of them as prisoners would enable them to dictate the terms of the peace.

The season, however, seemed likely to pass away without the accomplishment of their purpose. They would not be able to maintain the blockade through the winter.

Dispiriting reports of their prospects came to Athens from
the party with Demosthenes. Men began to regard Cleon
with evil eye for having induced the city to disdain the
Spartan propositions. For his self-justification he threw
the blame upon the officers employed upon the service, and
hastily boasted that, if *he* were in command he would soon
bring the affair to a satisfactory conclusion. Nicias, the
General-in-chief at Athens, unexpectedly took him at his
word, and offered to him the command, with any force he
would name. When this was pressed upon him, Cleon
would fain have withdrawn; but the. people, apparently
taken with the humour of the thing, would not allow him
to do so.

Cleon then carried himself through with the bravado
with which he had begun. He would take no Athenian
force at all; only some light troops of the allies, then at
Athens, and he would bring back the Spartans as his
prisoners within twenty days, or die in the attempt.
Acting in concert with Demosthenes, he made a descent
upon the island Sphacteria, pushed the Lacedæmonians to
a surrender, and brought them to Athens within the stipu-
lated time. The prisoners were thrown into chains, and
held to guarantee the soil of Attica from Spartan invasion.
Eventually nothing less than a peace on terms of great
advantage to Athens, was the price of their release.

This Navarino was an untoward event for the comic
designs of Aristophanes. But it will be seen that his wit
was not at a loss how to evade its force, or even to take
advantage of it for strokes of humour. Demosthenes and
Nicias figure as important characters in the comedy. They
are, together with Cleon himself, represented as slaves in
the household of a testy, selfish old man named DEMUS,
or 'People.' This 'Demus' is throughout the comedy a
sufficiently daring impersonation of the mighty Athenian
populace.

It is not a little strange, however, that while Aristophanes could thus venture to display before the Athenians
a most insulting caricature of themselves, he never ventures to call his 'character' CLEON *by his name*. The
occurrence of the name in a choric ode (line 900) is no

real exception. The reference there *need* not be to the character in the play. Throughout the comedy, the name of the person is adroitly avoided; he is 'THE PAPHLA-GONIAN,' or referred to by some equivalent description. It is true that editors, and doubtless from ancient times all manuscripts, set the name *Cleon* in the list of Dramatis Personæ, and before all the spoken parts. The translator has not ventured to alter the custom. But the fact as it concerns Aristophanes is worth notice.

With all respect to those who have suggested that this comedy should bear the title *Demagogues* instead of *Knights*, the translator sees no reason for the change, but rather the contrary. In the opening of *Acharnians* Dicæopolis is made to crow over a fine of five talents which Cleon had been made to pay on the prosecution of the Knights. It surely cannot be doubted that it was this very fact which directed Aristophanes to connect his attack on Cleon with that class. He has been careful to give a speciality to the Choral Odes, and the Parabasis, to make them appropriate in the mouths of these proud *Horsemen*. Of course it is to be understood that our English word *knight* is used as our only convenient word to signify a person of definite social and political status, who was bound to render his military service on horse-back.

In this comedy the reader is first introduced to a feature of Athenian, perhaps it should be said of Greek character, which is very remarkable, and plays a large part in all the other comedies. It is addiction to prophets and prophecies. In this respect alone does the professed belief in the Gods appear to have had any reality. Men under all circumstances live upon the hopes of the future, and have a strong desire to foreknow it. This great secret was in the possession of Apollo. For a considera-tion he was willing to impart it in terms more or less clear. This convenience was not reserved to kings and communities. The fortunes of individuals the most obscure might be told on application. The enigmatic oracles were so far what we should call Revelations: but there is no sign of any reverence being attached to them as words of

God. They might, we see, without any offence to public opinion be parodied, and doubtless forged. It appears that collections of such oracles were made, and much used by individuals as Books of Fate. Two such are here alluded to. That by Bacis, a Bœotian, was in high repute. Herodotus (vii. 77) quotes from it, with expressions of the highest confidence.

Nothing can come from Aristophanes which shall not bear marks of brilliant and versatile fancy and fine humour, but those who read this comedy, without the stimulus of strong anti-democratic prepossessions, must feel that these powers are overborne and darkly shaded by mere personal vituperation, which it has been sometimes irksome to translate. If there is one other circumstance in connection with this comedy which deserves remark, it is the fact, that The People, who as they sat on the benches of the theatre heard themselves so insolently treated, had the patience, one may say, the dignity, merely to be amused, and to sanction the award of the Judges, which gave to it the first prize.

Dramatis Personæ.

DEMUS.   *A crotchety old man, representing the Populace of Athens.*

DEMOSTHENES.

NICIAS.   } *Household servants of Demus.*

THE PAPHLAGONIAN, *or* CLEON.

THE SAUSAGE-SELLER, *afterwards* AGORACRITUS.

CHORUS, *of the order Knights.*

DEMOSTHENES *enters, muttering to himself.*

Dem. The curse of all the Gods upon this new-bought
    dog,
This Paphlagonian! 'Tis nothing else but 'flog,
Flog, flog,' for all the rest, since in an evil day
This slave came to the house.

Enter from the other side NICIAS, *also muttering.*

Nic.   A plague on him, I say,
And all his cunning lies, this Paphlagonian!
Dem. (recognising NICIAS). Poor fellow, how are you?
Nic.   Sadly; like you, poor man.
Dem. Then pitifully let us weep in unison.
Both. Ugh-ugh, ugh-ugh, ugh-ugh, ugh-ugh!
Dem.   Nay, nay; have done:
This whining serves no purpose. Can we not contrive
Some better plan than whimpering whereby to thrive?
Nic. What can it be? Speak you.
Dem.   No, you say it to me.
I will not cross you.
Nic.   No; that must not, cannot be.
I will say afterwards. Speak out; be not afraid.
Dem. 'The thing that I should say, I would that you
    had said.' [1]
Nic. I have not got the pluck; I can't. I want in fact
The power to speak it with Euripides's tact.
Dem. No 'watercresses,' [2] pray! Suggest some sort of
    notion
That has in it a hint of master-quitting motion.
Nic. Then speak the words 'a,' 'way,' the two pronounced
    like one.

---

[1] A quotation from the *Hippolytus* of Euripides.
[2] Equivalent to 'no Euripides.' See note, *Achar.* l. 405.

F

Dem. ' Away.'.

Nic.   Now after it, express the sound of ' run.'

Dem. So ?—' run.'

Nic.   Aye; slowly say ' away;' and after, place
The ' run;' and then repeat, increasing still the pace.

Dem. A, way, run, away—runaway.

Nic.   Like you it fast ?

Dem. 'Tis well at first, but apt to burn the skin [1] at last !

Nic. Why then there's nothing left us but to say our
        prayers
At some god's image, for redress in our affairs.

Dem. Image ? Do you believe in gods ?

Nic.   ·   Aye, verily.

Dem. What token have you ?

Nic.   That they have a spite at me.
Is not that reason ? [2]

Dem.   Excellent : I'm satisfied.

Nic. Then something in another quarter must be tried.

Dem. Shall I explain the matter to the audience ?

Nic. 'Twere well. But let us first make trial of their
        sense,
Beseeching them to show by some distinctive token
That they approve what we are doing and have spoken.
                    [*Audience signifies approbation.*

Dem. Now will I speak. We have a master, you should
        know,
Churlish in temper, bean-fed, and by no means slow
To wrath, DEMUS of Pnyx; a humorous old man,
And rather dull. No longer than the month began
He bought and brought us here a Paphlagonian [3] slave,
A tanner, lying rogue, and most consummate knave.

---

[1] Runaway slaves who were recovered were branded.—*Birds*, 729.

[2] This smart argument is attributed to Diogenes, as used by him to
answer an Impertinent, enquiring whether he ' believed there are Gods ? '
' Of course I do; for I believe you are an object of aversion to them.'

[3] It is evident that many of the Greek slaves were brought from Asia
Minor: hence the names Lydian, Phrygian, Paphlagonian, or ' Midas '
were used indiscriminately and in contempt for *slaves,* as in our time
' nigger.'

No sooner come but, measuring the old man's ways,
He set to wheedle, fawn on, flatter him, and plays
Upon his weaknesses with petty gifts. 'Please you
To wash,' he'll say, 'when you've despatched a case or two;'
'Dear Sir, a mouthful, just a sip;' 'pray take the fee;'
'Ah, you are ready for your supper, Sir, I see.'
Then, catching whatsoever we have cooked with care,
. My Paphlagonian hands it in with special air.
Only two days ago at Pylus I had got
A mess of Spartan broth just ready in the pot,
When round my rascal comes before it could be known,
And, smiling, serves it up as if it were his own.
He will not let us see our master but at distance;
And never suffers us to render him assistance;
But with a leather thong stands while the master sups
To whisk the buzzers off that gather round the cups;
And entertains his ear the while with prophecies,
For mightily the old man likes that sort of lies.
And when he sees the master fooled to his content,
Pushes the game on which his roguish heart is bent:
He has some story trumped upon a false pretence
To tell of us; and we are whipped by consequence.
He'll filch a present from a fellow-slave by dint
Of impudence in asking, followed by the hint—
'You know what came to Hylas when he dared deny me.
I'll have you flogged to death, unless you gratify me.'
And so we give it him. Now what is to be done?

Nic. Good fellow, there is nothing for it but—to run.

Dem. But nothing can escape this Paphlagonian,
His eyes are everywhere, his legs have such a span,
One is in Pylus, and the other in the Pnyx;
His hands—wherever there is anything that sticks;
Only his mind is constant; always fixed on theft.

Nic. Then we had better die, for nothing else is left.
How may we do it in most manly fashion? How?

Dem. Eh, how?

Nic.   Drink bull's blood! that is manly you'll allow
After Themistocles?[1]

_____

[1] This is a vague story, not confirmed by Thucydides, indeed discredited by his silence.

Dem. A bumper to 'Good Luck'
Were better: and therefrom some wise thought might
    one pluck.
Nic. Neat wine! for shame, your heart is ever upon
    drink.[1]
How can a man bemused with wine be fit to think?
Dem. Out on your wishiwashiness! you water sot!
Wine dull the wits?—the only thing that it does not!
What will you find to put a man in better trim?
See, when a man has drunk the world goes well with him;
He carries out his plans; he feels that he can spend;
He wins his battles and has heart to help a friend.
But go you in and bring me out a stoup of wine.
I'll wet my intellect and think of something fine.
Nic. What will your drinking do for us? No good I
    fear.
Dem. Fear not: go fetch it. I will lie and wait you
    here.
Only let me be drunk and you will see the rout
Of thoughts, and plots, and plans that I will throw you out.
      [NICIAS *goes in, and returns with a stoup*
        of wine.
Nic. Bravo! I've filched the wine, and managed to
    avoid
All observation.
Dem. How was Paphlagon employed?
Nic. Snoring upon his back; for lying on a heap
Of untanned skins, the knave has drunk himself to sleep.
Dem. Fill me a bumper,—neat.
Nic. There.—Luck be in the draught.
Dem. (*after drinking*) Ha! ha! Good Genius, I thank
    thee for the craft!
Nic. What is it? tell me.
Dem. Go: steal me his Book of Fate.
While he's asleep.
Nic. But mine may not be fortunate.
      [*Exit* NICIAS.

---

[1] It is likely the real soldiers Demosthenes and Nicias, to the knowledge
of the public, differed as here represented in their principles and habits
in the matter of wine.

Dem. Methinks I'll take meanwhile another cup of wine,
To wet my intellect and think of something fine.

Re-enter NICIAS.

Nic. I've got it. · Oh how heavily the rascal sleeps.
I've got the very one, the oracle he keeps
So closely.
Dem. Oh, you clever dog.   Here, give it up,
And let me read.   Meanwhile do you refill the cup.
Let's see.   What have we here?—oh! oracles indeed!
The cup, the cup, I say, give me the cup with speed.
Nic. Ha! ha! what says the oracle?
Dem.   Here, fill again.
Nic. What! is *that* written there? and is it written
      plain?
Dem. Oh, Bacis!¹
Nic.   What is that?
Dem.   A cup here in a winking.
Nic. Bacis has prophesied a good deal about drinking.
Dem. Ha! Paphlagonian rogue, is this what you had got,
And kept, in terror for yourself, so closely?
Nic.   What?
Dem. Here is prognosticated what his end will be.
Nic. What will it?
Dem.   What?—'tis written unmistakeably.
A lint-dealer² will be the first to guide the State.
Nic. One 'dealer,' that is: who is next? does it relate?
Dem. A sheep-dealer² should be the second who shall rise.
Nic. Two dealers these. Of him what say the prophecies?
Dem. That he must reign until a more disgusting man
Is found to take his place.   The Paphlagonian,
The leather-dealer, next turns up, the greedy maw,
The bellower with lungs to keep a flood in awe.
Nic. The leather-dealer, then, was called up to abate
The sheep-dealer.

---

¹ A Greek 'Merlin,' under whose name passed a collection of oracles in great repute.
² Eucrates and Lysicles; two leaders of the Democratic party before Cleon.   The fiction of the drama is defied by the introduction of these allusions: we are not here in the domestic troubles of the household of old Demus, but launched on Athenian party politics.

Dem.   Aye, so.

Nic.   That is unfortunate :
There's not a dealer left to put him in the shade.

Dem. Oh, yes; there still is one of quite a startling
        trade. .

Nic. What is he ? tell me.

Dem.   Shall I ?

Nic.   Yes.

Dem.   A man that deals
In sausages is found to trip the tanner's heels.

Nic. A sausage-dealer ? Neptune ! what a calling too.
Where shall we find the man ?

Dem.   We'll see what we can do.

            [*A man carrying the implements of street
                sausage-seller seen approaching.*

Nic. Nay: see you; here he comes, by Providential plan
Led to the market-place.

Dem.   Oh, happy sausage-man !
Come up, sweet soul; come here, for thou art born to be
Our saviour and the city's.

                Enter SAUSAGE-SELLER.

Sau.   What want you of me ?
What is all this about ?

Dem.   Come here and learn the fate
Which lifts you upwards to a most sublime estate.

Nic. Do you expound to him the oracle's good will.
I'll go and see if yonder knave is sleeping still.

                        [*Exit* NICIAS.

Dem. Set down your goods; but first with reverence pro-
        found
Adore the blessed Gods and humbly kiss the ground.

Sau. So; there : what is it ?

Dem.   Man supremely fortunate,
Humble to-day, to be to-morrow more than great,
Captain of Athens.

Sau.   Pooh ! you're joking : let me go
And wash my tripe.

Dem.   Tripe! fool; see you row after row,
That mass of people?[1]

Sau.   Yes, I see them.

Dem.   All the herd
In market, ports, and Pnyx must wait upon your word:
You'll shut and open prisons, spend the State's resources;
'Tis yours to make and break commanders of the forces;
The senate will lie abject underneath your heels,
And in the Prytaneum you will have your meals.

Sau. I shall?

Dem. Aye, you. And yet you have not seen the whole.
Set down your dresser, mount upon your chopping-bole,
Now, look the islands round.

Sau.   I see them great and small.

Dem. And marts, exchanges, merchantmen?

Sau.   I see them all.

Dem. How great your fortune! carry now your eye—the
        right—
To Caria; on the left, Chalcedon is in sight.

Sau. Shall I be fortunate if I contract a squint?

Dem. Nay, but these all may be to you a mint.
For you must be the head; the oracle is plain.

Sau. How can a sausage-factor be the man to reign?

Dem. That is the virtue of it: you are from the crowd,
A very raggamuffin, confident and loud.

Sau. I cannot think that I am fit for dignity.

Dem. Nonsense, I say; for where can your unfitness be?
I fancy that you think there is some spark of worth
About you now. I ask, are you of gentle birth?

Sau. Not I, but of the basest.

Dem.   Happy in your fate.
It is the warrant for advancement in the State.

Sau. But, Sir, I have no education but a touch
Of letters; and, in truth, of them I know not much.

Dem. Not much is all too much; that is a fault indeed!
Effective leading of the masses does not need

---

[1] The actor no doubt pointed towards the benches of the spectators.
The people whose good temper and sense could be content only to laugh
at this deliberate and hearty insult deserve our respect.

The character and gifts which studied arts enhance,
But falls, of right, to Coarseness and to Ignorance.
The Gods have marked you out to this high future born.
I pray you do not leave and lose it in your scorn.

 Sau. What says the oracle?

 Dem.   It is the choicest bit
Of chequered light and shade, and enigmatic wit :—

> When hooked Tan-eagle stooping to his prey
> Would silly Dragon, blood-fed, bear away,
> The Paphlagonian's garlic brine is dead,
> And glory crowns intestine-seller's head
> Unless he will sell sausages instead.

 Sau. But what is this to me? explain what you have
   said.

 Dem. Tan-eagle is of course the Paphlagonian.

 Sau. Why is he hooked?

 Dem.   That is to represent the man
With ever-busy hands clawing unrighteous gain.

 Sau. Then what means dragon?

 Dem.   That is absolutely plain.
Is not the dragon long? so is a sausage too.
The dragon feeds on blood : what does a sausage do?
'Tis said, unless he lets himself be fobbed with words,
The dragon's fortune shall be better than the bird's.

 Sau. I like the oracle, but can't conceive how I
Should manage the affairs of a democracy.

 Dem. Nothing is easier. You know your trade. The
   fact is,
You've but to follow out your ordinary practice.
Throw everything together, keep the mixture stirred,
Humour the people's taste, throw in a wily word
To give a pleasant flavour. All a man can want
To lead a populace you have—voice dissonant,
Mean birth and vulgar manners; your success is made :
The oracles concur; the Pythian gives his aid.
Put, then, a chaplet on, make sacrifice with prayer
To Stupid,[1] and to meet the enemy prepare.

---

[1] A divinity, apparently, made for the occasion.

Sau. But who will be my friends ? The rich men fear his
  power,
The poorer sort bewildered in his presence cower.

Dem. There are the KNIGHTS, a thousand valiant men
  and true,
They hate him, and will frankly aid and comfort you ;
Among the citizens all men of worth and sense,
And every honest fellow in this audience.
I will be with you : and the Gods will aid our task.
So fear you not : for you will not behold his mask.
The artists for our stage, poor terror-stricken creatures,
Dared not supply us with that image of his features.
No matter.[1] (*pointing towards the audience.*)
  These are shrewd, and they will know the man.
         [NICIAS *runs in.*

Nic. Alackaday, here comes the Paphlagonian !

Enter CLEON.

Cleon. By the twelve gods, you two shall answer for your
  crime.
You plot against the people, and have done long time.
Ha, ha ! what means this cup ?[2] It is Chalcidian.
Soh ! Chalcis shall rebel ?—You see, I know your plan.
You shall be ruined. Ah, you villains, you shall die.
    [*The Sausage-seller is intimidated and slinks
     aside.*

Dem. Stop, don't desert us, Sausage-man : why do you
  fly ?
  Valiant Horsemen, to the rescue !—
    Simon,[3] now your squadrons bring.
  On the right, Panætius[3] forward !
    Will you not support the wing ?

---

[1] Not only would not the artists make the mask to represent Cleon,
according to custom when any public character was introduced upon the
stage, but the actor declined to take the part. It was therefore borne by
Aristophanes himself with his face smeared with wine-lees. So says
tradition.

[2] The cup brought out of the house by Nicias.

[3] At this time captains of the two divisions of Horse or ' Knights.'

Courage ! now the men are coming ;
> turn and stand on your defence.

See, the dust which they are raising.
> Stand and drive the fellow hence. ✓

Enter Chorus.

Cho.   Hit the rascal ; rank-confounder,
> public-money-taking cheat,

Plunder-swallow, Tax-Charybdis,
> rascal, rascal, I repeat ;

Twenty times a day a rascal.
> Follow, hit him, kick him out ;

Loathe the fellow just we do.
> Up and at him with a shout.

Stop the passage, pray be careful,
> he'll escape you ; for the man

Knows how Eucrates before him
> went the shortest way to—bran.[1]

Cleon. (*appealing to the audience*).

Ancients of the Courts of Justice,
> brothers of three-obol zeal,

Whom, by roaring right or wrong, I
> furnish with a daily meal,

Help me : I am being beaten,
> victim of a shameful plot.

Chorus.   You are served for gulping down the
> shares you did not get by lot.

All the men in state employment
> who will have account to render

You delight to handle, just like
> figs when they are growing tender ;

One is hard, another softer,
> here is one about to fall.

So you search and pinch the victims :
> if you find among them all

---

[1] Eucrates (see l. 117) was a miller, and did not avoid roguery ; his flour became 'bran' ; he brought his 'noble to ninepence ;' being detected in some corruption, he fled the country to escape the penal consequences.

One that like a sheep is simple,
        trembling at the thought of law,
Holding courts and men of business
        in a stupid kind of awe,
Him you drag from Chersonesus,
        fling him down and bind him fast,
Twist his throat behind his shoulder
        and secure a rich repast.

Cleon.   You to fall upon me also !
        I am beaten then for you !
When I was about to say that,
        it was nothing less than due,
That the city should set up a
        monument upon the heights
To record her estimation
        of the valour of our Knights.

Chorus.   Lying varlet, cringing fellow.
        see you how he tries to sneak ?
Does he think he has·to cozen
        men in second childhood weak ?
If by this device he wins it,
        we a counter-stroke must try ;
If he drop his head to push me,
        he shall butt upon the thigh.

Cleon.   City, People, what a sort of
        beasts are banded to my hurt !

Chorus.   You to make an outcry who are
        bent the city to subvert !

Sausage-seller. I will fright you with my bellow.

Chorus.   That were ·wonderfully done ;
But in impudence surpass him
        and the victory is won,

Cleon.   I declare this is the fellow
        who is known in many trips
To have furnished stores and slops for
        sundry of the Spartan ships.

Saus.   I declare this is the man who
        to the Prytaneum goes
Empty-bellied, but comes from it
        filled as everybody knows.

Dem.   Aye and, not contented, filches
                    from it bread and meat and fish,
Such as Pericles had never
                    set before him in a dish.

Cleon.   Knaves! ye shall die: no more ado.
Sau.   I'll bellow down three such as you.
Cleon.   Bellow? I'll bellow you to death.
Sau.   Bah! I will roar you out of breath.
Cleon.   Get a command: I'll trip you up.
Sau.   I'll lash you as I would a pup.
Cleon.   I'll clip your wings for all your crowing.
Sau.   I'll mine the paths where you are going.
Cleon.   Now,—dare to look me in the face.
Sau.   Pooh! I am from the market-place.
Cleon.   Another word, and you'll be hurt.
Sau.   Speak, and I'll smother you with dirt.
Cleon.   I own to stealing: you'd be loth.
Sau.   By Mercury I pledge my oath
          Against the very men who see.
Cleon.   Ha! meddler, that belongs to me
          With barefaced perjury to cheat.
          But I'll inform the Prytanes
          You sacrilegiously possess
          The holy tithes of sausage-meat.
Chorus.   Loathsome brawler, where's the spot
          Where your arrogance is not?
          'Tis in Council-hall, and Court;
          Offices of every sort
          Welter with the noisome flood,
          Oh you stirrer of all mud.
You that have completely deafened
                    Athens with your endless din,
And sit on the rocks to watch [1] the
                    shoals of tribute coming in!
Cleon.   I know all about this matter,
                    whence you've patched it altogether.
Sau.   Truly, if you don't know how to
                    set a cunning patch in leather

---

[1] In the original the word is borrowed from the practice of an Ægæan-sea fisherman watching for 'thunnies' as for mackerel.

I'm no hand at sausage-making.
> You know how to cut a hide,
Though the bullock that it come from
> in a ditch of murrain died,
So that it shall cheat the bumpkins;
> they shall think it thick and stout,
But the wear of half a day shall
> spread it some six inches out.

Dem. So he cheated me, and all my
> Pergasæan neighbours voted,
Since they were no boots I came in,
> it was evident I boated.

Chorus.   'Twas Impudence of old,
> (On whom as on a friend
> The pleaders all depend)
> Who made thee first so bold
To pluck what golden fruit the Strangers bring :
See, Archeptolemus [1] sits sorrowing.
> But here comes one to my delight
> Whose foulness will eclipse you quite;
> Your master, it is plain to see,
> > In force of lung,
> > In reckless tongue,
> And every act of knavery.
But come, you Sir, in whom we feel
> this age is well reflected,
Display to us what bootless zeal
> is that, to be respected.

Sau. The man is such that, though I try,
> I can't be his traducer—

Cleon. But let me—

Sau.   No; by Jove; for I
> am quite as bad as you, Sir.

Cho. If that is not enough, aver
> that, in their generation,
Your fathers' fathers always were
> dregs of the population.

Cleon. But let me speak—

Sau.   You sha'nt : that's flat.

---

[1] In the original only ' the Son of Hippodamus;' the scoliast supplies the name, but without pointed explanation.

Cleon.   I will, by Jove, despite you.

Sau. Speak first? By Neptune, upon that I will begin
      to fight you.

Cleon. Oh! I shall burst—

Sau.   You sha'nt, I say.

Cho.   Nay, nay, 'tis my petition,
  If bursting really is his way,
      don't think of opposition.

Cleon.   On what do you set confidence
      that you should dare defy me?

Sau.   That I can speak; and have some sense
      in sauce-compounding. Try me.

Cleon.   You speak! A very dainty treat
      would you make of a question;
  To serve your raw and ragged meat
      for other folk's digestion.
  I know what happens with you all.
      For once you had a victim,
  A foreigner, the case was small,
      and handsomely you pick'd him;
  You muttered all the night and then,
      you walked the roads reciting;
  You gave your friends a specimen,
      but not by their inviting:
  Wine was not to be had so weak,
      you took to water-drinking.
  And then you think that you can speak!—
      the more fool you for thinking.

Sau.   What liquor was it aided you,
      the only living duper,
  To talk as no one else could do
      a city into stupor?

Cleon.   And whom will you presume to think
      my better or my equal?
  I'll eat my turbot hot, and drink
      a pot of wine for sequel;
  Neat wine, no water in it, I
      do not approve the mixture,
  And put our generals at Pylus
      in an awkward fixture.

Sau.　　And I will eat a dish of tripe,
　　　　　　With chitterlings to follow,
　　And staying not my mouth to wipe,
　　　　　　at one draught will I swallow
　　The broth they're boiled in : then I'll slit
　　　　　　the throat of every pleader ;
　　And Nicias [1] shall smart for it,
　　　　　　as I'm a dainty feeder.

Cho.　　In other things your moral tone
　　　　　　merits our approbation,
　　But drinking up the broth alone !—
　　　　　　should have some explanation.

Cleon.　Pooh ! you won't eat a dog-fish steak,
　　　　　　and tackle the Milesians.

Sau.　　I'll eat a side of ox, and make
　　　　　　the mines my own possessions.

Cleon.　I'll take you up and hind-before
　　　　　　Will pitch you doubled through the door.

Chorus.　By Neptune, that if you should do,
　　　　　　You'll after have to pitch me too.

Cleon.　The stocks shall hold you like a vice.

Sau.　　I'll have you tried for cowardice.

Cleon.　I'll tan your hide.

Sau.　　　　　　　　　I'll make your skin
　　　　A bag for thieves to put things in.

Cleon.　I'll peg you down.

Sau.　　　　　　　　Nay, you I'll chop.

Cleon.　I'll pluck you hairs.

Sau.　　　　　　　　I'll cut your crop.

Cho.　　Clap a ring upon his snout,
　　　　　　You may do it boldly, easily.
　　　　Catch his tongue and drag it out ;
　　　　　　Let us look if it be measly.
　　　　Fire, had we experience,
　　　　　　Might be feeble found to burn ;

---

[1] Bentley well makes a question whether Nicias, the soldier, is here intended : for he, with Demosthenes, is represented as abetting the Sausage-seller. In another comedy reference is made to another Nicias, one of the 'pleader' tribe.

These are feats of impudence
We had yet to live and learn.
Methinks that this
Is not amiss.
But at him, seize him,
Twist him, teaze him,
Do nothing small,
But let him have a heavy fall.
If he only yield a little,
stubborn though the hide and tough,
He will prove an arrant coward;
for I know him well enough.

Sau.　That he had been all his life long
till he was for better known;
When he put his sickle in the
harvest by another sown.
Now he has the ears he gathered
in the stocks exposed to dry,
And is looking for the people,
who he thinks will come to buy.[1]

Cleon.　You I fear not while the Senate
has direction of affairs,
And while Demus,[2] like a dummy
yonder sits and nothing cares.

Cho.　He says it! yet upon his cheek
There's not a tint of shame to speak.

Cleon.　May Cratinus spit upon me,
Morsimus teach me a part
In his play, if I don't hate you
frankly and with all my heart.

Chorus.　Oh, settler on each flower that yields
The sweet of bribes, in all the fields,

---

[1] In allusion to the Spartan prisoners: many of them were men connected with the best families in Sparta. It is said that they were ill-treated in order to induce their countrymen to be willing to make political sacrifices for their release.

[2] That is, the people sitting on the benches of the theatre. This at least is more like Aristophanes than Wieland's suggestion, that the character 'Demus' to be presently introduced, was already seen at the back of the stage.

Be made the pleasant theft to quit
As lightly as you swallowed it.
So will I sing the merry lay,
  ' Drink, for the luck that falls to-day.' [1]

Cleon. If you beat me in impudence,
             I'll own to the disgrace,
Nor share the feast of Jove from hence
             set in the market-place. [2]

Sau. I swear by every fisticuff,
             and every cut of knife
Which (and they have been quite enough)
             I have endured through life,
I'll beat you to your heart's content,
             or vainly I will own
Dog's meat has been the nutriment
             on which my bulk has grown.

Cleon. Fed on the meat of dogs you were !
             then how can you escape,
You utter scoundrel, when you dare
             contend with a dog-ape ?

Sau. Ha ! when I was a little boy
             I had my tricks to play
Upon the slaves in cook's employ :
             for instance, I would say,
' Ha ! ha ! a swallow; summer's nigh;
             he's flying up the street.'
And while they gaped into the sky,
             I'd filch a piece of meat.

Cho. A pretty piece of flesh ! as though
             you made a nettle-meal ! [3]
Before the swallows !   Did you so ?
             Such early days to steal !

---

[1] A song of Simonides.

[2] An image of Jupiter was set up in the market-place to admonish men to be honest in their dealings. It was understood that a proved rogue should be excommunicated from all part in the Deity's sacrificial feast. Cleon here assigns as against himself a different ground of unworthiness, namely, finding a man who could outdo him in impudence.

[3] The style of wit exhibited in this encounter is not worth much enquiry or comment. I own myself unsatisfied by the only explanation offered of this ' nettle-meal.' Nettles were used as food only when young in the *early* spring.

Sau. And then, if any stander-by
                    charged me with the offence,
I'd clap the meat beneath my thigh,
                    and swear my innocence.
A pleader once, who saw the game,
                    remarked when it was done,
' This lad will make his way to fame,
                    and govern everyone.'
Cho. And reason for it, on my word.
                    He knew what you had got;
He saw you steal it, and he heard
                    you swear that you had not.
Cleon. I'll make your courage somewhat small:
                    aye, aye, the pair of ye;
In tempest I am going to fall
                    and mingle earth and sea.
Sau. I'll reef my sausages and catch
                    the weather at my ease,
And not at yours.
Dem.   And I will watch
                    if we ship any seas.
Cleon. By Ceres, I will not endure
                    to see the public robbed:
Some hundred talents, I am sure,
                    you villain, you have fobbed.
Cho. Look out, and slack the sheet; I see a
                    cyclone of accusation.
Cleon.[1] Ten talents had from Potidæa,
                    I have on information.
Sau. Will you take one of them yourself,
                    and let proceedings stop?
Cho. Aye, willingly.   Let out a reef;
                    the wind begins to drop.
Cleon.   Four hundred talents, less or more—
          I'll bring you to account for four.
Sau.   I twenty you, for service left,
          Besides a thousand for sheer theft.

---

[1] This dialogue is a contest of barefaced impudence. It is here brought to a climax by representing Cleon charging against the other a piece of corruption which in fact he had himself committed.

Cleon.   I'll challenge you; for I engage
           You come of cursed [1] parentage.
Sau.   Your grandfather was henchman to—
Cleon.   To what? to whom?
Sau.   To Byrsiné.[2]
Cleon.   Knave.
Sau.   Rogue.
Cho.   Strike manfully.
                    [SAU. *and* DEM. *beat* CLEON.
Cleon.   Oh! oh!
           They beat me in conspiracy.
Cho. (*to* SAU.). Oh, noble mass of flesh and bone,
                    oh, soul sublimely great,
    How have you dawned to be alone
                    the saviour of the state?
    You have so well and artfully
                    sustained the wordy fight.
    How can I make an eulogy
                    to match my soul's delight?
Cleon. By Ceres! this does not surprise me.   I'm aware
Where all these things were pinned and glued upon the
        square.
    Cho. Oh, dear! he's talking wheelwright; can't you do
        it too?
Sau. Ah, ah! he went to Argos; I know what to do.
To win the Argives?—Nonsense.   For his private ends,
It was to forge a compact with his Spartan friends.
I know what sort of metal was in chiefest use,
And how they welded chains—to let the captives loose.
    Cho. That's giving smith for wheelwright.   Capital!
        bravo!
    Sau. And there were people here who struck in blow for
        blow.
Nay, send me not your friends, your silver and your gold,
The Athenians shall know, the story shall be told.

---

[1] Meaning 'of the family of Megacles,' reputed to be under a curse for
having slain the adherents of Cylon at the altar of Minerva.

[2] Put for Myrrhiné, wife of Hippias, to imply the charge of giving aid
and comfort to 'the tyrants.'   'Myrrhiné' might signify 'having the
odour of myrtle '—' Byrsiné' 'having the odour of a tan-yard.'

Cleon. I'll to the Council-hall. Aye, I will bring to light
Your vile intrigues, your plots, your meetings in the night,
Your secret dealings with the King, and what you squeeze
From your Bœotian vats.
    Sau.   What is the price of cheese ?
    Cleon. By Hercules ! I'll rack you.
                      [*Exit* CLEON, *infuriated.*
    Cho.   Now is the time for you
To show your mettle.   What do you propose to do ?
For he, I know, will rush into the Council-hall
And smother us with calumnies, and make a brawl.
    Sau. And I will follow him.   But here awhile be laid
The meat which I have brought, and sausage-chopping
          blade.
    Cho. A moment—on your neck smear you some little fat,
That you may slip his calumnies.
    Sau.   Well thought of, that ;
And like a trainer.
    Cho.   Eat these knobs of garlic.
    Sau.   Why ?
    Cho. To mettle you for fight.   Make haste.
    Sau.   No sluggard I.
    Cho. Now bite, abuse, accuse, and let the spurs go home,[1]
And come back having made a meal upon his comb.
        Now go you and fulfil
        The utmost of my will.
        Jove of the market-square
        Have you in constant care ;
        And having won the day,
    Come back with many garlands gay.
                    [*Exeunt.*

PARABASIS.

    Cho.   And now, the theme to change,
        Ye who, with ample range,
        Judge every taste and style,
        Attently hear our anapests awhile.

---

[1] Four lines above the Chorus uses the language of a trainer preparing
a wrestler ; here, that of cock-fighting, a favourite Athenian amusement.

If any one of the elder poets
　　　who put comedies on to your stage,
Had asked *us* [1] to recite his verses,
　　　we should have been very loth to engage
In his service.　But this poet
　　　comes to us with a different claim.
Certain men he marks for hatred;
　　　we have a thorough disgust for the same:
While he shows the spirit and courage
　　　well becoming a valiant knight,
Who will face all storm and tempest
　　　while he does his battle for right.
Much surprise exists among you,
　　　so he says, and many have sought,
Why his claims to have a chorus [2]
　　　up to this time had never been brought.
We are charged with his explanation.
　　　It was not any folly, he says,
But a sad conviction, which has
　　　stood in the way of his offering plays.
Muses and maidens many are hard to
　　　please; and coyer than Comedy none.
Many indeed have been her suitors;
　　　few who have found in her will to be won.
Then, he says, that your critical favour
　　　has too much of an annual cast:
Those who have won it in earlier days have
　　　found, to their sorrow, it does not last.

---

[1] Under ordinary circumstances it would have been an insult to a class who even in democratic Athens had a recognised position as the ‘higher order’ to introduce *the Knights* as the Chorus of a comedy. Aristophanes here offers his explanation for doing so. The emphasis of restriction upon the original word ἡμᾶς in this place does not appear to have been noticed by the scoliast and commentators or translators who have followed.

[2] In the ordinary course a dramatic poet having composed his play, ‘asked for a chorus’; that is to say, he offered his composition to one of the Choregi, whose duty it was to be at the cost of putting the play upon the stage. The three comedies of Aristophanes which had been already represented were not offered to the Choregus, or the public, in his own name.

He observed what Magnes had to
          bear when his crown was gathering grey ;
He who had carried off more prizes
          than any other man of his day.
He who went through all the gamut,
          one while Harping, then as a Bird,
Lydian, Palmer-worm, or as dipped in
          Frog-colour,[1] always merrily heard,
Pleased you not in his later days, for
          he could not for ever be young :
So you cast away the old man,
          when the merry jest failed on his tongue.
He remembers too, Cratinus,[2]
          flowing once in the glory of force
Through a soil that broke before him :
          how he swept in his violent course
Oaks and planes and all opposers :
          then, at meetings of jovial souls,
'Fig-shod Doro' was the favourite
          song they chanted over their bowls ;
That, and 'Craftsmen hymn-composers.'
          Such was he then in the flush of bloom :
Now, without a pang, you see him
          poor, and drivelling down to his tomb.
Tuneless, unstrung, from the lyre its
          amber stops are dropping away.
So the old man, like a Connas,[3]
          dully maunders into decay.
On his brow the chaplet withers,
          on his lips is a deadly thirst :
He, who in the Prytaneum   [first ;
          should have drunk with the honoured and

---

[1] These are allusions to the names of comedies of Magnes.

[2] Cratinus was at this time ninety-six years old. Probably he was not grateful for Aristophanes's style of patronage and commiseration. At any rate, with a comedy entitled *The Wine-flask* he carried off the first prize in the next year against Aristophanes himself, with his favourite production *Clouds*.

[3] Connas was a flute-player, who, though he won the honours of his art in the Olympic contests, spent his latter days in unrelieved poverty.

He, who in this [1] Temple of Bacchus
      should have sat the mark of all eyes,
Waking the thought of his ancient glories,
      shame to you, a driveller dies.
And Crates too, from your whimsical tastes,
      what has the poor man not had to bear?
Who, at the least [2] expense, has sent you
      feasted full of capital fare:
Mincing though his lips are, he can
      cook tit-bits for the many or few;
Sometimes falling, sometimes otherwise,
      he alone has favour with you.
These examples scared the poet.
      Furthermore, he made the remark,
One should learn to row before one
      undertakes to govern the bark.
Now do you, respecting these his
      reasons and prudential fears,
Send him with eleven oars [3] forwards,
      gladdened in heart with spirited cheers.
Semichorus. Neptune, thou horseman king,
      Who lov'st the coursers' whinnying,
      And clatter of their brazen feet,
      And blue-stemmed galleys fleet,
        And youths all emulous
      To be the foremost and to vie
      In the splendour of their chariotry—
        (May it not ruin us!)
Lord of the golden trident, to our Chorus come,
Oh, dolphin-driver, shrined in Sunium,
And in Geræstus worshipped, Saturn's son,
Most loved and reverenced by Phormion,[4]

---

[1] The theatre.

[2] At the least expense of wit, it is said, because his comedies were remarkably short.

[3] This expression is not unanimously and conclusively accounted for; but it represents some then well-known mark of honour.

[4] An enterprising and successful officer at sea.—*Vide* Table at the year 420.

And, as our fortunes now appear,
Of all Gods most unto Athenians dear.
Cho. We would speak our [1] fathers' praises.
     Men they were, to tell their tale,
Worthy of the land that bore them,
     worthy of the Temple veil.[2]
Wheresoever battle called them,
     on the land or on the sea,
Won they glory for the city,
     bringing home a victory.
Never one of them was known to
     count the foes that stood in front;
But a soul that bore them forward
     made them bear the battle's brunt.
If one fell upon the shoulder,
     he would wipe away the stain,
Disallow it was a fall, and
     grapple with his man again.
Did one lead some expedition,
     and come back victorious,
He would ask no public mess,[3] or
     beg it of Cleænetus.
Now, unless they have their messes,
     and a preference of place,
They decline to fight your battles.
     We will ask this as a grace,
For our city and religion
     only let us freely fight.
Nothing further will we ask you,
     save it be this little right,

---

[1] As the foregoing Ode and that which follows are in character for 'Horsemen,' so here it must be understood that the 'Chorus' are speaking restrictively of *their* fathers, the Knights.

[2] A veil or curtain, the object of much care, upon which were embroidered the acts of Gods and heroes, and in later times, the acts of distinguished Athenian citizens; it was carried in procession at the festival Panathenæa, but usually hung in the Temple of the Goddess.

[3] In the Prytaneum, as guests of the State. It has already been invidiously observed of Cleon, that he not only had this privilege but abused it. It was a privilege much coveted and envied.

When the peace is re-established,
　　　　and we all may live at ease,
Let us not be grudged to wear our
　　　　hair, and comb it if we please.[1]
Semichorus. Pallas, our city's queen,
　　　Under whose guardian sway is seen
　　　The holiest land, and given to it
　　　Man's best in might, in war, in wit,
　　　　Hither; and bring with thee,
　　　Friend to the Knights, against all foes
　　　Our trusty aid in battle blows,
　　　　Our help-mate Victory.
　　　Come, Pallas, come, if ever on our side
　　　Thou willest to sustain our native pride,
　　　Regard thou us in these men's eyes,
　　　And let us carry off the victor's prize.[2]
Chorus. What we feel about our horses
　　　　we would willingly relate.
They deserve our warmest praises,
　　　　for their service has been great.
Many times in march and action
　　　　have they borne us stoutly on:
Still their feats on land are little
　　　　worthy of comparison
With their conduct on the transports;
　　　　when they bravely leaped on board,
Bought their mugs with leeks and onions
　　　　for the voyage to be stored;
Then they seized the oars and plied them
　　　　just like ordinary men,
Shouting as they bent upon them,
　　　　'Hippapai,—that stroke again,'
'Now go to it,'—'what's the matter,
　　　　Samphora,[3] you shirk your oar?'

---

[1] Like our Cavaliers, the Knights cherished their locks: it was an aristocratic fashion not approved by the people. Probably it was a Spartan fashion. When a vidette from Xerxes went to reconnoitre the Spartans encamped at Thermopylæ, he saw them, some engaged in athletic exercise, some combing their hair.

[2] For the best comedy at this festival.

[3] A frequent name given to a horse.

Then they leapt upon the Isthmus.[1]
           Soon as they had touched the shore,
Colts began to kick their beds up,
           and to look for overcoats,
Others caught the crabs, and eat them,
           just as they would Poland oats ;
Digging for them, if one did not
           from his burrow pop his head.
So Theorus tells a story
           that a crab[2] of Corinth said,
' Neptune, 'tis beyond endurance,
           neither on the land nor sea,
Can I get beyond the clutches
           of this hungry cavalry.'

Enter SAUSAGE-SELLER.

Cho. Oh, most beloved of men, and least to be repressed,
How have I been for thee by anxious thoughts possessed.
But since you have returned safely, it seems, and well,
How went the matter with you, we beseech you, tell.
  Sau. Then, in a word, I am the Council-conqueror !
  Cho.   Oh ! tidings worthy shouting for !
Oh, speaker of good words, of deeds beyond expression
        The doer !   Of the facts
        Put me in full possession ;
        For these are acts
      No journey would be long to hear.
        Speak then ; be bold ;
        Your story will be told
        Into a well-pleased ear.
  Sau. In truth 'tis worth your while to hear how matters
      went.
Soon as he left this place I followed to prevent

---

[1] Aristophanes humorously transfers to the horses an affair in ·
200 Knights were engaged, having been embarked with 4,000 infantry, for
a sudden descent on the coast of Corinth. It occurred only a few months
before the production of this comedy.

[2] The allusion is to a man named Carcinus—that is ' Crab '—who had
made himself obnoxious to the Knights.

Advantage from his start.   He, when he got within,
At once broke forth in thunders with a horrent din.
To overwhelm the Knights he flung at them—what not ?
Whole cliffs of words ; and made it seem there was a plot.
The Council quickly answered to the seed of lies ;
Mustard it looked ; and from knit brows glared angry eyes.
When that I knew and saw it so profoundly stirred,
Implicitly believing all the lies it heard,
' Tag,' said I, ' Rag and Bobtail, Thimble-rig and Plant,[1]
And thou, oh Market-place, that ever wast my haunt
From earliest days, inspire me now with daring force,
A fluent tongue, and tone of impudence of course.'
Here, somewhere on my right I heard a sound which I
Interpreted for favour ; whereupon I cry,
' Oh Council, I esteem my fortune very great
That I the first am here good tidings to relate.
For never since the war's commencement have there been
Anchovies so abundant as may now be seen.'—
All countenances brightened as my news was heard,
I seized my time and added underneath a word
For wise men—' It were well to clear the shops of dishes
That each might get one's obole's worth of little fishes.'
They clapped their hands, with open mouths on me intent.
Whereon the Paphlagonian, knowing what it meant,
And what would please the Council—said, upon the shift,
' We owe the Goddess thanks for this most welcome gift,
And therefore I propose a hundred beeves be slain.'
Whereon at once the Council fell to him again.
But I, unwilling to be worsted, said ' 'Twas mean ;
Make it,' said I, ' two hundred,' and outshot him clean.
' And further to the Huntress[2] vow,' suggested I,
' A thousand goats to-morrow, if a man may buy
Sardines a hundred for the obole.'   In a trice
The Council all was bent to hang on my advice.

---

[1] These are to be understood as the patron Gods, or *Guardian Genii*, of
the Sausage-seller, whom he is invoking.   The tame, trading associations
of ' Market-place ' with us, of course give no adequate idea of that City
centre where all the idle and mischievous of the lowest class congregated
for their daily amusement.
[2] Artemis or Diana.

He heard amazed, and babbling out some stuff,
Met from the officers with treatment rather rough:
They dragged him from his place, while all the clamorous
        crowd
Were talking of anchovies. ' Might he be allowed,'—
' A herald had come in '—he only wished to say
' What were the Spartan overtures for peace,'—but nay,
With one accord they shouted, ' Peace ! that's very nice !
Anchovies you should say : for they have heard the price ;
We want no peace.   No ; let the war go on.'   And so
They cried upon the president to let them go.
And then they leapt the rails.   But I had slipped away
To buy up all the fennel to be had to-day ;
Which I bestowed in presents, as it was required,
For fish sauce.   How I was applauded and admired,
It needs not to describe.   Suffice it, that it means
I've bought the Council for an obole's worth of greens.

     Cho.   In this business your address
              Is a pledge of all success.
              Yonder wily rogue hath found
              There's a rogue upon the ground
                Who can teach him,
                Overreach him ;
              And in his especial game
              Put his knaveries to shame.
              But consider, now you know him
              Once again how you may throw him,
                Ere you take the prize.
              We —but that you understand—
              Shall be always close at hand,
                Very staunch allies.

                      [CLEON *is seen approaching.*

  Sau. Here comes the Paphlagonian trundling the wave
That is to overwhelm us.   Ah, but he looks brave,
Ready to drink me.

                Enter CLEON.

  Cleon.   If there yet remain a lie
In me unused, it shall go hard but you shall die.

Sau. I like your threats; your smoky fustian charms
  me too;
It sets me dancing—so—hey, cock-a-doodle-doo!

Cleon. By Ceres, I will eat you, that shall be your death,
Clean off the earth, or never draw another breath.

Sau. Eh? eat me, did you say? But I will drink you first,
And when I've swallowed the last drop of you I'll burst.

Cleon. I swear it, by the seat of honour which I won
For what I did at Pylus, you shall be undone.

Sau. The seat of honour! you! But I will see you cast
Headlong from that, and sitting last among the last.

Cleon. By heaven I'll have you put into the pillory.

Sau. Hah! you are angry. Bring some food.[1] What
  shall it be?
What like you best? A purse?

Cleon.   I'll claw your bowels out.

Sau. I'll pare the public mess in which you thrust your
  snout.

Cleon. I'll have you before DEMUS;[2] you shall have your
  due.

Sau. I'll with you; I can lay it on as thick as you.

Cleon. What does he care for you? You do not know his
  bent;
But I can fool him to his very heart's content.

Sau. You fancy DEMUS is your private property.

Cleon. I know the bits he relishes: leave that to me.

Sau. And like a wicked nurse, you chew for him one bit
And swallow three yourself.

Cleon.   That is the trick of it.
But let us in to DEMUS.

Sau.   Good, I follow you.
Let nothing stop us.

Cleon.   DEMUS, pray come out.

Sau.   Aye, do:
Come out.

---

[1] With allusion to a proverb, 'Beware of approaching a hungry man,
because he is apt to be snappish.

[2] The General Assembly of the People, impersonated.

Cleon.   Come out, my DEMEY dear, and you shall know
How I'm insulted.

> [DEMUS *appears from the doors at the*
> *back of the stage.*

Demus.   Who are these that clamour?   Go,
You've torn my olive branch.[1]—My Paphlagonian,
What have they done to you?

· *Cleon.*   I'm beaten by this man
And these young puppies.

Demus.   Why?

Cleon.   Because I love you, dear.

Demus (to Sau.). And who on earth are you?

Sau.   · *His* rival 'twill appear: ·
For long since I have been your lover and desired
To do you services; as others have aspired,
Men of good stamp: but he prevented us: for you
Will not admit to favour honest men and true;
But give yourself to tanners, cutters-up-of-hides.
To cobblers, chandlers, and I don't know whom besides.

Cleon. For I take care of DEMUS.

Sau.   How so?   What d'ye mean?

Cleon. At Pylus I slipped by the Generals, as was seen,
Took ship and brought the Spartans back.

Sau.   Just as I took
For him a mess of pottage which I did not cook.

Cleon.   Now call a meeting, DEMUS; put it to the test
Which is the most devoted to your interest?
And let it be decreed on me your love you fix.

Sau. Let him decide: but anywhere but in the Pnyx.[2]

----

[1] The Eiresioné; a branch of olive usually placed near or over the
door of a private house, probably in its origin having some significance of
Peace and Welcome; and so in some distant degree related to the 'bush'
hung out from an inn; whence the proverb, 'Good wine needs no
bush.'   It is apparently intended to signify the captiousness of Demus,
that he begins by laying a charge against somebody for something.

[2] It was the 'Council' or 'Senate of Five Hundred,' before whom
took place that scene described by the Sausage-seller, when he comes back
to the Chorus describing himself as Council-conqueror, l. 573.   Here
Cleon moves the appeal to the whole 'demus' or Populace in General
Assembly, described in the opening of *Acharnians.*

Demus. It must be in the Pnyx : I cannot sit elsewhere.
Sau. I'm ruined then : for he's an idiot when there.
Cho.   Out all your cables, and belay:
          And strike no blow that he can parry.
     He has the art to find a way
          Where men of duller wit miscarry.
     Assume a full and dashing style :
     Be firm and on your guard the while,
     Prepared to break his bold attack :
     And push him as he staggers back.[1]
               [*The scene is changed, and the characters ar-*
                    ranged so as to represent a popular meet-
                    ing in the Pnyx. DEMUS, *however, is the*
                    single representative of 'THE PEOPLE.'

Cleon. To the Lady Athenæa
               this my prayer I make and crave,
     If I have towards this DEMUS
               been the most attentive slave,
     (Always saving Lysicles and
               Cinna and Salabaccho),[2]
     As it is at present, may I,
               doing nothing, always go
     To the public hall for dinner.
               If I entertain a thought
     Short of pure affection to you ;
               if indeed I have not fought
     One against a thousand for you,
               may my death avenge your wrongs,
     Be my body sawn in pieces,
               and cut into leather thongs.
Sau. If I do not love you, DEMUS,
               do not as my father treat,
     May I too be chopped to atoms,
               and boiled up for sausage-meat.

---

[1] The figure seems to be drawn from a manœuvre of naval combat
wherein one vessel waits the attack of the other, with a heavy weight
suspended from a cross-beam ; the effect of the fallen weight is to be
followed by an attack with the prow.

[2] Lysicles, or the 'sheep-dealer' referred to l. 119, as People's favourite
before Cleon. The two others are women notorious and infamous.

If you don't believe it, scrape me
    with some cheese into a pie,
Put a flesh-hook in my body;
    drag me out and let me die.
Cleon. Let the pledges of my love be
    taken into fair account.
Who has brought to your exchequer
    wealth to such a great amount?
Some I racked, and some I strangled,
    some I asked it of as due;
What cared I about who owned it
    so I had to give to you.
Sau. That is but a trifle, DEMUS,
    I will do for you as much;
Serve your table with the loaves which
    I from other people clutch.
His regard for you is nothing,
    that I undertake to show,
But his loving for the corner
    where your pleasant embers glow.
You, for token, you, whose sabre
    slew the Medes at Marathon,
And for us a theme of glory
    not to be exhausted won,
You, without a care, he suffers
    here to sit upon the stones.[1]
I have brought for you a cushion,
    to relieve your aching bones:
Do, I beg you, rise a moment
    and sit softly upon this;
Pray do not be galled and blistered
    as you were at Salamis.
Demus (accepting a cushion and much gratified). Who
   are you?   Are you descended
    from the good Harmodius?
It is nobly done of you, to
    show us your affection thus.

---

[1] The meeting of the whole people in the Pnyx was of course in the
open air: see the opening of the *Acharnians.* It appears there was no
accommodation for sitters but the native rock or stone benches.

Cleon. What a very mean attention
     to him puts you at your ease!
Sau. You no doubt have often caught your
     fish with cheaper bait than these.
Cleon. I will stake my life upon it,
     never did the man appear
Who regarded more your comfort,
     or to whom you are so dear.
Sau. 'Comfort' quotha! Yet you see him
     eight years stifled up in huts,
Creeping into dog-deserted
     holes and empty water-butts.[1]
Yet when Archeptolemus [2] came,
     bringing overtures for truce,
You expelled him from the city,
     treating him with gross abuse.
Cleon. Should not DEMUS lord it over
     all the Greeks? for, is it not
Prophesied about his future,
     that it is his coming lot
As a judge in Arcady to
     earn five oboles for the day?
Only let him wait a little,
     I will try to make a way—
Foul, if fair is insufficient—
     how he may achieve the three.[3]
Sau. You will try: but not that he may
     be the lord of Arcady,
But that you may plunder more, and
     finger bribes from the allies:
While good DEMUS, war-perplexed and
     with a mist before his eyes,

---

[1] When the rural population retired before the Peloponnesian invaders within the walls of Athens, they were put to great straits for accommodation.

[2] As appears from this place the name of a deputy from Sparta who brought overtures from Sparta soon after the affair of Pylos.

[3] The dicast's pay at Athens was now two oboles; it is therefore the difference which is here meant.

Shall not see your rascal doings,
                or at least has no escape,
And by gross corruption shall be
                held to you with mouth agape.
But if ever peace should come, and
                he get out into the fields,
Taste a dish of furmity, or
                know the fruit an olive yields,
He will know what he has lost by
                taking wages,[1] and return
Keen and angry : then the manner
                of his vengeance you will learn :
This you know and so beguile him,
                dealing out your prophecies.
Cleon. Is it not too bad that you should
                rail on me and tell such lies ?
When my services to Athens
                and the people have been such
That Themistocles did never
                for the city half as much.
Sau. Hear him, Argos ![2] You comparing
                merits with Themistocles !
He, that when the city's cup might
                barely touch the lips with ease,
Made it full and brimming over : ˎ
                served her as a morning dish
With Piræus,[3] and supplied her
                with a double stock of fish.
You, his match, would make the city
                in your fashion small enough,
Cross-walling,[4] and feeding her with
                windy food of Prophet's stuff.
He, 'tis true, was banished—you are   ˎ
                feeding on a double mess.

---

[1] Either as dicast in the courts, or as military pay.
[2] Words from a drama of Euripides.
[3] Themistocles taught the Athenians the value of Piræus as a port,
and fortified it.
[4] These words seem to indicate that Cleon had proposed some plan for
a cross-wall, probably to reduce the line of defence : but it does not
appear that any other record of such a design remains.

Cleon. For the love I bear you, DEMUS,
            must I hear this foul address?
Demus (*to Cleon*). Hold your tongue and don't be saucy.
            Know that you have had your day.
    All too long have you escaped me,
            cheating in your sneaking way.
Sau.   Yes, my DEMEY, he is stinking;
      Ever upon plunder thinking.
      While your mouth is catching flies
      Both his busy hands he plies;
      Here a tender sprout he robs
      From the peculator's jobs; [1]
      There he dips to get a scoop
      Out of your exchequer soup.
Cleon. I will show your peculation;
      Thirty thousand defalcation.
Sau.   Pooh! your rowing is a joke,
      Smacking water, missing stroke.
      Felon shall the people know you,
      Bribed to cheat them I will show you.
      What did Mitylene give
         For your voice the other day?
      Forty minæ, as I live—
         How much more I cannot say.
Cho.   Oh! born to aid the human race,
         I bless that tongue. Your blows redouble:
      Then step into the highest place:
         All will obey you without trouble.
      You have the Trident; [2] if you strike,
      You may be wealthy as you like.

---

[1] The sources of Athenian revenue were various: they are summed in one line of *Wasps* (Gr. 659, Transl. 419–20). The collection of these in any form must have involved a great number of officials, through whose hands money passed. These were all liable to pass their accounts. Those who had peculated even grossly might contrive to pass through this ordeal by making influential people sharers in the plunder. It is suggested that Cleon thus enriched himself. The figure seems to be that of regarding the accountable man as a fine head of cauliflower, of which Cleon had the stripping.

[2] The instrument and symbol of Neptune, wherewith he had power to shake the earth to its foundations.

Quit not your man; you have him fast;
With sides like yours he must be cast.
Cleon. Hold there, my friends; it is not so;
   and you are much deceived;
For by my hand, by Neptune, yes!
   a deed has been achieved
Enough to stop the mouths of all
   of those who dare revile us,
As long as there remains a shield
   of those I took at Pylus.
Sau. The shields, say you?—You give me there
   a handle to my mind.
Why, when you offered them, were not
   the handles left behind? [1]
Is that your love to DEMUS?—No:
   it was his dark intent
To baulk you if you wished to bring
   this rogue to punishment.
For ever at his heels a band
   of tanner-lads one sees,
The honey-dealers live next them,
   and then the men of cheese;
They understand each other, they:
   and if you ever took
Some act of his amiss, and had
   an oyster-shellish look, [2]
No doubt about it, we shall find
   they are engaged to steal
The shields, some night, and occupy
   the passes to—our meal.
Demus. Alackaday! and they have got
   the handles on them still!
And, with this base deception,
   you have treated me so ill?

---

[1] When arms were dedicated as votive offerings it was usual and proper to render them unserviceable, lest they should fall into the hands of enemies. It appears that Cleon in offering the shields had neglected this precaution.

[2] Threatening him, like Themistocles, with ostracism.

Cleon. Good Sir, I beg you not to give
              your faith too readily,
Or think that you will ever find
              a better friend than me.
I ever was the one to find
              a plot, and nothing stirred
Within the city, but I made
              my voice directly heard.
Sau. Aye, truly. Like the cunning men
              who fish for eels ; they take
No victims when the pond is clear :
              but stir it with a rake
Until the mud comes up ; why then
              they catch ; and so do you.
The city must be troubled, that
              you may your game pursue.
But come now, only answer this :
              for all the hides you sell,
Did ever you present to him
              you say you love so well
A shoe-sole ?
Demus.   By Apollo, no.
Sau. (*to* DEMUS).   Ah ! then you see him there,
And what he is.—But these I've brought.—Pray, Sir, accept
    a pair.   [SAU. *gives* DEMUS *a pair of shoes.*
Demus. Of all the men I know, you are
              the one whose conduct shows
The kindest interest in us,
              the city, and our toes.
Cleon. 'Tis hard a single pair of shoes
              should have such great effect,
And all that you have had from me
              you should not recollect.
Sau. And you have seen how he for clothes
              is put to sorry shift,
Nor thought a coat with sleeves might be
              a seasonable gift,
In winter too !—But here is one,
              my modest offering.

Demus. It did not strike Themistocles
                to find me such a thing!
A bright idea, too, was that,
                Piræus! but compare it
With this invention, and I think
                the overcoat will bear it.
Cleon. Alas, what jack-an-apish tricks
                you use to circumvent me!
Sau. I do not use such monkey-tricks
                as you yourself have lent me.
Cleon. I'll not be beat in fawning, I.
                Pray you, accept this cloak:
Sir, it becomes you.
        [*Giving* Demus *a cloak from his own shoulders.*
(*To* Sau.)   Rascal there! now you may go and choke.
Demus. Out on you! faugh! you smell so ill
                of tannery, I hate you.
Sau. Ah, that's the reason he puts on
                the cloak, to suffocate you.
He had a like design before.
                You must remember when
The assafœtida was cheap?
Demus.   Of course I do: what then?
Sau. He made it cheap, that men might buy
                it, compassing your death.
For dicasts in the courts would kill
                each other with their breath.
Cleon. What foolery is this you try,
                you villain foul and base?
Sau. The Goddess has commanded me
                to put you out of face.
Cleon. That shall you not—I'll see to it.
There is a galley you shall fit;[1]
'Tis old and wanting some repair—
May ruin you—that's your affair.
And I will see 'tis not forgotten,
The sail you go with shall be rotten.

---

[1] By way of tax upon property the richer citizens were called upon to fit out ships for service. Probably enough, as here indicated, this was sometimes made a means of oppression and wreaking personal spite.

Chorus. Beware! the man is boiling hot,
   And will be over. Check the pot.
   Take off some fire, and from the brew
   A ladleful of threats or two.
Cleon. My vengeance will be sweet when you shun
   The pressure of a ' contribution.'
   For I will see you are not missed
   In making out the ' Wealthy List.'
Sau. Your threats I answer with a—wish.
   All hissing be the jelly-fish
   Within the frying-pan, when you
   In Council have a thing to do
   For the Milesians ; and therein
   A talent, as your price, to win.
   May you intend to finish eating
   The jelly-fish before the meeting ;
   But just as you are setting to,
   May some one call for you; and you,
   Eager to get the talent, poke
    Too large a piece into your swallow,
       And choke!
    That is my prayer.
Cho.   By Jove, by Ceres, and Apollo!
    But this is rare!
Demus. True. And he is besides a thorough People's man
As ever was. But you, you Paphlagonian,
Who say you love me—faugh! your kisses poison me—
There's garlic in them. But you shall no longer be
Steward of mine. Give me the ring.
 Cleon (giving the ring).   There. But know this,
Me from the stewardship rashly should you dismiss,
A greater knave than I must come into my place.
 Demus (looking at the ring). This cannot be my ring.
     So far as I can trace,
 It bears another sign.
Sau.   What was the sign?
Demus.   A leaf[1]
Of fat beef cooked.

---

[1] Vide *Acharnians*, l. 967.

Sau.   This is not such.

Demus.   What! not the beef?
What then?

Sau.   A cormorant agape, to speak or dine.

Demus. Ah! bah!

Sau.   What?

Demus.   Off with it. It is no ring of mine.
Cleonymus [1] will own it.

    (*Giving another ring*). Take you this, and charge
To rule my house.

Cleon.   Not so, till you have heard at large
My oracles, good Sir.

Sau.   And mine.·

Cleon.   In mine 'tis said
That you shall rule the world with roses on your head.

Sau. In mine, that clothed in purple and embroidery,
Crowned, in a golden car, you shall chase Smecythé.[2]

Cleon. Fetch yours that he may hear.

Sau.   Of course.

Demus (*to* CLEON).   And let us see
Yours too.

Cleon. I will.

Sau.   And I, for what should hinder me?

                                             [*Exeunt.*

Chorus. Delightful will the dawning be
      To us and all posterity
      That brings the day when we shall see
          Cleon's clean overthrow.
      And yet there are, as I am told,
      A certain few morose and old,
      Who haunt the Mart,[3] where suits are sold,
          Who say they think not so.

---

[1] *Acharnians*, l. 79.

[2] If from the original the words 'and master' were added, it would
only turn twilight into absolute darkness, which the scoliast's glimmer of
light does not dispel. Smecythé is said to have been a king of Thrace.

[3] So I understand Δεῖγμα τῶν δικῶν. The Deigma was a sample-hall
or sort of Merchants' Exchange at Piræus, but Aristophanes here adding
'of suits or causes' indicates I think the Court of Heliæa, where 'justice'
was bought and sold.

'If this man never had appeared,
To be by all the city feared,'—
   For so runs their demurrer—
'We never should have had at hand
Two articles in great demand—
   A Pestle, and a Stirrer.' [1]
For me, I often have admired
Under what master he acquired
The music of a hog; but they
Who were his fellow-scholars say
He was so slack to learn as lad
   To touch the lyre and sing,
That all concluded that he had
   No gift for fingering.
In vain his master would employ
   Each artifice and shift;
Till, angered at the last, 'This boy,'
Said he, 'will never, never learn
To touch a lyre: his only turn
   Is—fingering a gift.' [2]

Re-enter CLEON *and* SAUSAGE-SELLER, *each loaded with
oracles.*

Cleon. See you what I have here.   But much is left
   behind.
Sau. See you what I have here; a sample of their kind.
Demus. What are they?
Cleon.   Oracles.
Demus.   What, all?
Cleon.   You think it much?
By Jupiter, I have a coffer filled with such.
Sau. Besides an upper room, two blocks of buildings, I.
Demus. Who made all these predictions?
Cleon.   Bacis mine are by.

---

[1] In *Peace* Cleon is again called a 'pestle'; the other article
commonly means a 'ladle,' but here and below a ladle especially for
stirring the ingredients of soup while boiling.

[2] Aristophanes is not responsible for the exact play on words here
given: he has his own, which is untranslatable, between 'Doristi,' in
the Dorian mode, and 'Doro-dokisti,' 'fingering gifts.'

Demus. And yours?

Sau.   By Glanis, Bacis' brother : elder too.

Demus. But what are they about?

Cleon.   Athens, Pylus, and you,
And me and everything.

Demus.   Of what have yours to tell?

Sau. Of Athens, lentils, Sparta, shoals of mackerel ;
Of market-men who cheat us in the weight of bread ;
Of you, of me.

Demus.   Make haste and let me hear them read.
Especially that one in which I take delight,
How, like an eagle,[1] I through clouds shall take my flight.

Cleon. True for you : but attend to me while I recite :—

> Son of Erectheus, mark the import grave
> Of words Apollo speaks from out his cave
> Over the holy tripod unto thee.
> Keep carefully the Sacred Dog, saith he,
> Sharp-toothed, wide-jawed. For thee does he purvey,
> Barking most frightfully, supplies of pay ;
> Which else would fail. The Daws, his enemies,
> Pursue the good Dog with ill-omened cries.

Demus. By Ceres, I see not to what this jingle draws :
What business has Erectheus with a dog and daws?

Cleon. I am the dog ; for you I bark so loud : and, see,
Phœbus desires that you will keep the dog—that's me.

Sau. That is not what the prophet, but the dog, dictates,
Who gnaws at oracles just as he does your gates.
I have an oracle that speaks of him aright.

Demus. Read it. But let me get a stone, and hold it tight,
For fear the oracle about the dog should bite.

Sau.   Son of Erectheus, mark that stealthy dog,
> That Cerberus, who, with an eye to prog,
> Fawns on you while you sup, and snaps a fish
> Unless you keep your eye upon the dish.
> By night about the larder will he prowl,
> And carry off an Island[1] like a fowl.

Demus. By Neptune, Glanis is by much the better seer.

Cleon. Reserve your judgment for a little while, and hear.

---

[1] See Comedy *Birds*, l. 943.

[2] The dominion of Athens over the Islands, nominally independent
offered many occasions to corrupt demagogues for taking bribes.

A wife in holy Athens bears a Lion,
Who, for the People, many gnats will fly on,
As for his whelps: him keep you and environ
With wall of wood and towers of massive iron.

Demus (*to* SAU.). Have you a notion what this means?
Sau.　　　　　　　　　　　　By Phœbus, none.
Cleon. Surely the meaning is as patent as the sun.
The God desires that you will have a care for me;
For I to you am Lion.
Sau.　　　　　　　One thing willingly
That here appears he fain would smother if he could:
Namely, what is the 'iron,' what the 'wall of wood,'
In which Apollo bids the man be kept in ward.
Demus. How has the God shown that?
Sau.　　　　　　　　　He means the stocks [1] afford,
With pillory attached, the place where he should be.
Demus. This oracle will be fulfilled, it seems to me.

Cleon. Believe him not, for envious Ravens croak,
But love the Hawk, and let him still invoke
Grateful remembrance of the daring deed
Which brought you home the Crows of Spartan breed.

Sau. A deed he did when drunk. But here's a prophecy
About the fleet; to which 'twere well you should apply
Your best attention.
Demus.　　　　　　I attend; so read, and say
First, how the men who man my ships shall get their pay.

Sau. Yon stealthy dog-and-fox, Aegides, mark,
Swift, and his bite will come before his bark.

You see the drift?
Demus.　　　　　Philostratus, it may be guessed.
Sau. Not so: but yonder rogue has always in request
Swift ships upon exchequer-service. Phœbus now
Enjoins you that demand of his to disallow. [2]

---

[1] The application of the words to the stocks is not as far-fetched as it would seem. Herodotus, ix. 37. ξύλῳ σιδηροδέτῳ is used to describe the stocks from which Hegesistratus escaped by cutting off the blade of his foot.

[2] If there is little wit in this oracle and its exposition, there is here a stroke in behalf of political honesty which it is creditable to Aristophanes to have made in the presence of the Athenian people. They were in the habit of sending ships round to the islands, ostensibly to protect their commerce and to receive the contributions which each city or community

Demus. Why call the ship a ' dog-and-fox ' ?

Sau.   The ship is quick ;
So is the dog.

Demus.   But what of ' fox ' ? 'tis there I stick.

Sau. The foxes represent the men-at-arms, for they
Will always eat the grapes that come across their way.

Demus. That may be so. But where shall these same
                    foxes get
Their pay ?

Sau.   Leave that to me ; I will provide that yet.

Cleon. I have an oracle, and that is hearing's worth,
That you shall be an eagle, King of all the earth—

Sau. The Red Sea is included in *my* prophet's plan,
And lunch while you decide a case at Ecbatan.

Cleon. But I have had a dream, and there the Goddess
              · seemed
To hold a spoon, and from it health and plenty streamed.

Sau. And so have I, by Jove. I saw the Goddess stand,
An owl upon her head, a bucket in her hand :
Therefrom upon your several heads she let to trickle,
On yours ambrosia, on that man's garlic-pickle.

Demus. I see your Glanis is the veritable sage.
Myself to you I trust to govern my old age,
And bring me up again.

Cleon.   Nay, I beseech you, stay :
I'll find you barley and your dinner every day.

Demus. ' Barley ! ' don't mention it, the very name dis-
                    pleases :
I've been too much your dupe, yours and Theophanes's.

Cleon. It shall be barley-meal.

Sau.   I'll give you cakes and fish,
All ready fried ; and nothing else to do or wish
But eat.

---

made to the League in lieu of personal services. Dishonest commanders
coveted this employment, as it gave them great opportunities for exacting
' presents ' for themselves and their crews. The suggestion of Aristophanes's oracle is that this nefarious practice should be discontinued.
Perhaps he did not venture to make his oracle speak more plainly. Two
or three of these ' oracles ' are here omitted, as formed upon mere puns,
with very little humour.

Demus.   Then lose no time about it.   For the rest,
Which ever of you two shall furnish me the best,
To him will I consign the reins of government.

Cleon. I'll be the first to run.

Sau.   Not you : that's my intent.

          [*Exeunt* CLEON *and* SAU.

Chorus. You, DEMUS, have a nice domain ;
          For all men fear you, and you reign
               As though you were a king.
          And yet it takes but little skill
          To make you follow where one will :
          For flattery is your delight,
          And you may be bamboozled quite.
          The cunning orator will find
          Your mouth is open, and your mind
               Is gone wool-gathering.

Demus. Your hair [1] is longer than your wits,
          If you suppose my foolish fits
               Outrun my own control.
          Though I am fond of sitting still
          And tippling day by day my fill,
          I like an officer-in-chief
          Of mine to be an arrant thief.
          When he has gathered up a stock,
          I've nothing else to do but knock
               The pursy fellow's poll.

Chorus. If you are artful as you say,
          And that the subtle game you play,
               You needs must be a winner ;
          If thus upon your man you fix,
          And stall your oxen in the Pnyx,
          Against the day when fish is bad,
          Or cannot for your means be had,
          Then pick one from the feeding cribs,
          An ox with fat upon his ribs,
               And kill him for your dinner.

Demus. Do I not shrewdly circumvent
          The rogues who come with full intent

---

[1] See l. 540.

To plunder me by stealth?
I watch my time; I mark my fox;
And then I make the ballot-box,
Which gave them power, disgorge its votes: [1]
I put a feather down their throats.
Knowing exactly what they stole,
I make them give me back the whole
Of their ill-gotten wealth.

Enter CLEON, *carrying a chair*, SAUSAGE-SELLER *a table
and each a supper-box.*

Cleon. Out of my way!
Sau.   Be hanged!
Cleon.   This age I've been preparing
All I can think of, DEMUS, for your better faring.
Sau. An age!—I've been a thousand in the same employment.
Demus. And I have spent a million—waiting for enjoyment,
And am disgusted with you both.
Sau.   What's to be done
You understand.
Demus.   Explain, what?
Sau.   Let us run:
Placed for a fair start from the barrier let us try   ·
Which will do most for your advantage—he or I.
Demus. Well.
Sau.   I'm ready.
Demus.   Run.
Cleon.   He shan't slip by, as I did. [2]
Demus. Between the two to-day I shall be well provided.
Cleon. See you, I am the first to bring you forth a chair.
Sau. But not a table; I am far the foremost there.
Cleon. Here is a cake of grain from Pylus.
Sau.   Here a sippet,
Made by Minerva's ivory hand: I pray you dip it.

---

[1] That is, by a popular vote, I cause the recall of an appointment to office which had been given by a popular vote.
[2] See his boast, line 690.

Cleon. And here is some pea-soup, high-coloured, rich,
and hot;
Pallas, who fought with us at Pylus, stirred the pot.

Sau. The Goddess has a care for you, it is well seen:
Over your head she pours this broth, a full tureen.

Demus. The city would not be worth living in, I ween,
If she above my head held less than a tureen.

Cleon. Our Lady Fright-the-host[1] has sent this steak to
you.

Sau. Our Lady Noble-Sire[1] presents this tripe and stew.

Demus. We thank her, she remembers that her veil with
pleasure.

Sau. And pray Sir, taste this cup, mixed with the nicest
measure—
Just three to two.

Demus.   And bears it well upon my word!
How sweet!

Sau.   Tritogenes herself put in the third.[2]

Cleon. I beg you to accept a slice of my rich cake.

Sau. This cake, the whole of mine, I beg of you to take.

Cleon. Ha, ha, look you at this. You cannot give him hare.

Sau. Alas, I cannot. How can I procure it? where?
(*aside*) Oh, Wit! suggest some trick to make the fault's
amends.

Cleon. You see it?

Sau.   Never mind: for hither come my friends.

Cleon. Who are they?

Sau.   Legates, and their purses carry double.

Cleon. Where? where?

Sau.   What's that to you? don't give the
strangers trouble.

[*Cleon passes to the side of the* Sausage-
seller *to endeavour to see the 'Legates.'*
Sau. *seizes the opportunity to take*
Cleon's *dish of hare.*

[1] Titles for Minerva, probably invented in derision of such conceits
in general.

[2] That is, the third measure of water to two of wine. We may infer
from this place that such proportions of wine and water were considered
handsome.

Dear DEMEY, on this dish of hare vouchsafe to dine.

Cleon. Oh ! oh ! you artful thief, and you have stolen mine.

Sau. As you did those from Pylus.

Demus.   Answer me this question:
Whence did you get this happy filching-it suggestion ?

Sau. The Goddess gave me that, and I directly—took it.

Cleon. I hunted him the hare.

Sau.   I was the one to cook it.[1]

Demus. Away !   My thanks are only due to him who
          brought it.

Cleon. I am outdone in impudence—who would have
          thought it ?

Sau. But which of us has done the better to provide
For you and for your palate ? Pray you, Sir, decide.

Demus. To what criterion may I my judgment trust,
And give the audience assurance I am just ?

Sau. I will suggest one.   Search my canteen of provi-
          sion,
And then examine his.   I fear not the decision.

Demus (*looking into* SAUSAGE-SELLER'S *provision-box*).
Ha, ha ! what shall I find ?—

Sau.   ˙   Nothing !—my Daddy dear;
My offerings to you have made the cupboard clear.

Demus. The cupboard tells the truth that DEMUS is your
          care.

Sau. Try now the Paphlagonian's.   What see you there ?

Demus. All sorts of dainty things ;—a monstrous cake—
          how nice !
And yet he only gave me such a little slice !

Sau. That ever was his way.   Whatever he could clutch,
The little went to you, while he enjoyed the much.

Demus. The rascal that you were to steal, and cheat me
          too !
And I had honoured and bestowed so much on you.

---

[1] The wit in this line is keen and happy.   Aristophanes naturally puts
into the mouth of his Paphlagonian just what Demosthenes, the general,
might be supposed to urge against the real Cleon in regard to the Lacedæmonian captives : 'I was at the pains and risk of hunting the hare,'
while the Sausage-seller adopts what would be the nonchalant answer of
Cleon : 'But I served it up.'

Cleon. 'Twas for the city's good that I have played the
knave.

Demus. Give up to him the chaplet.

Sau. Quickly, quickly, slave.

Cleon. Not so : an oracle from Phœbus has related
By whom, and whom alone, I am to be abated.

Sau. Telling my name distinctly.

Cleon. I should like to see
How far your tokens with the oracle agree.
To test it, I will put you on examination.
In what school, as a boy, had you your education ?

Sau. The Shambles were my school : with fist-cuffs I was
broken.

Cleon. Ah ! say you ? How my mind misgives about the
token.
What art of fence learnt you in any other place ?

Sau. To steal ; deny on oath ; and look you in the face.

Cleon. Oh Lycian Apollo ! what must be my fate ?
What calling did you follow when at man's estate ?

Sau. Sold sausages.

Cleon. Alas ! I am undone. 'Tis slight
The hope that yet remains ere I am ruined quite.
Answer me only this. In the market-place did you,
Or at the city-gates, that sausage-trade pursue ?

Sau. Where else but at the gates, where they buy salted
stuff.

Cleon. Alas ! the prophet's words are only sure enough !
Bear off the hapless wretch !—Away : my sun has set.
And, chaplet, fare thee well ; though all unwilling yet
I part with thee : Thee shall another now possess,
No greater thief perhaps, but rogue with more success.[1]

[*Exit* CLEON.[2]

Sau. Hellanian Jove ! the honour of the day is thine !

---

[1] A parody from a line in Euripides, where Alcestis takes leave of her
marriage-bed.

[2] Dramatically Cleon should leave the stage here ; though in the
original there are two or three touches which imply that he is still
present ; these, however, the translator has ventured to suppress, and to
make some other slight abbreviations.

Demosthenes. And I salute thee. But bethink, the stroke
                    was mine.
That made a man of you.
    Demus.   Your name, Sir: what is it?
    Sau. 'Tis AGORACRITUS.[1]
    Demus.   Myself then I commit
To AGORACRITUS.
    Agoracritus.   And I will you provide
As never citizen of Catch-flies[2] did beside.   [*Exeunt.*
    Chorus.   I have lain awake at night,
                Thinking how Cleonymus,
                Spending less than most of us,
                Manages his appetite.
                Only let him (people say)
                Dine with those who can afford
                To put plenty on their board,
                He will never move away :
                They will say, (unless 'tis fable)
                ' Eat the viands without stint,
                But for heaven's sake take the hint,
                Do have mercy on the table ! '[3]
It is said the ships in port have
                had a meeting for debate,
Where an ancient Galley took
                upon her to expostulate.
' Ladies, have you heard the doings
                in the city touching us ?
'Tis reported, that a nasty
                fellow named Hyperbolus[4]

---

[1] By this name the ' Sausage-seller' appears to the end of the comedy.
As the name is untranslated, it does not seem necessary to give the line
which pretends to point its significance : more especially as the explanation
presents difficulties to the critics.

[2] ' Athens,' he should have said. Aristophanes's word seems to be the
same as the French ' Gobe-mouches.'

[3] As the point of this epigram seems to have been sometimes at least
missed, it may be well to fortify the idea by reference to the very well-
known lines :—

        Cum te, nate, fames ignota ad littora vectum
        Accisis coget dapibus consumere mensas.—*Æn.* vii. 124.

[4] A lamp-manufacturer, and leading man in the democratic party. See
Clouds, l. 945.

Has demanded that a hundred
   of us should be sent with him,
On a business to Chalcedon.'—
   This made all of them look prim.
Then spoke up a little craft, who
   yet had known no master's hand;
'Heaven forbid that I should ever
   go to sea in his command.
Rather than submit to such a
   captain upon any terms,
I would die of age in harbour
   and be eaten up by worms.
He have Nauson's tight Nauphante![1]
   God forbid he ever should!
Never! as I am a galley
   built of honest pitch and wood.
If a thing so out of reason
   Athens should be pleased to grant,
We must sail to the Theseum,
   there to sit all suppliant:
Or invoke The Venerable
   Goddesses[2] to shield our fame.
We at least will never aid him
   on the city to bring shame.
He has barrows for his lamp-trade,
   let him go to sea in those;
They are good enough to take him
   on his voyage to the crows.'

Enter AGORACRITUS.

Agor. Hushed be every sound of evil;
   let all legal processes stay.
Shut the Courts of Justice, for our
   city is bent on its holiday.
For this happy change of fortune,
   let this audience shout to the sky.

---

[1] The name of a ship.
[2] An euphemism for 'The Furies.'

Cho. Glorious light of holy Athens,
                 all the islands' friend and ally,
        Will your news diffuse the smell of
                 victims through the neighbourhood ? [1]
Ag. I have happily boiled up Demus ; [2]
                 he is changed from bad into good.
Cho. Oh deviser of wonderful notions,
                 where at present may he be found ?
Ag. His abode is in the city of
                 antique Athens, violet-crowned. [3]
Cho. When may we see him ? what is he dressed in ?
                 what sort of person has he turned out ?
Ag. As when with Aristides or Mil-
                 tiades he sat drinking a bout.
        You shall see him ; for I hear some
                 sounding as of an opening door.
        So prepare your throats to welcome
                 Athens seen in the fashions of yore.
                 [*Scene changes to a representation of Athens in
                 the olden time, and* DEMUS *appears with
                 his hair dressed with crobulon, surmounted
                 by a golden grasshopper—like a fine old
                 Attic gentleman, All of the olden time.*
Cho. Glistening Athens, crowned with violets,
                 envy of all for thy glory and worth,
        Take to thyself the monarch of Greece, and
                 of the whole inhabited earth.
Ag. There you see him with his grasshopper,
                 such in form as our grandfathers went,
        Smelling not of fish-shells [4] but of
                 truces and most delicate scent.
Cho. Hail, oh king of all the Grecians !
                 and you too ! for by you are done
        Deeds most worthy of our city, and
                 of our trophy at Marathon.

----

[1] Shall the city feast on the meat of sacrifices at the public cost ?

[2] An allusion to the myth of Medea, who induced the daughters of Pelias so to treat their father, as a method of restoring him from age to youth.

[3] See *Acharnians*, l. 584.

[4] A small shell used as ' pebbles ' for judicial voting.

Demus. My Agoracritus, my dearest friend and best,
Your boiling has done good that cannot be expressed.

Ag. Good sir, if you but knew how very sad and odd
You were before it, you would reckon me a God.

Demus. What did I do ? What was I like ? Do tell me,
　　　pray.

Ag. For instance, at the Meeting, should a speaker say,
' DEMUS, the love of you preoccupies my breast;
Believe it, I alone study your interest : '
On such a preface you would clap your wings and crow :
Or like a bull-calf shake your horns.

Demus. 　　　　　　　　　　　Eh ; did I so ?

Ag. Of course he went away with what he liked from
　　　you.

Dem. Eh? that I did; did I? and yet I never knew.

Ag. And then, by Jupiter, the ears upon your poll
Expanded and contracted like a parasol.

Demus. And was I such a fool? To think that I should
　　　dote !

Ag. Two orators should be contending for your vote :
One urges building ships, and asks the money, ' Nay,
'Twere better,' says the.other, ' spent in soldiers' pay.'
The man who asked for pay would rapidly eclipse
The efforts of the man who asked for building ships.
Why do you hang your head? Why cannot you stand
　　　still ?

Demus. I am ashamed to think of what I did so ill.

Ag. Nay, do not grieve. It was not you that did amiss;
You were misled by others. Come now, tell me this :
Suppose some scurril pleader should concluding say,
' Condemn this man ; the fine will find you meal to-day ;
Or let him off, if you have no desire to feed.'
What will you do with him who ventures thus to plead ?

Demus. I'll lift him in the air, and throw him in the pit,
With a weight about his neck,—Hyperbolus to wit.

Ag. That's spoken like a man of honesty and sense.
But for administration, how will you commence?

Demus. I'll see to it that men who in the galleys pull,
When they come into port receive their pay in full.

Ag. For that there's many a hardy fellow owes you
    thanks.

Demus. Then will I have no'jobbing in my soldiers' ranks.
By time and worth of services, and not by grace,
My citizens shall win and keep the higher place.

  Ag. That will abate Cleonymus, 'tis to be feared.

Demus. Then no one shall be heard until he gets a beard.

Ag. That strikes at Cleisthenes' and Strato's arguments.

Demus. It is the boys, I mean, lads of uncommon scents.
Who babble to each other fashionable cant:
' A clever fellow Phæax : carries all with rant,
Syncretic to a fault, and so original,
His crousis is superb : no having him at all.'
Long speeches and decrees I will forbid from hence :
And not to hunt shall be a capital offence.

  Ag. 'Twill be well done.

Demus.   For yonder Paphlagonian,
What shall we do with him ?

  Ag.   Not much to hurt the man.
Give him my ancient trade : he might have harder fate.
Let him sell sausages before the city-gate :
And air his ribaldry among the riff-raff there.

  Demus. Well thought of. For yourself, come in and take
      the chair
Vacated by that villain at my public mess;
And, for a mark of honour, take this festal dress. [*Exeunt.*

CLOUDS.

INTRODUCTION.

In this comedy Aristophanes has for ever connected his name with that of Socrates, and that in a way more to the credit of his wit than of his candour.

More fortunate in that respect than Cleon, SOCRATES is known to us as painted by another and friendly hand. When *Clouds* was being represented at Athens, there was a little boy of six years old who was to live and redeem Socrates from the outrageous misrepresentations of Aristophanes. Whatever might otherwise, on the credit of this author, have been accepted as fact, thanks to Plato, we may confidently assert that Socrates was *not* the master of a school of starveling disciples with whom he lived in community; that it is odious that his name should be connected with the idea of filching and petty trickeries; that there never was a man who more emphatically lifted his voice in behalf of truth and right, or more earnestly denounced every attempt to confound right and wrong. Let it be that *at* Athens there were unprincipled ' Sophists ' who, at least as a trick of rhetoric, undertook to teach the art of making the worse appear the better reason, Socrates was not one of them. It is inconceivable that a man of such sagacity as Aristophanes could have been mistaken on that point.

Had the obvious purport of this comedy been no more than a witty exposure of those Sophists, no more need have been said than to make this protest on the part of Socrates personally. But the animus of Aristophanes goes much farther. There is a studied attempt to stimulate hatred and even violence against Socrates as an unbeliever in the popular Gods, to confound him with, and overwhelm him in, the obloquy of Diagoras the Melian. More: it is not merely sophistical rhetoric which is the butt of the

comedian's shafts, but the pursuit of learning generally.
Geometry, geography, astronomy, all pursuit of physical
knowledge, are equally sneered at, not from the point of
one who had or cared to have better knowledge, but with
the disposition which, even to our own time, animates the
man of mere æsthetic literature to decry the later births
of science. With this there is combined in the comedy a
parade of zeal to rehabilitate education on the better, the
old-fashioned system. When, however, we look to the
features of this education, it will be seen to be confined
to the moral discipline of order, obedience, and respectful-
ness, the mere cultivation of the taste, included under the
general term μουσική, and bodily exercise.

What is the meaning of the part taken by Aristophanes?
and why was his zeal for this education connected with an
assault upon Socrates? We may find an answer to these
questions by regarding Aristophanes as nothing more than
a spokesman and partisan of the retrograde school of his
day. He lived in the generation and in the very focus of
great changes, social, political, and intellectual. It is
everywhere evident that he most cordially hated the
changes social and political. Does it not follow that he
equally suspected and hated the movement of intellect
too? That he really misliked the spread of education, or
at any rate would have confined it to the cultivation of
taste? In this idea we may find a key not only to this
comedy, but to sentiments scattered elsewhere. Naturally
enough, he would identify Socrates with the school of pro-
gress; he would regard him as a dangerous man before
whose spirit of criticism the venerable traditions of the
past, with their supposed guarantees for social order,
would crumble away. Aristophanes was sagacious enough.
He was almost a generation before his time in detecting
that there was a side on which Socrates might be discredited with a remarkably superstitious populace. He
bent himself to the attack with unusual earnestness. He
was proportionately chagrined by failure. The dramatic
judges and people did not share the feelings which the
comedian kept in reserve. The caricature which he put
upon the stage did not answer to the features of the

Socrates known to all.   It required a violent and reactionary revolution in the interest of Aristophanes's politics
before Meletus succeeded in an attack upon the lines
opened twenty years before by Aristophanes.   The comedy
failed ; its author had even the mortification of seeing the
first prize carried off by the veteran Cratinus, the 'driveller'
whom he had insolently patronised in the Parabasis of
Knights.

As a mere argument against Sophistry, the plot of the
comedy cannot be commended.   Strepsiades, a thickwitted
yeoman, is, to begin with, an unprincipled rogue.   Being
rich in land, he has been màtched with a lady of family
and breeding ; he grudges all outlay in maintaining his
wife and son in any condition above that of the coarse
farmer ; spending seems to him to be ruin.   He conceives
the idea of avoiding that evil by simply cheating his
creditors.   It seems that he has heard of the power of
rhetoric to prove that black is white : in search of such
power, to be used against his creditors, he goes to the Sophists.   Whether the result proves anything to the discredit of the school reflective readers will judge.   Some
observations on the part and character assigned to
Pheidippides are postponed to the end of the comedy, that
the fresh reader may form in the perusal his own unbiassed
impressions.

Failing to obtain the prize, Aristophanes reproduced
this comedy, probably with some alterations, in the following year ; but that comedy which has come down to us is
fortunately the *First Clouds*, with the small exception of
some angry lines prefacing the Parabasis.   These lines,
however, are not here translated, as for other reasons, so
because, however interesting to the student of the Greek
Drama, they could not be made so to the English reader.

Dramatis Personæ.

STREPSIADES, *an Attic yeoman.*

PHEIDIPPIDES, *son of Strepsiades.*

SERVANT *of Strepsiades.*

SOCRATES.

DISCIPLES *of Socrates.*

CHÆREPHON, *a sophist.*

CHORUS OF CLOUDS.

RIGHT-REASON.

WRONG-REASON.

PASIAS, *creditor of Strepsiades.*

WITNESS.

AMYNIAS, *creditor of Pheidippides, a broken-down racing-man.*

SCENE.—*In the house*[1] *of Strepsiades.* STREPSIADES, PHEI-
DIPPIDES, *and house-slaves, in bed.*

Strepsiades. This night is everlasting while I lie awake.
Oh dear! Oh Jupiter! will the day never break?
And yet I'm sure I heard the cock crow long ago.
But here these slaves lie snoring. 'T used not to be so.
Plague on the war! for other reasons as for this,
One can't correct one's servants when they do amiss.[2]
And that nice son of mine—there's nothing breaks his rest,
But there he sleeps, and five good blankets make his nest.
Well, if it must be so, close be the bed-clothes drawn,
I'll try to snore in chorus.—No! there is the dawn.
I cannot sleep. I'm eaten up with thoughts of duns,
Mangers, and mortgages. This work is all my son's.
Aye, he must be a gentleman; and have his horse—
His riding horse—and drive a handsome pair of course.
He dreams of horses. I am dying day by day
With watching of the moon still wane and wane away,
While interest is growing.—
(To a slave in bed).   Fellow, strike a light.
Bring me the ledger. I should like to know my plight,
The number of my creditors, and calculate
The interest now due. Come, let me see the state.—
'To Pasias twelve minæ.' How did that arise?
To buy the nag that has the star between his eyes.[3]
I'd rather that a stone had knocked out one of mine!
    Pheidippides (speaking in his sleep). Philon,[4] you're going
      wrong: keep to your proper line.—

---

[1] Perhaps this should be a court partially open to the sky; the beds
being under a colonnade; so that from the place a view may be had of
the Phrontisterion or Meditation-hall of Socrates and his fellows.

[2] They would run away and find protection with the enemy.

[3] This is really not the 'mark' by which Aristophanes has distinguished
this horse; but it seemed more material to force some connection between
the mark and malediction of Strepsiades, than to preserve the numeral
'κοππα.'

[4] The name either of one of his horses, or of the driver in a race.

Streps. See there! 'tis that which brings me ruin and
    disgrace;
Even in sleep he dreams of nothing but a race.
    Pheid. (*still asleep*). How many heats do war-appointed
      chariots run?
    Streps. 'Tis many heats that you are driving me, my
      son.
What's next to Pasias?—Amynias I see.
' Item, a pair of wheels and body—minæ three.'
    Pheid. (*as before*). Let the colt have his roll, and take
      him to his stall.
    Streps. ' Roll' do you say, young dog? You've rolled
      me out of all.
Some creditors have got their judgments, and the rest
Ask for security, at least for interest.
    Pheid. (*waking*). Why do you, father, toss and fidget all
      the night?
    Streps. I've bailiffs in the bed who never cease to bite.
    Pheid. Good man, I wish you'd let one get a wink ot
      sleep.
    Streps. Sleep on then : but the day is coming when this
      heap
Of debts will lay no little burden on your head.
                    [PHEIDIPPIDES *falls asleep again.*
A plague on match-makers! would that one had been dead
Before she matched me with thy mother! I was well
Before I learnt to know foul linen by the smell;
Living a country farmer's life; richly at ease
Among my grapes, and flocks of sheep, and hives of bees.
Then I must be the fool to wed a city dame!
Of Megacles of Megacles my lady came.
A haughty dainty Cœsyra,[1] she married me
Rank from my wine-vats, cheese-press, sheep-shearing!
    but she,
All perfumes, saffron, pretty kisses at our meeting,
Extravagant in dress, and delicate in eating.

---

[1] The name of the wife of Alcmæon; here taken to represent a lady
of very aristocratic connections.

I will not say that she was idle: nay, she span.[1]
But she was more than active: such a race she ran
That, holding up my coat in irony, I'd say,
The rate you go will use you up before your day.

Slave. The lamp is going out for want of oil.

Streps.   You scamp,
What did you mean by lighting such a thirsty lamp?
Come here, I'll stripe your skin.

Slave.   Why should you stripe my skin?

Streps. Because you put a wick of double thickness in.—
Then when we had this son, I and my lady had
Some wrangles on the point how we should name the lad.
Nothing but 'hippus' could her horsey fancy please—
Xanthippus, or Charippus, or Callippides.
I would have had 'Pheidonides;'[2] the name my sire
Bore with respect. Long time this kept us both on fire.
We settled it at last, by way of compromise,
Pheidippides. Then newer contests would arise;
For she would take the child and say in early days,
'When you are grown a man and drive a pair of bays
Like Megacles, and wear a splendid suit:' but I,
'When you go out to fetch the goats home by and bye,
In leather jerkin as your father does.' But nay,
He never would attend to what I had to say.
And so at last has brought upon my whole estate
A galloping consumption.—After much debate
Within my mind to-night, I've hit upon a course—
It is the only one—a most superb resource;
By which, if I can bring this heady youngster to it,
All may be well. I'll wake him. Aye, but how to do it?
How shall I wake him gently? Dear Pheidippides,
Pheidy, my boy—

Pheid. (drowsily). What, father?

Streps.   Kiss me if you please;
Give me your hand.

---

[1] We must suppose that her spinning was 'fancy' work: while the husband's coat was ragged.

[2] Hippus, signifying horse, as the compound of a name would imply some pretension to the habits of gentlemen of good estate. Pheidon signifies sparing or parsimonious. Pheidonides 'the son of a *careful* man.'

Pheid.   So, why ?

Streps.   Do you love me, my lad ?

Pheid. By Neptune of the horse, I do.

Streps.   You'll drive me mad.

Not ' of the horse ' I beg : for 'tis to him I owe
The weight of trouble which has brought my fortune low.
But if you really love your father as you say,
Hear and obey me, boy.

Pheid.   In what shall I obey ?

Streps. Give up the course of life that you are now
          pursuing,
And learn as I would wish.

Pheid.   What would you have me doing ?

Streps. But will you do it ?

Pheid.   Yes, by Bacchus.

Streps.   Then look here ;

You see that little door and little mansion near.

Pheid. I see it : what of that ?

Streps.   'Tis Meditation-hall ;

Where shrewd wits meditate on matters great and small
There live the men who teach that the o'erarching sky,
Is one great oven ; [1] men its constant coal supply.
They are the men who teach you for a little pay
The art to make the right or wrong side win the day.

Pheid. Who are these men ?

Streps.   By name I do not know them all,

But Meditants they are, and quite respectable.

Pheid. Bah, rogues ! the men who set all reason at de-
          fiance,

The shoeless, meagre-faced pretenders to a science ;
Like that poor devil Socrates and—what's his name ?
That Chærephon.

Streps.   Hush, hush ! don't be a fool ; for shame.
But, if you father's meal-chest may deserve your care,
Give up your stable-life and be a scholar there.

---

[1] The cosmical theory that the sky is a solid firmament over-arching
the earth suggested to the wits that the earth is the floor of an oven, and
the Gods the bakers. This had been represented before the Athenian
audience by the comic poet Crates in a comedy called *Panoptæ.*

Pheid. Not I, if you would give me—though—'twere
　　　worth the gaining—
The Phasian thorough-breds Leogoras is training.

Streps. My dearest, dearest boy, I do beseech you, go:
Do go and learn.

Pheid. 　　　　　　What is it you would have me know?

Streps. 'Tis said they have two Reasons, both exceeding
　　　strong—
The Reason for the Right, and Reason for the Wrong.
This latter one, they say, will put a decent face,—
Aye, bring you winner through the most dishonest case.
Now, if you'll learn me *that*, with confidence I'll rob all
My creditors, and never pay another obole.

Pheid. It cannot be.　How could a man of my connection
Endure the being seen with such a bad complexion?

Streps. By Ceres then you may despatch yourself from
　　　hence,
Pole-horse and hack! you shall not live at my expense.
Out of this house you go: pack off to feed the crows.

Pheid. The noble Megacles, I venture to suppose,
Will not permit it that his kinsman shall remain
Without a horse. I go: and treat you with disdain. [*Exit.*

Streps. I'm not the man to lie because I have been
　　　thrown.
No! praying to the Gods, I'll learn what may be known
At Meditation-hall myself. I own, 'tis late
To learn the niceties of logical debate
Now that my apprehension is becoming slow
And memory failing; notwithstanding I must go.
Why do I hesitate when matters are so grave?
Why don't I knock?—I will.—What hoa! within there!
　　　Slave!　　　　　　　　　　　　　　　　[*knocks.*

DISCIPLE, *looking out.*

Dis. Who's knocking at the door?

Streps. 　　　　　　　　Strepsiades, good sir.
Pheido's son of Cicynna.

Dis. 　　　　　　　Then, by Jupiter,
It was a clownish trick your coming with a dash on
The door in such an unpremeditated fashion:
A great conception has miscarried.

K

Streps.   Pray forgive :
For buried in the country 'tis my hap to live.
But what was that which came to such untimely fate ?
  Dis. That may we but among our own communicate.
  Streps. Then safely you may say : the purpose of my call
Is to be entered at your MEDITATION-HALL.
  Dis. I'll tell you.   But the thing must be observed as
       one
Of our close mysteries.   'Twas asked of CHÆREPHON
By SOCRATES, How many times the little thing
A flea would measure its own foot's length in the spring,
Which just before had happened, as they lay in bed,
From CHÆREPHON's eyebrow to SOCRATES's head ?
  Streps. How did he measure it ?
  Dis.   With great dexterity :
Having first melted wax, he lightly took the flea
And in the fluid dipped its feet.   The wax grew cold
And gave to CHÆREPHON a perfect flea's foot mould,
Just like a Persian slipper, easily applied
To measure the dimensions of the insect's stride.
  Streps. King Jupiter, how exquisite ! With such a mind
One might be sure to leave one's creditors behind.
  Dis. No meal was in our chest for supper yesternight.
  Streps. Granted.   What dainty art supplied your appe-
       tite ?
  Dis. First laying dust upon his problem board, he took
A spit; one end of which he bent into a hook ;[1]
He takes me his dividers—while we're looking on,
A little jacket, left upon the bench, was gone!
  Streps. Who's Thales that we talk of him !   Undo the
      door,
And let me all the wonders of the place explore;
Pray you, undo the door, and show me SOCRATES.
       [*Doors of the Hall are thrown open, and dis-
        cover gaunt Students in various occupa-
        tions and strange attitudes.*
Oh, Hercules ! what sort of animals are these ?

---

[1] To make an instrument wherewith to operate on the clothes of some
unwary scholar in this school.   The stealing of clothes seems to have
been in ancient times the substitute for picking pockets.

Dis. What think you they are like? what moves you to
   such wonder?

Streps. Like the Laconians whom famine had brought
   under
At Pylos.[1] Why do those men look upon the ground?

Dis. Upon inquiry subterrestrial they are bound.

Streps. What? looking after truffles? Pity that they
   should;
I know a place where they are plentiful and good.

   [*Some of the Students come about* STREP-
      SIADES *and the Disciple.*

Dis. Go in: lest SOCRATES should chance to come this
   way.

Streps. No, no, not yet; I beg of you to let them stay.
I wish to let them know about my small affair.

Dis. They may not squander time here in the open air.

Streps. (*seeing some of the scientific apparatus*). By all the
   Gods, inform me what can these things be?

Dis. That is astronomy.

Streps.   And this?

Dis.   Geometry.

Streps. What is the use of it?

Dis.   To measure out the land.

Streps. What? the allotments?

Dis.   No, the whole.

Streps.   I understand,
Sharing the whole among the citizens there are:
A useful measure that, and very popular.

Dis. (*showing a map of the world*). Here is a plan of all
   the earth. Eh! do you see?
Here's Athens.

Streps.   What d'ye say? It's not like it to me.
I do not see the dicasts sitting in their courts.

Dis. 'Tis really Attica, its places and its ports.

Streps. Where is Cicynna? and my fellow-townsmen
   there?

Dis. 'Tis here: and here's Euboea stretched out long and
   fair.

---

[1] The prisoners emaciated by famine, whom Cleon brought from
Sphacteria.

Streps. ' Stretched ' say you—racked by us and Pericles.[1]
Where's Lacedæmon ?

Dis.   Here : as everybody sees.

Streps. How very close to us !   I beg you'll meditate
To put at greater distance such a noxious state.

Dis. By Jove, it cannot be.

Streps.   A whipping for your fee !
But who is that up yonder, in the basket ?

Dis.   HE.

Streps. Who's *he* ?

Dis.   Why, SOCRATES.[2]

Streps.   Oh, SOCRATES !   Good man,
I wish you'd shout to him, and call him if you can.

Dis. Call him yourself; I have not leisure for it.

Streps.   Ho !
My jewel, SOCRATES.

Soc. (*from the basket.*) Mortal, why call you so ?

Streps. But tell me first, I beg, what you are doing there ?

Soc. Considering the sun, and walking on the air.

Streps. Then is it from your crate exalted to a height
That you disdain the Gods ?   For if on earth, you might[3]—

Soc. Nay, if I had not hung my observation high,
How could I have detected things 'twixt earth and sky?
'Tis therefore that I blend with air, to which 'tis kin,
Mind's subtle essence.   So the higher truths we win.
It needs must be : for earth draws with constraining thirst
The dew-beads which from earnest Contemplation burst.
Just as with cardamums—

Streps.   What say you about wet ?
That Contemplation causes cardamums to sweat ?
But, prithee, SOCRATES, come down to help me through
The difficulties which have brought me here to you.

Soc. What may you want ?

---

[1] The inhabitants of Euboea had tried to throw off the yoke of Athens.
They were reduced by Pericles.

[2] In the stage arrangements Socrates is exhibited swinging in a large
basket from the roof.

[3] If the text is not corrupt, it is not clear what is the drift of the
broken sentiment.   I suppose the suggestion to be something like—
' might suffer as a blasphemer.'

Streps.   To learn to speak : for I'm distressed
By duns inordinate and compound interest ;
While all my property I see in mortgage going.

Soc. But how came you so much in debt without your
    knowing ?

Streps. A horse disease consumes me eating at all seasons.
So pray instruct me in the one of your two Reasons,
The reason for not paying. You shall have your fee,
I swear by all the Gods, whatever it may be.

Soc. Swear ? by what Gods ? the Gods are not a coin to
    pass.

Streps. By what then do you swear ? by something
    worse than brass ?
By iron ? such as that which is called Byzantine ? [1]

Soc. Will you be made acquainted with the true Divine,
The genuine ?

Streps.   By Jove, I would, if such there is.

Soc. To hold communication with our Deities,
The Clouds ?

Streps.   Indeed I would.

Soc.   Then please you to sit down
Upon the sacred couch.

Streps.   I'm sitting.

Soc.   Take the crown.

Streps. Why should I have the chaplet, SOCRATES ? alas !
I'm going to be sacrificed like Athamas. [2]

Soc. 'Tis your initiation ; think you nothing of it :
'Tis what we do to all.

Streps.   But what will be the profit ?

Soc. You will be such a speaker ! rattle ! pepper ! dust ! [3]

    [*A basket full of mason's rubbish is emptied
      over* STREPSIADES.

Hold fast.

Streps.   By Jupiter, under this shower I must.

---

[1] None of the '*iron* coin' of Byzantium has survived to testify to its
existence.

[2] In a drama of Sophocles Athamas is introduced with a chaplet upon
his head in view to his being sacrificed.

[3] It is not easy to see how the original words here used signify anything
to the purpose. Probably they had acquired a 'cant' meaning as far
from the original as our words 'beak,' 'fence,' &c. The scoliasts say

Soc. Let this elder hear in silence,
　　　　　　let him hear my invocation.
　　Air! thou lord of realms unmeasured
　　　　　　round our earthy habitation;
　　Splendid Æther! Clouds majestic,
　　　　　　bringing flashing light and thunder,
　　Rise before the meditant, who
　　　　　　bows to you with reverent wonder.
Streps. Let me wrap my cloak about me,
　　　　　　I shall get a thorough wetting;
　　I have not my leather cap here—
　　　　　　'twas unlucky my forgetting.
Soc. Clouds, of highest honour worthy,
　　　　　　come, your glory manifesting,
　　Whether upon the snowy peaks of
　　　　　　hoar Olympus you are resting;
　　Or in your Ocean father's gardens
　　　　　　with the nymphs a dance ye hold ·
　　Or from the mouths of Nile are drawing
　　　　　　water in your ewers of gold;
　　Or ye hang o'er lake Mæotis;
　　　　　　or on Mimas' peakèd ice:
　　Graciously attend my prayers, and
　　　　　　pleased accept this sacrifice.

CHORUS OF CLOUDS
(*heard as the voices of women at a distance*).
　　Rise we everflowing Clouds,
　　Visible in misty shrouds,
　　From our parent Ocean-beds,
　　　Where billows hoarsely roar:
　　Rise we to the tree-capt heads
　　　Of mountains high and hoar.
　　Thence to behold the beacon towers,
　　The holy earth, its fruits and flowers,
　　To see the ancient rivers sweep,
　　And hear the bellowings of the deep.

-----

that the rubbish poured over Strepsiades represents the 'salted meal' poured on the head of a victim at the altar. But it seems more like a baptism or other ceremony of initiation parodied.

For Æther's never-wearied eye
　　　Flames in the sky
　　　With lustrous rays.
Shake off the darkness of the storm,
Unveil your own immortal form
　　　On earth afar to gaze.
Soc. Great and gracious Clouds, ye heard me.
　　　　　Stirring with a song like bees
When the mother leads them swarming,
　　　　come the blessed Deities.
Chorus.　Bearers of the gracious rain,
　　　Maidens gather all your train,
　　　Let us see the shining land [1]
　　　Which Pallas loves of old,
　　　Hardily by Cecrops manned,
　　　Home of the rites untold.
The cell of Mysteries is there,[2]
And lofty shrines, and offerings fair,
The blessed gathering to their feasts,
And victims garlanded, and priests
Through all the circle of the sun;
　　　But chief that one,
　　　The joy and grace
Of Bacchus,[3] when the spring comes in,
When dance and song and piping din
　　　Make life in all the place.
Streps. Jupiter! but who can these be
　　　　　making such a solemn hymning?
SOCRATES, I do implore you,
　　　　　tell me; are they hero-women?
Soc. Nay, but they are clouds of heaven,
　　　　　great divinities for those
Who are not disposed to labour.
　　　　　Unto us do they disclose

---

[1] Attica.

[2] The holy house of Demeter (Ceres) at Eleusis, where the Mysteries of Eleusis were celebrated.

[3] The Bacchic or Dionysian Festivals, at which dramatic contests took place. The first, Lenæa, about the end of February; the second or 'great festival in the city,' when allies and foreigners were present, at the end of March or beginning of April.

Arts of logic, power of judgment,
                    requisites for an oration,
Catching, hitting, controverting,
                    and creating a sensation.[1]
Streps. Since my soul has heard their voices,
                    even now it longs to caper,
Make refinements on a trifle,
                    fiddle-faddle about vapour,
Thirsts to put two little notions
                    into active opposition.
If it may be, with the ladies
                    let me come to open vision.
Soc. Look you now toward Mount Parnes—
                    I can see them now descending
Quietly—
Streps.   Where? prithee, show me.
Soc.   Now they are obliquely tending
Through the thickets and the hollows—
Streps.   How is it I do not see?
Soc. Yonder by the gorge—
Streps.   Ah! now I
                    almost fancy that must be—
Soc. Surely now you see, unless your
                    eyes are glued with plumtree gum.[2]
            [*The chorus of women, dressed as* CLOUDS,
                now enter the Orchestra.
Streps. Aye, by Jove, the honoured ladies!
                    Everywhere they come, they come.
Soc. Truly had you not a notion
                    these were goddesses?
Streps.   Not I.
I supposed that they were mist or
                    vapour floating in the sky.

---

[1] As the art of Rhetoric became a fashionable study, its professors multiplied and refined the terms of their art. We have no true English equivalents for them: mere etymological translations will not give the ideas.

[2] This expression of the idea here meant is borrowed from a well-known passage in *Hamlet*. A more literal translation would import an idea not easily intelligible.

Soc. Ah, you did not know how many
        in the scientific ranks
Have their living from the clouds, as
        poets, prophets, mountebanks ;
Idlers with their signet rings, their
        dirty nails and bushy hair ;
All the class of speculators,
        who contrive to live on air.
Streps. Yes, I know; you mean the sort of
        versifiers who discourse
Of the ' moist clouds ray averting,
        rushing on with mighty force,'
' Locks of Typho hundred-headed,'
        ' wind-born tempests, airy, wet,'
' Swimming-birds with hooked talons ; ' [1]
        as rewards for which they get
Turbot slices good and mighty,
        dainty shares of thrushes' fat.
Soc. Don't you think they quite deserve it ?
Streps.   Tell me how it happens that
These are just like mortal women,
        if the clouds they really be ?
Clouds are not at all like women.
Soc.   What are clouds like that you see ?
Streps. 'Tisn't easy quite exactly
        to describe what one supposes ;
Puffy fleeces, say ; not women :
        but these clouds of yours have noses.
Soc. Answer now to what I ask you.
Streps.   Ask it, if not very hard.
Soc. Saw you never cloud that pictured
        centaur, lion, wolf, or pard ?
Streps. Often, doubtless; what of that tho' ?
Soc.   They can change their forms at pleasure.
If they see some dirty fellow
        growing hair beyond all measure,
Like the son of Xenophontes,
        he shall see himself reflected
In the likeness of a centaur.

---

[1] Probably descriptions of clouds by dithyrambic poets.

Streps.   What if Simon is detected
    Plundering the public treasure?
Soc.   Him they as a wolf display.
Streps. When Cleonymus [1] was throwing
                    yesterday his shield away,
    Were they deer to show him timid?
Soc.   ··   Doubtlessly; and therefore these
    Took the shape of women since they
                    caught a sight of Cleisthenes. [2]
Streps. Welcome, then, my mistresses, and
                    if at all such thing can be,
    Wake your heaven-commeasured voices,
                    universal queens, for me.
Chorus. Welcome, father; welcome relic
                    of a former generation,
    Youthful student in the arts of
                    subtle ratiocination!
    Thou, too, priest of tittle-tattle,
                    make thy wishes known to us,
    For no misty speculatist,
                    saving only Prodicus, [3]
    Has such willing ear of us; for
                    thy conceit is very great,
    Proudly mean is all thy raiment,
                    and thy countenance elate.
Streps. Earth! how solemn is their talking!
                    quite amazes one, it does.
Soc. These are your true Deities, for
                    all the rest are simple buzz.
Streps. Jupiter upon Olympus
                    we a god must surely call?
Soc. Nonsense! who is Jupiter? there
                    is no Jupiter at all.
Streps. Not a Jupiter? who rains, then?
                    Let your teaching start at this.

---

[1] *Acharnians,* l. 79.

[2] Cleisthenes is frequently reflected on for foppishness and effeminacy.
Birds, l. 790.

[3] Prodicus of Ceos, a sophist then at Athens, who undertook to teach
his pupil a rule of reason applicable to every case: the fee for admission
to each of his lectures was 50 drachmas.

Soc. These do.   I will give you tokens
           of it which you cannot miss.
When no clouds were present, did you
           ever see it raining, pray?
But your Jupiter should rain when
           all the clouds are gone away.
Streps. By Apollo! you have neatly
           put your argument tôgether.
Who, then, makes the thunder? tell me,
           for I tremble in such weather.
Soc. These do; rolling on each other.
Streps.   You are not ashamed to say it?
   How?
Soc.   When they are filled with water,
           and are driven to convey it,
Tottering beneath their burden,
           they are very apt to stumble
Over one another and to
           make a clatter when they tumble.
Streps. If it be not Jove who drives them,
           who compels the clouds to go?
Soc. 'Tis the mighty Whirl [1] of Æther.
Streps.   Whirl? eh?—that I did not know!
So, then, Jove exists no longer,
           but this WHIRL is king instead.
Whence, however, comes the lightning
           terrible to strike one dead?
Clearly it is Jupiter who
           hurls about the burning flashes,
And especially reduces
           wicked perjurers to ashes.
Soc. Simple son of Saturn's reign, and
           born a day before the moon; [2]

---

[1] Referring, probably, to a doctrine of Protagoras, or some other physical philosopher, who supposed that the action of the universe was sustained by an inherent, perpetual and circular motion or 'Dinos.' But 'Dinos' also was the name of some large vase or vessel, referred to in the end, line 1410.

[2]   'Did first Arcadia her Pelasgus bear,
           Pelasgus elder than the moon.'
     Translation by Dean Milman, *Quart. Rev.*, vol. lxxxix. p. 180.

How can you believe such fables?
>> I will disabuse you soon.
If he strikes the perjurers, how
>> is it Simon is before us?
And Cleonymus? how is it
>> he has not consumed Theorus?
All of these we know are perjured.
>> Neither does he spare to strike
Sunium of Athens, or a
>> temple of his own alike.
Just as he will shiver oak-trees,
>> glories of the forest.   Why?
How have they deserved it? have the
>> oaks committed perjury?

Streps. That I cannot answer; but you
>> seem to me to speak with reason.
After all, what is the lightning?

Soc.   Passing through a parching season,
Needs must be the wind is heated
>> and unnaturally dry;
So it gets enclosed among the
>> clouds that float about the sky;
There it blows them up like bladders.
>> If there be a little force
Then applied: eh? what will happen?
>> An explosion comes of course!
What with all the noise and chafing
>> in the struggle to get out,
It will set itself on fire; there
>> cannot be the slightest doubt.

Streps. No, by Jove! and that is just what
>> happened to me with a haggis:
I was cooking for some friends, and
>> did'nt slit it where the bag is;
Just as I had served it up, and
>> we were going to begin,
Crack it went, and threw a juice which
>> blinded me and burnt my skin.

Chorus. Thou, whose soul for its perfection
    in the school of wisdom seeks,
 High in honour shalt thou be
    among Athenians and Greeks.
 Only be a Meditator,
    not from any hardness flinching,
 Not by any labour broken,
    not by cold however pinching;
 Never care to break your fast,
    abstain from wine and exercise;
 Look on such indulgences as
    something much beneath the wise.
 As becomes a man of sense,
    consider this a perfect life,
 To be busy, thoughtful, and to
    get the best in wordy strife.
Streps. As to spirit, never fear me.
     · Mine's a heart that mocks at grief;
 Hardy, frugal, I've a stomach
    which can dine upon a leaf.
 Thought and sleeplessness will never
    give me any trouble. Pooh!
 I'm an anvil, and upon me
    you may cut a bar in two.
Soc. You determined not to credit
    any other Gods than we;
 Firstly Chaos, Clouds the second,
    thirdly Tongue; these only three?
Streps. Not if I should meet them would I
    enter into conversation,
 Nor upon their altars offer
    victim, incense, or libation.
Chorus. Fear not now to ask a favour.
    Since you pay us honour due,
 And are anxious to be clever,
    we'll do anything for you.
Streps. Ladies, it is little I shall
    ask of your according smiles;
 'Tis that I may distance all the
    Greeks in speaking twenty miles.

Chorus. Be contented, you shall have it:
                    Not a speaker from to-day
    Half so many striking things, or
                    so victorious shall say,
Streps. 'Tisn't striking things I care for;
                    what I want is to defeat
    Justice, and to make the ruin
                    of my creditors complete.
Chorus. You shall have your utmost wishes;
                    'tis a modest thing you ask.
    Take my servants for your teachers,
                    and apply you to your task.
Streps. In reliance on your favour
                    I will do it, for those horses
    And that marriage with my madam
                    lay upon me strongest forces.
        Let them now do what they like
        With my body: they may strike,
        Wet it, dry it, starve it thin,
        Broil it, freeze it, flay my skin.
        So I slip the debts that thrall me,
        I consent that men shall call me
        Daring, prater, pushing, pert,
        Lie-compounder, mass of dirt,
        Snappish, pettifogger, hack,
        Fox, bore, thong, dissembler, clack,
        Oily, coxcomb, shuffler, patcher,
        Foul, vexatious, dainty-catcher.
        I care not if those who meet me
        With such titles like to greet me.
        They may do just what they please;
        Cut me into sausages,
        By Demeter, if they will,
        Meditators' mouths to fill.
Chorus.   He seems not disposed to shirk,
        But is ready for our work.
            Make yourself content,
        Only be obedient;
        And you shall attain a name
            Wide as heaven in fame.

Streps.　　　What must I go through?

Chorus.　　　No man, while you stay with me,
　　　　　　　Happier in life than you!

Streps.　　　Shall I such a fortune see?

Chorus.　　There will be such troops of clients at your door
Rushing, crushing, your assistance to implore;
Actions and cross-actions, pleas and counter-pleas,
Worthy of you, bringing talents for the fees.
　　(*To Socrates*). Take in hand the elder; let him go to
　　　　　　　　school;
Try him; see if he is clever or a fool.

Soc. Come, let me know your mind, that I may judge
　　　your bent,
And see if there is any need to supplement
Your native force by novel engines in support.

Streps. Do you suppose that I am going to scale a fort?

Soc. No; but my questions go to see how far your mind
Is furnished as to memory.

Streps.　　　　　　　　'Tis of double kind:
I well remember if a person is my debtor;
But if a creditor—I am a sad forgetter.

Soc. Have you a talent for collecting in and stating
What is before you?

Streps.　　　　　No: but for appropriating.

Soc. How can you ever learn?

Streps.　　　　　　　　　Oh, well enough.

Soc.　　　　　　　　　　　　　Suppose
I throw some inference before you, such as those
In Meteorics, will your apprehension catch it?

Streps. Must I treat wisdom as a dog does garbage?
　　　　　snatch it!

Soc. The man is stupid and intensely ignorant.—
I fear, old gentleman, some stripes are what you want,
Come tell me what you'd do if you were beaten?

Streps.　　　　　　　　　　　　Why—
I'm beaten:—then I call on one to testify:
And bring in proper time my action for assault.[1]

---

[1] Strepsiades supposes himself being put through an elementary course
of common law.

Soc. Now, sir, strip off your coat.

Streps.   Eh! where am I in fault?

Soc. When pupils enter here the clothes are always left.

Streps. But I have no intention to commit a theft.[1]

Soc. Nonsense: put down the coat.

Streps.   Do tell me this one thing:
If to my studies I severe attention bring,
Which of you shall I most resemble?

Soc.   CHÆREPHON.

Streps. A man it makes one think of death to look upon.[2]

Soc. Do learn to hold your tongue, sir: quickly here this
        way,
And follow after me.

Streps.   Nay, sir, I pray you stay,
And give into my hands a piece of honey cake,
For I—I feel and fear as if about to make
A visit to Trophonius.[3]

Soc.   Go on before:
Why are you hanging back to poke about the door?

Chorus.   Go, with your heart so stout,
            And fortune bear thee out.

                    [*Exeunt* SOCRATES, STREPSIADES, *and*
                        Disciples.

            Good luck to him who spares
            No pains for truth; but dares,
                In ages's dull decline,
            His paling mind to dye
            With younger thoughts and try
                Wisdom's stern discipline.

---

[1] Because, say the commentators, burglars left their clothes behind them when they entered a house.

[2] On account of his emaciated appearance.

[3] The oracle of Trophonius was in a cave. Those who entered took a honied cake to appease the serpents. It was observed that those who entered the cave always returned sad.

PARABASIS,

Semichorus. Sovereign on high
   Over all Gods, I call
   Jove to our festival.
  Then Him who doth the trident ply,
  Sternly to shake the earth and bitter sea.
   And thee, great-named, who feedest all,
  Æther, most worshipful, our proper sire.
  And Him, the Charioteer, whose fire
    Glows for the earth; with equal love
    Esteemed by men and Gods above
   A mighty deity!
Chorus. Oh, most clever audience,
    pray you give us your attention.
  Where you give us great offence
    we will scruple not to mention.
  Unto us, and us alone,
    you neglect to bring oblation.
  Yet no Deity, you'll own,
    tenders more the state's salvation.
  If, in prudence's disdain,
    ye contemplate some excursion,
  Then, in thunder or in rain,
    we proclaim our strong aversion.
  When for general of late
    you were bent to choose the tanner
  (Whom all Gods agree to hate),
    in a most decided manner
  We our high displeasure showed;
    with the lightning there was thunder:
  Then the moon forsook the road;
    and the sun, to show your blunder,

---

    [1] Cleon.

   L

Drew his wick within his lamp;
   showing his determination
Not to light you if that scamp
   Cleon held the situation.
Yet you chose him not the less!
   But it happens, when the city's
Counsel is but foolishness,
   that some Deity makes it his
Business to redress it by
   turning error into profit.
Bad as is this policy,
   you may get advantage of it.
Let this cormorant be caught
   at his bribes and peculation,
And to pillory be brought;
   it is his befitting station.
If his office comes to this,
   we will be the first confessing
That which you have done amiss
   has come out the city's blessing.

Semichorus. Come, glory-crowned
   Phœbus, and leave the while
   Thy lofty-peakèd isle;
And thou, whom Lydian maids surround,
Come from thy golden house of Ephesus.
 Come, thou, who o'er this city's pile
Castest thy shield, Athené, to thine own.
And thou, among thy revellers known,
Where on Parnassian rocks at night
They follow on thy leading light,
   Come, Bacchus, unto us.

Chorus. Just as we were coming out   [us;
   chanced it that the Moon was nigh
Learning what we were about,
   she has sent a message by us.
After you and your allies
   are with all good wishes greeted,
She declares with some surprise
   that she finds herself ill-treated.

She has served you in the night,
>   not in words, but very clearly;
Saving each in torches' light
>   twelve or thirteen drachmas yearly:
Some one stepping from his porch
>   (he goes out to visit nightly)
Says, ' You need not buy a torch,
>   for the moon is shining brightly.'
Such, and more, her favours are,
>   as she says with much assurance,
Yet you have your calendar
>   disarranged beyond endurance.
All the Gods are out of sorts
>   from confusion thence arising.[1]
You are squabbling in your courts
>   when you should be sacrificing.
So, upon the ancient days
>   disappointed of a dinner,
They will turn on her, she says,
>   and reproach her as the sinner.
Oftentimes again when we,
>   at a time by all agreed on,
Fast with mourning, it may be
>   for a Memnon or Sarpedon,
You are at high holiday !
>   We may hint it was this hap led
Some rough Gods to take away
>   from Hyperbolus his chaplet,
When he was Remembrancer.[2]
>   Let it fix his observation
That the Gods their feasts prefer
>   by a lunar regulation.

---

[1] The grievance of the Moon arose from a rearrangement of the Athenian calendar under the direction of Meton. By the intercalation of a month, or one lunation, at certain intervals the solar and lunar periods were made to coincide in a cycle of nineteen years. The alteration caused some uncertainty and misunderstanding as to annual celebrations. If their places *in the year* were kept, the day would fall in an unusual month. If kept *to the month*, the month itself would not always follow its predecessor in the old order. Hence the disappointment and displeasure of the Gods.

[2] Hyperbolus was one of two deputies to the Amphictyonic Council,

Enter SOCRATES.

Soc. By Respiration! Chaos! Atmosphere, my God!
I never saw a man so absolute a clod,
Blockhead so thick or so much lacking memory!
Try you to furnish him with some slight matters, he
Forgets before he learns.   I'll try in open day.
STREPSIADES, come out and bring your bed this way.
   Streps. (*within.*)   The bugs won't suffer me.
   Soc.   Make haste; and pay attention.

Enter STREPSIADES, *carrying a truckle bed.*

Put the bed down.
   Streps.   Yes, sir.
   Soc.   Be good enough to mention
What you would know that you have not already learned.
Measures? or Rhythm? or Verses, how they should be
     turned?
   Streps. By all means about Measures.   No long time ago
A mealman cheated me of half a peck, I know:
   Soc. I asked not of such measures; but which you
     prefer:
A verse in trimeter, or in tetrameter?[1]
   Streps. There's nothing beats a gallon!
   Soc.   Nonsense.
   Streps.   Will you stake
A wager on that point, four measures do not make
A gallon?
   Soc.   You're a blockhead! you learn rhythms indeed!
   Streps. And what may rhythms do to help a man to
     feed?
   Soc. Nay, but in conversation an accomplished man
Of course should show that he is competent to scan.

---

and bore the office of 'Hieromnemon' or 'Sacred Remembrancer'; as
such it was his distinction to wear a chaplet.   It appears that on a late
occasion as he was returning home his chaplet was blown off by the
wind.
  [1] That is, of 'Three-measure' or 'Four-measure.'

And have it at his fingers' ends how many feet are
Admissible in ' war-dance ' or ' dactylic ' metre.

Streps. Dactylic fingers' ends! why, every body knows,
What fingers are—I do. It isn't things like those
I want to know.

Soc.　　　　　　What then?

Streps.　　　　　　　　　Why *that* :—the thick and thin
Wrong-Reason.

Soc.　　　　　　But 'tis not with that that we begin.
With males of quadrupeds 'tis proper to commence.

Streps. I know the males, unless I've lost my common
　　　　　sense:
Crios, Tragos, Tauros, Kuōn, Alectruōn—[1]

Soc. Ah, there! stay, don't you see how you are over-
　　　　　thrown?
Alectruōn you say at once for *cock* and *hen.*

Streps. By Neptune that I do! How should I say it
　　　　　then?

Soc. *Alectruaina*, female, and *Alector*, male.

Streps. Alectruaina! Be the atmosphere my bail!
I am so much obliged for being taught it thus;
I'll put two doles of meal into your Cardopus.

Soc. Ah! there again the Cardopus is feminine.
And you were wrong.

Streps.　　　　　How did I make it masculine?

Soc. Just like Cleonymus.

Streps.　　　　　How so? explain.

Soc.　　　　　　　　　　In ' us ';
So Cardopus would be just like Cleonymus.

---

[1] 'Ram, Buck, Bull, Dog, Cock,' evidently the first elements of Gram-
mar. As it is impossible to carry out the corrective instructions here
given, if the English equivalent of ' Alectruon' is used, in this case, and
in ' Cardopus,' the original words are retained. ' Cardopus' signifies a
kneading-trough. A noun ending in *os* (or, as in the latinised form, in *us*)
is generally masculine, but *cardopus* formed one exception. The addition
of the definite article in Greek, enabled Socrates to recognise that Strepsiades has assigned the right gender; but it appears that he, perhaps
representing some grammarians of the day, would have had the noun
reformed into a feminine termination, in *é*. The terminations ' *ōr* ' and
' *aina* ' are by rule respectively masculine and feminine.

Streps. Cleonymus has not a Cardopus at all,
But kneads his meal up in a pipkin round and small :
But how must I hereafter say it ?

Soc.   Cardopé ;
Just as you call your wife or daughter Sostraté.

Streps. So, Cardopé the feminine ?

Soc.   Yes, that's the name.

Streps. If so, I ought to make Cleonymé [1] the same.

Soc. Now as to Proper Nouns, or human names, they
          should
As masculines and feminines be understood.

Streps. I know the feminines. ·

Soc.   Say some, that I may know.

Streps. Lucilla, Philinna, Demetria, and so.—

Soc. And which are masculine ?

Streps.   They make a largish class,
Philoxenus, Melesias, Amynias.

Soc. Why these, you varlet, are not masculines at all.

Streps. Not masculines ! how so ?

Soc.   Having a wish to call
Amynias to you, what, tell me, would you say.

Streps. What would I say ? why, ' Here this way,
          Amynia.'

Soc. See there you make a woman [2] of him !

Streps.   Right enough ;
He never fights.   But wherefore should I learn this stuff
That everybody knows ? what is the use of it ?

Soc. 'Tis of no use.   Lie down.

Streps.   For what ?

Soc.   To whet your wit
By meditation.

Streps.   Not abed, I do implore.
If lie I must, do let it be upon the floor.

Soc. No, no, it cannot be allowed.

Streps.   I go my way
Unto the bugs ! Ah what a penalty to pay.

---

[1] To mark his want of manliness.

[2] The terminations ' a ' or ' é ' are feminine.   But the vocative case of
a masculine in ' as ' or ' és ' drops the final consonant, and gives occasion
to Socrates to make his reproof, probably at the cost of some Amynias
well known to the audience.

Soc.   Now meditate, and inside out
    Turn your conjectures.   If a doubt
        Raises debate,
    And checks the stream; then take a theme
        Less obstinate.
    But let no mind-seducing sleep
    One moment o'er your eyelids creep.

Streps.   Oh dear, oh dear! oh dear, oh dear!

Soc.   What is the matter, let me hear.

Streps.   The bugs, the bugs! The bed is filled
    With bugs and I am being killed.
        Here while I am lying thinking,
        In my nostrils they are stinking,
        Of my very life blood drinking,
        They at least are never winking,
        And I am gradually sinking.

Soc.   Good man, don't grieve so very sadly.

Streps.   Eh? not when I am treated badly?
        My money's gone, my colour too,
        My spirit's gone, gone is my shoe,
        And last, like some lone sentinel,
            While with a tune
        I try my sorrows to dispel,
        Gone too *I* shall be very soon.

                          [A silence.

Soc. What are you doing? are you meditating?

Streps.   I?
By Neptune, yes.

  Soc.   And what your mind may occupy?

Streps. How much the bugs will leave when they begin
    their fast.

Soc. An evil death to you!

Streps.   That, sir, is come; and past.

Soc. Pooh, milksop: wrap the blanket round your head
    and catch
A pure abstraction, some repudiative fetch.

Streps. The blanket is of wool; I would that it had sent
Into my mind some very fleecing sentiment.

                      [Silence again.

Soc. Come now, I'll see this man, and hów his matter
        goes.
You sir; are you asleep ?
Streps.   Not I; Apollo knows.
Soc. Have you got anything ?
Streps.   No, not a ray of light.
Soc. Then slip beneath the clothes and think with all
        your might.
Streps. But what about? do mention something,
        SOCRATES.
Soc. Choose your own subject : you have but yourself to
        please.
Streps. I want to know, a thousand times you've heard
        me say it,
About the Interest; how I may never pay it.
Soc. Then wrap the clothes about you and pursue the
        thought.
Resolve it into atoms, and let each be brought
To several introspection by the inward eye.
Streps. Oh dear !—
Soc.   Be quiet.   If it comes to nothing,—why,
Let it depart; and give the sentiment a shift :
Again seize on a thought and follow up its drift.
Streps. Dear SOCRATES.
Soc.   Eh? what?
Streps.   My mind is in commotion;
I've got a practical repudiative notion.
Soc. Declare it.
Streps.   Tell me now.
Soc.   What tell you?
Streps.   If I buy
A witch of Thessaly, I'll draw down from the sky
The moon some night, and shut her in a round strong box,
Such as we use for mirrors, fasten it with locks—
Soc. How would that help you?
Streps.   How? if I could but restrain
The rising of the moon, I never should again
Have interest to pay.
Soc.   I don't see why, I own.
Streps. Because it was on monthly terms I took the loan.

Soc. That's pretty.   Try another problem for your wit.
You owe five talents, say : a clerk writes out the writ :
How may you cancel it ?

  Streps.   Upon the thought I'll enter.

Soc. Keep not your sentiment too closely to its centre :
Give it the air, and let it wheel about your head,
As though it were a chafer fastened to a thread. [*A silence.*

Streps. I've got a clever plan for cancelling the writ.
You'll own it such.

  Soc.   What is its nature ? tell me it.

Streps. You know that sort of stone the oddment-dealers
        sell,
A pretty thing, and you can see through it quite well,
'Tis used for lighting fires.

  Soc.   The lens you mean ?

  Streps.   Aye, so.

Soc. Well what about it ?

  Streps.   If I had it I would go
Upon the sunny side, some distance from the clerk,
And fast as he could write—would melt out every mark.[1]

Soc. That's clever, by the Graces !

  Streps.   I am gratified
To think how that five-talent writ was put aside.

Soc. Now, quickly hit me this.

  Streps.   What ?

  Soc.   How a man may parry
The judgment in an action, where he must miscarry
For lack of witnesses ?

  Streps.   That method's very short.

Soc. What is it ?

  Streps.   I'll explain.   I'll wait about the court,
Until they call the case that's next preceding mine,
Then I'll run out and hang myself upon a line.

Soc. That would'nt do.

  Streps.   It would : for I will wage my head
No one would carry on the case when I was dead.

  Soc. You drivel.   I will have no more to do with you.

---

[1] The clerk would use the common instrument of the time, a stylus, or
bodkin to write upon a tablet covered with a thin coating of wax.

Streps. Why, SOCRATES? Nay, by the Gods, I pray
      you, do.

Soc. You're so forgetful, that one's teaching goes for
      nought.

Now, tell me if you can, the first thing you were taught.

Streps. The first thing—let me see—the first thing—ah,
      I know.

What is the thing? the thing in which we knead our
      dough?

Oh, dear! what is the thing?

Soc.   Out with you, feed the crows!

A dotard with more dulness than a body knows.

               [SOCRATES *in disgust ascends to his basket.*

Streps. I have not learnt to quibble; I am ruined quite.

What shall I do? Oh, Clouds, advise me in my plight.

Cho. Old man, if you have got a son to serve the turn,

We would advise that you should send him here to learn.

Streps. Oh yes, I have a son, a pretty fellow too:

But he declines to learn: so what am I to do?

Cho. But you permit it?

Streps.   Yes; he's stout, and puffed with pride,

And comes of haughty people by his mother's side.

I'll go for him: and if he still is obstinate,

I'll turn him out of doors: and so, I beg you, wait.

                      [*Exit* STREPSIADES.

Chorus (*addressing* SOCRATES).

    See you what a living you will make of this?

    That is all the giving of us deities.

    Lacking self-possession, that excited man

    Lies at your discretion: snap him while you can.

    Such a chance neglected, you are not to learn,

    When you least expect it, takes another turn.

STREPSIADES : PHEIDIPPIDES.

Streps. Here, by the Mist, you do not stay: go, if you
      please,

And eat the marble colonnades of Megacles.

Pheid. What is the matter? by Olympian Jupiter,

I do believe that you are rather crazy, sir.

Streps. Ha-ha! ' Olympian Jupiter!' I can't but laugh—
Believing Jupiter! and you! a full-grown calf.
    Pheid. Why do you laugh at that?
    Streps.   To think that you're a child
So much behind the times: no wonder that I smiled.
But come, I'll teach you what will make a man of you.
But you are not to tell it further if I do.
    Pheid. Eh? what?
    Streps.   You swore ' by Jupiter ' just now.
    Pheid.   I did;
What then?
    Streps. You see how learning helps one to be rid
Of lies. There is no Jupiter.
    Pheid.   Indeed! who then?
    Streps. Jove is deposed and Whirl is King of Gods and
         men!
    Pheid. You're joking.
    Streps.   Not at all: I say 'tis true, young man.
    Pheid. Who talks this nonsense?
    Streps.   SOCRATES the MELIAN: [1]
And CHÆREPHON, who knows the footmarks of a flea.
    Pheid. What? are you, father, really crazed to that
         degree
That you believe these moping madmen?
    Streps.   Hush, my boy.
In speaking of such men do not these terms employ,
Long-headed men, who hold it waste to spend their means
On oil, soap, shaving, anything that cleans.
But you are wasting mine as though you thought me dead.
But come and be their pupil in your father's stead.
    Pheid. What can one learn of value from such men as
         those?
    Streps. Eh? everything you may, that anybody knows.
You'll know yourself to be the booby that you are.
Wait here till I come back; I am not going far.
                                  [*Exit.*

---

[1] Socrates had no connection with Melos. The epithet is here used in order to throw upon Socrates the popular ill-fame of Diagoras, *the Melian*. Diagoras was apparently a man much before his age. Having openly scorned the traditional theology, he was persecuted as an atheist.

Pheid. Alas! my father is beside himself.   Shall I
Take him before the courts? [1] or, seeing he will die,
Look for an undertaker?

    Re-enter STREPSIADES *carrying a cock and a hen.*

    Streps. (*showing the cock*).   I should like to know
What you call this, my lad?
    Pheid.   Alectruŏn.
    Streps.   So, so.
And this (*showing the hen*)?
    Pheid.   Alectru̯ŏn.
    Streps.   Ridiculous indeed!
What? both the same? In future, pray, with better heed,
Call this *Alectruaina*,—this one *Alectŏr*.
    Pheid. Alectruaina?   And is this the precious store ·
Of learning you have gathered from the Sons of Earth! [2]
    Streps. Aye is it: and besides much more of equal
           worth.
But, more's the plague of it, that everything I'm told
Goes faster out than in, for I have got too old.
    Pheid. And is it then for this your upper coat is gone?
    Streps. Not gone exactly, but—I scorn to put it on.
    Pheid. And how have you consumed the shoes in which
           you stood?
    Streps. Like Pericles's talents they are gone—'for
           good.' [3]
But come, come; let us go.   Set off the 'little sense'
Against an act of filial obedience.
For I remember when you were a babbling child,
Some six years old, and how your winning ways beguiled
Your silly father with his first court fee [4] to part
To buy you at Diasia a little cart.

---

[1] The equivalent to our 'taking out a statute of lunacy.'

[2] 'Gegeneis,' that is 'Giants'; the allusion is to the conspiracy of the 'Giants' to displace Jupiter and the other denizens of Heaven.

[3] In rendering an account of some public money which had passed through his hands, Pericles set down some talents as spent 'for a proper purpose.' The account was allowed without further question. It was understood that they had been spent in bribes at Sparta.

[4] The oboles which he had received for a day's service as dicast.

Pheid. Hereafter you will much regret this step I doubt.

Streps. Enough, if you obey.—Here, SOCRATES ! come
    out.

I've brought my son to you, but much against his will.

Soc. (*from his hanging basket*). A babe in knowledge, who
    has yet to climb the hill.

But in the court of wisdom suitor [1] let us hope,

Pheid. You'd be a *w*agged *th*uit, if hung upon a *w*ope.

Streps. Out on you ! You revile the master of the school.

Soc. ' Upon a *w*ope ' indeed ! Observe the lisping fool.

How can a man like that be taught to cross an action,

To handle witnesses, or prove to satisfaction

That black is white by nice degrees of shade?—and yet

Hyperbolus acquired the art to bilk a debt,

And only paid a talent as his master's fee.

Streps. Teach him. Be not afraid. He's sharp enough
    you'll see.

I tell you when he was, oh, such a little boy,

He used to cut out boats, and he could any toy ;

And made a little house, and glued it all together,

And little waggons too he made with strips of leather,

And wonderful the frogs out of pomegranate rinds.

Ah, if he could but learn those reasons of two kinds :

The Reason for the Right and Reason for the Wrong,

Which always shows itself insuperably strong.

Or, let him keep to that, learn *that* at any rate.

Soc. He shall be taught them both, by hearing them
    debate.

Streps. I'll go ; but recollect, he shall be taught and
    must,

To answer any case however true and just.

                  [*Exit* STREPSIADES.

---

[1] A slight variation on the original is here made in order to retain a
play upon words, and the reference to the shabby clothes of Socrates. It
appears from the reply of Pheidippides that it was then the habit of
young gentlemen of fashion to be affected or slovenly in pronunciation.
Probably the actor who personated this young man had throughout given
the drawl or proper mispronunciations ; but it does not seem worth
while to write them except in this instance.

Enter RIGHT-REASON *and* WRONG-REASON, *suspended in
baskets and dressed as fighting-cocks.*

Right-Reason. Come on : I do not think you fear,
    Let the spectators see your face.

Wrong-Reason. Just where you please : the more to hear,
    The more will witness your disgrace.

R. R. Disgrace me ! will you ! who are you ?

W. R. I'm Reason.

R. R.   Aye, the worser too !

W. R. And you the better, so you say.
    But I will beat you.

R. R.   In what way ?

W. R. By sentiments of new invention.

R. R. Aye, such I know have won attention ;
    For these are fools (*towards the audience*).

W. R.   Because they're wise.

R. R. I'll overthrow you.

W. R.   What your art ?

R. R. Mere righteousness.

W. R.   But I'll devise
    Good reason on the other part.
    I say the thing does not exist.

R. R. Not righteousness ?

W. R.   If so, where is 't ?

R. R. Among the Gods.

W. R.   Nay, sure it died
    When Jupiter his father tied.

R. R. Oh ! frightful ! this is worse and worse.
    I'm sick—

W. R.   And old and want a nurse.

R. R. You profligate and shameless hound !

W. R. Your words are roses ; I'm beholden.

R. R You low buffoon !

W. R.   I'm lily crowned.

R. R. You strike your father !

W. R.   That is golden.

R. R. You heretofore were trimmed with lead.[1]

W. R. But now wear gold about my head.

---

[1] No further explanation of this expression is given than 'had in dishonour.'

R. R. Sir, your audacity is great.

W. R. Your fashions, sir, are out of date.

R. R. The rising youth decline to go,
     Through you, to schools.
   Athenians will one day know,
     And rue it, what you teach the fools.

W. R. Your raiment is the worse for use.

R. R. And yours, I see, is very spruce.
   Though once a beggar dressed in rags
     As Telephus [1] you used to greet us,
   And hoarded your scrap-hints in bags
     Picked up from Pandeletus.

W. R. What clever things—*R. R.* Infatuation!

W. R. Do you recall?—*R. R.* The city's too;
   Which, to its ruin, leaves to you
     The rising generation.

W. R. Then will you, Saturn, keep a school
     For this man's education?

R. R. If he desires a healthy rule,
     And not mere declamation!

W. R. (*to* PHEID.) Come; leave his dotage till it's spent.

R. R. You will regret if you consent.

Chorus. Now leave your virulent debate,
     And tell us how to educate.
   You, sir, explain the ancient plan;
   You—how to make the modern man:
   That, having heard your several schemes,
   He may elect as good it seems.

R. R.   I am quite willing.

W. R.   So am I.

Chorus. Which shall begin and which reply?

W. R. Let him begin.   Then from his stuff
   · I'll pick conceptions new and trim
   Shall make me dainty shafts enough
     To settle him.
   Or, if at last he dares to grunt,
     I will let loose a hornets' nest
   Of notions on him, rear and front,
     And lay him in eternal rest.

---

[1] The allusion is to the drama of Euripides, in which Telephus is represented as a beggar. See *Acharnians*, l. 368.

Chorus.   With mental throes, and wordy twists,
Here meet two shrewd antagonists
       To win a day.
Each, as the other, confident;
Which has the best in argument
       Will they display.
The cause is great, the lists are free,
    And Wisdom is the prize.
On her the friends who follow me
    Have set their constant eyes.
Thou, who didst our elders crown with
       noble morals, as·with bays,
Show thy dispositions, and the
       voice, in which thou gloriest, raise. .

R. R.   I will tell the ancient fashions,
       how your fathers trained their youth;
When men listened to my words of
       justice, soberness, and truth.
Seemly boys were made to walk the
       streets in silence all together,
Bare-foot, bare-backed; shining, snowing,
       whatsoever was the weather.
So they sought their music-master's;
       where they learnt by his assistance,
'Pallas, sacker of the cities,'   ·
       or, 'The cry that sounds at distance,' [1]
With their harmony according
       to the strict primæval version.
For if any played his pranks or
       ventured on his own insertion,
Turns, and trills, and variations,
       such as Phrynis has invented,
Stripes informed the innovator
       'twas a taste to be repented.
In the School of Exercises,
       motion, posture, voice, and eye,
All were cared for, all were ruled to
       manliness and modesty.

---

[1] The initial lines of old martial songs.

Daintiness was not permitted:
        none would take the lettuce-heart,
Or partake his herb until his
        seniors had had their part.
Fish was not for striplings' palates.
        Noisy levity was stopped.
Woe to him who crossed his legs,
W. R.   when
        you were all grasshopper-topped![1]
Kept ' Boufonia ' and ' Dipolia,'
        and Cecides was your poet!
R. R. Such our training was; I call the
        men of Marathon to show it.
Now you teach your tender boys to
        muffle themselves up in clothing.
Wherefore, lad, elect for me, and
        look upon this rogue with loathing.
You will learn to scorn the warm baths,
        and eschew the market-place.
Made a jest of, you will have an
        honest blush upon your face.
You, when elder men are come in,
        will know how to yield a seat.
You will think it shame your parents
        disrespectfully to treat.
Never call your father ' Japet,'[2]
        or withhold a reverence due,
Scorn-requiting him who spent his
        love and substance upon you.
All your character an image
        of a proud and worthy shame,
Not by wanton word or gesture
        will you smirch an honoured name.

---

[1] Thucydides mentions, among habits which had passed away, the fashion of wearing the hair in a knot, brooched with golden grasshoppers, probably symbolic of their claim to be Autochthones, 'children of the soil.' It must be understood that the religious feasts here referred to had passed away, as ' May-games ' or 'pilgrimages to Canterbury ' with us.

[2] One of the Titan sons of Heaven and Earth, father of Atlas and Prometheus. It will be seen that the order of these lines is slightly changed.

W. R. Help us, Bacchus! if you listen
<blockquote>to this ancient proser, you will</blockquote>
Oust Hippocrates's litter,[1]
<blockquote>boys will call you 'water-gruel.'</blockquote>

R. R. You will be in good condition
<blockquote>for the boxing, wrestling, races;</blockquote>
Much unlike our modern idlers
<blockquote>chaffing in the market-places.</blockquote>
Undisturbed by petty actions,
<blockquote>spun into perplexities,</blockquote>
You in the Academy [2] will
<blockquote>run beneath the olive trees,</blockquote>
For yourself and your companion
<blockquote>twining chaplets by the way,</blockquote>
Redolent of ivy-berries
<blockquote>and of happy holiday;</blockquote>
When the poplar buds are bursting,
<blockquote>when ye glory in the spring,</blockquote>
When the breeze is in the leaves and
<blockquote>Plane to Elm is whispering.</blockquote>

<blockquote>Take my counsel; give your thought
To do the things I say you ought.
Broad and strong your chest shall be,
Your complexion bright to see,
You shall have your arms well hung,
Stalwart shoulders, slender tongue.
Otherwise, be as the rest,
Notable for narrow chest,
Sallow skin and feeble knees,
Monstrous tongue and—long decrees.</blockquote>

<blockquote><blockquote>And finally receive</blockquote>
That Good is but a make-believe;
<blockquote>That foul is fair,</blockquote>
And Honour is not anywhere.</blockquote>

Chorus. Sweet is the air that breathes from thy discourse,
Thou, whose firm feet with undiminished force
The castled steep of wisdom love to climb;
Oh happy were the men of olden time.

---

[1] The sons, or as by a little perversion of the original word they were called the 'pigs,' of Hippocrates passed as a proverb for 'boobies.'
[2] The grove Academia.

Now thou, whose Muse has smiling airs to catch
Our preference, come forth to meet thy match.
So well hath he sustained the ancient ways,
That thou some unsuspected points must raise
To wrest our judgment unto his defeat;
Or earn thyself the scorn that boasters meet.

W. R.   I really have been almost choked
     waiting for his conclusion :
And long with reasonable views
     to put him to confusion.
I know that I have got the name
     among the Meditators
Of ' worser ' Reason.   Why ? Because,
     the first of good debaters,
I dared to meet old saws and laws
     with open contradiction.
What ? if I take the weaker side
     and yet induce conviction ?
It is a talent better worth
     than any money gaining.
See now, how I will overthrow
     this boasted plan of training.
At once, I cannot understand
     what ground he has for viewing
Our Baths with such disfavour that
     warm water must be ruin !

R. R.   It is a most disgraceful thing,
     and makes a man a coward !

W. R.   Stay there : I have you round the waist,
     and you are overpowered.
Of all the sons of Jupiter,
     tell me, who was the bravest ?
And, as to hardships, underwent
     by far the most and gravest ?

R. R.   For me, I reckon Hercules
     the best among the bold ones.

W. R.   And who, pray, ever thought the baths [1]
     of Hercules were cold ones ?
Yet never was there braver man.

---

[1] The Thermæ, ' warm springs,' Thermopylæ, were said to have been produced by Minerva for the refreshment of Hercules.

R. R.   This is the common babble
          That empties the Gymnasium
                    and fills the Baths with rabble.
W. R. Then he proscribes the Market-place,
                    where all the wise and witty
          Meet as in common Council on
                    the business of the City.
          He calls the habit bad; but I
                    affirm it for the best; or
          Assure yourselves that Homer would
                    have never called his Nestor
          The ' market-man,'[1] the Councillor,
                    as others of good credit.
          I pass, however, to the ' tongue ';
                    for lads he seems to dread it :
          That cannot I at all approve.
                    But that which is the oddest,
          Is his enforced prescription that
                    a young man should be modest !
          For Modesty, (and if you can,
                    confute me and deny it)
          You never saw or heard of man
                    who got advantage by it.
R. R. Aye many ! Peleus[2] got a sword
                    with beasts to do his battle.
W. R. Poor devil for his modesty !
                    a broad sword : and was that all ?
          Hyperbolus,[3] and not for lamps,
                    nor modesty's reward, sir,
          Has got his thousands, sterling cash :
                    and not a simple sword, sir.

---

[1] ' Agora,' the market-place. ' Agoretes,' the designation of Nestor. Our habits do not afford a pair of kindred words in the same relation.

[2] Peleus having been slandered, like Joseph in the house of Potiphar, was exposed to the risk of becoming the prey of wild beasts in a wilderness. The Gods sent to him a sword forged by Vulcan for his self-defence.

[3] Referred to in the *Peace* as successor of Cleon. He was a lamp-dealer, and had the repute of having enriched himself by the fraud of secretly loading his lamps with lead, and selling them by weight as solid brass. It must be supposed that he also was not famous for his modesty.

You doat, old man.—But, modest youth,
    I'd have you think at starting
How many pleasant things in life
    you never can have part in ;
Wife, children, Cottabus, good wine,
    fish dinners, fun and laughter !
And if all these are gone away,
    is life worth living after ?
Well, be it so.   Be virtuous ;
    at least intend to be it ;
But under some temptation slip,
    and let a tattler see it :
You're ruined quite.   You cannot speak.
    You have no word to offer.
Take part with me, and be yourself,
    a wag, a scamp, a scoffer.
You are detected in the act ;
    ' detected '—but what matter ?
Your words are stout, you face it out :—
    it all goes off in chatter.
Or, at the worst, some God has done
    the like : and you cut short all
Reflections on your virtue by
    alleging—you are mortal.
R. R. Your art may make him profligate ;
    but can you heal the sorrow,
That comes as sure as night on day
    on Profligacy's morrow ?
W. R. Pooh, Profligacy's sorrow ! there
    you show yourself but queasy :
If I can satisfy you that
    these pains are very easy ?
R. R. I'll hold my tongue hereafter.
W. R.   Say,
Our learned pleaders what are they ?
R. R. They're profligates.
W. R.   And what are those
Who for the Tragic stage compose ?
R. R. They're profligates.

W. R.   The people's choice,
Directors of the public voice?
R. R.   They're profligates.
W. R.   You see that these
Endure the pains you fear with ease.
Now look the audience round, and see,
Which find you in majority?
R. R.   I'm looking round.
W. R.   Which have it? say.
R. R.   The profligates must have the day.
I know that fellow sitting there,
And this one with the length of hair.
W. R.   Say, have you had enough of it?
R. R.   Aye.   I am beaten, and submit.

                                   [*Combatants withdrawn.*

STREPSIADES, SOCRATES, PHEIDIPPIDES.

Soc. Have you determined? will you take your stripling
          hence?
Or shall he learn of me the art of eloquence?
Streps. Teach him, and spare him not.   You'll sharpen
          up one cheek
That he may like a thorough pettifogger speak.
The other you shall whet that he may bear a part
Not undistinguished in the higher branch of art.
Soc. Fear not: a perfect sophist you shall have him
          back.
Pheid. And, as I fear, a pale-faced miserable hack.
Cho. Go now.
Pheid.   Unless I judge amiss,
One day you will repent of this.

                                   [*Exeunt.*

Chorus. We, the Clouds, think right to mention
                    what you, Judges, may expect
     If we meet with kind attention,
                    And your judgment is correct.[1]

---

[1] That is to say, in assigning the prize in the dramatic contest to this
comedy.

When you set about your cropping,
>> breaking up your fallowed swards,
You shall have our early dropping;
>> others not till afterwards.
When your vines put out their promise,
>> we will care that they shall get
Not too little moisture from us,
>> nor be surfeited with wet.
But if you should venture scorning
>> Our Divinity,—beware!
We accord you timely warning
>> how your insolence shall fare.
You henceforth shall never bring in
>> pleasant produce from your farm:
Volley after volley flinging,
>> we will try to do a harm
To the vine and olive setting:
>> we will batter them to sticks:
We will never cease from wetting
>> when we see you making bricks.
Then a hail shall crack your tiling,
>> big as pebble-stones at least.
And when you are spruce and smiling,
>> looking for your marriage-feast,
We will set the rivers swelling
>> all the night; and you shall say,
'Would that Egypt were my dwelling'!¹—
>> —If you judge amiss to-day.

Enter STREPSIADES, *carrying a sack of meal.*

Streps. The fifth, the fourth, the third, and after that
>> the second,
And after that, of all the days that can be reckoned,
The one in all the month I hate and fear the worst,
Aye, then comes that abominable 'last-and-first'!²

---

¹ In Egypt, says Herodotus, it *never* rains.

² Strepsiades is looking forward to the first of the month, when his debt and interest would become due. The Greeks reckoned the days of the month *towards* a point in advance. So the last four days of the

My creditors are pledged, for so at least they swear,
To see me ruined, though I ask them to forbear :
' Good Sir, a little time ; ' ' you will take less than that ; '
' Remit it ; ' but they are unanimous and flat
In their refusals.   ' That,' say they, ' is not the way
' To get our own again.'   And they must needs display
Suspicion of me !   Say—I am a rogue ; in short,
That they will 'court' me. Well, then, let them go to court.
I do not care about it if Pheidippides
Has learnt the art of speaking.   Be it as they please ;
I soon will know.   I'll knock at Meditation-hall.
Boy, boy !—

 Soc.   Strepsiades ? Ha ; is it you who call ?
Good morning to you.

 Streps.   Worthy Sir, the same to you.
And I have brought, you see, the master's proper due.

        [*Deposits the sack of meal.*

How fares my son with you ? and is he yet complete in
His studies ?

 Soc. Perfectly.

 Streps.   Good, by most mighty Cheating !

 Soc. He can defeat with ease the strongest action known.

 Streps. If witnesses were present when I took the loan ?

 Soc. A thousand if you like ; it makes the case so clear.

 Streps. If that be so, I must sing out my hearty cheer.

   Woe to the money that's lent !
   Woe to the men who lend it !
   Hey, for the money that's spent ;
    I am the man who spend it.
   Money put out is gain,
    Interest makes it double ;
   Paying it back is pain ;
    I will have no such trouble.
   I have a son, and he a tongue
   With double edge, and trimly hung,

---

month were the 5th, 4th, 3rd, and 2nd before the first. This day was
expressed by a compound phrase, which, without etymological accuracy,
is here rendered ' last-and-first.'   The original has this plurality of
form : it will be seen by the sequel that it was necessary to preserve and
emphasize it.

Born to support his house and name,
And bring my enemies to shame.
Go, bring him hither; run.
Here, to thy father, son!

Enter PHEIDIPPIDES.

Soc. See, here he is.
Streps.   This is a joy!
Soc. Take him and go.
Streps.   Ha! ha! my boy!
How charmed I am to see your white and yellow tint!
One sees at once there is repudiation in't,
And contradiction. You have caught the local fashion—
'What say you, Sir? nay, pray, don't get into a passion;
You say that you are injured. Doubtless; I see through
    it;
Yes, injury there is, and *you're* the man to do it.'
You have upon your face the thorough Attic sneer.
You've ruined, you must save, me.
    Pheid.   What is it you fear?
Streps. The first-and-last day.
    Pheid.   Eh? how call you that a day?
Streps. 'Tis when my creditors will pay the fees,[1] they
            say.
Pheid. Then must they lose the fees. 'Tis patent as the
            sun;
Two days are clearly *two*, and never can be *one*.
Streps. They cannot.
    Pheid.   No; unless you are disposed to own
A woman may at once be young girl and old crone.
Streps. But yet it is the law.
    Pheid.   People have not the gift,
Reading the law, to see its drift.
    Streps.   What is its drift?
Pheid. Old Solon had an eye to popularity.
Streps. But what is 'last-and-first' to that? I cannot
            see.

---

[1] To commence an action the plaintiff paid in to the proper officer the
Court-cost by way of deposit; if he gained his cause he recovered the
amount from the defendant.

Pheid. On two days, 'last and first,' the summons should
      be made;
The first day of the moon the fees were to be paid.
  Streps. Why did he add the 'first'?
  Pheid.   Dull man! that the defendant
Upon the former day might pay and make an end on't;
That failing, on the morrow when the moon is new,
The rigour of the law should make him pay his due.
  Streps. Why do the magistrates accept the fees so soon
Upon the 'last-and-first,' and not on the new moon?
  Pheid. It seems to me, they act like tasters at a table;
They like to taste the fees as soon as they are able,
And so they get them in a whole day in advance.
  Streps. (*contemptuously toward the audience*). Poor people,
      There you sit in blessed ignorance!
That men of sense may use you; number, nothing more;
Blocks as it were, or sheep, or barrels in a store.
So that, with none to listen but myself, I raise
My self-congratulating voice in songs of praise.

        Happy man Strepsiades is!
        Clever (that's as nature pleases).
        Only see what he has done—
        Educated such a son!
        All our neighbours envious
        Will be talking of us thus;
        When the plaintiffs are defeated,
        When the creditors are cheated.
        But come you in, my boy, and dine;
        The dishes are prepared, and wine.

                    [*Exeunt.*

Enter PASIAS, *a Creditor, with his* WITNESS.

  Pasias. Why should a man be bound to throw away his
      own?
He is not. But it had been well to let alone
This traffic, and have borne the shame of saying 'no,'
Rather than serve a friend and then be treated so.
See, here am I obliged, all for this money's sake,
To drag you here to be my witness, and to make

A fellow-townsman enemy.   But while I live
My country shall not be ashamed of me.[1]   I'll give
The summons to Strepsiades.

Enter STREPSIADES.

Streps.   What's this about?

Pas. The last-and-first.

Streps. (*appealing to the witness*). He said, and you will
　　　bear me out,
Two days.   What debt are you pretending to enforce?

Pas. Twelve minæ which you borrowed for the star-
　　　marked horse.

Streps. A horse! you know I hold all horsing in disgust.

Pas. You swore, by all the Gods, you would redeem the
　　　trust.

Streps. By Jove, that was before Pheidippides had
　　　learned
The counter-logic which cannot be overturned.

Pas. You do not therefore mean to try repudiation?

Streps. How else should I be answered for his education?

Pas. On oath before the Gods, if called, will you demur to
The justice of my claim?

Streps.   What Gods do you refer to?

Pas. Jove, Mercury, and Neptune.

Streps.   Jove! I have you there.
I'll pledge three oboles extra for the chance[2] to swear.

Pas. Perish the perjurer! out on your impudence!

Streps. Some salt would do you good to flavour you with
　　　sense.

Pas. Scoffer.

Streps.   You'll take six pecks.

---

[1] That is, for any falling off from the Athenian character for litigiousness.
[2] In defect of witnesses on the part of the plaintiff in an action for money,
the defendant would be put upon his oath.   Diagoras, referred to before
(note, p. 155), is said to have renounced his faith in the traditional Deities
in consequence of such an incident.   On suing for a sum of money he had
lent he was met by the oath of the defendant denying the fact of the
loan.

Pas.   By Jupiter the Great,
And all the Gods, you'll not escape me at that rate !

Streps. I'm tickled at your Gods.   To men of sense like
            us,
Swearing by Jupiter is quite ridiculous.

Pas. Some day you'll pay for this. But answer, yes or no,
Do you intend to pay your debt? and I will go.

Streps. Stay here a moment and I will distinctly say.

                            [STREPS. *goes into the house.*

Pas. What, think you, will he do ?

Witness.   I think that he will pay.

          [STREPSIADES *returns with a kneading-trough.*

Streps. Let anyone who says that there is money due
Tell me what this is.

Pas.   That ? a *Cardopus.*

Streps.   And you
Ask me for money ! No.   I'll pay no obolus
To one who calls a *Cardopé* a *Cardopus.*

Pas. You'll not refund ?

Streps.   Not if I know it ; you may go,
And speedily.

Pas.   I will : but for a surety know,
As I'm alive I'll pay the fees and start the suit.

                        [*Exeunt* PASIAS *and* WITNESS.

Streps. You'll lose your dozen minæ and the fees to
            boot.
And yet, in truth, I'm sorry you should suffer thus
For your simplicity in saying *Cardopus.*

                    Enter AMYNIAS.

Amyn. Woes me, woes me !

Streps.   Whence come such mourning notes as these ?
Or was it one of Carcinus's [1] Deities ?

Amyn. What's that you ask? I am a man in deep
            dejection,
If you would know.

---

[1] Carcinus had introduced in Tragedy some deity or hero making
unseemly lamentation. Some of the lines which here follow are said to
be either quoted or parodied from Carcinus. Hence, it seems probable, the
reference to 'Tlepolemus,' a character in one of these dramas.

Streps.   Then do not scatter the infection.

Amyn. Oh utter breakdown of my horses! Oh cursed spite

Of luck! oh Pallas, thou hast ruined me outright.

Streps. What? has Tlepolemus wrought you a grief so sore?

Amyn. Fling not your scoffs at me, but bid your son restore

The money he has had, as well for honesty,

As that my fortune seems to have deserted me.

Streps. What money might that be?

Amyn.   He had it as a loan.

Streps. Your fortune does appear extremely bad, I own.

Amyn. I've had a heavy fall; indeed I drove too fast.

Streps. You're rambling, like a man who has been donkey-cast.

Amyn. And is it rambling to demand my own again?

Streps. You cannot be quite sound, that's obvious.

Amyn.   What then?

Streps. Your brain is shaken.

Amyn.   'Tis as clear to me that you

Will be in court unless you pay me what is due.

Streps. Tell me, I beg, if you suppose that Jupiter

Rains water new each time? or, do you, Sir, prefer

The view that 'tis the sun which through the nether air

Draws the same water back?

Amyn.   I neither know nor care.

Streps. And can you ask your money back without compunction

When you know nothing of the meteoric function?

Amyn. Nay if you really are at fault for it, at least

Pay me the interest.

Streps.   Tell me what sort of beast

Is Interest?

Amyn.   What else but that the little store

Of money month by month and day by day grows more

And more as time flows gently on.

Streps.   Nicely explained!

Now tell me, if you think the sea at all has gained

Upon its ancient bulk?

Amyn.   By Jupiter, not it,
It is but common sense to think so,—not a bit.
  Streps. Then, blockhead, if with all the rivers ever
          flowing
Into the sea, you say, it never yet is growing,
Can you desire to make your stock of money more?
Go follow up your own pursuit: there is the door.
Hey there! bring me a whip.

                    [STREPSIADES *lashes* AMYNIAS.
  Amyn.   I do—I do protest.
  Streps. Get up; you're lazy, Sir; and hang behind the
          rest.
  Amyn. Nay, this is insolence.
  Streps.   I'll make you show your paces.
I'll tickle you and make you tighten up the traces.

                              [*Exit* AMYNIAS.
So, So! You're running now. I thought that I could
          move you,
You and your rattle-traps. A breathing will improve you.
                                        [*Exit.*

  Chorus. How sad is this propensity to cheat!
              Therewith infected, this old man
          With tricks his creditors will treat
              And rob them if he can.
          Before the day is out, a something will
              This scheming sharper overtake,
          And for his aim conceived so ill
              A fair requital make.
          He'll find, methinks, that which he went to seek.
              His son will prove a clever wight,
          With capability to speak
              In honesty's despite.
          So much that he shall get the best,
          Whoever may with him contest;
          Although he dresses with all art,
          The pure and simple scoundrel's part.
          And he, the father, wish in vain
          He had a wordless son again.
          [STREPSIADES *running, followed by* PHEIDIPPIDES.
  Streps. Oh! oh!

Here neighbours, kinsmen, fellow-townsmen, run to me,
Defend me; I am being beaten shamefully.
Oh! oh! my wretched head; you hit me in the face;
Villain, you strike your father?

Pheid.   Yes, that is the case.

Streps. You see, that he confesses it.

Pheid.   ·   Oh yes, they heard.

Streps. You villain, you! you parricide, you gallows-bird!

Pheid. Repeat the words, and any more you can produce,
There's nothing pleases me so much as such abuse.

Streps. You infamous!

Pheid.   Another rose.

Streps.   You strike your father!

Pheid. That I admit, by Jove: I justify it rather.

Streps. You profligate, how will you justify such sin?

Pheid. That I'll explain; and speaking undertake to
      win.

Streps. You'll argue that, and win?

Pheid.   Aye, that will I with ease.
And of the Reasons you may take which one you please.

Streps. What Reasons? eh?

Pheid.   The *Worse* and *Better*.

Streps.   'Twas to fruit
I had you taught the art to beat an honest suit,
If you will undertake to prove by arguing
That beating fathers is a fit and proper thing!

Pheid. That thesis I will take and make so very clear
You cannot answer it.

Streps.   That should I like to hear.

Chorus. Old man, if you your ground would hold
    Against a man so shrewd and bold,
      Look well on either hand.
    He never would have been so bad,
    Be sure, unless he felt he had
      Some ground on which to stand.
    But you should tell the Chorus first,
      What spark between you two
    To such a flame of discord burst.
      So, that proceed to do.

Streps. Aye, truly; I will tell you that:
   And he was the beginner.
'Twas thus.   We both at table sat
   (You know we went to dinner).
Amongst the kind of melodies
   There's one I'm fond of hearing,
A ballad of Simonides,
   About the ram and shearing.
'Sing that and try this lyre of mine,'
   Said I: but in a passion
He said that singing with your wine
   Was quite gone out of fashion.
Pheid. 'Tis so.   And when I spoke in vain,
   A thrashing was quite proper,
To teach you not to entertain
   A guest like a grasshopper.[1]
Streps. Aye, that he said within: and he's
   Quite willing you should know it.
He said, besides, Simonides
   Was but a middling poet.
'Twas trying to be treated thus,
   But willing to content him,
I, asking for some Æschylus,
   The myrtle-chaplet sent him.[2]
'The prince of bards is Æschylus,'
   Said he, in tone sarcastic,
'But turbulent, precipitous,
   And something too bombastic.'
To hear him speak in such a way,
   Of course was most provoking,
But I restrained myself to say,
   Albeit nearly choking,
'The moderns write with greater ease,
   And taste beyond correction,
Pray favour me with one of these,
   And make your own selection.'

---

[1] The Cicada, the chirping of which seems to have been regarded as cheerful.

[2] The chaplet was passed to the guest who was going to sing or recite: he, it appears, passed it on as a 'call' on another of the party.

Therewith he took Euripides,
    And sung a horrid fable,
Made up of immoralities.
    Of course I left the table.
I made him feel, while they were hot,
    My scorn and indignation.
He answered me : and so we got
    To sharp recrimination.
Then leaping up quite suddenly,
    He struck and got me under ;
And kicked and strangled me : that I
    Am living is a wonder !

Pheid.   He disapproved Euripides !
    It was quite right to strike him :
A man of such abilities
    That there is no one like him !

Streps.   Abilities !—but I abstain,
    I must not speak too lightly,
Or he will set on me again.

Pheid.   And serve you very rightly.

Chorus.   Now, all young men are in a flutter
To hear what this sharp lad will utter.
If he his case should win,
    And justify his deed ; for me
    I would not at a single pea
Appraise an old man's skin.
It is your business, engineer
    Of forces in debate,
To make your arguments appear
    To have the greater weight.

Pheid.   'Tis pleasant living in the reign
    Of mental revolutions,
And looking with sublime disdain
    On ancient institutions.
When I was occupied about
    The going of my horses,
I could not speak three words without
    Missing my proper courses;
But since my father stopped me there,
    And I have been expanding,

N

By studious thought and constant care,
   My powers of understanding,
I undertake to prove the right
   Of sons to beat a father.

Streps.   Then drive again with all your might;
   For very much I'd rather
Maintain four horses, car and all,
   Than bear the filial beating.

Pheid.   You interrupt me. I recall
   The point that I was treating.
Pray did you ever beat your son?—
   I wait for your reply, Sir.

Streps.   Of course I did—'twas kindly done
   To make you grow up wiser.

Pheid.   Since kindness then in beating lies,
   I am not an abuser,
If I beat you to make you wise,
   But simply kind to you, Sir.
Why should your body be reserved
   From stripes although you need 'em,
And mine exposed? I'm tender nerved
   And born like you in freedom.
Children may cry: 'tis not denied.
   Then why not fathers? Say you,
The law approves the blows applied
   To make a child obey you.
But are not dotards children twice?
   And if you find them swerving
From wisdom's common way to vice,
   Of stripes much more deserving?

Streps.   But such a law was never heard
   As gave a son permission
To beat his father—   .

Pheid.   Stay: a word:
   Who made the prohibition?
If such there be. At any rate,
   Who makes a father free, Sir,
To beat his son, if obstinate?
   But men like you or me, Sir.

Then what forbids that any day,
 And at a public meeting,
I make a law that sons shall pay,
 In kind, their fathers' beating.
The law shall not, we will agree,
 Have ex-post-facto action,
But beatings had before shall be
 Without their satisfaction.
Cocks beat their fathers when they please,
 And creatures game and tame do!
Except in making of decrees,
 Are we not all the same too?

Streps. If precedents you go to search
  Among the hens and chickens,
 Go you and roost upon a perch
  And live on dunghill pickings.

Pheid. The ratios are not alike,
ϽοϨ And Socrates would say it.

Streps. Then you be cautious how you strike,
  Or you perhaps may pay it.

Pheid. How so?

Streps.   Your rights are on your son;
  Treat him as you were treated.

Pheid. But if I never should have one,
  My rights would be defeated.

Streps. He's right, my friends. I will be taught:
  His arguments affect me.
 And if I do not what I ought,
  May't please him to correct me.

Pheid. One striking sentiment hear yet.

Streps. I yield you all my senses.

Pheid. And you may think without regret
  On your experiences.

Streps. How so? they have been sad indeed;
  And how can they be other?

Pheid. As I beat you—I pray you heed—
  I now will beat—MY MOTHER.

Streps. What do you say?—What can you mean?
  Such monstrous deed was never seen!

Pheid.   If with the Reason for the Wrong
           I make it clear by process strong
           That mothers should be beaten too ? —

Streps.   There would be nothing else to do
           But that foul Wrong to take,
               And SOCRATES with it ;
           And one long leap to make
               Into the Bottomless Pit.[1]

And this then is, ye Clouds, the recompense I meet
For having laid myself devoutly at your feet ?

Cho. Nay, friend, you have none other than yourself to
           blame   .
For having turned aside to ways of evil aim.

Streps. Why did you warn me not before it was too late,
But let the poor old man be quite infatuate ?

Cho. Ever it is our way, when we behold a man
Bent upon evil courses, to abet his plan ;
Till through misfortunes we can lead him to the mind
In reverence to the Gods his certain strength to find.

Streps. Your words to me, oh Clouds, are bitter, but most
           just.
I should not have attempted to belie a trust,
And cheat my friends.   But now, aid me, my dearest son,
To wreak my wrongs on Socrates and Chærephon.

Pheid. I cannot lend myself to wrong my masters, Sir.

Streps. Nay, nay, but reverence our Guardian Jupiter.

Pheid. Our Guardian Jupiter ! again that musty creed
Is there a Jupiter ?

Streps.   There is.

Pheid.   .   There's not indeed ;
Since Jupiter is driven out and Whirl is king !

Streps. Jove's not deposed.   True, once I thought this
           whirling [2] thing
Was truly Jove and King.   I was a monstrous fool.

Pheid. I'll take my leave of you to let your folly cool.

                                            [*Exit.*

---

[1] See note at the end on the character of Pheidippides.—The Pit. See
note, *Plutus*, 381.

[2] A modification is here made in order to give to the reader some idea

Streps. How came such madness on my silly brain to
    seize,
That I should throw away the Gods for SOCRATES ?
But, dearest Mercury, be not too much enraged,
That I, the fool, was with such chatterers engaged.
Advise me, shall I risk a process and indict them ?
Or do you know a better manner to requite them ?
                 [*Applies his ear to an image of Mercury.*
' Appeal not to the law,' you say ; aye, very good ;—
' But burn the house which holds the prating brotherhood.'
Fetch out the ladder, Xanthias, and bring an axe ;
Mount to the roof and strike its timbers till it cracks.
Quick, let your zeal appear by hastening its fall ;
And pluck about their ears their Meditation-hall.
Bring me a lighted torch, I'll make some pretty ruins,
Which shall for me requite the coxcombs for their doings.
First Disciple (*rushing out*). Ho, ho, there !
Streps.   Go, my torch, and do thy business blazing.
1st Dis. Hulloa, Sir, what are you about ?
Streps.   I'm simply raising
A nice discussion with the rafters of this dwelling.
2nd Dis. (*rushing out*). Ah ! who was that who threw
        the blazing torch which fell in ?
Streps. The man whose coat you stole.
2nd Dis.   You'll ruin us, my friend.
Streps. Exactly : 'tis the very thing which I intend,
Unless the mattock should my ardent wishes check,
Or I by some unlucky fall should break my neck.

      Enter SOCRATES *and* CHÆREPHON.

Soc. Hey ! you Sir, on the roof, what are you doing there?
Streps. Contemplating the sun, and walking on the air.[1]
Soc. Oh, my misfortune !   I am being suffocated.
Chær. And I, unhappily, am being incremated.

---

answerable to the self-justifying allegation of Socrates. It is supposed
that he referred to a large sort of vase called by the same name as 'whirl'
or ' vortex.' It is at least supposable that he may have referred to some
' turnabout' representation of Mercury near the door, such as that
alluded to in *Plutus*, 1153, especially as we see directly afterwards that
Strepsiades does address ' Mercury' and apparently receives an answer.
  [1] Vide line 198.

Streps. Why did ye dare the Gods on Science' lofty
   height?
Why of the Moon demand how she dispenses light?
For many reasons, follow, strike, and pelt, and ply them,
But chiefly to avenge the Gods insulted by them.
   Chorus. Let us depart.   Lead on the way,
      For we have danced enough to-day.

The moral crisis of the comedy and the character assigned to Pheidippides seem to have been often misapprehended. It is assumed that
Pheidippides is a profligate; whose moral corruption the Sophists have
completed, so that he at last beats his father and justifies it. Not so.
He is no profligate. His father was a rogue from the beginning, but
Aristophanes has been careful to preserve the son from all assent to his
father's knavish intentions. His worst fault is a touch of that Megacles'
blood, which .... ses him to the aristocratic taste for horseflesh. Strepsiades, who ... churl, does not like to spend money on such tastes. He
would like to redeem it by defrauding his creditors; creditors whom
Aristophanes has been careful to make not common money-lenders. Notwithstanding that he has such a father, Pheidippides carries his filial duty
so far as to consent to become a scholar of the Sophists. But it is with
his own aim, not with his father's. It is to obtain the faculty which he
will use to redeem his father from his infatuation. He comes out
accomplished in the art of maintaining either side of a question. He
practises this upon his father even to justify father-beating. But even
this, as Pheidippides finds, does not open the old man's eyes to the
immorality of the rogue-rhetoric which he is invoking against his creditors. It is not until Pheidippides goes on to justify *mother-beating* that
Strepsiades is corrected. Then the work of Pheidippides is done; his
father recognises his son's good purpose and principle, and confidently
asks him to join in the onslaught upon the Sophists. But the taste of
Aristophanes withdraws him from so mean an action. The Sophists had
done Strepsiades no wrong. They had not corrupted his principles or
his son's. But they had enabled his son to vindicate the fundamental
principles of morality, so that such a rogue as Strepsiades should become
sensible of duty. In truth, the part and character assigned to Pheidippides is remarkably *Socratic*. He is corrective; indirectly corrective;
he is an embodiment of that most delicate moral habit Εἰρωνεία. He
plays a part, and assumes a character, not his own, in order effectually to
convict another of false principles. Viewed in this light, the character of
Pheidippides is the most original which Aristophanes put upon the stage.
It is conceived and carried out with admirable art. It is true that this
view interferes with the construction of the comedy as an argument
against Socrates. But what of that? Aristophanes appropriately supplies the deficiency of moral force by recommending the application of
'mattock' and 'torch.' The Athenians were not persuaded, and the
dramatist was deeply mortified.

WASPS.

INTRODUCTION.

This comedy was produced in the year following Aristophanes' great disappointment with *Clouds*. The introduction, put into the mouth of Xanthias, seems to bear marks of chagrin and resentment. The poet had flown at the highest game, at Euripides and popular taste in poetic art, at Cleon and the demagogues, at Socrates and the professors of science. But the reception given to his pieces had not answered to his hopes. Probably the ambition of Aristophanes looked for more success than the mere crowning of his Chorus; he hoped to stem and turn public opinion. He now told himself that his themes had been too high for the audience which he had to please. On the present occasion they should look for 'nothing very great,' an argument not above common understandings.

The result is what has been pronounced 'the feeblest of the pieces of Aristophanes.' Yet, as this comedy contains at least a strain of humour, not only equal to the best of Aristophanes, but rarely surpassed by any humourist, such an epithet must at least be restricted to its comparative force. The humorous conception which especially characterises it has been followed by Racine in 'Les Plaideurs.' But the piece is prolix and unequal; unequal in the worst form, in that it falls off; so much so, that the translator, addressing himself to the fastidious English reader, has not here ventured to carry the translation beyond the break for the Parabasis, and even to that point has taken great liberty of abridgment; greater, he is well aware, than will be readily conceded to him by those whose taste has been already Aristophanised. Carried to the point which is here translated, the comedy arrives at a climax of humour which could not be sustained through a second part, unless indeed the old Dicast was himself to appear before the

court as *a defendant*. It seems as if the poet had really
intended this, but that the plot was too long for his space.
But, as it is, to produce the old man under the tutelage of
his son, tipsy upon the stage, and with all the follies and
vices of a *roué* young man, is a downfall in moral which
vexes one. Better, one must feel, that he should have
continued for ever the rigid old Dicast, through whose
incorruptible fingers, at least, no rogue ever slipped.

For the elucidation of the comedy it does not seem
necessary to enter into any detail of the judicial system of
the Athenians, beyond what will be supplied by the comedy
and some notes.

Besides the high court of Areopagus, there were the ordinary tribunals. All citizens were qualified to sit upon their
judicial benches. Under an official president, the office of
these *dicasts* was doubtless more like that of jurymen with
us than judges : those who were willing to act gave their
names in to a public officer; lot determined to which court
each man should be appointed; he received a ticket bearing the number of his court for the day. It does not
seem that the number of dicasts in any court was limited.
For the day's service, or for each cause, each dicast received the fixed fee of three oboles. It was probably in
consequence of the war pressing all the population into the
city, that the number of applicants for this pittance, by
way of eking out a livelihood, was enormous. A line in this
comedy (Greek 662, Trans. 442) is quoted as authority for
the number, 6,000. If it were not for the distinct word of
Aristophanes that these were ' dicasts,' one would suppose
that it must include all those who received pay for attending public meetings at the Pnyx.[1]

There is no need to dilate upon the vicious consequences
of such a judicial system; this is just what the satirist
proposes to expose.

The comedy obtained the first prize.

---

[1] Clinton, Fast. Hell. p. 70, estimates the usual attendance at the
Pnyx at about 6,000; being rather less than one in three of the adult
male citizens.

Dramatis Personæ.

LOVE-CLEON.

HATE-CLEON, *son of Love-Cleon.*

XANTHIAS.
SOSIAS. } *Slaves in the household of Love-Cleon.*

CHORUS of DICASTS, *dressed as Wasps.*

BOYS, *attending on Chorus.*

A DOG.

Dog SEIZER, *a mute person.*

Xanthias. Hold, while I give the audience to understand
That this is no great matter which we have in hand.
We task no simple wits, we strike at no high prey,
But just present the men and thoughts of every day.
Our master, yonder, on the roof, and fast asleep—
An independent man—has set us here to keep
Strict watch upon his father, who requires a warder,
As being subject to a curious disorder—
You will not guess it: try.—Amynias, I hear,
Suggests, the love of dicing. No: he is not near.
   Sosias. By Jove, he judges others' ailments by his own.
   Xan. But it begins with Love; I let so much be known.
' The love of drinking,' Sosia whispers to his neighbour.
   Sos. Nay, that's an ailment under which good fellows
      labour.
   Xan. Nicostratus says—but you're all beside the mark ;
You will not hit it. Come, I'll lead you through the dark.
'Tis love of Court-work ; yes, administering law.
If not the first upon the bench, you never saw
Man so distracted. If he sleeps, he's dreaming,
And ever wakes with his three fingers closed, as seeming
To drop a ballot in an urn. A cock that crew
Some hour or so after the sun was down, he knew,
Had been corrupted by some rogue to make him late.
Supper is scarcely cleared away, when he can wait
No longer ; calls for shoes, is off, his place to keep,
And, like a limpet, on a column drops asleep.
That he may never want a pebble for his votes,
He keeps a shingle-beach at home : so much he dotes.
His son, in grief at this, has tried what counsel could
To move him from his fancy ; but it did no good.

A course of water-treatment failed; then Corybanting [1]
Impelled him to the new court with a timbrel ranting.
Religion and its rites proved unavailing thus;
We took him to the shrine of Æsculapius,[2]
Crossing the water; there we laid him down at night,
But he appeared in Chancery [3] with morning light.
Since that, we keep him in the house; but still he found
Means to escape us through the sewers underground.
Whereon we looked for every hole, and stuffed them all
With shards and rags. But he drove pegs into the wall,
Whereon, supported like a daw or parrakeet,
He clambered down and made his way into the street.
Thus driven to our last resource, besides the setting
A constant guard, we have enclosed the house with netting.
The old man's name is Love-Cleon, as well it may;
His son is Hate-Cleon, high-minded in his way.

     Hate-Cleon (*calling from the outside*). Heigh! slave, are
            you asleep?
     Xan. and *Sos.*   What, Sir?
     H.-C.   Come here—by Jove!—
My father—run—has got into the bath-room stove,
And hides himself, and runs about it like a mouse;
Look to the funnel, else he'll get upon the house.
Lean you against the door.
                   [Xanthias *runs out and returns.*
     Sos.   Aye, Sir.
     H.-C.   I hear a scraping
I' the chimney (*looking up*). Who are you?
     Love-Cleon (*appearing out of the chimney*). Only the smoke
            escaping.
     H.-C. The smoke! what! bring me here a slab—the
            kitchen table.
                [Hate-Cleon *ascends to the roof, drives*
                   Love-Cleon *down, and puts the table*
                   upon the vent.

---

[1] The Corybantes were priests of Cybele. Their rites were those of madmen dancing. It appears that a course of this was sometimes prescribed medically. It must be understood, too, that the water-treatment was at once medical and religious.

[2] At Ægina.

[3] Within the Cancelli or railing which separated the dicasts in their court from the suitors and public.

A log above—there now : escape if you are able.
The door,—man, push with all your might. I'll help you
　　too.
Look to the bolts: beware, he'll break the cross bar through.
　　　　　　[LOVE-CLEON *inside, trying to force the door.*
L.-C. You wretches, let me out. I will—I must—in short,
Dracontides will be acquitted by the court.
H.-C. And that you could not bear.
L.-C.　　　　　　　　　　At Delphi I was told
If ever a defendant should slip through my hold
And get acquitted through an act of mine, that I
Should pine away.
H.-C.　　　　　Apollo ! what a prophecy !
L.-C. I do beseech you let me out; I shall be dead.
H.-C. By Neptune, never. That is positively said.
L.-C. Then I will gnaw the net.
H.-C.　　　　　　　　　But that you cannot do :
You have no teeth.
L.-C.　　　　　How can I make an end of you?
Give me a dagger or a verdict-board.[1]
H.-C.　　　　　　　　　　He's bent
On mischief.
L.-C.　　　　No, but let me out : I only meant,
To-day is market-day, and I should like to sell
The ass and panniers.
H.-C.　　　　　　　I can do that just as well.
Xan. It is a trick to make you let him pass the gate.
H.-C. He does not take his fish, for I perceive the bait.
Fetch me some stones to block the door. By Jove; I'd
　　rather
Be set to counter-wall Scione [2] than my father.
Sos. Now he has not a hole through which a mouse
　　could creep,
Why may we not lay down, and get a snatch of sleep?
H.-C. No no: his bench-fellows thinking to find him
　　waking,
Will soon be here.

---

[1] That which is here represented as a weapon for murder is a tablet on
which the President would mark the result of the Dicasts' votes.

[2] A city on the peninsula Pallene, which, having revolted from Athens,
was now being blockaded by the Athenians.

Sos.   How so? The day is scarcely breaking.

H.-C. Pooh! they are late this morning. Commonly they come

Soon after midnight, by their lantern-light, and hum

Some new-old-fashioned catch of Phrynicus.

Sos.   Why not

Despatch a flight of pebble-stones amongst the lot?

H.-C. As well to meddle with a nest of wasps as such

Old men, distempered. They have got a sting, whose touch

Is of the keenest; and they use it, dashing, crying,

Like sparks about one's head from kindled brushwood flying.

Sos. That would not frighten me. If I had got the stones,

I would disperse a swarm of such judicial drones.

      [*Exit* Hate-Cleon. Xanthias *and* Sosias
        sit down before the door, and fall asleep.

Enter Chorus, *attended by* Boys *carrying lanterns.*

Chorus. Come on, come on. Why, Comias,
    we do not step together.

By Jove you are not what you were
    when you were tough as leather.

Charinades would beat you now.
    What ho! my Strymodorus,

The model dicast of our day,
    and any time before us,

Where's Chabes? where's Euergides?
    Ah, there they are behind me.

And is that all that now is left
    of Chabes to remind me

Of *that* night in Byzantium?
    (to think how one remembers)

We stole the baker's kneading-trough
    and turned it into embers

To cook our greens. But come along:
    Here is a smell of honey.

Laches will be arraigned to-day
    and he, they say, has money.

So Cleon warned us yesterday
    to come this morning early,
And bring with us a store of wrath
    to keep us three days surly.
So quicken step; and let the light
    be everywhere directed,
That anyone who is about
    may be at once suspected.
Boy. Mud—father, look, or you will stick.
Choregus. Pick up a straw and clear your wick.
Boy. My finger can do that: look here.
Choreg. Your finger, fool: and oil so dear.
Look at the growth upon the wick,
    and notice how it sputters:
Within four days I say there will
    be water in the gutters.
Aye, here is our companion's house.
    But what can ail our neighbour?
He was not wont to be a slug,
    or hanger-back from labour.
 What can it mean? not at his door?
 I never knew it so before.
 It may be he has lost his shoes;
  Or, in the dark, has tripped within
 And hurt his toe, or got a bruise;
  And inflammation has set in.
 And, at his years, to get a fall!
  He will be missed.   He had a heart
 For hardness that could beat us all.
  One never knew him take the part
 Of pity: when the rest of us
 Were well-nigh soft and credulous,
 He would hold out, and be alone.
 ' My friend,' he'd say, ' you soak a stone.'
 There was a man—it may be that—
  Slipped through our fingers yesterday,
 Swearing he was a ' democrat,'
  And useful in the spying way.
 That may have made our neighbour fret—
 A likely man enough—and yet
o

   May keep him fevered in his bed.
   But, neighbour, drive such care away,
   And do not die Remorse's prey.
    Pity it were that you were dead,
   When we shall have before the court
    A man upon the Thracian treason;
   And very rich they say. In short,
    Get up, and help us to have reason.

Love-Cleon (*within*).

   I, pining here, my friends, have heard,
   Yes, through a crevice, every word.
   But ah, I cannot join your song,
    For I am guarded here and barred.
    What can I do? 'tis very hard;
   I can't get out, although I long
   To join you at the voting-urn,
   And do some man an evil turn.
   Oh Jupiter, with lightning-stroke
   Convert me into sudden smoke:
   Resolve the solid thing I am
    Into a Proxeniades,
   Or son of sillus;—something sham;
    Two vapouring inanities!
   Or, of thy pity, let thy flashes
   Reduce my body into ashes;
   And these be caught away and blown,
    To be in brine and acid stored.
   Or make me at the least, the stone,[1]
    On which the dicasts' votes are poured.

Cho. But what is this restraint about?
   Who dares to bar your coming out?
    Do say; and be not nervous.

L.-C. Hush! softly:—'Tis my son: he's here,
   Or sleeping somewhere very near;
    I fear he may observe us.

Cho. But, silly, wherefore is it done?
   What object in it has your son?

---

[1] When the dicasts had put their voting-pebbles into one or other of the urns, these were emptied upon a stone in front of the president, and counted.

Why should you so accuse him?

L.-C. He says, I shall not go to court;
And undertakes my whole support;
But stiffly I refuse him.

Cho. Because you spoke unpleasant truth
About the navy, dares the youth
To set us at defiance?

L.-C. I'm very certain he would not,
Unless there were some horrid plot,
On which he has reliance.

Cho. But you must think about a plan
For getting down without his knowing.

L.-C. Do only tell me how I can;
So anxious am I to be going.

Cho. There is a hole, which if you please
You may enlarge and burrow through it.

L.-C. Aye, but the wall is not a cheese:
At present not a mite could do it.

Cho. Remember you outdid us all
At Naxos [1] with that feat of daring,
When you slipped down the city wall,
The spits, which you had stolen, bearing.

L.-C. Aye, I remember; but I feel
That this and that are divers cases:
Then I was young, and I could steal,
And let who would come on my traces;
And nobody was then alarmed;
· But here are watchers fully armed,
Set here and there,
To cut off my retreat.
Two of them stand
With a spit in each hand,
As though I were
A cat with stolen meat.

Cho. But think on some contrivance. See,
The day is breaking, busy bee.

---

[1] Besieged and reduced about fifty years before. It is noticed by
Thucydides as the first of the independent republics reduced to absolute
subjection by the Athenians after the Persian War.

L.-C.   This net must be surmounted, I
    must gnaw its cords asunder.

Cho.   Aye, gnaw away; and all defy
    to bring your proud soul under.

L.-C.   There, there; 'tis done, but mind my son,
    make no incautious cheering.

Cho.   I'm in the trim to deal with him;
    so venture, nothing fearing.
  Now get a rope, and make it fast
    upon some hook or pin, do.
  A loop beneath your shoulders cast
    and drop down from the window.

L.-C.   But what if these two men should wake
    while I in air am dangling?
  For they might come above and make
    some sport of me by angling.

Cho.   We will defend you, might and main,
    with all our ancient mettle.
  They shall not pull you up again;
    leave us with them to settle.

L.-C.   Then I will venture it.   But see,
    if there be fatal failing,
  Do pick me up and bury me
    beneath the dicasts' railing.[1]

    [HATE-CLEON *rushes in, and wakes the Slaves.*

H.-C.   Wake up, you dog.

Sos.   Eh? what sir?—what?

H.-C.   I hear some voices humming.

Sos.   What? surely has the old man got—

H.-C.   —a rope, and he is coming
  Down from the window while you gape.

Sos. (*to L.-C.*)   Ha! I will show you which is
  The way that you shall not escape.

H.-C. (*to Xanth.*)   Go, run and take some switches,
  And from the other window reach,—
    you need not stint in thwacking;
  This rover we perhaps may teach
    the simple art of backing.

---

    [1] See note [3], p. 190.

L.-C. To aid, all who intend to be
    this year before us suitors;
 Or you will lose a friend in me
    by these my persecutors.
   [HATE-CLEON *and Slaves try to prevent his descent.*
Chorus. Wherefore longer, wherefore should the
    bilious anger be repressed,
 Which is always ready when a
    fool disturbs a hornets' nest:
    Only such will dare it;
    Sharply stinging,
    Vengeance bringing,
    Draw, and do not spare it.
 Children, throw your coats away, and
    run as quickly as you can;
 Shout for Cleon; tell him we have
    got a monster of a man,
 Who is preaching novel doctrine,
    and subversion of the State;
 Saying, Dicasts are a nuisance,
    which the City should abate.
H.-C. Nay, but hear me, my good fellows,
    wherefore should you clamour so?
Cho. Heaven shall hear and split before we
    let our bench-companion go.
    [*Struggle for possession of* LOVE-CLEON.
Xan. Hercules! what stings they carry!
Cho.   They shall be the death of you.
 All in order, full of fury,   [through.
    draw your stings and pierce them
Xan. See you, Master, what a weapon
    each one to the battle brings?
 I am frightened at the look of
    these abominable stings.
Cho. Then unhand our old companion;
    if you do not, I foretell,
 You shall wish you were a tortoise
    comfortably cased in shell.
L.-C. Bitter-hearted wasps, be at them,
    fellow-dicasts, worthy friends,

Some of you about their eyes, and
                    some about their finger-ends.
H.-C. Hold him fast, you Lydian mongrels;
                    if you let him get away,
Shod in fetters you shall breakfast
                    upon nothing-broth to-day.
Let them bounce, say I, and crackle;
                    kindled fig-leaves do the like.
Cho. Loose the man directly: you will
                    suffer for it if I strike.
L.-C. Cecrops! do you see this outrage?
                    I am in these villains' grip,
Who have often filled a bucket
                    with their tears beneath my whip.
Cho. Truly this is one among the
                    sorrows which to age belong.
Here we see two men who do their
                    venerable master wrong;
Quite forgetting all the coats and
                    waistcoats they have had of him,
All the caps, and all the shoes to
                    shield their feet in winter grim;
All the purchase of his money!
                    Now we see the shameless dogs,
Lost to every decent feeling,
                    have no sense of ancient clogs.
L.-C. You ungracious beast, release me:
                    surely you cannot forget
That one day, when in the vineyard
                    unexpectedly we met;
Grapes you had been stealing, when I
                    led you to the olive tree;
Where I gave you such a flogging,
                    that the others stood to see,
Pale with envy!—yet do you no
                    proper gratitude display!
Now unhand me, you and you,
                    before my son here runs away.
H.-C. Thrash them; smash them, Xanthias, and
                    drive the creatures from the place.

Xan. Aye, Sir; that I'm doing; but some
     smoke would better suit the case.
Sos. Hang you, hornets; vanish: will you?
     take this crack upon your crown.
Xan. That has settled them: I knew that
     we in time must put them down.
       [*Chorus draw off beaten.*

Cho. We must bow; and you must reign!
   None so poor but they can see
   I am cozened; and again
    Come the days of tyranny,
   If with wickedness and pride
   You may set the laws aside.
   Not that you are eloquent,
   And have won us to consent:
   But because, and simply that,
   You must needs be Autocrat.
H.-C. Can we not without a battle,
     aye, without this noise and pother,
  Quietly discuss the case, and
     come to terms with one another?
Cho. I discuss with you—a traitor,
   Monarch-lover, people-hater,
   Friend of Brasidas, who wear
    Fringes on your skirts like those!
   Aye, and cultivate the hair
   Up to and beneath your nose![1]
H.-C. Better give my father up, and
     be at once from trouble freed!
Cho. Softly, Sir; that calculation
     indicates more haste than speed.
  You are pleased to think of ease; but
     when the prosecutor tells,
  Thus and thus you said and did; and
     your conspirators compels—
H.-C. Answer, by the Gods, I beg you,
     will you take yourselves away?
  If not I will stop and beat you
     and be beaten all the day.

----

[1] These fashions were odious to the Chorus as being 'Spartan.'

Cho.   Never!—Think not that of me,
              When you threaten Tyranny.
H.-C. Everything is Tyranny;
                    and every man Conspirator!
        Whatsoever be his crime, 'tis
                    that a man must answer for.
        Some while since it was a word we
                    had not heard for fifty years;
        Now the name of Salt-fish is not
                    rung so often in our ears.
        Even in the market-place the
                    term is vollied at one's head;
        If a man would buy a turbot
                    and declines a sole instead,
        He who has the soles upon his
                    fish-board will at once exclaim,
        'By his marketing 'tis clear that
                    Tyranny is this man's aim.'
        If a man who buys anchovies
                    ask for fennel for the sauce,
        'Fennel quotha'—says a coster-
                    monger, looking very cross,
        'Why should such as you want fennel?
                    'tis a tyrant's dainty dish;
        'Is the city to be taxed to
                    find you sauces for your fish?'
        Now, if I would get my father
                    to give up this way of life,
        Early-getting-up-to-nourish-
                    pettifogging-spite-and-strife;
        And to be a gentleman; I
                    am to bear the obloquy
        Of conspiring to evert the
                    order of Democracy.
L.-C. Justly too.   For pigeon's milk should
                    not entice me to give up
        Such a life as I have chosen.
                    Do not think I care to sup
        Daintily on skate and eels: a
                    dish which better hits my taste

Is a pretty little quarrel,
>   cooked into a suit in haste.

H.-C. Yes, I know these are your pleasures:
>   but I pledge my word to this,

I will prove, if you will listen
>   quietly, you judge amiss.

L.-C. I, a dicast, judge amiss!

H.-C.   Aye, that you are the jest of those
Whom you only do not worship,
>   while they lead you by the nose.

Slave you are, and do not know it.

L.-C.   Slave indeed! I'm not a slave.
I am lord of all.

H.-C. Not you, Sir.   You are but the working knave
Of the men you think you govern.
>   What advantage have you got
From receiving all the harvest
>   fruits of Greece? I ask you what?

L.-C. Much I say, and I am willing by that issue to abide.

H.-C. So am I. So now release him;
>   and these ancients shall decide.

Chorus.   Now our pupil is upon test,
>   Risking all to win this contest.
>   He must striking skill employ
>   To gainsay this headstrong boy.

L.-C.   What if I fail in my intent,
>   And his the better argument?

Chorus.   I shall say that all our number
>   Are but so much ancient lumber,
>   Proper butts for random wit,
>   Things to look at, only fit
>   To carry walkingsticks and clothes,
>   Empty shells of broken oaths.

But, oh thou, on whom are all our
>   hopes of saving our dignity hung,

Open the case with tact displaying
>   all the powers of a voluble tongue.

L.-C. This I start from, this is the thesis
>   which I undertake to debate,

That the Dicasts' own dominion
>   is nothing less than a royal estate.

Who so blessed as the dicast?
             Find me an animal, if you can,
Half so pampered or so terrible,
             more especially if an old man.
Soon as he leaves his bed in the morning,
             and creeps off to the sacred space,
Strapping fellows six foot high will
             humbly watch him and wait on his pace.
Presently I shall feel the fawning
             courteous touch of a delicate hand,
That has filched the public monies.
             Then when I stop the suppliants stand,
Making lament with broken voices :—
             'Kind Sir, father, pity and spare :
If you ever were in office and   [share :
             should have fingered more than your
If you ever have cheated your comrades
             when engaged to market for mess.'
This shall be said by a man who but when
             he had some such favour to press
Never since I was born has seen me.—
H.-C.   I will make a memorial note.
' *Supplications.*'
L.-C.   Then, when entered,
             thus besought to promise a vote,
First I wipe away ill humour ;
             then I undertake to forget
Every promise of support which
             I may have made to the people I met.
Then comes hearing all the various
             tones in which their fear is expressed.
What is the art and shift of wheedling
             which to a dicast is *not* addressed?
Some their poverty fall to bewailing,
             and supply in pitiful tone
Woes fictitious added to true griefs
             till they almost equal my own.
Some have got a wondrous story ;
             some with Æsop try to beguile ;
Some with a biting jest attempt to
             carry my temper off with a smile.

All this proving unavailing,   [stage,
    then are the children brought on the
Little girls and boys all standing,
    one in his arms of the tenderest age.
I give them my whole attention.
    All of them in symphony cry.
Treating me like his God, the father
    falls to supplicating,—'If I
Hear the voice of a lamb with pleasure,
    will I pity the voice of his boy?
If the squeaking of sucking pigs is
    such a sound as I rather enjoy,
May the cry of his little daughter
    move me just to—pass his account!
Surely a man so tender-hearted
    will not stick for a little amount.'
Then will we relent a little.
    Could I not in mockery sing,
When I see rich rascals cringeing? .
    Is not this to be more than a king?
H.-C. That I note again—your '*mockery.*'
    But, Sir, I am longing to hear,
How the benefits you derive from
    governing Greece are made to appear.
L.-C. If before our court Æagrus [1]
    has to establish his innocence,
He must give us a recitation
    from his 'Niobe' in his defence.
If a piper gets acquitted,
    he of course must pay for the sport
By a melody played as an afterpiece
    at the breaking up of the court.
Should a father make his will and
    constitute his daughter his heir,
And by testament signed and sealed in
    lawful form and manner declare
Such or such a friend shall marry her;
    we can say 'A fig for the seal:
We will find the girl a husband:'
    this we do without any appeal.

---

[1] A tragic actor.

II.-C. And commit a great iniquity.

L.-C.   Such is a dicast's common employ:
    You would have me leave it, and call the
            sum of my constant profit and joy
  Service!   Slavery!

II.-C.   Speak your fill.

L.-C.   As to power to have my will,
    Only Jupiter is my match!
    One indeed may often catch
    Words that might be meant for him,
    Or for me, when I am grim.
    As when 'tis said with awe and wonder
    'Hark! the court is launching thunder!'
    Yes, I fling my fiery brands,
    And your proudest kiss my hands.
    You too tremble at my breath,
      Aye, by Ceres, that is true.
    But, I take it on my death,
      I am not afraid of you.

Chorus. We never listened to discourse
    So lucid and so full of force.

L.-C. He thought, may be, to pick the grapes while I
    was out.[1]
For that he knew my strength there cannot be a doubt.

Chorus. He took his points up one by one
    With perfect ease, omitting none.
    I seemed transported from the place,
    And while I listened to the case,
    To be a dicast and addressed
    Within the Islands of the Blest.

L.-C. You see he is exhausted, lost in his surprise.
Nothing but whips to-day shall flit before his eyes.

Chorus. All that a wily man can do
    You must attempt, young man, if you
    Intend escaping. You will find
    My disposition hard to grind;

---

[1] Meaning 'to have it all his own way';—as a vineyard robber would
if the owner left his vines unwatched.

And the mill you get should be of the best,
> flinty stone and thoroughly dressed,
To reduce what I feel of angry zeal
> against the mind you have expressed.
H.-C. High the aim and hard the task is
> on this stage to try to abate
Mischief anciently engendered,
> grown now into the life of the State.
Yet, oh Father, son of Saturn—
L.-C. Stop, you sir! no 'fathering' here:
I am a Slave, say you; and if you
> do not make that perfectly clear,
You shall die, though I must fast for it.[1]
> I will not be pitiful now.
H.-C. Nay good Daddy, do but hear me:
> pray unknit that terrible brow.
Now, to begin with, reckon roughly—
> not with pebbles but on your hand—
At what figure for the total
> may our public revenue stand.
Contributions from the cities,
> taxes, with per-centage, fines,
Court-dues, port-dues, tolls at market,
> sales of public property, mines.
Shall I say two thousand talents?
> Put the dicasts' pay for a year—
(Some six thousand [2] all included) a
> hundred and fifty talents or near.
L.-C. Dicasts do not draw a tenth then?
H.-C. No; but what becomes of the rest?
L.-C. That rewards the zeal of those whose
> love for the People is never at rest.
H.-C. Yes, my father, these are the men who [guides.
> cozen you, whom you take for your

---

[1] Those who had committed homicide were not allowed any portion from the public sacrifices.

[2] 6,000 men at 3 oboles, would draw 18,000 oboles per diem, or half a talent. The 'business' days being reckoned at 300 in the year, the sum named is accounted for.

They will take in bribes from the cities [1]
   well-nigh fifty talents besides.
You are content with scraps and parings;
   they go off with the bulk of the prize.
This is a course that all may reckon on;
   so much so that, when the allies
See that the rabble of judges are lean and
   do not share with the rest in the sweets,
You they treat as Connus's vote; [2] but
   rush to load the others with treats,
Baskets of salt-fish, wine, embroidery,
   pillows, honey, sesame, cheese,
Goblets, clothing, liquors, chaplets,
   and in fact whatever they please.
But to you, the lord of empire,
   will they give for the matter of that
Not so much as a head of garlic,
   if you wish to flavour a sprat.
L.-C. Right, by Jupiter! Not so long since
   Eucharides denied to me three.
But you wear me out with waiting
   for your proof of my slavery.
H.-C. Slavery! what is it else when those who
   hold high offices carry away,
By themselves and by their flatterers,
   every post of credit and pay?
While you take your mean three oboles:
   aye, and requite the disburser with thanks,
You, who won them watching, marching,
   fighting every day in our ranks.
Then to bow and take your orders—
   yes, that throttles me more than it all—

---

[1] Meaning especially the island cities in nominal confederacy with, but really in subjection to, Athens.

[2] The explanations of this expression are so far-fetched that it seems better to rest under the conviction that we do not know who *this* Connus was, nor why his 'vote' proverbially expressed that which was of no importance. In the previous year Ameipsias had presented a comedy with the title 'Connus.' It is possible that there may be some allusion to that.

From some insolent son of Cineas !
　　　So—he saunters into the hall,
Posing his body into an attitude,
　　　ere he deems it proper to say,
' Dicasts, be in the court to-morrow
　　　something after the break o' the day.
None will be allowed their oboles
　　　who come after the close of the gate.'
He, however, will take his drachma,[1]
　　　come Sir Counsel never so late.
All, beside his share in a present,
　　　fingered by his magistrate friend,
To compound an affair of roguery.
　　　They soon bring the case to an end.
Two men saw through the log of timber.
　　　You meanwhile may sit in the sun,
Look to the bursar for your oboles,
　　　and know nothing of what has been done.
L.-C. Thus they serve me !　Do they really ?
　　　There is something that troubles my breast.
What can it be ?　I own that I am
　　　deeply moved at what you suggest.
H.-C. While there is wealth galore for all of you.
　　　That indeed is easily seen.
Shame it is these fellows should manage you ;
　　　wheel you about just like a machine.
From Sardinia up to Pontus
　　　how many cities call you their lord ?
Yet you are wearing a coat all threadbare !
　　　Is it the best that you can afford ?
No ! but it squares with your allowance,
　　　dropped like oil on the point of a hair.
Poor you are, almost to starving :
　　　'tis their meaning to keep you there.
Why ?—I will tell you.　'Tis that, knowing
　　　where is the hand by which you are fed,
You may be ready to seize and worry
　　　anyone *they* may happen to dread.

---

[1] Value six oboles : a fee to counsel ; of whom it appears the number was limited.

Look you; if they really wished it,
　　　you might all be living at ease.
Are there not a thousand cities, all
　　　bound to supply whatever you please?
Why not make them nourish our people,
　　　giving to every city its score?
Twenty thousand men would thus have
　　　everything they could wish for and more;
As becomes the men of Marathon.
　　　Now like men who look for a stray
Olive where others have picked the trees, you
　　　dog the heels of the man with the pay.

L.-C. What can this be? Is it palsy
　　　dully creeping over my hand?
See, the knife is dropping from it.
　　　—I feel scarcely able to stand.

H.-C. Presently some dark fears disturb them.
　　　Then they think to give you a treat.
You shall have Euboea;[1] or they
　　　promise you fifty measures of wheat.
What have you had? Some bushels of barley,
　　　doled to you a quart at a time.
While your citizen-claim to take it
　　　seemed to be regarded a crime.
　　　Therefore have I shut you up:
Bent to bar your way to those
Who but lead you by the nose.
　　　I will for your needs provide,
　　　In person, plate, and cup:
　　　Amply they shall be supplied
With everything that you can think,
Excepting bursar's milk to drink.

Chorus. To give everyone his credit,
'Twas wisely said, whoever said it,
' Reserve your judgment, till you may
Hear what both parties have to say.'
So have I heard, and I protest
Your argument is much the best.

---

[1] That the inhabitants of Euboea shall be dispossessed of their island, and that it shall be assigned in lots to needy Athenian citizens.

I feel my anger pacified,
And with my stick 'tis laid aside.
And you, my own judicial mate,
Listen, and be not obstinate.
　I would for me some friend would feel,
　Or kinsman, such a lively zeal,
　　And offer me the like provision.
　Some Deity for you must care,
　And make this thing his own affair.
　　Accept the kind interposition.

H.-C.　To find him all that suits his age,
As coat and blanket, I engage,
　　　　And groats for gruel.
But why this silence so profound?
To give no sign, to make no sound,
　　　　Methinks, is cruel.

Chorus.　His silence marks the self-reproof
　　That now is going on within.
He feels that to have held aloof,
　　When you were urging, is a sin.
And probably he will from hence
Change, and live like a man of sense.

L.-C.　Ah, me! ah, me! (*with tragic energy*)
H.-C.　　　　　　　　　My father, why
Bursts from thy lips that bitter cry?

L.-C.　Recall, my son, recall, deny
　　Your promises, and spare me, spare.
I long for them indeed, but I
　　Would fain be there, be there
Among them when the herald cries,
'Who has not voted let him rise!'
Then will I rise to be the last
My vote into the urn to cast.—
Quickly, my soul!—Dark thought, begone!
Avaunt, avaunt! Let me pass on.
Ah no, I cannot bear the thought—
　　By Hercules, I might have left
The dicasts' benches, when there's brought
CLEON before us—for a theft!

H.-C. Father, I do beseech you, listen to your son.

P

L.-C. What should I listen to? say anything but one.

H.-C. 'But one,'—what's that?

L.-C.   That I resign the dicasts' bench;
Hades decide it ere I yield to such a wrench.

H.-C. Since you have pleasure in it, prithee go not hence
Abroad for your enjoyment, but at home dispense
Justice among your household.

L.-C.   Nonsense!—what about?

H.-C. Our household matters. If the servant-girl goes out
By stealth and leaves the door ajar; that is a case
For simple fine.   So did you in the other place.
And all may be so well and reasonably done.
On sunny mornings you will court it in the sun:
But if it snows or rains, avoiding colds and mire,
You comfortably hold your court before the fire.
And should it happen that some morning you lie late,
You will not have to fear the closing of the gate.

L.-C. Aye, that will do.

H.-C.   Besides, if any case should last
Inordinately long, you are not bound to fast,
Worried yourself and worrying the speaker too.   [do.

L.-C. What! take a snack between? But that will never
How can I, going through the process of digestion,
Decide, as heretofore, the merits of a question?

H.-C. Tut, better. 'Tis observed when evidence conflicts
A dicast ruminates; and barely then convicts.

L.-C. Agreed. But one thing is not settled as I would:
Where shall I draw the pay?

H.-C.   From me.

L.-C.   Aye, very good.
I take the fee myself.   There will be none to play
The trick Lysistratus served me the other day:
He took the drachma,[1] and in order to arrange,
He went aside into a fishmonger's for change.
I popped it in my mouth as usual, for I thought
They were three oboles;[2] but in truth the rogue had
          brought

---

[1] Value, six oboles, the pay of two dicasts.

[2] If the oboles were in silver coin, they would not much differ in size
and appearance from fish-scales

Three mullet's-scales !   I spat the things away,
And prosecuted him.

    H.-C.   And what had he to say ?

    L.-C. He said I was a cock, and had of course a gizzard
Which could digest a coin, or anything that is hard.

    H.-C. You see how much you gain by change.

    L.-C.   'Twas not so small.
But fetch the things.

    H.-C. Aye, wait and I will bring them all.

                             [*Exit* HATE-CLEON.

    L.-C. How strange this is ! For I have heard 'twas said
        of old,
The time should come when we Athenians should hold
Courts in our private houses, when a man should build
A court before his door.   These things are now fulfilled.

Re-enter HATE-CLEON, *with various articles for the Court.*

    H.-C. See here. What can you want ? Have I not every-
        thing ?
A brazier too with fire, I thought it well to bring
To keep the gruel warm.

    L.-C.   'Tis just as I could wish ;
For if I have a cold and should be feverish
I still can earn the wages, supping while I sit.
Why bring a cock, though ? what can be the use of it ?

    H.-C. It is to wake you up in case you should be dozing,
When any speaker is unusually prosing.
But sit you down.   The sooner you are in your place,
The quicker I shall be in bringing on a case.

    L.-C. Then call one.   I am only waiting to begin.

    H.-C. Then—let me see—what case shall be the first
        called in ?
What has been done within the house, which we can
        settle ?
The kitchen-maid has burnt the bottom of a kettle—

    L.-C. Hold, hold ! how fortunate that we had not begun !
We have not got a railing.   What should we have done ?
The thing of most importance, so we always reckoned.

    H.-C. By Jupiter, we've not.   I'll get one in a second.

                            [*Turns to go out.*

How very strange, this slavery to prejudice!

[*He is met by* XANTHIAS, *dragging in a great dog.*

Xan. Hang ye—to think of keeping such a dog as this.

H.-C. Eh, what's the matter?

Xan.   What? a great Sicilian cheese
This dog, this villain SEIZER, has contrived to seize.
He stole it from the pantry.

H.-C.   Good: we'll have the brute
Into my father's court, and you shall prosecute.

Xan. Not I. The other dog will do it with good will,
If anyone will sign and introduce the bill.

H.-C. Go then, and bring them both.   [*Exit.*

Xan.   I will. [*Ties up* SEIZER, *and exit.*

Re-enter HATE-CLEON *with a gate.*

L.-C.   Eh, what? and why?
What have you there?

H.-C.   The pigs have lent it from their stye,
A gate, Sir, for your railing.

L.-C.   Prithee do make haste:
I'm looking for a fine.

H.-C.   Where will you have them placed,
The forms for verdicts and—

L.-C.   Plague on the man, what next?
You squander all the day. I really am perplexed.
Do call a case.

H.-C.   I will.

H.-C.   What is the first?

H.-C.   Aye, so—
To think I had forgotten them: but I will go—

L.-C. Where are you going now?

H.-C.   To fetch the voting-urns.

L.-C. No, no: the gruel jug and cups will serve the turns.

H.-C. Aye, excellently well. So fetch us myrtle boughs
And incense; that we may begin with proper vows.

Chorus. With thankful prayers, and streaming wine
          Will I address the Powers Divine,
          For gladness that the strife is past,
          And after war ye two are fast
              In concord bound.

H.-C.   Away, ill-omened sound.

Chorus.   Apollo, prosper with success
This man's design for peace.
Make all discordance cease;
And all of us be pleased to bless.

H.-C.   Oh, Lord and King, whose holy shrine
Neighbours this lowly door of mine,
This sacrifice be pleased to take,
Here offered for my father's sake.
Let him be softened and unlearn
All tempers too austere and stern.
Accept this must, and blend a touch
Of honey with his wrath too much.
His sympathies do thou dispose
More to defendants than to those
Who prosecute : and give him tears
For those who cry to him with fears.
To wrath no more inclined,
May he the suppliant heed,
And weed, Aguieus,[1] weed
The nettle from his mind.

Chorus.   Your prayers are ours ; and one in voice,
Will we in your new power rejoice.
For we perceive that you
Tender the People's interest
With love more zealous than the rest,
At least of young men, do.

(*Scene arranged for a Court.*)

H.-C. If any, cited to the court, is at the door,
Come in.   When they begin, we shall admit no more.

L.-C. Now which is the defendant?   There, conviction
stares—

Xan. Hear the indictment.   Dog, of Cydathon, declares
That Seizer, of Æxoné, did with covetise
Unaided and alone eat a Sicilian cheese.
The penalty a collar made of fig-tree wood.

L.-C. An he be guilty, Sir, a dog's death is too good.

---

[1] An appellative of Apollo.

H.-C. Here Seizer, the defendant, is to meet the charge.

L.-C. Rascal, upon his features THIEF is written large.
I see his teeth, but I will not be put upon.
Where is the prosecutor, Dog of Cydathon?

Dog. Bough-Wough.

H.-C.   Ah there: another Seizer, for that matter:
Good dog enough no doubt to bark and lick a platter.

Sosias as court-keeper. Sit down, sir: hold your peace.
                    (*To* XANTHIAS.) Go up and prove your case.

L.-C. Aye so; I'll take a draught while you are changing
            place.

Xan. Your ears have heard the charge, good dicasts,
            which I lay
Against this Dog. A crime I will take leave to say
Of the most hideous type, not only against me
But all the gallant tars, by whom we rule the sea.
He ran into the corner,—took it at his ease,—
He gorged himself: in short, unsicelized the cheese.

L.-C. By Jove, it's manifest: his breath, I smell it here—
Ah, faugh—is rank of cheese: the scurvy dog, it's clear.

Xan. And gave me not a morsel, though I asked it.

L.-C.   What?
No share?

Xan.   No: though I was his partner, not a spot.
What can you look for from his generosity,
Who would not throw a morsel to a dog, that's me?

L.-C. 'Tis a hot rogue: hot as this gruel.

H.-C.   Father, nay,
Do not prejudge. Hear what the other has to say.

L.-C. But, my good sir, the case is clear, it bellows out.

Xan. By no means let him off. He is without a doubt
The most alone-devouring brute; he has no match;
He'll walk about a bowl to see if he can catch
The paring of a cheese. 'Tis time that he should grieve.
One thicket will not keep two men disposed to thieve.[1]
If he is not put down, my barking is in vain.
In short he must be; or I will not bark again.

L.-C. Ha, ha! 'tis well exposed. A mass of villanies.

---

[1] Where one foot-pad might gain a livelihood two would starve.

The whole thing's *thief*.   What think you, cock ?   Yes, he
    agrees.

H.-C. Ah, will you never soften, rugged as you are,
And always adverse to the prisoner at the bar ?

    Sosias. Come forward witnesses for SEIZER; Dish and
        Pot,
Pestle, Cheesegrater, Pan, Dutch-oven, and what not.

    H.-C. Go SEIZER up, and bring the truth to light of day.
Why don't you speak ?

    L.-C.   Because there's nothing he can say.

    H.-C. Nay, but it is with him as with Thucydides,[1]
That he is speechless struck when he should make his
    pleas.

Give way; for I will undertake the Dog's defence.

To answer for a Dog, oppressed with false pretence,
Judges, is hard.   But I will try.   For he is good,
And keeps the wolves at distance from the neighbourhood.

    L.-C. Thief and conspirator.

    H.-C.   One that will never sleep
When ravening beasts are prowling round your flock of
    sheep.

    L.-C. But what has that to do with eating up the cheese?

    H.-C. He watches at your door and is prepared to seize
Ill-willers to you.   'Tis in fact a dog of merit.
Perhaps he stole.   But what of that? why should one
    ferret
For such slight faults?   He cannot sing.[2]

    L.-C.   I wish the knave
Had never learnt to write a speech : for that would save
Our time and temper.

    H.-C.   Let the witnesses appear.
You, Cheesegrater, come forward, let his worship hear.
Speak up : for you were in the pantry at the time
When this event took place which is alleged as crime.
Did you not for the soldiers grate the cheese you had ?
Now, clear your throat, and answer like an honest lad.
He says he did.

---

[1] The son of Milesias.   See *Acharnians*, l. 658.
[2] See p. 203, lines 369–372.

L.-C.   Why then, by Jove, he lies.

H.-C.   Oh, Sir,
Have pity on an undeserving sufferer!
This SEIZER is a shifty dog and he will sup
On any odds and ends he chances to pick up.
Whereas this other dog is always in the yard
Observing those who come, and looking very hard
At all they bring; whereof he always asks a share;
And if they do not give it, bites them then and there.[1]

    L.-C. Ah, something is the matter—I am—I am reeling.
What can have happened? I have got a touch of feeling.

    H.-C. Aye, father, I implore you do regard, do spare,
And do not ruin him. Where are the puppies? where?
Get up, you little dogs, and try your best at helping
To move his stony heart by whining and by yelping.

                           [The puppies yelp.

    L.-C. Get down, get down, get down.

    H.-C.   Aye, then I will get down.
But what has seemed a smile has often hid a frown,
When you have said those words. I get down not the
    less.

    L.-C. A plague! There's something bad in drinking I
    confess.
Ah, what? Have I been shedding tears? aye, sure enough.
That can be nothing but this water-gruel stuff.

    H.-C. Then really he escapes?

    L.-C.   'Tis very hard to say.

    H.-C. Yes, dearest father, turn you to the better way,
This.—Take the pebble. Shut your eyes and run
To the absolving urn, yes, to the hinder one.

    L.-C. No, no. My finger has not skill to touch that note.

    H.-C. Come, come, I'll lead you round—the shortest way
    —to vote.

                  [HATE-CLEON leads him.

---

[1] The humour of the 'Twa Dogs' was enhanced to the audience by
the fact that they are a very palpable caricature of Laches and Cleon.
Laches had had a command on the Sicilian coast, and was supposed to
have taken some 'presents.' As in *The Knights* Cleon is not put on the
stage in his own name, so here it is to be observed that 'The Other dog'
is unnamed. But these four lines are sufficient to identify him.

L.-C. Is this the nearest?

H.-C.   Yes.

L.-C.   I put the pebble in.[1]

H.-C. (*aside*) Acquitted! yes, he does not know it: and
    we win.

L.-C. I empt the urns.—How has it gone?

H.-C.   That we shall see
When I have counted votes.—Ha, SEIZER, you are free.
What ails you, father?

L.-C.   Water. I shall faint away.

H.-C. Hold up, hold up, dear Sir.

L.-C.   But tell me truly, say,
Is he acquitted?

H.-C.   Yes.

L.-C.   Ah! then I am no more.

H.-C. Nay, take it not to heart; come rise you from the
    floor.

L.-C. How shall I answer to my conscience for the
    deed?
That ever vote of mine a prisoner has freed.
What will become of me?   Forgive me, Powers Divine:
A deed against my will should not be reckoned mine.

H.-C. Do not reproach yourself. Good father, you shall
    fare
Right nobly. I will take you with me everywhere;
To supper, banquet, play, procession, every sight;
Hereafter you shall spend your days in all delight.
Hyperbolus with all his pride of wealth shall know
We snap our fingers at him.

L.-C.   Be it so. I go.

---

[1] In the Courts the urns to receive the pebbles were so arranged that
the one nearest to the dicasts was for the votes of those who confirmed
the charge, the further one for the votes of acquittal. In our case Hate-
Cleon has led his father (obviously to the audience) *round* the table on
which the urns were set, so that unwittingly Love-Cleon acquits the
prisoner while depositing his pebble in the 'nearest' urn.

PEACE.

INTRODUCTION.

In *political* order this comedy follows *Acharnians* and *Knights*. The appeal for peace made in *Acharnians* found no favour with the Athenian people. Before the end of that year Cleon and Demosthenes had brought to Athens the Spartans who had surrendered at Pylos. Even before the actual surrender, as has been said, the Lacedæmonians made overtures for peace, which were ineffectual. After the possession of such hostages the Athenians were too elated to listen to any terms the Confederates could unite to offer. So the war went on, though with no great energy and with no signal advantage on either side. One Spartan indeed, Brasidas, manifested a political and military ability which, had it been supported at Sparta, might have led his country to a political position which would have changed the course of Grecian history. But Sparta was not Rome, and did not answer to the genius and ambition of Brasidas. Inflated doubtless by the result of his stroke of energy at Pylos, Cleon went to confront this dangerous Spartan, where he was intriguing to undermine Athenian influence, in Thrace. There, at Amphipolis, in a very slight affair, on the part of Cleon miserably mismanaged, they fell, both of them, Cleon and Brasidas. The consequence was that the principal parties on both sides were disposed to come to terms. The Lacedæmonians met with difficulties interposed by their confederates the Corinthians and Bœotians : but driven to act independently, in order to redeem their relatives from the Athenian war-prisons, they agreed to a truce for fifty years.

Immediately after the great Dionysian festival at Athens, to which persons representing all the states lately at war would come to see the new tragic and comic dramas,

this treaty was to come into operation. Exactly for such
an occasion this comedy, *Peace*, seems to have been composed.   But, strange to say, if our text (in line 955 Greek,
795 trans.) is correct, it was not brought out until two
years later.   Even if some circumstances should have prevented its being produced on the actual occasion of peace,
it is unaccountable that Aristophanes should have inserted
a line, which in the face of the audience who knew they
had been at peace, included the last two years in the
period of war-suffering.   It is true that *we* reckon the
years of the war to the surrender of Athens as if they were
continuous ; and so does Thucydides, who saw the renewal
of the contest; but this could not have been the view in
the thirteenth year, when the peace made two years before
must have seemed stable and permanent.

If any reader of the *Clouds* has accepted in simple faith
the indignation of Aristophanes at the implied scepticism
of Socrates, he will be startled at the handling of MERCURY,
as a character in the play.   This, however, is only a pre-
lude to the manner in which the popular Gods will be
treated in the remaining comedies.   It is remarkable
among the phenomena of superstition that the people who
could bear and enjoy this impudent profaneness, should
a few years afterwards have been thrown into a phrenzy of
horror at the secret and sudden mutilation of the statues
of this very God. That very incident it was, which, affecting
the career and ambition of Alcibiades, indirectly operated
to rekindle the Peloponnesian War as between Athens and
Sparta.

In the Parabasis Aristophanes takes credit to himself
for effecting certain reformations in the taste of the Comic
drama.   It seems not difficult to illustrate from his own
comedies every fault in taste which he reproves.   One
thing at least never offended his taste, namely dirt, un-
mitigated ultra-Swiftian noisomeness. The reader of the
original has to pass through a perfect bog of it in the introduction to this comedy. Of course it is removed here. I
should have been glad to have escaped every the slightest
suggestion of it by retrenching the whole of the opening

scene. But the character and quest of TRYGÆUS must be explained. He must go to heaven in search of Peace. In parody of Bellerophon upon Pegasus, he must be carried there on a Beetle ; the Beetle therefore must be introduced. I hope the reader will not regret having made acquaintance with it.

TRYGÆUS *of Athmonos, an Attic vinegrower.*

DAUGHTERS *of Trygæus.*

SLAVES *of Trygæus.*

MERCURY.

WAR.

CONFUSION.

HIEROCLES *of Oreum, a Seer.*

A Maker of Sickles.

A Maker of Helmet-crests.

A Maker of Spear-shafts.

First Boy, *Son of Lamachus.*

Second Boy, *Son of Cleonymus.*

CHORUS *of Athmonean farmers.*

PEACE.

OPORA. } *mute persons.*

THEORIA.

SCENE.—*House of* TRYGÆUS : *two* SLAVES *feeding with dirt-cakes a monstrous Beetle, confined in a stye off the stage.*

First Slave. A pudding for the beetle.
Second Slave.   Here it is.
1*st S.*   Make haste
And give it to the brute.
2*nd S.*   And may he never taste
A sweeter morsel.
1*st S.*   Make another—quick—and let it
Be strong.
2*nd S.*   Here's one.
1*st S.*   But where's the other? has he eat it?
2*nd S.* Aye; snatched it, rolled with his feet, and gulped
        it whole.
1*st S.* More; more and larger.
2*nd S.*   Faugh! it won't be said I stole
The sweetmeats from the pudding.
1*st S.*   More, I tell you; more.
2*nd S.* Not I, until I get a nose without a bore.
Take the whole tub of it.
                *[Gives the tub of filth to his fellow, who
                empties it into the stye.*
1*st S.*   Ugh! you go with it, beast.
2*nd S.* (*looking over the stye*). I'll peep to see if he is
        glutted with his feast.—
Eat till you burst yourself.—How the thing works its jaws,
And wheels its head, and roundabouts its horrid claws,
Just as one coils a cable.—Each God has his pet; [1]
Which of them has this filthy thing I quite forget:
Not Venus, nor the Graces.
1*st S.*   Who then?
2*nd S.*   I'll be bound
It is a monster-sign of Jove-upon-the-ground. [2]

---

[1] As Jupiter the eagle, Juno the peacock.
[2] It seems that Pausanias mentions an altar dedicated to Jupiter under
the title 'Cataibates' the 'Descender.'

1st S. Now one of you spectators will have asked, no
  doubt—
Some smart conceited youth—what is all this about?
'What is this beetle for?' and some one at his side—
A shrewd Ionian—will briskly have replied,
'It must be Cleon, man; I know it by the stink.'—
But I must now go in and give the beetle drink.

          [*Exit* FIRST SLAVE.

 Slave. And I to boys, to mannikins, to men, to those
Who are yet older, to the eldest will disclose
Our history.—My master is completely cracked;
Not with a common madness, such as yours; in fact,
'Tis quite a new invention in the way of craze.
So—will he stand all day, with open mouth, agaze
Up to the sky, to rail on Jupiter, and say,
'Jove, lay thy besom down, and sweep not Greece away.' [1]
 Trygæus (behind the scene). Ahi! Ahi!
 Slave. Hush, hush.   I hear his voice.
 Try. (as before).   Oh, Jupiter, beware!
What wilt thou make our people suffer?   Have a care,
Or all the cities will but emptied nutshells be.
 Slave. You hear.   That is a sample of his lunacy.
When first he felt the action of disordered bile,
Here would he stand alone, and mutter all the while:—
'How might a man contrive to get straight up to Jove?'
So made he little ladders, on the which he strove
To clamber up to heaven; until he met a check,
Falling upon his head, and nearly broke his neck.
But yesterday, gone to his wit's end for inventions,
He brought a beetle back Ætnæan in dimensions,
Which I must groom, forsooth;—and patting it, says he,
'My little Pegasus, my noble winged one, see
You bear me straight to Jove.'—But 'twill not be amiss
To see what it is doing.

       [*Looks into the stye, and starts back.*

---

[1] A learned friend called my attention to the parallel of this forcible
expression in Isaiah xiv. 23, as rendered in our Translation and in the
Vulgate.   The Septuagint altogether changes the idea.   Pursuing at my
desire enquiry into this variation, he informs me that it arises from
the use of a word, the root of which is debateable amongst Hebrew
scholars.

What a sight is this !
My master in the air !—Run neighbours, run : alack,
My master is astride upon the beetle's back.

Enter TRYGÆUS, *on the Beetle.*

Try.   Easy now, steady ;
                Gently, my neddy ;
                Trust not at first
                To the fire of a burst
                Over-confiding ;
                But quietly gliding,
Wait a bit—wait till it comes to a push.
                Soon with a rustle
                Each fibre and muscle
                Warmed to the course
                Will double its force,
                Supplied with sweat,
                Dripping with wet ;
Then, with the fling of your wing, we will off with a rush.
         But breathe not in my face, my lad—
Slave. My lord, my master, you are mad.
Try. Hush, hush.
Slave. Where are you going through the air ?
Try.   It is for all the Greeks I'm flying,
          A venture yet unheard of trying.
Slave. But why so mad ? what do you there ?
Try.   Tush ! tush !   Forbear ill words to utter,
          Or make unseemly cry or mutter ;
          But tell all men to hold their peace,
          And make all open sewers to cease.[1]
Slave. I will not hold my peace until you tell me, Sir,
Where you intend to fly.
Try.   Where ? but to Jupiter
In heaven.
Slave.   And what to do ?
Try.   To know what end he seeks
Fomenting this embittered strife among the Greeks ?

---

[1] Lest his dirt-feeding beetle should be enticed down,

Slave. But if he will not say ?

Try.   Why, then 'tis plain indeed
That he holds treasonable commerce with the Mede.
I will indict him for betraying Greece.

Slave.   Not you,
While I'm a living man.

Try.   There's nothing else to do.

Slave. Here, children, here : to heaven is your father
                 stealing ;
You will be orphans ; try the force of your appealing.

Enter little GIRLS, *daughters of* TRYGÆUS.

Girls. Father, oh father, and can it be true ?
         Rumour has borne us a story that you
         Are flying up where nobody knows,
         Sillily travelling off to the crows.[1]
         Say, if you love me, father dear,
         Is there truth in the story we hear ?

Try.   So seems it, girls : but, ah !
                 Truth is, my heart has bled
         When you have said ' Papa '
                 So coaxingly, for bread ;
         And I—no, not a spot
         Rain-size of coin had got.
         But if I reach the skies
                 And do my business there,
         A bun of double size
                 Shall be my children's fare.

Girl. But, Pappy, how came you to think of such a thing
As getting to the Gods upon a beetle's wing ?

Try. It is the only beast on wings that has succeeded
In getting to the Gods : in Æsop you may read it.

Girl. I never can believe the filthy thing was able
To mount up to the Gods : it is a silly fable.

-----

[1] This phrase is of constant recurrence in this language of common
life, sometimes as a mere petty malediction, sometimes, as in this
instance, with a comical pertinence. It suggests the wish for a death of
disgrace to the person addressed, the gibbet, cross, or pit, where the body
would be left exposed.

Try. 'Twas once upon a time, her wrath would not be
    foiled,
She spilt the eagle's eggs, and all of them were spoiled.[1]

Girl. 'Twere better you had borrowed Pegasus awhile
To come before the Gods in higher tragic style.

Try. But how could I provide the food for such a steed?

Girl. Be careful lest you fall; that would be sad indeed;
For if you should be lamed, Euripides some day
May make a plot for you, and put you in a play.

Try. Leave me to see to that.   And so good-bye to you
And all whose interest my labour has in view.

    Forward, my Pegasus, proudly advancing,
    Prick up your ears to the rattle entrancing,
    Where the gay gold on your trappings is glancing.
          Pegasus, forward!

    [TRYGÆUS *ascends out of sight. Exeunt bystanders.*

SCENE.—*The Palace of Jupiter, on a platform above the
    stage.*   TRYGÆUS *enters upon his beetle.*

Try. Dramatic machinist, this is beyond a joke;
Mind what you are about before my neck is broke.
Surely the Gods' abode is somewhere hereabout.
Ah, yes, I see the house of Jove to end my doubt.
Who is the porter here? Heigh, answer if you please.

    [MERCURY *puts his head out of the door.*

Mer. Whence comes this smell of mortal? (*recognising*
    TRYGÆUS.) Eh! King Hercules!
What have we here?

Try.   A hippocanthar.[2]

Mer.   Impudent,
Audacious, refuse, scum of scum!   Oh to invent
A name to fit thy filthiness.   How didst thou come?
How callest thou thyself? wilt thou not answer?

Try.   Scum.

---

[1] The Eagle preyed on the young of the Beetle. The Beetle ascended
to the nest of the Eagle and rolled out her eggs. She appealed to Jupiter,
who bade her deposit her eggs in his own bosom. Then came the Beetle
and buzzed about Jupiter's head. He rose to brush the insect away,
forgetting the eggs; they rolled out and were broken. A wrong-doer is
not secure from vengeance even if he takes refuge in the bosom of God
himself.

[2] Meaning a horse-beetle, or huge beetle; a parody on Hippo-centaur.

Mer. Who are your people?

Try.   *Scum.*

Mer.   To whom owe you a birth?
Who is your father?

Try.   *Scum.*

Mer.   ⁛   I vow by holy Earth,
There's nothing for it but that you shall die the death
Unless you tell your name without another breath.

Try. TRYGÆUS the Athmonian, grower of good wine:
No sycophant, nor meddler in affairs not mine.

Mer. What is your business here?

Try.   To bring these chops to you.

Mer. How did you come, you rogue?

Try.   You change your point of view:
I am not *Scum*, you greedy?—Go, call Jupiter.

Mer. Ah, dear! that after all you should not find him,
         Sir!
The Gods all emigrated only yesterday.

Try. What! where on earth?

Mer.   On earth!

Try.   Well, where?

Mer.   Far, far away.
In short, into the heaven's very farthest zone.

Try. Then how is it that you are left behind alone?

Mer. The remnant of their furniture, the earthenware,
Tables and tankards, are committed to my care.

Try. But what could have induced the Gods to emi-
         grate?

Mer. The Greeks have brought them to a most distem-
         pered state;
So much so, that, before they quitted this domain,
They gave it up to WAR; with nothing to restrain
His doing what he likes with you folks down below.
Meantime they have withdrawn as far as they can go,
That they may neither see the struggles of your nation,
Nor be exposed to listen to your supplication.

Try. But tell me why the Gods treat us in such a way.

Mer. Because you both are so intent on war, while they
For proper truce have made occasions numberless.
But so it was, when those Laconics had success,

' By Castor and by Pollux,' should we hear them say,
' Aye now the Attican his penalty shall pay ;'
But when a turn of fortune flattered Attic pride,
And overtures for peace came from the other side,
Your cry was, ' By Athené, we shall be betrayed ;
' By Jove we must not let a hasty peace be made.
' When Pylos is secured then let them come again.'

   Try. On our side, I admit, this always was the strain.

   Mer. I doubt if eyes of yours will ever look upon
The face of PEACE again.

   Try.   Why not ? where is she gone ?

   Mer. Into a pit, where WAR has thrown her, dark and
       deep.

   Try. Where is it ?

   Mer.   Here below : and you may see the heap
Of mighty stones that he has piled on it, that you
May never more recover her.

   Try.   What will he do ?
What means he we should suffer ?

   Mer.   That I cannot say ;
Except that in the evening he brought yesterday
A monstrous Mortar.

   Try.   Wherefore ?

   Mer.   I believe that it is
A part of his intent therein to bray your cities.
But I must get away, for, judging by the din,
I fancy WAR himself is coming from within.

                        [*Exit* MERCURY.

   Try. Ah ! this is frightful. Let me fly : for I too hear
The ring and bellow of the Mortar coming near.

  Enter WAR, *who sets upon the stage a huge brazen mortar.*

   War. Oh, mortals, mortals, mortals ; what have ye to
       bear !
What racking of the jaws do I for you prepare !

   Try. Apollo ! what a breadth of mortar ! Ah, that
       glance :
What woe and mischief is there in War's countenance !
And this is truly He whom man in reason flies,
The terrible, the stalwart, sturdy on his thighs.

War (*putting prason* (*leeks*) *into the mortar*).
Three measures, Prasiæ,[1]—not three but five of sorrow,
Nay, mete her many tens :—for her there is no morrow.

Try. At any rate for us there was no trouble there ;
'Tis altogether a Laconian affair.

War (*putting in garlic, produce of Megara*).
Ho ! Megara, the happy garlic plots possessing,
So shalt thou bruised be into a salad dressing.

Try. Alackaday ! indeed how many and how sore
The lamentations are for Megara in store.

War (*slicing Sicilian cheeses into the mortar*).
Ho ! Sicily, and thou shalt perish without pity.

Try.[2] Oh how wilt thou be pounded, miserable city.

War. And now I will infuse a jar of Attic honey.

Try. Oh spare the Attic, Sir; it were sad waste of
          money,
Do use some other kind.

War.   Here, Sir, you slave, Confusion.

Enter Confusion.

Conf. Sir, did you call ?

War.   What are you gaping for ? contusion ?
                    [*hits him a heavy blow with the fist.*

Conf. My ribs ! that was a heavy one : there were I
          know
Some knobs of garlic [3] in the fist that struck that blow.

War. Run, bring me here a Pestle.

Conf.   That we have not got :
It was but yesterday we settled on this spot.

War. Run quickly then to Athens, fetch me one from
          thence.

Conf. Aye, for I know the cost of disobedience.
                              [*Exit* Confusion.

---

[1] A small town on the coast of Laconia, taken and destroyed in the
second year of the war.

[2] In the texts this line is continued to War; but the sentiment as
well as the symmetry of the lines seem to require that it should be given
to Trygæus.

[3] With allusion at once to the pungent flavour of the bulb and to the
practice of loading the fist with metal to make the blow heavier.

Try. Now, poor Humanity, you see the risk we run :
And we must settle sharply what is to be done.
For if that man upon his errand shall have found
A Pestle for his purpose, he will sit and pound
The Cities at his leisure.   Bacchus, stand our friend,
And break the fellow's neck before his journey's end.

Re-enter CONFUSION.

War. Well ?
Conf.   Yes, Sir.—
War.   Where is it ?
Conf.   The Tanner what's-his-name,
The Pestle [1] of all Greece, was dead before I came.
   Try. In happy time, good lady Pallas, was he dead,
Before we had that salad-dressing on our head.
   War. Then go to Lacedæmon, surely you can find
One for the purpose there.
Conf.   Yes, Sir.

                                          [*Exit.*
War.   And quickly, mind.
   Try. What will become of us, my friends ? for now,
         alas !
Things have arrived at an exceeding ticklish pass.
Those who in Samothrace have been initiated
Will pray [2]—The fellow's ankles may be dislocated.

Re-enter CONFUSION.

Conf. Oh dear ! I am unlucky, most unfortunate.
War. Have you not brought it then ?
Conf.   Again I was too late.
The Spartan [3] pestle is no more.
War.   How so ?

---

[1] Cleon died before Amphipolis nearly three years before this comedy
was exhibited.   Vide *Knights*, l. 010.
[2] Those who had been initiated in the mysteries of the Cabiri were
reputed to be assured of answer to prayer.
[3] Brasidas ; he was slain at the same time and place as Cleon.

Conf.   Employed
On loan by certain folks in Thrace it was destroyed.

   Try. Castor and Pollux too, well have ye done your
      parts.
All may be well as yet.   Mortals, lift up your hearts.

   War. Then take these things away and put them on the
      shelf;
I will go in and make a Pestle for myself.

                [*Exeunt* WAR *and* CONFUSION.

TRYGÆUS and CHORUS.[1]

   Try. From business and from battles now that we are
      free,
This is a breathing space, a happy time, when we
Before another Pestle [2] hinders, men of Greece,
May draw back into light that all-belovèd PEACE.
Come ye that plough the land, and ye that plough the sea,
Come smiths and artisans of every degree,
Come from the mainland, from the Islands great and
    small,
Come neighbours, foreigners, come hither and come all;
   Bring your mattocks, levers, cables,
          bring the will to work in haste;
   Luck[3] is in the undertaking,
          'tis the cup that we may taste.
   Chorus. Hither come, each honest man who
          has a zeal for our salvation.
   Now if ever let there be a
          gathering of the Grecian nation.
   Quit of blood-empurpled troubles,
          quit of military fuss;
   For a day has dawned upon us
          hated-much-of-Lamachus.[4]

---

  [1] How or when the Chorus finds its way to Trygœus it is not easy to
conjecture.
  [2] Supposed to allude to Alcibiades.
  [3] The pledge of the first cup appears to have been something like
'Here's to our Good Fortune.'
  [4] See *Acharnians.* He was one of the seventeen commissioners from
Athens who signed the terms of truce at Lacedæmon two years before
this.

Pray direct our operations;
             tell us how we should begin;
For I feel so stout about it
             that I never will give in,
Till we manage with our tackle
             to get up before our eyes
This the greatest and most vineyard-
             loving of the Deities.
             [*During the singing of these words the
                  members of the Chorus are dancing.*

Try. Do be quiet; your excessive
             spirits else will be our ruin:
You will waken War to fury
             when he knows what we are doing.
Chorus. Really this is such a pleasure.
             It was quite another thing
When the summons came to muster
             and three days' provisions bring.
Try. If you are not careful you will
             wake that Cerberus [1] below,
Who with bluster and with barking,
             as his manner was, you know,
When he was alive among us,
             will put something in our way
To prevent our drawing up this
             Goddess to the light of day.
Chorus. Dead or living there is not the
             being who shall pluck her back
If I can but once contrive to
             get her in my hands.
Try.   Alack!
You will be my death unless this
             noisy exultation ceases:
We shall have him running out and
             stamping all our plans to pieces.
Chorus. Let him stamp and let him trample,
             let him knead them into clay;

---

[1] Cleon.

I do not intend to put a
>> check upon my joy to-day.
>>> [*Chorus dances with increased energy.*

Try. What is this? oh, what can ail you?
>> do not, I beseech you, bring
> Ruin on our undertaking
>> by your foolish figuring.

Chorus. It is not my will to do it,
>> but my legs for very pleasure,
> Quite without my instigation,
>> fling themselves into a measure.

Try. Stop it, I beseech you, stop it,
>> dancing like a Bacchanal.

Chorus. There now, I have stopped.

Try.   You say so,
>> but you have not stopped at all.

Chorus. Just this figure let me finish;
>> I will not begin again.

Try. Be it so, if necessary;
>> after that you must refrain.

Chorus. We would not have danced a figure
>> if we could have aided you.

Try. You are just as bad as ever.
>> Really, men, it will not do.

Chorus. Just a leg—the right leg only—
>> let me fling and I have done.

Try. If you will not ask another,
>> I allow you just the one.

Chorus. Nay, the left must have its turn, it
>> cannot, will not be denied.
> I am so delighted, merry,
>> frolicsome and gratified.
> Not if I had cast away my
>> wrinkled skin and load of years,
> Should I be so happy as in
>> getting rid of shields and spears.

Try. Hold awhile in your rejoicing,
>> for we hardly know as yet
> How the thing may go; but when this
>> PEACE herself we really get,

Dance and sing, and laugh your fill,
Rove or sojourn at your will,
Lie abed, on holidays
Early rise to see the plays,
Take a friendly cup with us,
Pass the time at cottabus,[1]
Spend your time in all delight,
And 'Hurrah,' with all your might.

Chorus. Would that I could see that day
  After all I've undergone,
Bedding upon musty hay,
  Soldiering with Phormion![2]
Crusty as I used to be,
  In the court a judge severe,
  Sharp to speak and slow to hear;
That you never more shall see:
I will be an easy fellow,
  Younger than my teeth and hair,
Something soft and very mellow,
  When I'm quit of war and care.
We have had enough of drilling,
  In and out with spear and shield;
We have had enough of killing,
  Death at home, and wounds afield.
Only tell us how we may be
  useful to your plan,
Since good fortune has designed you
  for our leading man.

[*The scene shows the large stones over the
  pit where* PEACE *is buried.*

Try. See you these stones? I must contrive to move
them hence.

Re-enter MERCURY.

Mer. Ah! what are you about, you dirt and impudence?

---

[1] A favourite amusement requiring some little skill, by which a small quantity of wine was thrown from a cup so that it might fall upon, and depress to the legitimate point, a scale suspended on the balance.

See *Knights,* l. 522. Landing on the coast of Acarnania, he made some successful operations.

Try. Like Cillicon 'no harm.'[1]

Mer.   You rascal, you must die.

Try. Aye, if I have the lot: as you are MERCURY,
No doubt you will contrive it.[2]

Mer.   Think not of delay,
'Tis settled, you must die.

Try.   But when?

Mer.   This very day.

Try. But I have not laid in my stores for a campaign,
My barley and my cheese.[3]

Mer.   The case you know is plain:
For Jupiter has said, if anyone shall try
To dig up her who here is buried, he shall die.

Try. So I must die?

Mer.   You know it.

Try.   Lend me then a shilling,
To buy myself a pig; for I should be unwilling
To quit the world before I am initiate.[4]

Mer. Jove and his thunderbolt!

Try.   But you will not relate
What we are doing.

Mer.   That I must, or I shall rue it.

Try. Nay, by the chops I brought, I beg you not to
        do it.

Mer. Unhappy man, but Jove would knead me into dough
If I should fail with all exactitude to show
And to denounce these matters.

Try.   Clear away this storm,
Sweet little Mercury, and, prithee, don't inform.   ·

                                [*Turning to the Chorus.*

---

[1] Cillicon, intriguing to betray Miletus, was asked 'What he was about?' 'No harm,' he answered.

[2] The Athenians put to death only one malefactor a day. When several were under sentence, precedence for execution was determined by lot. Some official might have it in his power to arrange on whom the lot should fall. At any rate Mercury could manage that, as being the God whose specialty it was to regulate 'lots.'

[3] Trygœus affects to suppose that he is being ordered to join a regiment going on service before the enemy.

[4] Those who when living had been initiated in the Mysteries of Eleusis enjoyed in Hades perpetual light and other advantages. See *Frogs*, l. 133, 311.

Men, what ails you? what's the use of
                    standing dilly-dally thus?
Have you not a word to utter?
                    he's about denouncing us.
Chorus. MERCURY, my lord, I beg you
                    not to think of such a thing.
Is not pig a dainty dish?
If with that we ever had the
                    hap to gratify your wish,
In our present circumstances
                    that is worth remembering.
Try. Hear you how they coax and wheedle?
                    Listen to them, lord and king.
Chorus. Do not be ill-natured to the
                    fervour of our supplication.
Let her rise before our eyes.
Thou the most man-loving and mu-
                    nificent of Deities.
So we supplicants will ever
                    manifest our adoration
By redoubled sacrifices
                    and unparalleled dotation.
Try. Oh, have regard unto their cry, I supplicate you:
Since more than ever they desire to venerate you.
Mer. Since more than ever, they desire, you mean, to
        steal.
Try. Attend to me, for I have something to reveal.—
To overthrow the Gods there is a villain plot.
Mer. Well, tell me what it is.   I may believe or not.
Try. The plan is now matured, though long ago begun,
Between the Moon and that most good-for-nothing Sun
To bring upon the Gods a great humiliation,
By handing over Greece to foreign domination.
Mer. What is their motive?
Try.   What? 'Tis evident; because
We sacrifice to you, according to our laws,
But foreigners to them.[1]   They have it then in view,
'Tis not to be mistaken, to abolish you,

---

[1] The Greeks supposed that the Persians worshipped the Sun and
Moon. Herodotus (Erato. 97) says that Datis was ordered by his sovereign to spare the territory of the 'two Gods.'

And, filling all your places, to impropriate
All sacrificial dues that form the Gods' estate.

   Mer. The thing is quite apiece with their most thievish
      ways
In driving to cut off the corners of the days.[1]

   Try. By Jove 'tis true. Now you will join with us to
      save,
And draw, dear MERCURY, this lady from the cave;
So will we celebrate the great Panathenæa,
The Mysteries, Adonia, Diipolæa,
And all the rites of all the other Gods to Thee :
For thou alone shalt bear the honour, MERCURY.
And everywhere the Cities, finding the relief,
Will worship MERCURY, the saver-out-of-grief.
Then other things will follow.   But at present take
This trifle of a goblet, wherewithal to make
Libations.

   Mer.   'Tis my weakness ; I am soft of heart,
When goblets are in question.   You must do your part.
So now go in, my men, and heave the stones away.

   Chorus. We will : and you shall stand, you clever God,
      to say
What we shall do.   A master in the craft we know you ;
And that we are no lazy workmen we will show you.

   Try. Pray take the goblet, Sir, to make the due libation,
While I will pray the Gods to bless the operation.

   Mer.   The wine-drops fall :
                Be silent all.

   Try. So may the day on which these sacred drops we
      pour
To all the Greeks all good and joyous things restore.
And whoso on the rope shall lay a hearty strain,
Oh never may he have to carry shield again ;
But whoso chooses war,—from out his elbow-joints
May he employ his time in drawing arrow-points.

---

   [1] Aristophanes has here, for him, an unusually good pun between
ἁρματωλία, expert driving of a chariot, and ἁμαρτωλία, sinfulness.
The allusion of course is to eclipses and such variations of the sun's and
moon's period, as involve the making of calendar months and years longer
or shorter.

Chorus. Lady, if there be one who grudges winning thee,
Because he wishes to command a company,
May he experience Cleonymus's fare,
And, coming from the field, have left his honour there.

Try. If any knave by whom accoutrements are made
Wishes more battles, for the benefit of trade,
May robbers take him off and feed him with the horses.

Chorus. If one has hope to be Commander of the Forces,
And therefore will not lend a hand; or if he be
A slave who is deserting to the enemy,
Let him be whipped upon the wheel.—Ho! Paion,[1] Ho!
All fortune be with us.

Try.   Nay, do not say it so,
'Say ' Ho ' without the Paion,—*Paion* is too striking.

Chorus. I'll strike it out—Ho, Ho!—and say it to your
            liking.

Try. Now to the Graces, Seasons, Venus, Mercury—
Chorus. And Mars.
Try.   No, no.
Chorus.   Nor Enyalius?
Try.   Not I.
Chorus. Bend now the cables round the stone and make
            them tight,
And each one to his place to pull with all his might.

> [Chorus *and bystanders haul;* Mercury
>   *gives the time.*

Mer. Ho-e-yah.
Chorus. E-yah, fair.
Mer. Ho-e-yah.
Chorus. E-yah, stouter there.
Mer. Ho-e-yah.
Try.   Half the fellows are not working:
            You, Bœotians, are shirking.
Mer. E-yah, go.
Try. E-yah-o.
Chorus. You two hardly put a hand in.

---

[1] The word will be more generally recognised in the form of 'Pæan.'
It is a cry to Apollo, and stimulates to energy, as the middle-age cries
'St. George!' 'St. Denys!' By the form here adopted Aristophanes
gets a pun, as the same letters form the participle of the verb 'to strike.'

Try.   I'm at work with all my heart,
            Pulling till my arms will part.

Mer.   How is it the work is standing?

Chorus. You, Lamachus, why will you sit there to
            observe us?
The aspect of your dreadful Mormon[1] makes us nervous.

Mer. Those Argives are not drawing. I believe, in short,
They only make your griefs the matter of their sport,
And draw from either party mercenary meal.

Try. But there are the Laconians pulling with a zeal.

Mer. Those whom you see are men who work in wooden
            ware;
I undertake to say, no armourer is there.

Chorus. The men of Megara do nothing, though they
            groan
And struggle at the rope like puppies at a bone:
They're famine-struck.   But come, we're losing time, my
            men,
Now one and all together, at the work again.

Mer. Ho-e-yah.

Try. E-yah, fair.

Mer. Ho-e-yah.

Try. E-yah, Jupiter!

Cho. We hardly stir.

Try.   Shame it is that some are slacking,
            While the rest are almost cracking,
            Argives, you shall smart for this.

Mer. E-yah, go.

Try. E-yah-ho.

Cho.   There are somewhere hearts amiss.

Try.   You that love Peace, buckle to it.

Cho.   There are some who will not do it.

                    [*All give up pulling.*

Try. You men of Megara, you do us mischief: hence!
The Goddess hates your savour; for your rank offence
Is garlic.—Men of Athens, pray what are you doing?
Yes, busy in your law-courts, judging, pleading, suing,

---

[1] Mormon means generally a bugbear to frighten children, but is here
used in mockery of the 'Gorgon' bearing of Lamachus's shield.

You do no service here. I say, let go the rope,
Ye wrangling citizens. But if ye ever hope
To see the face of Peace, take this advice from me,
Shift and withdraw yourselves a little toward the sea.[1]

Cho.   Now neighbours, close; let none but those
     Who till the land touch cable.
Mer.   Aye, it will do, if left to you
     Who willing are, and able.
Cho.   He says we can: so let each man
     To work, and put his heart in't.
Try.   Work, farmers all, both great and small,
     For none else shall have part in't.
     [CHORUS *and* TRYGÆUS *only handle the ropes.*
     To work now fall, pull one, pull all.—
     Ah! there now she is nearing;
     Nay, never slack, though sinews crack,
     Hurrah! she is appearing.
     Ho-e-yo, away we go,
     Ho-e-yo, Ho-e-yo.
     [PEACE *is landed upon the stage, attended by*
     OPORA *and* THEORIA.

Try. Oh, Lady Cluster-giver, how shall I address you?
Where shall I find the *pipe* of word which shall express
    you?
When pipes of wine for us exist scarce in idea.
OPORA, fair befall thee! welcome, THEORIA,[2]
How pleasant is thy countenance! thy breath how nice!
Sweet with discharge-from-service and the oil of spice.

---

[1] If, as Brunck says, the point of this line is no more than to recommend
that policy which had been long ago prescribed by Themistocles, the air
of originality with which it is introduced is strange. Besides, one can
hardly think that in the time of Aristophanes Athens would have stood
in need of the advice, if he had been the man to give it.

[2] The names of these *Attendants on Peace* are left untranslated because
the translator knows no single words which would really represent them
to an English mind. The nearest single terms would perhaps be
'HARVEST' and 'HOLIDAY.' But OPORA must signify the season and
gathering of all fruits, and THEORIA, the exhibition of plays, and celebration of festivals with hymns and processions; such as the Athenian,
in time of peace, expected to have provided for the amusements of his
holiday at the public expense.

Mer. It does not, then, smell like a soldier's havresack?

Cho. I hate and utterly abjure both man and pack:
It smells of onions, bah! *her* breath of fruits, and plays
Of Sophocles, feasts, thrushes, piping, holidays,
Euripides's tit-bits—

Mer.   That is calumny;
She is not fond of snip-snap pettifoggery.   [juice,

Cho. Of ivy, straining-cloths dyed with the glorious
Flocks bleating in the homesteads, quarts in constant use,
And twenty other things as good.

Mer. (*looking towards the spectators*). How merrily
The Cities[1] reconciled talk of the days gone by :
Albeit many eyes are black, and half the nation
Are bringing bruises down by constant fomentation.

Try. Now cast your eyes around the theatre and give
A guess at each man's craft.

Mer.   Yon fellow, as I live,
The little man, you see him scratching at his head,
Whileome made crests for helmets, now his trade is dead.
That maker of wood shovels grinning pokes his thumb
Into the army-cutler's ribs; and *he* is glum.

Try. The sickle-maker cocks his finger at his neighbour,
The polisher of spear-shafts, who has lost his labour.

Mer. Now send the farmers home.

Try.   Hear, people, and obey.
Let all the farmers with their dead stock go away.
    Sword and spear will not be wanted.
                Peace is brimming everywhere.
    Go and fill the fields with labour,
                and with songs of joy the air.

Chorus. Day, for which all honest men and
                farmers have been sighing long,
    Now at last to see thee dawning
                tunes my language into song.
    How I yearn to see again the
                vine with cluster berries hung,
    And the fig-trees which I planted
                in the days when I was young.

---

[1] Among the strangers present at the feast would be representatives
of the States lately at war.

Try. To the Goddess, worthy neighbours,
        be our hearty praise addressed,
Who has sent our crests and gorgons
        in the lumber-room to rest.
Now, as fast as legs can carry,
        to the homestead and the field.
Lay your money out in dressing,
        'twill repay with double yield.
Mer. Neptune! what a troop assembles
        and by numbers is increased!
Close as barley-cake and keen as
        eaters at a common feast.
Try. Let your crusher be in order,
        let the prong gleam in the sun;
Fair and clean will be the alley
        and the work be deftly done.
Aye, my heart is there already,
        I am on the fret to stand
On the plot I worked from boyhood
        with the old fork in my hand.
      Think you how we used to live:
      Think, what Peace was wont to give;
      Mellow figs, or dried and pressed,
      Brow with wreath of myrtle dressed,
      Grape juice from the presses flowing,
      Violets by the fountain growing,
      Olives,—oh, their savour yet,
      Mingles longing with regret.
      PEACE, the giver of such treasure,
      Welcome with a grateful measure.
Chorus. Welcome, welcome, Peace returning,
        Now resume thy happy reign.
      Long for thee have we been yearning,
        Lead us to our fields again.
      Richly thou repayest toil
      Spent upon the willing soil:
      Yea, and freely will we spend,
      While we have thee, labour's friend.

      Thrifty joys but long enduring,
        Joys unbought by fear and care,

Dost thou give us, while assuring
  Healthful work and country fare.
There's a thrill among the vines ;
Gladness from the fig-tree shines ;
Every budding herb and tree
Laughs its welcome back to thee.
But, oh most benevolent of
   Gods, I wish you would explain,
Where the lady Peace has been, and
   why she left us in disdain ?

Mer. Most intelligent small farmers,
   you with ease will comprehend
How it happened that this lady
  came to an untimely end.
Phidias began the business,
  falling into your displeasure,[1]
Then was Pericles alarmed lest
  he should meet with equal measure.
Knowing as he did your temper,
  strong and stubborn in its ire,
He, before the trouble caught him,
  set the City all on fire.
It was but a spark he threw in,
  the Megarian decree :
But he blew it into war that
  raging far as eye could see
Filled the land of Greece with smoke and,
  overclouding all the skies,
Blinded friend and foe alike and
  brought the tears to many eyes.
Soon as knocks and counter-knocks had
  passed among the angry jars,[2]
There was none to stay the strife, and
  PEACE retired among the stars.

---

[1] The story told in explanation of these lines is this. Phidias was employed by the State to execute a work of art. He purloined some of the gold which was provided for him. Being detected he was banished. Pericles, conscious of misappropriating public treasure, diverted attention from himself by engaging the citizens with political ambition.

[2] Videlicet, earthen wine-jars, representing the States of Greece.

Try. Odd it is that I knew nothing
        of the facts which you have stated,
  Nor suspected Phidias and
        Peace in any way related!
Cho. Nor did I. What? *his* relation?
        but the fact would seem to show
  How it is she is good looking.
        But there's much one does not know!
Mer. See what followed : when the Cities,
        hitherto obedient,
  Saw you tearing at each other,
        only on your quarrel bent ;
  They set all their wits at work to
        shake you off and break away :
  For, said they, whoever wins or
        loses, *we* shall have to pay.
  Off they went to Lacedæmon,
        not without a weighty purse,
  Calculated to establish
        all the tales they would rehearse.
  False to friends as true to lucre,
        Spartan gentlemen were gained,
  Peace was foully thrown aside and
        War had license unrestrained.
  Spartan gains were farmers' losses ;
        for the men sent out to sea
  Eat the figs of honest fellows
        innocent as men could be.
Try. That was but a retribution.
        Was it not a Spartan hand
  Cut the cherished tree I set and
        raised upon my father's land ?
Cho. Figs indeed! It served them rightly :
        there was my six-bushel bin,
  What should these Laconians do, but
        with a stone they stove it in ?
Mer. Presently the country people,
        pushed within the City wall,
  Got entrapped in politics they
        did not understand at all.

Having not a fig to eat, or
        raisin-stone to throw away,
They misspent their time in hearing
        what the talkers had to say :
Rogues who knew their hearers' weakness,
        what a hungry man would stand.
How they railed at PEACE and drove her
        with a pitchfork from the land !
But when they could lay a finger
        on a rich and fat ally,
Who with profit could be plundered—
        They could give a reason *why* !
Some intrigue with Brasidas, if
        nothing better could be found.
You would turn upon the victim,
        and despatch him like a hound.
Pale and frightened sat the City,
        and, believing all they said,
Ever as the lie was greater
        snapped it up for sweeter bread.
All your foreign friends, perceiving
        who could do them mischief, ran
With a gag of gold to stop the
        mouth of any noisy man.
So while Greece was growing weaker,
        though you did not know the manner,
Richer grew the rogues among you.
        This was managed by the Tanner.[1]
Try. Stop, I beg you, Mercury, and
        let the wretched man alone.
Being down below, he is no
        longer ours, he is your own.[2]
        Grant him clever to contrive
        Mischief, when he was alive,
        Say, he chattered all the day,
        Say, he flattered to betray,

---

[1] Cleon.
[2] It was one of the offices of Mercury to convey the souls of the dead to Hades.

Say, he stirred sedition-broth,
Say, he ladled out the froth,
What you will;—but all your wit
  Vainly sounding,
  Back rebounding,
Will but your own subjects hit.
            [*Turning to address* PEACE.
Lady, why no word from thee?
Break that silence; speak to me.

Mer. She may not speak, at least before the audience,
For they have given her by far too grave offence.

Try. Perhaps she will vouchsafe to whisper in your ear?

Mer. (*speaking to* PEACE, *listening for her whispered
    answers and conveying them to the others*).

Aye, tell me what you think about them, lady dear,
You, who of all your sex most hate a buckler band.
—Ah, yes, I hear. Is that the charge? I understand.—
Now hear the reason why she holds you much to blame.
After the Pylos business she declares she came
Of her good will to bring a box of overtures;
But twice was she rejected in that hall of yours.

Try. There we were wrong. But beg her to forgive the
    crime;
For we in fact were leather-headed [1] at the time.

Mer. The Goddess bids me ask you, Who it is of late
That in the Pnyx has occupied your chair of state?

Try. Hyperbolus [2] at present occupies the place.
But, Lady, why is this? Why turn away your face?

Mer. She holds the populace in such abomination
For putting such a rascal in so high a station.

Try. We'll throw the man aside. But, happening as it
    then did
That they had lost their guardian, and were undefended,
The mob strapped on in haste the sword that came to hand.

Mer. What service he could do she cannot understand.

Try. Our counsels would be bettered.

Mer.   What could he confer?

---

[1] Under the influence of Cleon.
[2] *Knights*, l. 1164. *Clouds*, l. 945.

Try. It chanced he was a lantern manufacturer:
So, whereas heretofore we only groped our way,
His lantern to our council lends its kindly ray.

Mer. (*after listening to* PEACE, *laughs*). Ho! ho!
To think of what she bids me ask of you!

Try.   What is it?

Mer. Old matters she remembers from her former visit.
First, she would know how goes the world with Sophocles?

Try. Well; though he suffers from a very strange disease.

Mer. What is it?

Try.   He is changed into Simonides.

Mer. Simonides! How so?

Try.   Now he is growing old,
He'd go to sea upon a twig in search of gold.[1]

Mer. And is that clever man Cratinus[2] in good case?

Try. He died when last the Spartans overran the place.

Mer. Of what?

Try.   A swoon: poor man, he could not bear the guilt,
He saw a wine-jar broken and good liquor spilt.
And much beside has happened to our hurt and pain:
So, Lady, will we never let you go again.

Mer. Agreed: and you shall take OPORA for your mate.
In love live with her, and your clusters shall be great.
Take THEORIA to the Senate on your way;
And let them all the care they owe to her display.[3]

Try. Oh, happy Senators, how much soup will you
        swallow!
And in your roast and boiled for three whole days will
        wallow.
Dear MERCURY, farewell.

Mer.   Farewell, Humanity.
A pleasant journey to you; and remember me.

Try. Now homeward, homeward, Beetle, homeward let
        us fly.

---

[1] Simonides had the repute, and it was an evil repute, of being the first poet who regarded pay as well as credit for his verses. The reproach here is, that Sophocles had become too fond of money.

[2] *Knights*, l. 401. Cratinus then died in the year after his triumph over Aristophanes, at the age of 97.

[3] It would be the duty of the Senate to institute a three days' feast on the re-establishment of Peace.

Mer. Good man, it is not here.

Try.   Where is it gone ? and why ?

Mer. 'Tis harnessed to Jove's car to carry lightning out.

Try. Then how shall I go down ?

Mer.   Oh, very well, no doubt,
In company with PEACE.

Try.   Then, ladies, let us go ;
For many are the hearts that long for us below.

                                          [*Exeunt.*

PARABASIS.

Chorus. Fare you well.   In the meantime we will
            give up these things [1] to the property-man.
Ever about a playhouse rogues are
            watching to steal whatever they can.
Sir, I put them into your charge.   Now,
            if we can without giving offence,
We will address to the lookers-on a
            very few words of passable sense.
If your Playwright uses his Interlude
            as an occasion to force upon you
His self-praises, whip him, I say, for
            so shall he have no more than his due.
But, if ever a Comedy-maker,
            as the best in general fame,
Be entitled to honour, our Author
            thinks it fair to put in his claim.
When he began he found you amused with
            figures stale and silly as these :
Hercules baking, Runaways, Sharpers,
            wretches in rags and fighting with fleas.
Here was a slave who came in howling,
            there was another, his fellow, to say
How is your hide, man ?   Has the bristle-whip
            made an attack in battle-array ?

---

[1] The cables and implements wherewith Peace had been raised.

These were the rivals he supplanted :
   raising instead a fabric of art,
Where the thoughts and words were large, and
   polished with wit in every part.
Little men fear him not ; nor ever has
   woman by him been set on your stage.
His is the Hercules-vein, which, seeking
   subjects worthy his wit to engage,
Flies at the highest ; nothing daunted
   though he pass through a tannery yard :
Undiverted though by a kennel of
   threats and wrath his way may be barred.
First, I fought with the saw-toothed monster :
   lust and fury flashed from his eyes,
Round his head a hundred flatterers
   fondled him with slaver and lies ;
Out of his throat there came a roaring
   as of a dam that has broken away ;
Sea-calf was his smell, and his hide was
   scaled with the dirt of many a day.
Undismayed I engaged the Portent,
   doing battle for you and the isles.
Wherefore, not all undeserving,
   I may claim your favouring smiles.
Nor I think will you deny me
   such a measure of credit as this,—
What we looked for he has given us ;
   much that is good and little amiss.
Therefore, men and boys, stand by me,
  Let the bald fill up the chorus.
Every merry tongue will ply me,
  When the wine-cup is before us :
—Honour to the shining pate ;
  Bald [1] he is, and let him know it ;
  But his verses do not show it,
  For he is a worthy poet,

---

[1] Aristophanes among the comedians of course had not the monopoly of personalities.   It seems that Eupolis had quizzed him for his baldness ; which was the more noticeable as he was at this time only about six-and-twenty.

And withal a merry mate;
Fill his cup and heap his plate.

1st Semichorus. Away with wars, dear Muse, and link thy
  hand with mine
    To dance a measure.   It is thine
To glorify the spousals of the Gods above,
Their banquets and men's feasts : for such thy early love.[1]
    But certainly decline,
      If Carcinus should beg of thee
      To dance in his sons' company :
      Refuse to give them any aid,
      For they are villanously made,
      With length of neck and body short,
      Tame quails bred in a dingy court,
    Stage-carpenters.   Alas the day !
    Their father says, Who would have thought it,
  Just when he almost had a play
  A cruel cat one evening caught it.

2nd Semichorus. Such festal songs as might the bright-
  haired Graces please,
      When crowds are listening, such as these,
Let the wise Poet tune his soul and voice to sing,
What time the cheerful swallow brings with her the Spring,
      And Spring the tragedies ;
      If Morsimus has not to bore us,
      Nor yet Melanthius a chorus :
      His screaming notes I heard when he
      Exhibited a tragedy,
      He and his brother, Gorgon-throats
      To swallow dainty fish, he-goats,
    Matched in depravity and crime :
      Whom, Muse, reject with scorn and spitting ;
    And sport with me to make this time
    The feast of joyaunce that is fitting.

---

[1] The four first lines of this strophe and of that which follows are
adapted from lines of Stesichorus, the poet who is said to have invented
'Chorus.' Carcinus, Morsimus, and Melanthius were contemporary tragic
poets, of whom little more is now known than what Aristophanes says of
them.   The explanation given of the point in the first strophe is, that
Carcinus had succeeded in ' getting a chorus '—that is, the opportunity of
exhibiting a tragedy, the title of which was *The Mice.*   It was, however,
as we should say, hissed off the stage.

SCENE.—*House of* TRYGÆUS. TRYGÆUS *arrived from*
heaven, accompanied by PEACE, OPORA, *and* THEORIA,
SLAVE *and* CHORUS.

Try. That journey to the Gods was no slight under-
        taking;
And, I will fairly own it, that my legs are aching.
When I was up aloft and looked down upon you,
You men seemed very small; and yet 'tis certain, too,
As rogues you still were great when looked at from afar,
Yet still, the nearer seen the greater rogues you are.

Slave. What, master, are you come?

Try.   So heard I some one say.

Slave. How have you fared?

Try.   Badly about the legs; the way
Was long.

Slave.   Come, tell me.

Try.   What?

Slave.   When you were in the air,
Met you another man upon his travels there?

Try. Not I; except some souls, freed from their late
        abodes,
Some two or three, of crazy poets who write odes.

Slave. What were they doing?

Try.   Catching notions on the wing,
To introduce into some flimsy, cloudy thing.

Slave. And is there any truth in what is sometimes said,
About us being turned to stars when we are dead?

Try. No doubt of it.

Slave.   Who is the newest star that shines?

Try. Ion of Chios, he who made the pretty lines
About the Morning Star.   Immediately he came,
Among them, they in compliment gave him the name.

Slave. What sort of stars are those that shoot and
        quickly pass
As though they were on fire?

Try.   Stars of the richer class,
Who, after some convivialities, retire
With lanterns in their hands, and in the lanterns fire.

But now into the house conduct this lady fair,
Make warm some water quickly, fill the bath, prepare
A marriage-bed for us ; OPORA is to be
My bride this night.   This done, do you come back to me.
                              [*Exit* SLAVE, *with* OPORA.
And, Members of the Senate, you I charge with this—
The lady THEORIA.
                    [*A prytanis steps forward to receive* THEORIA.
                         See the prytanis !
How nimbly he came forward !   'Twere another thing
If I, without his bribe, had called on him to bring
Some matter into Council; then, ' Sir,' you would say,
' Impossible : the Council does not meet to-day.'
    Chorus.   Worthy man, and truly great,
                   Serviceable to the State
                        Is such a citizen.
Try.   Aye, aye, when vintage comes, you'll know me better
             then.
Chorus.   Nay, you are already known—
                   Born to be, and be alone,
                        All the nation's saver.
Try.   You'll say it when you know the new wine's fruity
             flavour.
Chorus. But come, what's next to do ?
Try.   To set us up a shrine
Where we with fitting rite may worship PEACE Divine.
So choose me out a sheep, and bring it in a trice,
And I will find an altar for the sacrifice.
    Chorus.   When God declares his will,
                       And Fortune ratifies it,
                   All must succeed ;
                   Need after need
                   Occasion brings, and still
                       Spontaneously supplies it.
Try. (*observing an altar at the side of the stage*).
                   That never was more true than now;
                   Here is an altar for our vow.
Chorus. Speed, then, your preparations while
                   The gusty gale of war is falling,
             For Providence begins to smile,
                   The happy ancient times recalling.

Try. Here is the basket, with the meal,
    The woollen fillet, and the steel,
    And here is fire; so what should keep
    Us waiting longer but the sheep?
Chorus. Up, stir yourselves, for if that Chæris
    Should chance to learn what business here is,
    He will without an invitation
    Come with his pipes and botheration;
    And then, I know, you'll be bestowing
    A something for his pipes and blowing.
Try. (*giving directions to the slave*). Take you the basket,
    with the water-stoup, and run
From left to right about the altar.
Slave.   It is done:
What next?
Try.   I dip this torch; you whirl it rapidly;
Offer some meal upon the altar; hand to me
The water-stoup; dip your own finger; now dispense
Handfuls of barley-corns among the audience.
Slave. Ready.
Try.   Let us commence the office:—'*Who is here?*'
The '*many and the good*,' it seems, do not appear!
Slave. Shall I not give to these,[1] who many are and good?
Try. Good do you reckon them?
Slave.   At any rate they stood,
When I upon their heads rained holy water down
Enough to have dispersed the rabble of a town.
Try. Now, let us pray; so let your idle babble cease.
    Goddess of our love and Queen,
        Honoured PEACE,
    Thou whom marriage-feast delights,
    And the dance upon the green,
    Deign accept our sacred rites.
    Lady, hear thy lovers crying,
    For their long-lost mistress sighing.
    Thirteen heavy years have worn us,
    Trouble and dissension torn us,
        Since we doated on thy charms.

---

[1] The audience.

Oh, receive us with a kiss,
Oh, embrace us, and dismiss
    Battle-cries and clash of arms.
Stay the carpings, stay the chatter,
When each other we bespatter;
Mingle us in heart and soul,   ·
Dropping love-juice in the bowl;
And let Gentleness fill up
Judgment's hot untempered cup.
Fill the market, as of yore,
With its rich and varied store,
Heaped in every pot and pan, its
Early cucumbers, pomegranates,
Jackets for the slaves between
Apples red and onions green.
Let Bœotians never cease
Bringing pigeons, ducks, and geese,
With the sweet Copaic eel.
Let us jostle round to deal
In the crowd with Teleas,[1]
Morychus, and Glaucetas,
And a score of others there
Looking out for dainty fare.
When the market has grown thin,
Let Melanthius come in,
Ask for eels, and finding none,
    Sing in tragic measure meet,
' Woe is me, I am undone,
    Widowed of my eels in beet;'[2]
Let bystanders see the jest.
So hearken, honoured Peace, and grant thy servant's quest.
  Slave. Take you the knife and kill the sheep as cookishly
As you can do it.
  Try.   But 'tis not permitted.
  Slave.   Why?

---

[1] *Birds,* l. 149.
[2] A parody of lines in the *Medea* of Melanthius.

S

Try. Peace is not pleased with slaughter, and it were a
          sin
With blood to stain her altar; but take you it in,
There kill it, and bring out the legs of mutton; so
A sheep's cost shall be saved in charges for the show.[1]

                                        [*Exit* SLAVE.

Chorus. 'Tis yours with proper care,
              Keeping your present station,
           To lay the wood,
           Just as you should,
           And other things prepare
              To perfect the oblation.

Try.   Have I not laid the faggots here
           As though I were a very seer?

Chorus. Aye, nothing can be lost on you;
              For yours that keen intelligence,
           All to provide and all to do
              As 'fits a man of nerve and sense.

Try.   This faggot makes a wondrous smoke,
           And Stilbides [2] is like to choke.
           I will supply my servant's lack,
           And put the table farther back.

Chorus. Oh, wondrous man! for it would shame us
           Not to extol a man so famous:
           For has he not the City saved,
           After such great adventures braved?
           So must he in each generation
           Be held the mark of emulation.

          Enter SLAVE, *carrying two haunches of mutton.*

Slave. Sir, I have done my work, and beg you take these
              haunches,
While I run for the incense and prepare the paunches.

Try.   Leave that to me, and stay; I've been expecting
              you.

Slave. Surely, I've not been long; and what am I to do?

---

[1] The humour of this speech of course lay in the fact, visible to the
audience, that they had no sheep.

[2] Trygæus, playing the part of a seer, speaks of himself *as* Stilbides.
Stilbides was *the* seer of the day.

Try. Look to the cooking well, for some one comes this
       way
Who has upon his head what seems a laurel-spray.
Who can it be ?
Slave.   He seems a coxcomb at his ease.
It is a Seer.
Try.   Ah, no ; 'tis only HIEROCLES.[1]
Slave. From Oreum?—It is. What can he want with us?
Try. To make our plans for peace occasion for a fuss.
Slave. Pooh, pooh ! he is attracted by the smell of food.
Try. That's very probable.   Seem not to see him.
Slave.   Good.

            Enter HIEROCLES.

Hier. What sacrifice is this? and to what Deity ?
Try. (*to slave*). Go on, and take no notice. Leave the loin
       to me.
Hier. Will ye not answer me?—To whom this pious care?
Try. The tail is doing well.
Slave.   Sweet Peace, but this is rare !
Hier. Now cut it up and let me have the primal slice.
Try. 'Twere best to cook it first.
Hier.   But this is very nice.
Try. (*to* HIER.) You meddle.
(*to the slave*) Where's the table? bring me the libation.
Hier. The tongue apart.[2]
Try.   We do not need the information.
Hier. But tell me—
Try.   Pray, sir, let these interruptions cease.
We are about a solemn sacrifice to PEACE.
Hier. Oh, hapless mortals and unwise—
Try.   Yourself to wit.
Hier. Who knowing not God's mind, or disregarding it,
Being men make terms with fierce-eyed monkeys—
Slave.   He-he-he.
Try. Why do you laugh?
Slave.   The fierce-eyed monkeys tickled me.

---

[1] In his own estimation unquestionably a seer.
[2] An Attic custom in sacrifice. See *Birds*, 1. 1611.

Hier. And, timid pigeons as you are, put confidence
In foxes full of guile and dangerous pretence.

Try. Coxcomb, I only wish your liver was as hot
As this is.

Hier.   Bacis,[1] if the nymphs deceive him not,   ·
Nor Bacis men, nor him again the nymphs—

Try.   .   God grant
A speedy choking to you with your silly rant.

Hier. The chains of Peace, I say, or Bacis is at fault,
Shall not be loosed before—

Try.   This wants a little salt.

Hier. The blessed Gods design that strife shall not
   abate
Till whelps shall see at birth, and wolves with sheep shall
   mate.

Try. What would you have us do ? maintain a constant
   pother ?
Or draw lots for it which of us should do the other
The greatest mischief? while, if rivalry should cease,
We might in concord share dominion over Greece.

Hier. Thou never wilt induce the crab to travel straight.

Try. Thou, after the event, shalt not vaticinate :
Nor eat thy suppers at the charges of the town.[2]

Hier. Thou canst not change the hedgehog's bristles into
   down.

Try. When will you stop your course of trickery and
   lies ?

Hier. What ordinance of God enjoins to burn the
   thighs ?

Try. That noted one which Homer long ago rehearsed—
' Whereas the hateful cloud of war was now dispersed,
' Peace took they in embrace and solemnly enshrined.
' Then did they burn the thighs and on the entrails dined,
' Draining their mighty cups. I was the author of it ;
' But no one gave a shining goblet to the prophet.'

---

[1] See *Knights*, l. 111 and 930.

[2] Seers, especially in time of war, were made much of and allowed their maintenance in the Prytaneum. As Trygæus had already secured peace, this entertainment for Hierocles would come to an end.

Hier. 'Tis nought to me : the Sibyl never said such
    things.

Try. Nay, but again Homer, the Master, wisely sings,
' Unbrothered, outlawed, houseless may he pass his life,
' Who sets his heart upon blood-chilling civil strife.'

Hier. A guileful kite is overhead. I say beware
Lest he should stoop on thee—

Try. (to slave).   Aye, surely, have a care;
For the blackpuddings 'tis an evil augury.
So, pour you out the wine and bring the meat to me.

Hier. So, so : then for myself I'll do the server's part.

Try. I pour, I pour. *(making libation.)*

Hier.   For me : and reach me here some heart.

Try. The blessed Gods design that it shall not be so.
They will that we should drink the wine, and you should
    go.
Deign, venerated PEACE, with us through life to stay—

Hier. Give me the tongue.

Try.   I wish you'd take your own away.

Hier. (taking the cup as if to help himself). I pour.

Try. (striking him). Take that for pouring.

Hier.   How long must I wait ?
Give me some liver.

Try.   Not till wolf and sheep shall mate.

Hier. Nay, by your knees, I pray.

Try.   In vain you clutch my gown :
Thou canst not change the hedgehog's bristles into down.
Spectators, join with us, and make the joy completer.

Hier. And what shall I do ?

Try.   Catch your Sibyl, man, and eat her.

Hier. By Earth, you too shall not be left to eat this
    dinner.
I'll fight for it ; and let it follow to the winner.

                    [*Seizes a piece of meat.*

Try. Hit him.

Hier.   I call on these to witness.

Try.   So do I,
That you're a greedy coxcomb. Hither, Slave, and ply
The stick about this Bacis.

                    [*Exit* HIEROCLES *running.*

Slave.   Hark, I'll make you drop
That sheepskin you have stolen.   Stop, you rascal, stop.

               [*Exeunt* SLAVE *and* TRYGÆUS, *pursuing*
               HIEROCLES.

Semichorus.   Happy, happy day !
       I may throw my shield away.
       Cheese and onion fare with fighting
       Is not such as I delight in.
       True enjoyment, to my thinking,
       Centres in a bout of drinking,
       When some good companions meet
       With a bright hearth at their feet,
       Fed with logs that have been lying
       All the sunny summer drying.
       There we gossip at our ease,
       Roasting nuts and parching peas.

There's nothing pleasanter than when the sowing time is done,
And God is giving rain, to have a neighbour say to one,
' Aye, truly, friend Comarchides, 'tis seasonable weather;
' What can we better do to-day than have a cup together?
' So, mistress, roast some haricots, a bushel at the least,
' A little corn will mend the fare and figs will make a feast.
' There's Manes [1] in the vineyard must be soaking to the skin ;
' 'Tis much too wet to prune the vines ; go, girl, and fetch him in.
' And bring me from the larder, boy, four fillets of a hare,
' A thrush, two finches and a dish of curds that should be there ;
' Unless the cat has got them; for I own I heard a clatter
' Last night, and did not give a thought to what might be the matter.
' So if you find them bring me three, and take your father one :
' And beg some boughs of myrtle from Æschinades, boy; run,

---

[1] The name of one of the farm-slaves.

' And as you go look in upon Charinades and say,
                ' We expect him here to day :
                ' While the rain of God is dressing
                ' Every field with fruitful blessing.'
    Semichorus.   That's a day of pleasure !
                When the cricket chirps his measure ;
                When I see along the lines
                Shoots upon the Lemnian vines
                ('Tis the first to ripen well).
                When the fig begins to swell ;
                Oh, and when the juice is sweet,
                How I smack and taste the treat !
                Then to cure all summer ails
                Thyme-tea is draught that never fails.
                I grow fat and say with reason,
                Blessings on the pleasant season!
'Tis better seeing than the Captain with his triple crest,
(Oh, how the Gods abhor him) in his scarlet mantle
    dressed.
He says it is of Sardian dye, but when the foe's in view,
The mantle and its master too are apt to change their
    hue.
The buzzard is the first to fly ; and, leading in the race,
You may observe his streaming crests, while *I* must keep
    my place !
But when they are at home again they treat us worst of
    all.
There's no one knows on whom the turn for service is to
    fall ;
One's in the list and out again.   Just when a man feels
    free,
He casts a careless eye upon the lists ;—and what to see ?
His name in full !—and he must go, poor fellow, to his
    sorrow ;
For no provision has been bought, and he must march to-
    morrow.
Though thus they treat us countrymen, 'tis not the game
    they play
With citizens, who take no shame their shields to throw
    away.

But, yes,—for all the wrong they've done, which I will not
   forget,
>   They shall pay the reckoning yet:
>   Lions in the city walls,
>   Foxes when the trumpet calls.

SCENE.—*House of* TRYGÆUS. *Preparations for a wedding
               feast.* TRYGÆUS, SLAVE.

Try. Well! such a company was surely never seen
To grace a wedding feast.
>   [*Taking from his helmet its horsehair crest,
>   and giving it to the slave.*
>   Here, sweep the tables clean.
This thing is useless now except to serve for brushes.
And now bring in the cakes, the rabbits, and the thrushes.

Enter SICKLE-MAKER *and* CASK-MAKER.

S. M. Where is TRYGÆUS?
Try.   Roasting thrushes, as you see.
S. M. Good Sir, the Peace you've made has set our busi-
               ness free;
And we are come to thank you.   Sickles would not bring
A groat apiece, but now they will fetch anything;
Yes, forty, fifty drachmas.   And here's a man who asks
And gets three drachmas freely for his country casks.
So, please you, on your marriage take in kindly part
These sickles, and this cask, the produce of our art.
Try. I thank you, put them down, and, pray you, take
               your places.
The supper is just ready.—Here is one whose face is
Significant of trouble!—'Tis the armourer.

Enter CREST *and* SPEAR-MAKERS.

Cr.-M. You've ruined me, TRYGÆUS.
Try.   What's the matter, Sir?
Are you crest-fallen?

Cr.-M.   You have quite undone our crafts,
Mine and my fellow's here who polishes spear-shafts.

Try. What is your price for these two crests ?

Cr.-M.   What will you give ?

Try. I'm half ashamed to say,—I know a man must
    live,—
The boss is good and must, as far as I can judge,
Have cost some little labour ; so I would not grudge
Two bushels of dried figs.   At least they'll serve the turn
Of table-brushes.

Cr.-M.   Take them ; I would rather earn
The figs than nothing.

Try.   Pooh ! I will not have them here.
Look you, they shed the hair.   A fig for them were dear.

Cr.-M. Shafter, let's go.

Try.   Don't think of it ; for he and I
May deal about the spears ; I am prepared to buy.

Shafter. What will you give ?

Try.   Saw them in-two, and I will take
A hundred for a groat.   Each one will make a stake.

Shaft. 'Tis insult, let us go.

Try.   Aye, do.
        [*Exeunt* CREST-MAKER *and* SHAFTER.
        What boys are these ?

Enter BOYS.

The children of my guests, who come to sing some glees.
'Tis well.   Come let me hear, to tune your voices up,
The song which you intend to sing us while we sup.

First Boy. I sing of men in armour proof.

Try.   I'll none of that :
Armour ! in time of peace, you ill-conditioned brat !

First B. Now when the foremost dashing
        Met the line embattled,
        Shield against shield was crashing,
        Bossy bucklers rattled.

Try.   Eh ! bucklers—I say, no,
       I will not have such stuff.

Boy.   Then were there cries of woe,
       And men said, Hold, enough.

Try.   By Bacchus, I will bring
   The tears into your eyes,
  If you persist to sing
   About those ' bossy ' cries.

Boy.   What shall I sing about ?

Try.   .   Slaying of beeves to eat,
  And laying viands out
   Both savoury and sweet.

Boy.   So many beeves and fat
   They slew, and from the car
  Loosing their hot steeds, sat
   As satiate with war.

Try.   Aye, satiate indeed.
   That's just what I should think.
  Sing how they sat to feed,
   And doubtless too to drink.

Boy.   Then buckled to again---

Try.   With good will I suppose.

Boy.   And rushing to the plain,
   A mighty shout arose.

Try. A plague upon you, boy, and on your battles too !
You only sing of wars.   And, pray, whose son are you?

 Boy. Who? I?

Try.   Yes, you.

Boy.   The son of Lamachus.

Try.   Eh-heigh !
I thought, to hear you sing, that you must be a spray
Of some war-monger stock.   Sing to the men of spears,
 Sir.
Where is Cleonymus's son among you ?

 2nd B.   Here, Sir.

Try. The son of that retiring man from whom you spring
Will keep quite clear of actions.   Let me hear you sing.

 Boy. With pride some Saian shows the shield
   I scatheless left upon the field—

Try. Do you sing that, you dog, before your father's
  face ?

---

[1] Aristophanes here uses some verses of Archilochus, composed in reference to his own conduct in having left too prematurely a field of battle against the Saians.

Boy (continues singing). My life I brought away—
Try.   You tell your sire's disgrace !
But let's go in, my boy, you'll not forget your part ;
Your father's son must have those verses well by heart.

> Good people all, fall to the fare ;
> There's plenty for your filling.
> It is not well to chew the air,
> For stones were made for milling,
> So come, with right good will, in
> And set your jaws at once to grind,
> The lower and the upper :
> White teeth their only value find
> When masticating supper.

Chorus. Leave that to us ; but you are right
In thus expatiating.

Try. For all who have an appetite
A dish of hare is waiting :
And pardon me for stating,
You will not often meet astray
Dumplings of dough or suet ;
So catch and eat them while you may,
Or you'll hereafter rue it.

> [*Exit* TRYGÆUS *to bring the Bride.*

Cho. Attention now : you go to bring
The bride and bridal party.
Fetch torches ; and let people sing,
With voices loud and hearty.
And pray we for the wealth of Greece.
May its barley crops increase ;
May the bounteous Powers divine
Bless the fig-tree and the vine ;
Give us honey in our hives ;
Give us children to our wives ;
All the good we had before,
And never to touch weapon more.

Re-enter TRYGÆUS, *leading* OPORA.

Try. Where the fields are green and free,
Lady, follow on with me,
Thou, to be mine honest wife,
We, to lead an honest life.

Cho.   Hymen, Hymenæus, O.
Semicho. Happy man, possessing
           Rightfully all blessing.
Cho.   Hymen, Hymenæus, O.
Semicho. What shall we do with the vine?
           Pluck the clusters; tread the wine.
Chorus. Up and bear the bridegroom home;
           For the vintage time is come.
                Hymen, Hymenæus, O,
           Free from care, and free from strife,
           Happy be your honest life.
                Hymen, Hymenæus, O.

                          [*Exeunt all in procession.*

BIRDS.

INTRODUCTION.

THIS comedy is not inspired by partisan politics or personal acrimony. It requires therefore little introduction
for those who have slight knowledge or interest in the
politics or public characters of Athens at the time in
question.

The opening scene and explanation offered to the
audience by EUELPIDES is really so little in harmony with
the middle and ending of the drama, that it seems as if
Aristophanes himself had set out with a design from which
he was early diverted by the unexpected creation of his
own humorous fancy.

Two Athenians, disgusted by the unending litigiousness
of their fellow-citizens, set out on their travels in quest of
a *quiet* city. With this view their first object is to find
Tereus. They counted upon his good offices in their behalf
on the ground that he had married an Athenian wife. It
is true the match had not been originally very happy;
but, as it would seem, all difficulties and jealousies had
been accommodated when Tereus, with his wife Procne, and
her sister Philomela, had been metamorphosed into Birds.
Tereus had become the EPOPS or Hoopoo. As such the
Athenians sought his assistance. For, with their powers
of locomotion, who should have such large knowledge of
the world as *the Birds*? If there was anywhere a quiet city,
the Birds must know it. With the help of a jackdaw and
raven as guides, they succeed in finding Tereus. Here, as
it seems for the first time, and independently, the idea
strikes Euelpides that it might be a pleasant end of their
journey to remain where they are and join the company
of the Birds. Peisthetærus, his companion, after some
silent thought, goes beyond him in conception :—'Why not
gather the Birds into a community, which shall supplant

the Olympian Gods, and draw to itself the reverence and
religious services of men ?' The Epops is delighted
with the proposal. The comedy proceeds with the carrying out of the idea. The 'quiet city' plan is dropped.
Euelpides, who has done nothing more for the action than
make the aforesaid short suggestion, has no further work
to do; and is shortly dismissed from the stage, not to reappear. Peisthetærus alone does the work, and carries off
the undivided honours of the situation.

In the course of the comedy Aristophanes finds occasion
to introduce his favourite characters, an Informer, an
Oracle-monger, and two Poets, and, in spite of his satirical
observations in the Parabasis of *Peace,* a gluttonous
Hercules. The grand idea, however, of Peisthetærus is
crowned with success by the intervention of no less a
person than PROMETHEUS. An unclassical reader may
look for some explanation of the very extraordinary part
taken in the piece by this mythical person. No legend in
the Greek mythology is more engaging to the speculative
mind than that of Prometheus. It is enough, however, for
this place to say, that he appears broadly as the antagonist of Zeus, in whom the power and disposition of the
Gods is represented. He does not question the God's absolute title to power, or seek to meet it with direct force, as
the Titans had done. So far he is like the Satan of Milton
at a certain point: but there is this great difference in
Prometheus, that he is actuated by a beneficent disposition
towards the human race. The Gods, having given to man
a place upon earth, had malignantly left him the mere
victim of physical evils. Prometheus devotes himself to
redress this stinted and envious providence. That boon to
men which is most frequently referred to as the gift of
Prometheus is *fire.* But the arts of working in metals, do-
mestication of animals, building, writing—in short, all the
great conquests of civilisation—have been ascribed to him.
For this meddling with the will and empire of the Gods he
drew upon himself the displeasure and overwhelming vengeance of Zeus. On the whole he seems to represent the
power of knowledge in contrast with the power of original
material force. Natural forces originally possessed the

field, and stand still. Wisdom progresses, and converts evils into instruments of good. The legend of Prometheus illustrates the struggle of all times by which the weak establish their right and their good against the pride of brute force and arbitrary power; and more perhaps, the paradoxical law that moral victories are won only by the apparent defeat, dishonour, and suffering of the conqueror. However that be, it will be evident from the scene in this comedy that some such ideas about Prometheus, in relation to Zeus and to Humanity, must at the time have been in popular acceptation.

The piece obtained only the second prize. Would that we had the *Revellers* of Ameipsias, which in the opinion of the judges was a better comedy.

Dramatis Personæ.

PEISTHETÆRUS
EUELPIDES } *Citizens of Athens on their travels.*

TROCHILUS (*the Wren*), *Servant of the Epops.*

EPOPS (*Hoopoo*), *formerly Tereus king of Daulis, married to Procne,*
daughter of Pandion king of Attica.

CHORUS OF BIRDS.

Priest, *of the Birds.*

A Poet.

A Textuary, *collector and student of Oracles.*

METON, *The Geometrician.*

Political Agent.

Decree-dealer.

Heralds.

Messengers.

IRIS *of Olympus* (*the Rainbow*).

Father-beater.

CINESIAS, *the Dithyrambic Poet.*

Informer.

PROMETHEUS.

NEPTUNE.

HERCULES.

TRIBALLUS, *a barbarian God, who cannot speak Greek.*

Servant of PEISTHETÆRUS.

BASILEIA, *the royal authority of Jupiter.* A mute person.

SCENE.—PEISTHETÆRUS *and* EUELPIDES ; *the former hav-*
ing a raven attached to a string, the latter a jackdaw.
They observe and follow the motions and flight of the birds
in a wild and rocky place.

Euelpides (*to the jackdaw*). What! yonder by the tree, is
　　　that, say you, the track ?
Peisthetærus (*to the raven*). Burst you!—This bird of mine
　　　again is croaking ' back.'
Eu. What means this tramping up and down ? we shall
　　　be dead,
Making an endless journey, like a weaver's thread.
Peis. A thousand stadia round about have I obeyed
This raven's leading. 'Tis a fool's march I have made.
Eu. And I, poor fool, this jackdaw's : 'twas a silly trick;
I've scrambled till my nails are worn down to the quick.
Peis. And where on earth we are is more than I can say.
Eu. If we would turn back home, could you find out the
　　　way ?
Peis. From hence ? not Execestides [1] himself would
　　　know.
Eu. Woe! woe!
Peis. 　　　　At any rate, don't take the road to Woe.
Eu. He used us scurvily, that mad Philocrates
The poulterer, when he persuaded us that these,
Of all the birds, could show us where to have a word
With the Epops, that is Tereus, who became a bird.
For this jackdaw, this son of Tharrecleides,[2] he
Charged me an obole, and for yonder raven three ;
But both are good for nothing else but pecking—
　　　　　　　　　　　　(*To the daw.*) Ho!

---

[1] He, as it will afterwards appear, made claim to be admitted a citizen
of Athens, but was reputed to be of foreign birth from nobody-knows-
where ; *he* therefore, if anybody, should know the road from that spot to
Athens: with these characteristics of a foreign adventurer in Athens, he
is alluded to several times in the comedy, ll. 731, 1450.

[2] It is presumed known for garrulity.

What are you gaping for, eh? would you have us go
Under the rocks?—there is no path.

Peis.   Nor here a trace.

Eu. What has your raven got to say about the place?

Peis. Nothing.

Eu.   No hint about a road?

Peis.   No, for his tone
Remains the same; he'll gnaw my fingers to the bone.

Eu. (*towards the audience*). Good people present, is it not
         too bad that those
Who are disposed to make the journey ' to the crows,' [1]
Should fail to find the way? 'Tis so we are perplexed;
For, be it known, we are by a disorder vexed
Clean opposite to Saca's: [2] he, no citizen,
Fain would be one perforce; we, honourable men,
In tribe and family the equals of your best,
Disquieted by no one, not content to rest,
With all the speed we can our native country quit.
Not that we hate the city, or deny to it
The name of ' great and happy.' One may spend a life
And fortune there, we own, impartially in strife.
The grasshoppers sit singing but a month or two
Upon the fig-tree tops; at Athens, all life through
Men sit and sing among their common pleas. So we
Have started on our travels, carrying, as you see,
Basket, and vase, and myrtle,[3] till we find a spot
Where we may live in peace and processes are not.
At present our immediate object is to find
Tereus the Epops, trusting he may be so kind
As to inform us whether he has come to sight
Or hearsay of such city in his utmost flight.   .

Peis. Stay.

Eu.   What?

Peis.   Just now the raven croaked a sort of sign
Of something overhead.

Eu.   Aye, and this daw of mine

---

[1] See *Peace*, l. 86.

[2] Saca, or Thracian, like ' Phrygian' in the mouth of an Athenian, a term of contempt as signifying a 'slave.' It is here meant to apply to Acestor, a tragic poet, residing in Athens.

[3] Preparations for sacrifice as soon as they find a new settlement.

Is gaping upward, which, unless I judge amiss,
Means something. Birds must live in such a place as this:
A noise will prove it.

Peis. Strike your foot against the rock.

Eu. Strike your own head; 'twill make a double knock.

Peis. Then take a stone to hit with.

Eu. Well, to please you—'Boy'!

Peis. You call the EPOPS 'boy'? you should say 'EPOPOI.'

Eu. Ho, EPOPOI! what! will you make me knock again?

Enter TROCHILUS.

Tro. Who calls my master, and in such a noisy strain?

Eu. Apollo help us! what a stretch of beak is here!

Tro. Alas! these are some horrid bird-catchers I fear.

Eu. Fie on the word! you do us wrong.

Tro. Yes, ye shall die.

Eu. We are not men at all.

Tro. What then?

Eu. *The Timid,* I,
A Lybian bird.

Tro. Pooh, nonsense.

Eu. Truly.

Tro. Who is he?

Peis. The *Phasian Dirty.*

Eu. But, by all the Gods, tell me
What animal are you.

Tro. A slave-bird.

Eu. Were you, then,
Defeated by some cock in battle?

Tro. No; but when
My master was made EPOPS, I, at his request,
Also became a bird, to serve at his behest.

Eu. What! does a bird require a slave?

Tro. *He* does, at least;
For when he was a man, nor has the fancy ceased,
He learned to like anchovies, true Phaleric fish;
I often, therefore, have to run and fetch a dish.
Whilome he wishes porridge; then I have to trot
That he may be supplied with spoon and porridge-pot.

Eu. Good Trochilus, you know your duties well; so run
And call your master out.

Tro.   By Jove, it can't be done.
After some myrtle-berries and a score of worms,
My lord has dropped asleep.

Eu.   Wake him on any terms.

Tro. He will be very angry; but you shall be served;
I'll wake him.   [*Exit* TROCHILUS.

Peis.   Plague upon you! I am quite unnerved;
What mischief you have done!

Eu.   It is a pretty scrape;
For in my terror I have let the daw escape.

Peis. What! mean you, coward, you have let the jack-
          daw slip?

Eu. And did you loose the raven when I saw you trip?

Peis. Not I, by Jove.

Eu.   Where is it?

Peis.   Flown away.

Eu.   Oh, then
You did not loose it, most magnanimous of men.

                    EPOPS (*within*).

Epops. Undo the wood; let me go out.

                    Enter EPOPS.

Eu.   ·   Oh, Hercules!
What brute is this? what wings and triple crests are these?

Ep. Who ask for me?

Eu.   The Gods!—But you are much misused.

Ep. Is it my plumage, strangers, makes you so amused?
But once I was a man.

Eu.   We did not laugh at you.

Ep. At what, then, did you smile?

Peis.   That beak of yours, 'tis true,
Is most ridiculous.

Ep.   And yet in this array
Did Sophocles costume me, TEREUS, in his play.[1]

-----

[1] In a drama of Sophocles, Tereus undergoes the change into a bird.
It seems by the text that Aristophanes had here taken care to caricature
the costume in which the Tereus of the tragedy had been represented.

Eu. Then you are TEREUS? bird or portent?

Ep.   I am bird.

Eu. Where are your feathers?

Ep.   Cast.

Eu.   Has some disease occurred?

Ep. No; but we birds in winter regularly shed
Our feathers, and acquire another set instead.
But tell me who are you?

Eu.   Two mortals.

Ep.   Of what race?

Eu. Of that where ships are good.

Ep.   What! courtiers out of place?[1]

Eu. Nay, of another stamp; men who detest the court.

Ep. Does that seed grow there?

Eu.   You would find the crop but short.

Ep. What business might it be that brings you to tliis
          spot?

Eu. The wish to have some conference with you.

Ep.   On what?

Eu. Because you formerly were man, as we are yet,
And so, like us at present, you have been in debt;
Because there was the time when you, like us, have known
The joy of not repaying what you took on loan.
Then you became a bird and travelled upon wings
The breadth of earth and sea; so that you know all things
That bird or man can know. Therefore for information
We are your suppliants. Know you the place or nation
Where we may find a fleecy comfortable town,
In which, as in a blanket, we may settle down?

Ep. A city larger than the Cranaan[2] you would find?

Eu. Not larger, but much more according to our mind.

Ep. You wish aristocratic rule, 'tis manifest.

---

[1] This translation is nearer to the letter than to the meaning of the original. The 'Courts' to which allusion is made are the law courts; so the true meaning is 'are you then judges or jury who cannot find employment?' The answer made by Euelpides is apparently a pun on the word used by the Epops. The traditional interpreters give no other meaning to the word than that by which it is here rendered; but I suspect it is also the name of some herb. Then the rejoinder of the Epops has significance.

[2] That is to say 'than Athens.'

Eu. That son of Scellias [1] I utterly detest.

Ep. What sort of city is it that you would prefer ?

Eu. Where troubles, when they come, are of this character :—

At early dawn there comes a friend to me to say,
' By the Olympian Jove, you dine with me to-day,
You and your children, early : for I have in hand
To keep my wedding-day ; so, pray you, understand
I will take no denial ; or, remember this,
Don't think to help me when my fortune goes amiss.'

Ep. Your liking for misfortunes is extravagant ;
And yet I know a city just such as you want,
By the Red Sea.

Eu.   Not by the sea, or some fine day
The Salaminian [2] might appear within the bay
With summoners on board her.   Can you not suggest
Some city of the Greeks where one might live at rest ?

Ep. There's Lepreum of Elis, why not settle there ?

Eu. I never saw it ; but the place I cannot bear ;
It calls to mind Melanthius.

Ep.   Then why not try
Locris, and make your home among the Opuntii ?

Eu. I would not for a talent be Opuntius. [3]
What sort of life is this among the birds ?   Discuss ;
You know it well.

Ep.   One easily might find a worse.
To start with,—one is bound to live without a purse.

Eu. You take at once from life all that is counterfeit.

Ep. The gardens where we live provide us daily meat,
White sesamé and myrtle-berries are our fare.

Eu. You live on what they give a newly-married pair ! [4]

---

[1] The allusion to a citizen of Athens named Aristocrates here helps
Aristophanes to parry the charge of being an aristocrat.

[2] The *Salaminian* and the *Paralus* were two state vessels of the
Athenians used especially for carrying official persons. The allusion here
is perhaps particularly to the mission of the Salaminian to Sicily to bring
back Alcibiades to answer a charge of treason : an event which had
memorable influence on the future fortune of Athens.

[3] ' Opuntius ' means generally an Opuntian citizen ; but here also a
man of the name, well known as having only one eye.

[4] Sesamum entered into the composition of a kind of wedding-cake.

*Peis. (who has given little attention to the dialogue between
Ep. and Eu.)* Ha! if the birds would only do as I could
           teach,
A mighty stroke for empire is within their reach.

Ep. What would you have?

Peis.   What would I have? ye should forbear
Your flitting openmouthed here, there, and everywhere.
'Tis not respectable.   When any one refers,
Down among us, to such unsettled flutterers,
Asking, 'What bird is that?' then Teleas will say,
'The man's a bird of passage; he came here to-day
And will be off to-morrow; ever on the wing,
He's of no mark, nor ever sticks to anything.'

Ep. By Bacchus, your remark is just as it is witty.
What would you have us do?

Peis.   Lay out a single city.

Ep. And pray what sort of city could be built by birds?

Peis. What sort? oh, utterer of very idle words,
Look down!

Ep.   I'm looking down.

Peis.   Look up.

Ep.   I take the hint.

Peis. Now turn your neck.

Ep.   'Tis lucky if I do not squint.

Peis. What see you?

Ep.   Clouds and sky.

Peis.   But is not all this space
The pole of birds?

Ep.   The pole? how so?

Peis.   As one should say the 'place.'
But since this all is turned about, and to the whole
Is central, therefore is it rightly called 'the pole.' [1]
Here if you found your city, and enclose the same,
Then from this pole your polity shall take its name.
The human race like gnats will be at your direction,
And famine must reduce the Gods to your subjection.

Ep. How so?

---

[1] The author here labours for such puns as are to be had between πόλος, πόλις, πολῖται, and πολῖται : pole, city, rotates, citizens.

Peis.   The atmosphere lies intermediate
Between the earth and heaven ; as the Bœotian state
Lies between us and Delphi : just as we are bound
To ask a thoroughfare through the Bœotian ground ;
So, when the men below you offer sacrifice,
It lies with you to make the Gods at your device
Pay tribute ; otherwise, you disallow the thighs
To send their savour up through chaos and the skies.
 Ep. Ho ! ho !   By earth ! by trap ! by clouds ! by nets !
  I vow
So very neat a thought I never heard till now.
With your assistance and the other.birds' consent
I'll found the city.
 Peis.   Who will tell them our intent ?
 Ep. You shall : for though they were before barbarian,
They have at length from me acquired the tongue of man.
 Peis. How will you summon them ?
 Ep.   Oh !. with the greatest ease ;
I have no more to do than hop into the trees,
And call my nightingale.   Soon as they hear the sound
Of our united voices they will gather round.

 Peis. Proceed at once, dear bird ; let not the business fail,
But hop into the trees, and call your nightingale.
 Ep.   Up from thy slumbers, mate of mine ;
  Let forth the flood of strains divine,
  As when, the wonder of thy throat,
  Thou trillest Sorrow's bubbling note,
  For Itys [1] wailed with many a tear
  By thee and me.   The warbling clear
  Forth of the yew-tree's close-leaved tresses
  Issues, and mounting upward presses
  To Jove's own seats ; when golden-haired
  Apollo hears.   To answer dared,
  His ivory-fashioned lyre he takes,
  And such soul-touching chords awakes,
  That, as the melody advances,
  The Gods move forward to their dances ;

---

[1] Itys, the son of Tereus and Procne, killed by Procne in her fury at
the deceit and infidelity of Tereus.

And lips immortal deign to borrow
            And sing with thee
            In harmony
A marvellous sweet song of sorrow.
            [*The sound of a pipe behind the scene.*
Peis. King Jove ! how through one's soul the little bird's
      voice thrilled,
And all the thicket with its melody was filled.
  Eu. Hush !
  Peis.   What ?
  Eu.   Be quiet.
· *Peis.*   Why ?
  Eu.   List for another strain ;
The EPOPS is preparing to begin again.
  Ep. Epopoi, popopo, popoi, popoi !
            Io-io, ito-ito, ito-ito.
            Hither all of kindred feather ;
            Ye that on the fertile plain
            Share the sower's ample gain,
            Ye that on the barley feed,
            Ye that pick the dainty seed,
                  Swiftly winging,
                  Softly singing,
            Gather all your tribes together.

            Hither, hither, troop to us,
            Ye that multitudinous
            Twitter modestly around
            Clods upon the fallowed ground.
      Tio-tio-tio-tio-tio-tio-tio-tio.

            Shrubbery and garden quit,
            Ye that in the ivy sit,
            Quit the mountains, quit your fare,
            Arbutus and olive there.
                  Away, away.
                  My call obey.
            Trioto-trioto-trioto-to-brix.

            Leave the stinging gnats
                  Uncaught upon the fen ;
            Leave the dewy flats,

And pleasant Marathon ;
Come speckled attagen,
And come all ye
Who with the halcyon
Brood o'er the heaving sea.
Come to hear the news that's stirring,
All the slender-necks concurring,
There is come a shrewd adviser
On our revolution bent ;
He intends to make us wiser :
Come unto the parliament.
Hithero—hithero—hithero.

Cries of strange birds in the distance.
Torotoro—torotoro—torotinx.
Kikkabo—kikkabo,
Torotoro, torotoli—lililinx.

Peis. Do you see any bird ?
Eu.   None by Apollo, I,
Though I have gaped through every region of the sky.
Peis. The Epops, like a lory went into the tree
To sit on addled eggs, as far as I can see.

A bird coming.   Torotinx—torotinx.
Peis. Birds ! but bless you, my good fellow,
                    look at this one coming now !

              Enter Scarlet-wing bird.[1]

Eu. Bird, by Jove, it is ! what is it ?
                    Not a peacock anyhow.
Peis. He will tell us what the name is.
                    What is it you call this bird ?
Epops. 'Tis a foreign bird of which you
                    probably have never heard :
He inhabits lakes and marshes.
Peis.   'Tis a very handsome thing.
Ep. Your remark is very happy,
                    for we call him *Scarlet-wing.*

Eu. Look you !
Peis.   What ?
Eu.   Here comes another.

---

[1] Perhaps the Flamingo.

Enter Mede-bird.[1]

Peis.   Out of what outlandish place
Did a creature such as that is
                      bring his solemn form and face?
Ep. Mede is the bird's appellation.
Peis.   Mede indeed! but, very good.
How did he without a camel fly into this neighbourhood?
Eu. Here's another crested creature.

Enter another Epops, with ragged plumage.

Peis.   In the name of wonder, he's
Just like you, another EPOPS!
Ep.   'Tis the son of Philocles;[2]
I am father's father to him; just as it has come to pass
Callias had Hipponicus—Hipponicus Callias.
Peis. Then this bird is Callias; but
                      many feathers he has lost.
Ep. Aye, the sycophants have got 'em—
                      'tis his lineage's cost:
Something too the hens may pluck him.[3]

Enter another bird.

Peis.   Neptune! whence does this thing fall?
Particoloured what d'ye call him?
Ep.   This bird is the *Swallow-all.*
Peis. Has Cleonymus[4] a double?
                      yet, the truth must be confessed,
If it be Cleonymus, he has not thrown away his crest.
Tell me what is all this cresting?
                      Are they coming to the races?[5]

---

[1] Perhaps the Adjutant.

[2] Sophocles first introduced the Epops in his tragedy *Tereus*; Philocles subsequently produced another 'Tereus' with its Epops, bearing a sufficient likeness to that of Sophocles to establish the relationship here insinuated.

[3] Callias inherited the property and principles of one of the old Aristocratic families of Attica. Sycophants (in the modern sense) and '*hens*' had helped him to dilapidate his fortune.

[4] *Knights*, l. 1150, and *Acharnians*, l. 70.

[5] Young men of fashion attended a certain favourite race in full military costume with casque and crest. Whatever may be the point of the rejoinder, 'crests' must there mean the hill tops.

Ep. Nay but like the Carians they
     choose the crests for safer places.
Peis. What a plague of birds is gathered !
Eu.   By Apollo ! what a storm ;
 One can hardly see the way in
     for the curtain which they form.
Peis. Here by Jupiter is partridge,
     yonder is a guinea hen,
After kingfisher and widgeon,
 Eu.   What is that which follows then ?
Peis. That's the halcyon of Barbar—
Eu.   Is a barber then a bird ?
Peis. What besides is Sporgilus [1] ?—
     Ah ! here's the owl.
 Eu.   What ? How absurd !
Who has brought an owl to Athens ?
 Peis.   There's a brown-owl to the white,
 Magpie, pigeon, lark and turtle,
     dabchick, cuckoo, plover, kite,
 Woodpecker, and water wagtail,
     bottletit and dove and coot,
 Golden-crested wren and osprey,
     grouse and cormorant to boot.[2]
Eu. What a quantity of blackbirds !
     How they twitter, how they run
Hither, thither in confusion !
     They are screaming everyone.
Ah ! I think they mean to threaten,
     eyeing fiercely me and you,
And with open mouth advancing.
 Peis.   I'm of that opinion too !
Chorus. Popopopopopopoi.
     Where is he who called this meeting ?
     How and where may he be found ?

---

[1] Nothing is known about Sporgilus. Of course Aristophanes had too nice a sense of right to raise a laugh at anyone who did not deserve it: so—suggests a commentator—'Perhaps he was a greedy man,' or, as Wieland suggests, 'used blunt razors.'

[2] We have here from the 'partridge' four-and-twenty birds introduced into the orchestra; no doubt so costumed as to be recognised by the audience. From this point they constitute the Chorus.

Ep.   I am here upon the ground,
       Ready with a friendly greeting.
Chorus. Be then good enough to state,
       What's the subject for debate?
Ep. Something just, safe, pleasant, useful
       and for common interests;
For two men of great acuteness
       have arrived and are our guests.
Chorus. How so?—what's that?—say you?
Ep.   That two ancients of the human kind
Have arrived and bring the trunk[1] of
       something vast and well designed.
Chorus. Never since I was a chicken
       made you such a monstrous error:
What say you?
Ep.   Pray do not let the
       mention cause you so much terror.
Chorus. What's the scrape you've brought us into?
Ep.   Simply I have welcomed here
Two good men, to whom the welfare
       of this company is dear.
Chorus. 'Tis a fact that you have done it?
Ep.   And with pleasure you should know.
Chorus. And the two are now among us?
Ep.   Yes, if I myself am so.
Chorus. Betrayed we are and foully wronged
       By one who shared the feeding plains,
    To all that equally belonged.
       Our ancient statutes he disdains,
       And sacred oaths defies,
    Contriving upon us his snares to throw,
    And hand us to a tribe, the eternal foe
       Of everything that flies.
For the bird that has offended,—
       leave his reckoning to stand;
But the ancients, to my thinking,
       should be dealt with out of hand.
Let us tear them both in pieces.

---

[1] This term follows the original, and seems intended to signify something more pretentious than the 'root.'

Peis.   We must die.

Eu.   You are to blame.
Wherefore did you bring me with you?

Peis.   'Twas to follow me you came.

Eu. It was for my bitter weeping.

Peis.   That remark is scarcely wise:
How shall you contrive your weeping,
                    if they pick out both your eyes?

Chorus. Upon them! at them! in a ring
               Encircle them with bloody force:
               Make onslaught with embattled wing!
               For these two men must die of course,
                    And glut my beak with prey.
               No gloomy glen is there, nor airy cloud
               Nor hoary sea that can their persons shroud
                    And let them get away.
Pluck them; tear them; bite them, scare them:
                    do not let us be afraid.
Where is he who should command us?
                    let him lead the light brigade.[1]

Eu. Now it's coming: where am I to get to?

Peis.   Silly fellow, stay.

Eu. Stay—and let these horrid creatures
                    pull me into pieces!

Peis.   Pray,
How do you propose escaping?

Eu.   That's a different affair.

Peis. Then we must remain and fight it!
                    we have got the earthenware.

Eu. Earthenware! but what will that do?

Peis.   Owls at least will not come near it.[2]

Eu. But an eagle with his talons?

Peis.   I will take the spit and spear it.

----

[1] Aristophanes says 'right wing'; but he has a word which avoids any confusion of idea with a *bird's* wing. These strophes are clever parodies of the style of the tragedians.

[2] The earthenware is that which they brought from Athens for sacrificial vessels. The owls would recognise the *Attic* pottery and respect it.

Eu. How can we protect our eyes
    against such enemies as those ?
Peis. Take a dish or salad-bowl, and
    hold it up before your nose.
Eu. Ah, how wonderfully clever
    in expedients you are !
Nicias[1] was great in tactics,
    but you distance him by far.
Chorus. Forward : forward : put the beak in ;
    put it home and do not spare :
Pluck them ; slay them ; strike them ; flay them ;
    first knock down the earthenware.
Ep. Most unconscionable, listen :
    tell me, brutes, why ? what is this ?
Why should you attack these strangers,
    who have nothing done amiss ?
Why, without a provocation,
    should you hurt in limb or life
These two quiet men, the tribesmen
    and relations of my wife ?
Chorus. Why should we regard them more than
    wolves or other enemies ?
When shall we find foes deserving
    sharper recompense than these ?
Ep. Though they be our foes by nature,
    these are come with friendly mind
To instruct us in a scheme of
    great advantage to our kind.
Chorus. Who can credit we should hear of
    anything like that from those
Who have been through generations
    all our fathers' fathers' foes ?
Ep. Yet from enemies the wise get
    lessons of the greatest value.
What protects us more than caution ?
    That's a lesson never shall you

---

[1] Nicias was at this time engaged in command of the Athenian expedition to Sicily.

Learn from friends; a foe compels it:
   Not from any friendly powers
Learn the states to cherish navies,
   and to build their walls and towers:
So they learned to keep in surety
   children, houses and estate.
Chorus. It may be as well to hear you:
   one may learn from a debate.
Peis. (*to Eu.*) They, it seems, relent a little;
   stand at ease; we may retire.
Ep. (*to Chorus*). You may thank me for abating
   your unconscionable fire.
Chorus. Nay, we never could maintain an
   opposition to your wishes.
Peis. So then, Peace is more established;
   we may lay aside the dishes.
   Not the less I think it fit,
   Spear in hand—(I mean the spit),
   You and I should make the rounds
   Cautiously within our bounds.
   Keep the bowl within your sight.
   We should never think of flight.
Eu.   Certainly.   If we should fall
   Where could we find burial?
Peis.   Where they bury soldiers, like us
   Dying, in the Ceramicus.[1]
   That the state may bear the cost,
   We will say that we were lost,
   Fighting with the enemy
   Gallantly at Orneæ.[2]
Chorus.   Fall back into the loose array,
   And, soldier-like, your anger lay
   Beside your wrath.[3]   Let us know whence

---

[1] That is, a potter's field: no doubt originally a piece of exhausted land, and naturally enough applied to the purpose of a burial-ground. Here, obviously, the word has a merry allusion to the 'pots and pans' which the two heroes were now guarding.

[2] A town in Peloponnesus, but sounding to Greek ears as 'Bird-bury' would to ours.

[3] Compare *Wasps*, l. 487 :—
   'I feel my anger pacified,
   And with my stick 'tis laid aside.'

These men are come: on what pretence.
Hear, Epops, what I have to ask.

Ep.   To listen is a pleasant task.

Chorus.   What men are these? and whence are they?

Ep.   They are two strangers on their way
From clever Greece.

Chorus.   What fortune then
Amongst us birds has brought the men?

Ep.   The strong desire they have to share
Our mode of living in the air.
They wish to come and live with us,
In perfect intimacy.

Chorus.   Eh?
Have they got anything to say?

Ep.   Yes, that they have, and marvellous.

Chorus.   What? Does the man foresee some gain
That should induce him to remain?
Will our assistance serve his end
To crush a foe, or serve a friend?

Ep.   He sees, surpassing all belief,
A happiness for us. In brief,
All that is here and elsewhere too
By his account belongs to you.

Chorus.   Insane?

Ep.   A wit
Past telling it.

Chorus.   There's something in him?

Ep.   Fox complete.
Fine, double-bolted, shrewdness neat.

Chorus.   Oh bid, oh bid him utter
His views; for your account
Has made my fancy mount,
And I am in a flutter.

Ep. (*to Peis. and Eu.*) Come now, do you, and you, take
all your armour back,
And happily replace it in the kitchen rack.

(*to Peis.*) And now, do you explain to them the reason why
I have convoked this general parliament.

Peis.   Not I;
Till they accord to me, to make an end of strife,
The terms the tinker fellow settled with his wife—

'You shall not bite, item, nor scratch.'

Chorus.   ·   I will engage.

Peis. Confirm it with an oath.

Chorus.   I swear upon this stage.

On these conditions I will carry off the prize,[1]

By every judge's voice, and yours, whose ears and eyes

Bear witness.

Peis.   Be it so.

Chorus.   Whereas, if I transgress,

My best competitor shall have but one vote less.

HERALD..

Good people, hear.   The soldiers will go home with speed,

And pay attention to the notices they read.

Chorus.   'Tis man's whole nature to deceive.

          Speak not the less; you have my leave.

          May be that you have hit

          Some great advantage on my side,

          Some right inherent, undescried

          By my more humble wit.

          This if you see, unlock

          The secret to us all.

          The benefit, or great or small,

          Shall be in common stock.

     But whatever may be the business

                    which has induced your travelling here,

     Speak it boldly: we shall observe our

                    treaty of peace with honour clear.

Peis. I am anxious, Jupiter knows; and

                    my materials for a speech

     Nothing hinders being kneaded.

                    Bring me a chaplet,[2] slave, and reach

     Hither a ewer to lave my hands.

Eu.   Then are we going to dinner? or what?

Peis. (*aside to Eu.*) No: but I am going to open a

                    marvellous rich and excellent plot,

     Which shall captivate their fancy,

                    and put them into leading strings.

---

[1] That is, the prize for the best comedy of the festival: there were five official judges.

[2] Orators spoke crowned with a chaplet.

(*to Birds*). Most profoundly do I pity you,

        you who once on a time were kings—

Chorus. We were kings! of what?

Peis.   I say, *you :*

        Kings of all, aye kings of Me,

    Lords of Jupiter, kings of all that

        ever has been or can possibly be.

Does it not fall by primogeniture?

        You undoubtedly reckon your birth .

    Long to have preceded that of

        Time, or Titans, aye, of the Earth.

Chorus. Of the Earth?

Peis.   Aye, by Apollo!

Chorus.   That by Jupiter did I not know.

Peis. That is because you are not a scholar,

        in such matters are apt to be slow.

    You have neglected to con your Æsop,

        or you would have read or have heard

How, before the world was made, the

        top-knotted lark was the earliest bird.

When her father died she was puzzled, for

        after he had been five days dead,

There was no earth in which to bury him :

        so she buried him in her head.[1]

Ep. Ere the Earth and Gods existed,

        seeing that birds were in being and known,

    Surely we by primogeniture

        -    are entitled to sit on the throne.

Eu. Yea, by Apollo, but you must look to it ;

        cherish your beaks, for it seems to me,

    Jupiter will not tamely yield to the .

        bird that taps the hollow beech tree.

Peis. That with men in ancient times no

        Gods were allowed to interfere,

But that the rule of birds was admitted,

        there are signs exceedingly clear.

---

[1] Therefore out of her head grew the 'top-knot' or 'crest.' The fable ascribed to Æsop has not come down to us. The line that follows has been omitted because we have no known place which could represent the pun : it requires a name like 'Head-bury.'

Take the Cock as a first example.
　　　　　Over the Persians he held sway,
Ere Darius and Megabazus:
　　　　　Persian [1] he is called to this day.

Eu. Therefore just as the Great King does, and
　　　　　as one might in reason expect,
He alone of all the birds now
　　　　　carries the comb on his head erect. [2]

Peis. Nay, of that once great dominion
　　　　　some observance still is in force;
For as soon as he sings the day-break,
　　　　　up they jump as a matter of course;
Out in the dark they shuffle to business,
　　　　　braziers, potters, journeymen bakers,
Farriers, bagnio-keepers, curriers,
　　　　　martial and musical instrument makers.

Eu. I have a tale to tell of his crowing.
　　　　　Once to my sorrow it cost me the loss
Of a coat of superfine Phrygian wool,
　　　　　new it was with a beautiful gloss.
Being one of a party invited
　　　　　the nameday of a baby to keep,
As it happened I drank a little, and
　　　　　just for a minute had fallen asleep:
Hardly had I winked when some un-
　　　　　timely [3] cock must set up a crowing.
What could I do but think it sunrise
　　　　　and of course high time to be going
Home to Alimous?　So I do: but
　　　　　barely was I clear of the wall
When some footpad comes behind me,
　　　　　strikes me a blow on the head, and I fall.

---

[1] 'Persian fowl,' as we say 'Turkey-cock' or 'Guinea-fowl.'

[2] It is said the Persian king wore his tiara erect, his subjects theirs leaning backward.

[3] Failing to make any sense from the common reading of this line apposite to the story of Euelpides, I have ventured to guess a verbal emendation which in effect explains that the cock who woke Euelpides crowed unseasonably.

[4] For πρὶν ΔΕΙΠΝΕΙΝ I read πρὶν ΕΠΑΙΝΕΙΝ τοὺς ἄλλους, sc. ἀλεκτρυόνας. The word is used in the sense of 'to assent' by Aristophanes. 'Ορν. 1616; Λυσ. 70.

Just as I was about to shout, I
    felt a scarcely perceptible pull:
All was done in a minute, and I was
    eased of my coat of Phrygian wool.
Peis. All the Greeks were under the kite's rule.
Ep. Greeks?
Peis.   Aye, for it was under his reign
Men were taught to roll on the ground when
    kites are hovering over the plain.[1]
Eu. I remember one day rolling.
    flat on my back on seeing a kite,
When I swallowed[2] an obolus which was
    meant to pay for my supper at night.
Peis. Egypt then obeyed the cuckoo,
    Egypt and Phenicia too ;
People did not dare so much as
    reap their grain till he said ' cuckoo.'
Nay, so far were birds considered
    that we see our earlier kings,
As Menelaus or Agamemnon,
    always bore such a figure with wings
Sitting upon the top of their sceptres
    ready to take their share of a gift.
Eu. That explains a thing of which I
    own I could not fathom the drift.
Why our tragedy kings have always
    sceptres tipped with the aquiline tribe ;
Now I know they watch Lysicrates,
    hoping to get a part of his bribe.
Peis. But the most significant fact is,
    that the now possessor of power,
Jupiter, ever is represented
    having an eagle up to this hour;

---

[1] Brand, ' Popular Antiq., Omens,' quotes : ' Some bileve that yf the kyte or the puttock flie over the way afore them that they should fare well that daye.'

In many parts of England, magpies are saluted by taking off the hat, or a curtsey. It is to be feared that the magpies find that the politeness of the English is on the decline.

[2] Euelpides, like Love-Cleon, *Wasps*, l. 556, had the habit of carrying his money in his mouth.

So has his daughter an owl; and Apollo
        has a hawk for his lower degree.

Eu. Very well said; but can you tell us
        why this disposition should be?

Peis. That the bird may be in place to
        take to himself the Deity's rights,

When a victim is divided;
        so he gets the liver and lights.

None in those days swore by a God, but
        only the names of birds were in use;

Lampon, when he means deceiving,   [goose.' [1]
        keeps the fashion, and swears 'by the

Such was once your estimation!
        Now they say in the name of a fowl,

Silly as a goose, stupid as an owl;
Kill me the booby, knock him on the head.
Even in temples, with shame be it said,
Lurks some birdcatcher.[2]   Nets fall around you,
Springes entangle, cages impound you.
Sent by the hundred, hung up to dangle,
Over your bodies poulterers wrangle.
Comes in a buyer—he fingers and thumbs you;
Then comes the cook, who lards you and crumbs you,
Takes out your entrails, puts in instead
Onions and sage, suet, pepper and bread;
        Nor yet has he done;
A savoury liquid has he got,
Over your bodies he pours it hot,
        As though your flesh were carrion!

Chorus.   Oh, man, this is a sad, sad tale;
        And I with bitter tears bewail
          My fathers' baseness, who
        Let pass this brave inheritance.
        But you are come with happy chance
          To be my saviour; you
          Shall be my citadel:

---

[1] Μὰ Χῆνα, instead of μὰ Ζῆνα.
[2] The reference is here to a scene in the *Ion* of Euripides.

Myself and little ones from hence
    Entrusting to your providence,
        I will securely dwell.
Tell me, however, what's to be done; for
        life is not worth living, I see,
If no method can be hit on
        for regaining our sovereignty.
Peis. First, then, there must be a city,
        built by birds and common to all;
Round the city and the suburbs
        you will enclose the air with a wall,
Ramparted with massive brickwork
        of the Babylonian sort.
Ep. Oh, Cebriones and Porphyrion![1]
        will it not be a terrible fort!
Peis. After this is finished, you will
        send a herald to Jupiter
Asking back the empire from him.
        If then he makes any demur,
Temporising or refusing,
        and does not acknowledge his wrong,
Then proclaim a holy war; for
        you at least are ready and strong.
As the Gods are in the habit of
        coming down from the upper abodes
On their feasting expeditions,
        you will refuse the use of the roads.
Then you will send another herald
        duly commissioned to let the world know
You are kings, and therefore entitled to
        all that men have been wont to bestow
Hitherto upon their sovereigns :
        you, at any rate, call for the best:
Let them, if they think it proper,
        still to the Deities offer the rest:
Pair the Gods and Birds together;
        so when Venus her dues shall take,
Let the bald coot have some barley :
        let there be some peas for the drake,

---

[1] The names of Giants engaged in the war with the Gods.

When a sheep is slain to Neptune :
    when the ox to Hercules falls,
Honied cake should go to the cormorant :
    when for his ram great Jupiter calls,
First to the wren of the golden coronet
    let them slaughter a masculine gnat.

Eu. Exquisite thought ! a gnat to be slaughtered !
    let great Jupiter thunder at that.

Ep. How should men be taught to treat us as
    Gods, not daws, as we come and we go,
Travelling through the air on pinions ?

Peis.   Nonsense, doth not Mercury so ?
Does not many a god beside him ?
    Victory flies upon golden wings :
And Love, by Jove : and Iris flew,
    ' like a timorous dove,' as Homer sings.

Ep. Will not Jupiter, in his anger,
    send among us his thundering bolts ? [1]

Peis. What if men who live below you,
    showing themselves to be nothing but dolts,
Still insist on the gods of Olympus
    and reply to your title with scorn ?
Then you will send a cloud of seed-eating
    sparrows and other birds into their corn :
And let Ceres, when they are famine-struck,
    give to her worshippers measures of grain.

Ep. Nay, she will give them reasons why she
    should from any such measures abstain.

Peis. Let the eyes of all their plough steers
    be at once pecked out by the crows ;
Likewise of their sheep ; that they may
    choose between you, as friends or as foes.
Then let Apollo descend to cure them :
    he, however, will ask for his fee.

Eu. Not till I have sold my two steers ;
    that I beg as a favour to me.

---

[1] It is observed that Peisthetærus does not reply to the question of the Epops. Because, says Wieland, he could give him no satisfaction. Reise, however, suggests what would have answered very well for an intermediate line, ' He cannot do it for the want of an eagle to carry his weapons.'

Peis. If, however, their Life, their Deity,
       they will see and honour in you,
You their Earth, their Time, their Neptune,
       then to them will all blessings accrue.
Ep. Tell me one of them.
Peis.   If, for instance,
       locusts attack the bud of the vine,
On such food a troop of buzzards
       and of owls will be happy to dine.
If the palmer-worm and the maggot
       threaten to make their figs disappear,
Send a band of thrushes among them;
       soon will the trees be thoroughly clear.
Ep. How can we contrive to enrich them,
       so that their utmost wish may be crowned ?
Peis. That you may do by indicating [1]
       where the richest mines may be found :
Merchants too may learn from the augurs
       when to make a prosperous trip ;
No more will the pilot be in
       danger of losing himself or his ship.
Ep. Pilots, how so ?
Peis.   When an augur
       is required to tell in advance,
What will be the state of the weather ;
       it will not be a matter of chance :
One of your birds will pre-instruct him—
       ' Do not think of putting to sea,
' There is such a tempest brewing,' or
       ' Sail, for you will do fortunately.'
Eu. I will buy a hoy and sail her.
       I decline to dally with you.
Peis. Then you can disclose the treasures
       hidden of old where nobody knew,
Save, as they commonly say, some ' little bird.'
Eu.   No, no. I will part with the hoy ;
I will have a spade and mattock,
       digging for urns is a better employ.

---

[1] This and following services of birds refer to the common custom of drawing auguries from the appearance or flight of birds.

Ep. How shall birds supply men's bodies with
   Health, who assuredly dwells with the Blest?

Peis. Only give them wealth in abundance;
   that they will own is health of the best.

Peis. Never at any rate is there a poor man
   whose condition is thoroughly sound.

Ep. How shall we make them attain to old age?
   that in Olympus is certainly found.
 Must they all of them die in childhood?

Peis.   You may give them three centuries more.

Ep. Where shall we get them?

Peis.   Where shall you get them?
   From your special property store.
 Do you not know that the croaking raven
   lives through five generations of ours?

Eu. How much better than Jupiter is it that
   birds should be the dominant powers!

Peis. Better!—there will be no need of building
  Temples of marble: no need of gilding
  Doors for the temples.   Gods such as these
  Will live in the bushes and holly trees.
  Birds of the highest degree will reside
  In the boughs of the olive-tree for pride.
  We shall not go for a voice divine
  To Delphi or to Ammon's shrine;
  But by the arbutus we shall stand,
  Or by the wild-olives, barley in hand,
   Making our prayer:
  At the simple cost of a handful of seed
  They will give us whatever we need
   In answer to our pious care.

Cho. Thou who once wast most detested,
   but art now the most dear of old men,
 Never can I, while I have my senses,
   dream of rejecting your counsel again.
  By your words made strong to dare,
  I have threatened and I swear,
  If you to me as I to you
  Will faithful be, guileless and true,
  And with a true intent
  Acting with one consent,

Against the Gods will go; not long
Shall they my sceptre treat with wrong.
All that must be done by mainforce
          we will be directed to do;
Yours it is to give the counsel;
          therein we depend upon you.

Ep. This is no time for sleeping, now the thing is
          planned:
Leave that to Nicias.   Do something out of hand.
Meantime I beg of you to come into my nest;
Partake my sticks and straw and feel yourself my guest.
And, if I may presume, your name, Sir?

Peis.   If you please;
My name is PEISTHETÆRUS.

Ep.   His?

Peis.   EUELPIDES.
Of THRIA.

Ep.   Welcome both.

Peis.   We thank you.

Ep.   In, I pray.

Peis. We will: show us the road.

Ep.   Go on.

Peis.   Heigh, you sir, stay.
There's this: you all have wings, but we are pinionless:
How can we live with you? 'tis more than I can guess.

Ep. Oh; easily.

Peis.   Besides, the case is monitory
Of the Eagle and the Fox, as Æsop tells the story.[1]

Ep. Nay, do not be afraid: there is a root we know,
Which, taken as a drug, will cause your wings to grow.

Peis. If so, we will go in.   Heigh! Xanthias,[2] quick,
          pack;
You, Manodorus[2] put the luggage on your back.

Cho. (*to Ep.*)   Stay, hearken, Sir.

Ep.   To what?

---

[1] The scoliast tells us no more than that this is a fable of Archilochus
and *not* of Æsop.

[2] These are common names of slaves: either two such had come
with the Athenians, or Peisthetærus addresses ideal slaves while doing
the work himself.

Cho.   Go you and entertain
The strangers handsomely; no stinting of the grain.
But, prithee, let the Muses' darling come the while,
The sweet-voiced NIGHTINGALE, our waiting to beguile.

 Peis. I join in that petition; be it kindly heard.
Grant it, by Jove, and from the thicket call the bird.
By all the Gods I beg it, call her without fail;
That we too may behold the charming NIGHTINGALE.

 Ep. You wish it?—I will not refuse in such a case.
PROCNE, come forth, and let the strangers see your face.

 Enter NIGHTINGALE (*a woman's figure with the bird's mask*).

 Peis. Oh Jupiter the honoured! what a lovely creature:
So soft, so fair, such pretty trinkets.
 Eu.   I beseech her
To let me have a kiss.
 Peis.   You blockhead; but her lips
Are like two spits.
 Eu.   But one might manage as one strips
The top shell from an egg: and so—
 Ep.   But we delay.
Let us be going.
 Peis.   Aye: and Fortune lead the way.

       [*Exeunt* EP., PEIS., EU.

PARABASIS.

Chorus (*to the Nightingale*).

   My dainty one, above
   All birds my choice for love,
   My mate, to whom belongs
   Chief part in all my songs:
   And art thou come again
   With thy enchanting strain,
   Seen in some bosky vale,
   My own, my Nightingale?
   Oh then come forth and fill
   Thy musical pipe to trill
   A spring-tide melody.
   So lead the strain with me.

        [*To the Audience.*

Listen, ye men who grope in twilight,
                clayborn structures of fictile art,
Leaves of the forest, punies, ye who
                come like shadows and so depart,
Wingless insects, born for suffering,
                men whose being is but a dream,
Listen to us, the true immortals,
                whose it is to be and not seem,
Children of air, whom age never creeps on,
                contemplators of infinite things:
Ye shall know by what we tell you,
                from their very original springs,
All about Birds and Gods and Rivers,
                of Chaos too and Erebus.
So that with this information,
                ye may take leave of Prodicus.[1]
Chaos was, and Night and Erebus;
                these with Tartarus occupied space:
All was blackness; Earth as yet nor
                Atmosphere nor Heaven had place,
In the boundless tracts of Erebus
                first did raven-pinioned Night
Lay a wind-egg; from which ripely
                Love, the charming, sprang into light.
On his back were feathered wings like   [wind.
                glistening gold and the whirls of the
Mated he with wingèd Chaos;
                hard by Tartarus nestled our kind.
We were the first born; born or ever
                brooding Love had begotten a race,
Which in their turn, with each other mating,
                bore as their progeny into space
Heaven, and Ocean, Earth and all the
                infinite Beings called divine.
Thus we are, by primogeniture,
                first in all the immortal line.

---

[1] A sophist, professor of natural philosophy: in the *Clouds*, l. 326, Aristophanes connects him with Socrates.

That we were by Love engendered
>needs for proof but very few words.
We have wings like him; but further
>what would lovers do without birds?
Mortal men for their convenience
>owe to us well-nigh everything.
First we announce to them the Seasons,
>such as Autumn, Winter, and Spring.
When the crane departs for Lybia
>then the sowing they know is to do;
Then the seaman, hanging his rudder,   [through;
>settles to sleep for the whole night
Then should they weave a coat for Orestes,[1]
>lest in the cold he be driven to steal.
Afterwards comes the kite, another
>change in the time of year to reveal;
Then from the sheep you take its spring fleece;
>after that comes the swallow to say
Sell your great coat and provide some
>dress that is fit for midsummer day.
Ammon, Delphi, and Dodona,
>Phœbus Apollo are we to you.
'What do the Birds say' is the question
>first to be answered whatever you do.
Whether it be to buy or sell: or
>earn your living or take to a wife;
Everything is 'a bird'[2] to you that
>betrays the shadow of coming life;
A phrase, a sneeze, two people meeting,
>a sound, a slave, an ass is a 'bird.'
So, that we are your prophet Apollo,
>is too clear for another word.
Take us as Gods, and for your uses
>You will have in us Prophets, Muses,

---

[1] Orestes was a noted footpad, whose ill offices are invoked by the Chorus in the *Acharnians*, l. 1032. Euelpides (466–476) has described *how* such as he provided themselves with clothing according to the season.

[2] From the usage of drawing auguries from *birds*, omens in general, from whatever source derived, passed under the general name '*bird*.'

Winter, summer, wind and weather,
To your liking altogether.
We shall not retire for state
Up to the clouds like Jove the Great:
But residing handily by you
We shall hear, and not deny you
All that you may wish to possess;
Health and wealth and happiness,
Length of days, a state of peace,
Laughter that shall never cease,
Constant feasting, dances, youth,
With milk of birds : so that in truth
　　You and your heirs
　　Shall have no cares
　　But how to live
On the very abundance of wealth we give.

Semichorus. Muse of the copse,[1]
　　Tio-tio-tio-tio-tio-tio-tinx,
Haunting with me the glade,
　　Or wooded mountain-tops,
　　Tio-tio-tio-tio-tinx,
Beneath the ash-tree's full-leaved shade,
　　Tio-tio-tio-tio.
Oft have I blended with thine my note,
Pouring the strain from my brown-feathered throat.
The Holy Mother [2] has heard with pleasure,
And Pan leapt up to the sacred measure.
　　To-to-to-to-to-to-tinx.
　　Then, like a bee
Feeding upon ambrosial meat,
Phrynichus [3] has gathered the sweet,
　　And borne away a melody.
　　Tio-tio-tio-tinx.

Cho. If now one of you, spectators,
　　　　of our life is emulous,
And desires to end his days in
　　　　comfort, let him come to us.

---

[1] Hotibius is energetic upon this ode :—' Dispeream nisi hæc a luscinia canantur.' ' Death o' me, but this is the nightingale's song ! '

[2] Cybele, or Rhea, the Mother of the Gods.

[3] Not the Tragedian, but a Lyric poet of the same name.

X

Much, that under law's provisions,
       is in bad repute with you,
Is among us birds regarded
       as the proper thing to do.
You think that to beat his father
       is disgraceful to a son;
That with *us* is thought quite decent:
       so that one of us shall run
Straight upon his father, saying,
       ' Cock your spur if you will fight.'
If a rascal slave of yours has
       earned some branding marks by flight,
He would be described among us
       as a speckled attagen;
A Phrygian slave a frygilus, and
       Execestides might then
Show his ancestors and cousins;
       while another in a scrape
Might, while law was looking for him,
       play the partridge and escape.[1]
Semicho.   So the swan sings,
       Tio-tio-tio.
     Praise to Apollo high-
Sounding, with clash of wings,
       Tio-tio-tiotinx.
     Sitting where Hebrus' streams flow by.
       Tio-tio-tio-tio,
Up, through the clouds that float in the air,
Up springs the cry. In weald and in lair
   All creatures cower; the waters lie
   Abashed beneath a breathless sky.
       To-to-to-to-totinx.

---

[1] It is just to Aristophanes to say, that these lines are but slightly rendered, because we can neither satisfactorily identify the birds, nor know the characteristics of the persons alluded to. The old commentators, in explaining the allusion to the *partridge,* ascribe to it the habit of throwing itself upon its back and covering itself with litter, when pressed by the sportsman. For Execestides, *vide* l. 4. It must be understood that the words here freely rendered by *ancestors* and *cousins* were also, like *frygilus* and *attagen,* the names of certain birds.

With awe profound
Olympus hears: the royal faces
Are darkened.   But Olympian Graces
And Muses catch the dying sound.
Tio-tio-tio-tiotinx.

Cho. Take my word, I do assure you
            that of all the handy things,
Nothing would be half so pleasant
            as to grow a pair of wings.
Just suppose that one of you had
            such appendages as these,
When he comes to see and hear the
            chorus in the tragedies;
When his interest was failing,
            and his hunger getting keen,
Would he not his wings expanding
            take a hop and leave the scene?
Presently refreshed with luncheon
            we should have him dropping in,
In the very nick of time to
            see the comedy begin.
Nothing can exceed their value:
            there's Diotrephes in sight,
Who had only wicker bottles [1]
            to assist him in his flight;
See how he has mounted with them;
            first he was an overseer,
Then a captain; now he is the
            loudest-crowing chanticleer.

PEISTHETÆRUS *and* EUELPIDES, *with wings*: EPOPS.

Peis. (*amused at the appearance of* EUEL.) And is it come
            to this! excuse me, on my word,
I never saw a thing so utterly absurd.

Eu. What are you laughing at?

Peis.   Your wings.   Have you a notion
What you are like with your new instruments of motion?

---

[1] A reference to the trade by which Diotrephes had made his fortune.

Just like a limner's goose, drawn at the cheapest rate.

 Eu. And you are like a blackbird bald about the pate.

 Peis. If so they sketch us, 'tis, as said by Æschylus,

' Not other's feathers, but our own,'[1] have marred us thus.

 Ep. But come, what shall we do ?

 Peis.   First we should take in hand

To find a name for our new city, something grand :

Then we should offer sacrifice.

 Eu.   I think the same.

 Ep. Well said : consider what shall be the city's name.

 Peis. What say you then to *Sparta* as a name of dread ?

 Eu. Broom-string ![2] I would not use it for a truckle
  bed.

 Peis. What shall it be ?

 Eu.   It should, in altitudes so rare

Of clouds and meteors, be something—with an air.

 Peis. What think you of HIGH-CUCKOOBURY ?

 Ep.   Capital !

An admirable hit, and dignified withal.

 Eu. HIGH-CUCKOOBURY, where Theagenes holds fees,

And where lie those estates talked of by Æschines.

Is it not so ?

 Peis.   Nay more : 'tis that Phlegræan field

Where braggart Gods compelled the Sons of Earth to yield.[3]

 Eu. A jewel of a city.   What God shall we choose

To be its guardian ? and the woven veil [4] be whose ?

 Peis. Minerva Polias ? why not ?

 Eu.   'Twould be a pity :

How shall it ever be a well-conducted city,

Whose God, a woman born, prefers to stand at ease

In arms, and leaves the woman's work to Cleisthenes ?[5]

---

[1] Æschylus, referring it to an old Lybian fable, has expressed the well-known image of an eagle wounded by an arrow feathered from its own wing.

[2] Unless there is corruption of the text, there seems to be here a laboured and ineffective play upon the meaning of the word ' Sparta ' as a rope made of the broom-shrub.

[3] Not only as imaginary as the ' estates ' of those men, but as the Wars of the Gods with the Giants.

[4] See note, *Knights,* l. 526.

[5] See *Clouds,* l. 320.

Peis. But who shall have the charge to guard the
citadel ?

Ep. That will a bird of ours do marvellously well,
Of Persian family and very high repute,
The very chick of Mars.[1]

Eu. The lordly chick will suit ;
He is the very God to stand upon a wall.

Peis. But come, to business ; go, as I appoint you all.
Do you, EUELPIDES, go out into the air,
Fly to the battlements and help the workers there ;
Bring limestone, strip and stir the mortar, see 'tis thick,
Fall from the ladder, pick the bucket up ; be quick ;
Tell off and set the guards ; don't let a fire be seen ;
Run round and ring a bell, and drop asleep between.
Select a herald for the Gods and let him go :
Despatch another to the men that live below :
And then come back to me.

Eu. (*in manner declining to go*). And you the while shall
stay,

With—my best wishes !

Peis. My good fellow, go I pray,
For else I shall get nothing done. For, myself, I
Must sacrifice to these new deities and try
To find a priest who can a good procession group.

[*Exit* EUELPIDES.

Here, boy, take up the basket ; you, bring on the stoup.

Chorus. I am thoroughly with you,
Quite approving all you do.
Costly acts and splendid sights
Be our novel worship rites.
Also let a sheep be slain
For Gratitude. In joyful strain
High let the Pythian hymn ascend,
And Chæris with his pipe attend.

---

[1] The Cock.

Enter a PIPER (*who, having the mask of a raven and the leather mouthpiece then used by pipers, begins an air*); *and
a* PRIEST.

   Peis. You sir, stop blowing.   Hercules! what have we
     now?
I have seen many things and odd, but I allow
Never a raven with a leather on his chin!
   Ep. Attend your duty, Priest.   Let sacrifice begin.
   Priest. I will:—but let the basket-bearer come this way.
            So let us pray
        To Vesta of the painted feather,
          And to the Kite with guardian pens,
        To all Olympian Birds together,
          Both cocks and hens.
   Cho.   King of Pelargus, Sun-hawk, hail.
   Priest.   Unto Latona-Quail,
        To Swan the Pythian,
        And Goldfinch-Artemis,
        To Ostrich too, who is
        Mother of Gods and man.
   Cho.   Grant, Ostrich, mother of Cleocritus,
        Unto the HIGH-CUCKOOBURIANS health
        And abundance of wealth,
      And to the Chians with us.
   Peis.   I'm glad the Chians have a share.
   Priest.   To all heroic birds and their
        Descendants: to the Pelican,
       'The Dodo and the Cassowary,
        The Albatross and Ptarmigan,
        Caper-cailzie and Canary,
        Peacock, Buzzard, Cockatoo [1]—
   Peis. Off to the crows, man: that will do.
What need to call the eagles, vultures, all the lot
To dine upon the paltry victim we have got?
One kite would stoop and make the whole affair his own:
Off with your fillets; I will sacrifice alone.

---

  [1] The translator pleads the difficulty of a more exact rendering of this
litany into metre, and allows that he may not be scientifically correct in
identifying the birds named with those expressed by Aristophanes.

Priest.   Nay, pardon me, but stop,
              Just from the ewer's brim
         I'll sprinkle but a drop
              And sing a second hymn.
              It shall be rightly done ;
              I'll bid unto the feast
              The blessed ;—if at least
                   There is enough for—one !
              But that is to be feared ;
              The sacrifice is nothing now
                   But horns and beard.

Peis. Hear, winged Gods : to you we offer thus and vow—

Enter POET.

Poet. In strains to such a lofty subject due
              Sing, O Muse, HIGH-CUCKOOBURY :
              City of the free and merry—

Peis. Heigh !—what have we got here ?—and pray sir,
who are you ?

Poet. One whose lips distil the honey-drops of song,
              One who waits upon the Muses
              Constantly,—as Homer uses.

Peis. Methinks that for a slave your hair is rather long.

Poet. Not so : but all we singers of sweet lays
              Are busy servants of the Muses,
              For Homer that expression uses.

Peis. Your livery has done its work in better days.
But in the name of lunacy what brought you here ?

Poet. Something of verses; pretty things as will appear,
About HIGH-CUCKOOBURY : a dithyrambic strain,
For women's voices, in Simonides's vein.

Peis. Pray when did you compose the verses ?

Poet.   Long since, long,
This famous city was the subject of my song.

Peis. But was I not about its Tenth-Day [1] as you came
And have but even now given the babe a name.

Poet. Fame, with the Muses, flies far and is fleet
              As the twinkling of the courser's feet.

---

[1] 'Tenth-day' after birth was fixed by custom for giving the new-born
a name : it was of course a family festival.

Ætna's founder! Sire of kings
Co-titled with divinest things,[1]
A boon, a boon for me
According to thy high estate
And worthiness commensurate—
A boon becoming me and thee.

Peis. This nuisance will increase, unless we make a shift
To purchase his retirement with some sort of gift.
You sir, you have a cloak and coat; without more fuss
Strip off the cloak and give it to this Genius.
Accept the cloak; you seem to feel the cold to-day.

Poet.   Not all unwillingly the Muse
This gift from thee will take and use.
But let this verse of Pindar reach
Thy inner mind with power to teach—

Peis. The man seems not disposed to take himself away.

Poet.   Among the nomad Scythians straying
Was Strato, unpossessed
Of woven garment, like the rest;
For glory-less was cloak of skin
Unless he had a coat within.
You understand what I am saying?

Peis. I understand you want the little coat.   Strip you,
And give it up, to let the Poet have his due.
—Now, take it and retire.

Poet.   I will; and as I go
In lyric measure will I praise your city, so—
Oh, Golden-throned,[2] the frosty air
Whereto I came—hah! hah!
Snow-smitten plains, with harvests fair
Make known to fame.   Hurrah!

                                    [*Exit* POET.

Peis. By Jupiter, you have at last escaped the frost;
And we are rid of you, but at the jacket's cost.

---

[1] These lines are from Pindar, and refer to Hieron; his name admits the play upon the word ἱερῶν—'sacred things.' As introduced here they are mere fustian, as intended no doubt. Probably Aristophanes in this place did not mean so much to parody the lyric poets, as to attribute to his ' Poet' impudent plagiarism.

[2] That is, Apollo.

I did not think to have that sort of bore appear,
Or that our city's fame so soon would reach his ear.
(*To the Priest.*)
But go you round the altar, sprinkle it again.
   Priest. Be silent every one!

Enter TEXTUARY.[1]

   Text.   Touch not the goat, refrain.
   Peis. And who are you?
   Text.   One who makes it his care to know
What things to come have been revealed.
   Peis.   Be hanged, sir; go.
   Text. Nay treat not holy things so loosely.   You may
       learn—
'Tis here, in Bacis,—things that obviously concern
HIGH-CUCKOOBURY.
   Peis.   Why then was it not propounded
Before the city was by my endeavour founded?
   Text. Divine restraint was on me.
   Peis.   Now at any rate
Tell me what fortune you for us vaticinate.
      𝔚𝔥𝔢𝔫 𝔚𝔬𝔩𝔟𝔢𝔰 𝔪𝔢𝔢𝔱 𝔥𝔬𝔞𝔯𝔶 𝔕𝔞𝔟𝔢𝔫𝔰 𝔞𝔫𝔡 𝔟𝔢𝔱𝔴𝔢𝔢𝔫
      𝔊𝔬𝔯𝔦𝔫𝔱𝔥 𝔞𝔫𝔡 𝔖𝔦𝔠𝔶𝔬𝔫 𝔱𝔬 𝔡𝔴𝔢𝔩𝔩 𝔞𝔯𝔢 𝔰𝔢𝔢𝔫—

   Peis. But what have I to do with Corinth?
   Text.   Riddlewise,
Clearly it is the Air which Bacis signifies.
      𝔉𝔦𝔯𝔰𝔱 𝔞𝔱 𝔓𝔞𝔫𝔡𝔬𝔯𝔞'𝔰 𝔞𝔩𝔱𝔞𝔯 𝔱𝔥𝔢𝔶 𝔰𝔥𝔞𝔩𝔩 𝔰𝔩𝔞𝔶
      𝔄 𝔴𝔥𝔦𝔱𝔢-𝔴𝔬𝔬𝔩𝔩𝔢𝔡 𝔕𝔞𝔪.   𝔄𝔫𝔡 𝔴𝔥𝔬𝔰𝔬 𝔦𝔫 𝔱𝔥𝔞𝔱 𝔡𝔞𝔶
      𝔖𝔥𝔞𝔩𝔩 𝔟𝔢 𝔪𝔶 𝔭𝔯𝔬𝔭𝔥𝔢𝔱 𝔞𝔫𝔡 𝔞𝔫𝔫𝔬𝔲𝔫𝔠𝔢 𝔱𝔥𝔦𝔰 𝔫𝔢𝔴𝔰
      𝔖𝔥𝔞𝔩𝔩 𝔥𝔞𝔟𝔢 𝔠𝔩𝔢𝔞𝔫 𝔩𝔦𝔫𝔢𝔫 𝔞𝔫𝔡 𝔞 𝔭𝔞𝔦𝔯 𝔬𝔣 𝔰𝔥𝔬𝔢𝔰.
   Peis. Are the shoes really in the writing?
   Text.   Take the book.
      𝔅𝔢𝔰𝔦𝔡𝔢𝔰 𝔱𝔥𝔢 𝔠𝔲𝔭 𝔞𝔫𝔡 𝔢𝔫𝔱𝔯𝔞𝔦𝔩𝔰 𝔦𝔫 𝔥𝔦𝔰 𝔥𝔞𝔫𝔡.
   Peis. The entrails—are they there?
   Text.   Pray take the text and look.

---

[1] We seem to have no word which describes the quality of this person. He is not a 'prophet;' because he pretends to no personal inspiration. Probably many collections of 'Oracles' were current. Such persons as the man now brought on to the stage made it their business to study these *revelations,* and were thus prepared to produce texts apposite to any occasion.

> If, favoured youth, thou dost as I command
> Thou shalt become an Eagle in the sky:
> But otherwise nor Eagle, Dove, nor Pie.

Peis. Is that there?

Text.   Take the book.

Peis.   These words, although divine,
Differ from some which *I* brought from Apollo's shrine.

> But when a man whom nobody invites
> Shall thrust himself upon your sacred rites,
> And ask for entrails; let the coxcomb take
> A buffet which shall cause his ribs to ache.

Text. For shame, you are but trifling.

Peis.   Pray you take the book.

> Nought for the Eagle in the sky abate
> To Lampon, or Diopithes, though he be 'the Great.'

Text. Is that there?

Peis.   Take the text.   Well, if you will not look,
Out to the crows, you vagabond.   [*Beats him.*

Text.   Oh spare me, spare—
                                   [*Runs out.*

Peis. Be off and favour others with your sacred ware.

Enter METON, *the Geometrician, with instruments.*

Met. I'm come among you—

Peis.   What? another pestilence?
What may your business be? Aye, what is your pretence?
What scheme have you? what boot has carried you this
     way?

Met. I wish to make a geometrical survey
Of air and to lay out enclosures in the sky.

Peis. Do tell me, by the Gods, who are you?

Met.   Who am I?
I'm METON, known in Greece, aye at Colonus too.

Peis. Now tell me, what are these things? what are
     they to do?

Met. Air-metres: for the air being in its extent
Most like an oven, I apply this instrument,—
You see its curve—setting, as is my wont,
The great dividers thus—you understand?

Peis.   I don't.

Met. Aye, thus I find a line, and when I let it fall,
Your circle is a square, and in the midst of all
There is the market-place ; the roads, you see, all run
Straight to the centre, like the rays about the sun.
Peis. The man's a Thales ?—METON.
Met.   What ?
Peis.   I am your friend ;
Believe me ; 'tis advice on which you may depend.
Met. Eh ? what's the matter ?
Peis.   As in Lacedæmon, here
They drive out foreigners.   Already as I fear
Blows must be stirring in the city ;—
Met.   What ? sedition ?
Peis. Oh no, not that.
Met.   What then ?
Peis.   A common disposition
To dress all coxcombs' jackets.
Met.   Jove ! I will not stay.
Peis. I hardly know if you have time to get away ;
They are upon you.   [*Beats him.*
Met.   Oh !   [*Exit.*
Peis.   I told you to prepare ;
Now go ; and take the measure of yourself elsewhere.

Enter POLITICAL AGENT.

Pol. Ag. Where are my hosts ? [1]
Peis.   Sardanapalus, who are you ?
Pol. I come, so named and ordered in assembly due,
As Agent to HIGH-CUCKOOBURY.
Peis.   Agent? so !
Who sent you here ?
Pol. (*Showing a paper*).   This sorry little scroll may
            show :
The words are Teleas's.

---

[1] The principal states of Greece were in the habit of sending political
agents to small cities and new settlements over which they arrogated any
political supremacy.   The business of these was to meddle with and
manage the internal policy of the place so as to make it subserve the
interests of the so-called mother state.   In all towns there would be
'proxeni,' 'public hosts,' whose business it was to entertain these officers,
or other persons of distinction having a public character.

Peis. (*confidentially*).   If you take your price,
You will feel free to go?
    Pol.   That would be very nice:
For, truth to say, I should take part in the debate;
For I have been engaged with Pharnaces [1] of late.
    Peis. (*beating him*).
Take your deserts and go.   You shall have double fees.
    Pol. What's this?
    Peis.   The payment for your speech on Pharnaces.
    Pol. I testify you use a Functionary thus.
    Peis. You and your voting ware [2] be off:—'tis scandalous;
They send their officers to meddle here, before
The city yet has served the Gods it will adore.

Enter DECREE-DEALER. [3]

    Deal.   'If a High-Cuckooburian shall do amiss
      To an Athenian'—

    Peis.   What villain scroll is this?
    Deal. I am a dealer in decrees, and come this way
To sell you the new laws.
    Peis.   'New laws,' eh? what are they?
    Deal.   High-Cuckooburians, it is hereby decreed,
      Shall use the weights and measures, and in law proceed
      As hath been duly ordered for the Olophyxians.

    Peis. And you—will have the measure of the Ototyxians. [4]
                             [*Beats him.*

    Deal. Heigh! what's the matter now?
    Peis.   Off with your litter; pack:
I'll give you laws indeed to carry on your back.
    Pol. Ag. I summon Peisthetærus at Munychion [5]
For insult.

---

[1] A Persian satrap with whom the citizen has been secretly intriguing.
[2] He had brought with him urns for collecting the votes in a popular assembly.
[3] This man's business was to copy out and sell the latest decrees of the People.
[4] Olophyxus, really the name of a town in Thrace: the parody upon it is formed on the sound 'ototoi,' an expression of grief used by Æschylus.
[5] A form of summons for the first court-day in the month of this name at Athens.

Peis. Ha! you rogue, I thought that you were gone.

Deal. 𝔦𝔣 𝔞𝔫𝔶 𝔬𝔫𝔢 𝔟𝔶 𝔣𝔬𝔯𝔠𝔢 𝔢𝔵𝔭𝔢𝔩 𝔞 𝔐𝔞𝔤𝔦𝔰𝔱𝔯𝔞𝔱𝔢,
𝔒𝔯 𝔬𝔟𝔢𝔯𝔱𝔩𝔶 𝔯𝔢𝔣𝔲𝔰𝔢 𝔱𝔬 𝔱𝔞𝔨𝔢 𝔞𝔫𝔡 𝔯𝔢𝔦𝔫𝔰𝔱𝔞𝔱𝔢
𝔄𝔠𝔠𝔬𝔯𝔡𝔦𝔫𝔤 𝔱𝔬 𝔠𝔬𝔫𝔳𝔢𝔫𝔱𝔦𝔬𝔫 𝔡𝔲𝔩𝔶 𝔰𝔢𝔱𝔱𝔩𝔢𝔡, 𝔰𝔦𝔤𝔫𝔢𝔡
𝔄𝔫𝔡 𝔭𝔬𝔰𝔱𝔢𝔡—

Peis. Vagabond, have you remained behind?

Pol. Ag. You will be ruined by the fine you'll have to pay.

Peis. Ha! ha! seize me the rogue: a minute, villain, stay.

[*The Chorus threatening an attack, the two
officers run off.*

Priest. Let us remove and find a corner more remote
Where we may serve our Gods and sacrifice the goat.

[*Exeunt.*

Semicho. Soon to me, the All-surveyor,
All-disposer, will all people
Offer sacrifice with prayer;
For I see all the earth, and keep all.
Guardian of the growing fruit,
I am on the watch to slay,
In the bud and in the shoot,
All the thousand tribes that prey
On gardens sweet with fruit and flower,
Greedier growing while they devour.
. And erst with battling wing,
I stoop from the sky
On venomous beast and creeping thing;
And they too die.

Chorus. You have heard a talent offered
by the city to the man
Who will knock upon the head
Diagoras [1] the Melian;
Likewise whoso kills a tyrant
(though he be already dead),
He shall have a talent also:
so the proclamation said.

---

[1] See notes, *Clouds*, ll. 716, 1126. Diagoras was an object of popular
hatred on account of his rejection of the mythical Deities. Perhaps the
proclamation against the old 'tyrants' was rather in the nature of an old
form gratifying to the self-respect of the populace.

Now do we proclaim it further,
  whoso kills Philocrates [1]
Shall receive a single talent;
  four however if he seize
And bring him living. He's the man who
  strings the finches in a row
And retails them seven a penny:
  further he is known to blow [2]
Thrushes in a shameful manner:
  also when the villain kills
Blackbirds he will dress their noses,
  putting feathers in their bills.
What is more, he catches pigeons,
  and his prisoners employs,
Fastened well in cunning nets, to
  act on others as decoys.
So we set this price upon him.
  Furthermore be warned and know
If you have got birds in cages,
  you at once shall let them go.
Otherwise we birds will catch you
  unawares, and you shall learn
What it is to be entrapped and
  made decoys of in your turn.

Semicho. Happy race of birds in feathers!
  We need not a cloak's assistance
  In the most severe of weathers.
  Us no ray shot from the distance
  Scorches in the summer-tide;
  When the fields are green and gay
  Bosomed in the leaves I hide:
  While the cricket shrills his lay
  Glorying in the midsummer heat.
  Then in winter I find a retreat
  With nymphs and spend the hours
  In merry-making
  Till forth with the Graces among the flowers
  I fly in the spring.

---

[1] The poulterer and bird-dealer mentioned l. 13.
[2] Probably a poulterer's artifice to make the birds look plump.

Cho. We would have the judges know what
    they will have if they are wise,
 And in this day's competition,
    they assign to us the prize.
Better gifts than Alexander [1]
    from the Goddesses could boast
Shall they have ; for every judge shall
    have what he will value most,
Laureatic owls [2] in plenty.
    In your purses they shall dwell,
Make their nests, and lay their eggs, and
    silver small-change chip.the shell.
In your houses you shall live at
    large, as do the Gods or kings ;
For when you construct your mansion,
    we will surely add the wings.[3]
When you have secured an office
    and are anxious to make of it
Something more to your advantage
    than the regulation profit,
We will send a little falcon,
    light of wing and keen of eye,
Not a tittle will he let go
    unappropriated by.
Lastly, when you feel at supper
    almost driven to a stop,
Courage ! and begin again, for
    we will furnish you a crop.

Enter PEISTHETÆRUS.

Peis. Our sacrifices, Birds, have had complete success;
But no one from the wall—and why I cannot guess—

---

[1] Otherwise ' Paris ; ' with reference to the rewards offered to him by
the three Goddesses when he was to assign the primacy of beauty among
them.

[2] Many of the silver coins of Attica bear the characteristic Owl of
Minerva. The silver was obtained from the rich mines of Mount Laurium
in Attica.

[3] This is not a *true* rendering of the idea of the original, which is ' we
will roof it to the eagle '—understood to be a sort of pinnacle.

Is come to tell us how that business is proceeding.
But ha ! I see—here comes one out of breath with speeding.

Enter MESSENGER.

 Mess. Where's PEIS—oh, ho, where, where's—PE-
  PEISTH—oh, where's—oh dear !
Where's PEISTHETÆRUS ? where's the governor ?
 Peis.   I'm here.
 Mess. Your wall's completely built.
 Peis.   .   That's well.
 Mess.   ·The work is splendid ;
Indeed, magnificent !—the breadth is so extended
That on the top Proxenides of Brag might meet
And pass Theagenes, horses and cars complete ;
And each horse like the Trojan !
 Peis.   Hercules ! the strength !
 Mess. Aye, and a hundred fathoms good it is in length ;
For I have measured it.
 Peis.   Oh, Neptune ! what a wall !
And who constructed it ?
 Mess.   The Birds have done it all.
They did not fetch from Egypt men to make the bricks,
Or masons to cut stones, or artisans to fix.
'Twas all done by themselves to my astonishment.
With stones for the foundation Lybia had sent
Her thirty thousand cranes ; [1] the bitterns then received
And dressed them with their beaks ; ten thousand storks
  upheaved
The clay for bricks ; moor-hens with water came and went,
With other river-birds.
 Peis.   But who brought the cement ?
 Mess. Herons, in bowls.

---

[1] Before making their long migratory flight the cranes were believed
to load themselves with stones by swallowing them, as is here expressed
in the original. To what purpose the stones ? A scoliast tells us. 'As
the cranes fly high and straight they could not well see what was below
them ; land, or water ? So when they wish to rest they drop a stone ; if
it falls upon the sea they must continue their flight, but if it strikes land
they may come down.'

Peis.   But how did they contrive to fill
The bowls with mud?

Mess.   'Twas done with admirable skill:
The geese, using their feet for shovels, backward struck
Mud to the bowls.

Peis.   What mayn't be done with feet!

Mess.   The duck,
Tucking her skirts within her girdle, found the knack
Of taking loads of bricks, like ducklings, on her back.[1]

Peis. So much for journeymen! hence, why should they
            be hired?
But say, who did the timber-work that was required?

Mess. Those clever carpenters the pelicans [2] did all.
To hear the noise you'd think it was an arsenal.
So all the circuit now is furnished with its gates;
And all the gates are barred; at each a warder waits.
Sentries are set and bells are rung at stated hours;
And birds to light the beacons sit upon the towers.
But I am so befouled with dust that I must run
And wash myself.   Do you see what is to be done.

                                [*Exit* MESSENGER.

Chorus (*to* PEIS. *in reverie*). You, Sir, what are you doing?
            Are you so amazed
At finding that the wall has been so quickly raised?

Peis. Aye, by the Gods I am. And well I may; for why?
The whole of the report appears to me a lie.
But see, here comes a sentry hitherward advancing
With speed and heat, as though he had been weapon-
            dancing.

            Enter 2nd MESSENGER.

Mess. Ho-ho! ho-ho! ho-ho!

Peis.   Is any news astir?

---

[1] The translator does not undertake to justify to a scholar the rendering
of these lines: he waits for light as to their real sense. The appreciative
taste of Brunck is followed in rejecting the line about the 'swallows.'
It wants the humour of broad absurdity that characterises all the other
assignments of work.

[2] The Greek gives an opportunity for pun between 'pelican' and
'hewing.'

                            Y

Mess. A very grievous thing: some God from Jupiter,
Before the jackdaws on the ramparts were aware,
Slipped through the city gates, and fled into the air.
    Peis. 'Tis an ill deed.   Which of the Gods?
    Mess.   We do not know;
But he had wings, 'tis certain.
    Peis.   Why were you so slow
In sending followers after?
    Mess.   Nay, we sent a rout:
Some thirty thousand hawks, horse-archers, are gone out.
And falcons, vultures, eagles, are upon the fret;
Kestrels and buzzards all, they have their talons set;
And all the air is sounding with the rush of wings.
It is not far from here.
    Peis.   Then we should have our slings
And bows.   Let every one go out immediately;
Shoot at him; spare him not: and bring a sling to me.
    Chorus.   The deed is done:
               War is begun,
               A war unheard,
               'Twixt God and Bird.
               Watch each with care
               The clouded air,
               The child, like us,
               Of Erebus;
               Lest, ere you spy,
               Some God slip by.
        Look sharply all the circuit round:
        For hark! I hear a whirring sound,
      As of a Deity on rushing wings not far.
    Peis. Heigh, madam! stop! where are you off?   Stop
        where you are.
Stand still.

Enter IRIS.

    Who are you? you must say; and whence you came?
    Iris. From the Olympian Gods came I.
    Peis.   And what's your name?
Helmet or Ship?[1]

----

[1] Because of her wings and feathers, he affects to take her for a sailing
ship—the Salaminian or Paralus, or a feathered helmet.

Iris.　　　　　　　　Swift IRIS.

Peis.　　　　　　　　　　Salaminian
Or Paralus?

Iris.　　What's this? (*spreading her wings to rise again.*)

Peis.　　　　　　　Heigh! let some bird who can,
Some buzzard, apprehend her.

Iris.　　　　　　　　　Say you 'apprehend'?
Apprehend me?—What's this? and whereto does it tend?

Peis. Towards grief for you.

Iris.　　　　　　　This is some great absurdity.

Peis. By which gates did you enter? baggage, answer me.

Iris. By Jove, I do not know. How should I know your
　　　gates?

Peis. There! you are witnesses how she prevaricates.
Did you request the daws to let you through the line?
Will you not answer? did the storks give you the sign?

Iris. What stuff is this?

Peis.　　　　　　You had no leave.

Iris.　　　　　　　　Are you not cracked?

Peis. No officer gave you the countersign in fact.

Iris. To me?—No.

Peis.　　　　　Then you fly in silence and defiance
Through Chaos and a city not in your alliance?

Iris. What other way is open for the Gods to go?

Peis. That is not my affair; I don't pretend to know;
You do not go by this. You trespass here to-day:
And were you twenty thousand Irises should pay
The penalty of death.

Iris.　　　　　　But I'm immortal.

Peis.　　　　　　　　　Pooh!
Death is, I say, the proper penalty for you.
A very grievous thing to bear it would be, truly,
If others should obey, but you Gods be unruly.
You must be taught to know your betters, and obey.
And where might you be piloting your wings, I pray?

Iris. I?—I am bearing down to men my father's will
That they should do high service to the Gods, and kill
Oxen and sheep, and let the savour, thick and rich,
Fill all the streets.

Peis.　　　　　　To which Gods do you mean?

Y 2

Iris.   To which?
To us, the Gods in heaven.

    Peis.   But are you Gods indeed?

    Iris. Pray, then, who else is God?

    Peis.   The BIRDS have now agreed
To be the Gods of men; and men it will behove
To sacrifice to them: by Jove, and not to Jove.

    Iris. Fool! fool! Beware thou stirr'st the Gods' most
              dreadful ire,
And Jove's just mattock should evert thy race; and fire
Should lap thee and thy houses in Licymnian flashes,
Leaving of thee alone a blackened heap of ashes.

    Peis. Hear you: allay these ebullitions: pray be quiet.
Am I a Lydian or a Phrygian slave [1] to fly at,
And terrify with bugbears? Think it not. But learn,
If Jupiter dares trouble me, that I will burn
By my fire-bearing eagles his high walls of pride
And houses of Amphion. I will send beside,
Porphyrion [2] birds, more than six hundred strong,
All clothed in leopard-skins. The time is not so long
But he can well remember one Porphyrion,
And what it cost him ere a stubborn fight was won.

    Iris. Wretch! perish with your words.

    Peis.   Off, off with you: despatch:
Quick, presto.

    Iris.   In my father you will find a match.

    Peis. Ah! bah! Be off, and wing it while you may and
           can;
Go play the trick of 'ashes' on some younger man.

                       [*Exit* IRIS.

   Chorus.   We do hereby
                    Henceforth deny
                    To Gods above,
                    The sons of Jove,
                    All right of road
                    Through our abode.

---

[1] Parodied from the *Alcestis* of Euripides.

[2] Here again is use made of the name of a bird, perhaps one of the Heron tribe, as identical with that of the Giant.

And disallow
All smoke or vow,
By mortals sent,
A passage through our firmament.
Peis. 'Tis strange that herald whom we sent to men
Has not come back.   Surely he will return again.

Enter HERALD, *returning from Men.*

Her. Oh, blessed PEISTHETÆRUS, wisest, cleverest,
Choice spirit, famous man, most blessed of the blest,—
Bid me go on.
 Peis.   What would you say ?
 Her.   This golden crown
All people send thee for thy wisdom's great renown.
 Peis. I take it : but from whence does all this praise
  arise ?
Her. Oh, founder of the famous city of the skies,
You know not then the honour you of men have got ;
And what devoted love is centred on this spot.
Before you founded this community men were
All Lacomaniacs ;[1] they chose to wear long hair,
To go without their meals, to carry scytales,
To dread the touch of soap as much as Socrates.
The fashion now is changed, it really is absurd,
For everybody's pleasure is to be a bird.
From bed the citizen at early morn resorts,
Like sparrows, to pick up the crumbs about the courts :[2]
The cause-list is his field on which he hunts for prey,
And finding verdicts gives employment for the day.
So far the crazy fancy runs that they will take
Their names from us : they have their Wren, and Hawke,
  and Drake,

---

[1] Other writers have noticed that there was at one time in Athens a fashion, a mania for imitating Spartan habits.

[2] It is not always possible to find equivalents for word-plays.   In the Greek the same word stands for 'feeding-ground' and 'law'; this gives Aristophanes his opportunity to make his usual stroke at the pleasure and profit which Athenians drew from the law-courts.

Their Martin, Swift, and Partridge, Coote and Jay, and
 Crowe,
Finch, Peacock, Pigeons, plenty, and a Gull I know.[1]
Then, all the songs that are in fashionable use
Have something of a ' Swallow,' ' Dove,' or ' Duck,' or
 ' Goose,'
Or ' wings,' or touch at least of ' feather,' for adorning.
Such is the state of things, but you should have this
 warning ;
We very soon shall have ten thousand of our friends
Desiring wings, or talons at their fingers' ends,
That they may be as vultures.   So you must provide
A store of wings for those who come here to reside.
 Peis. By Jupiter this is no time for standing still.
Go with all speed and fetch me baskets here, and fill
The hampers too with wings: and let a slave stand by
To hand them to me while all comers I supply.

 Cho. Our city soon is like to be,
   As men say, multitudinous.
 Peis. Only let Fortune prosper us.
 Cho. They yearn toward our community.
 Peis. Haste, will ye not obey my orders ?
 Cho. The man who dwells within our borders
   What is there not to bless !
   With wisdom, love, ambrosial graces
   And quietness, on whose calm face is
   The beam of happiness.
 Peis. (*to slave.*) How sluggishly you serve your master :
   Do try to move a little faster.[2]
 Cho. Let some one fetch these feather-cases.
   I pray you stir the man to go :
   Give him a handsome buffet—so.
   He is a donkey in his paces.

---

[1] The idea in these lines has been adapted rather than translated. In
the original the bird-names are nick-names, by which persons were
already known to the audience, or which are here offered to them by
Aristophanes.

[2] It should be remembered that these lyrics were the accompaniment
of a dance movement, on the comic effect of which it may be that the
dramatist here relies.

Peis.　Ah, Manes is a coward slave.

Cho.　Do you lay out the wings you have
　　　　According to a plan;
　　　　Poetic here, prophetic there;
　　　　Sea-wings apart, that each may wear
　　　　Just what becomes the man.

Peis.　By all the screech-owls! you shall pay
　　　　For creeping in this lazy way.

FATHER-BEATER (*heard singing before he enters*).

F.-B.　Oh give me but to soar
　　　　An Eagle, high and free,
　　　　Above the surge and roar
　　　　Of the blue and barren sea.

Peis. 'Twas nothing but the truth we heard the herald
　　say,
For here comes one who sings of Eagles on the way.

Enter FATHER-BEATER.

F.-B. There would be nothing half so pleasant as to
　　fly;
With all my heart I long the life of birds to try;
I feel quite flighty, having such desires to be
Admitted to the laws of your community.

　　Peis. What laws? the Birds have many.

　　F.-B.　　　　　　　　　　　All of them: but one
Especially I long for: that which gives a son
The right to choke or peck his father; since, in fact,
To kill him is with you an honourable act.

　　Peis. By Jupiter, we think it quite a manly trick
For one to beat his father, being but a chick.[1]

　　F.-B. 'Tis that which brings me here: I wish to suf-
　　focate
My father and possess the whole of the estate.

　　Peis. But there's a law amongst the Birds in high repute,
The tables of the storks preserve the institute,
Enjoining them, that, when the father on his side
The early wants of all the storklings has supplied

---

[1] Cockfighting was a favourite amusement with Athenians.

Till they can fly alone, they shall requite in kind,
And thenceforth the old father's maintenance shall find.

F.-B. By Jupiter, my journey here will prove a rather
Too costly pleasure, if I must maintain my father.

Peis. Oh not at all: for, since you came with kind
          intent,
I will receive you as an orphan; and present
A feathered gift to you; with this advice, (not bad
Though nothing new, for I received it when a lad)
' Do not ill treat your father.'—Take now for a shield
The wing of this brave cock, and let your right hand wield
This spur; suppose yourself to have that warrior's crest.
Now go, make marches, keep the guard, and do your best
To live upon your pay.   Since wars with you agree,
Fly off to Thrace and fight; and let your father be.

F.-B. By Bacchus you say well: and frankly I defer
To your good counsel.

Peis.   Wisely done, by Jupiter.
                              [*Exit* FATHER-BEATER.

          Enter CINESIAS, *the Dithyrambic Poet.*

Cin.   Up to Olympus flying
          On wings, light wings; and melodies
          Now one and now another trying.

Peis. This will require a load of wings to make it rise.

Cin.   I venture all,
          And fear nor weariness nor fall.

Peis. We bid Cinesias, the linden-wand,[1] good cheer:
But wherefore has your lame leg circled to our sphere?

Cin.   It is because I long
          To be a nightingale of thrilling song.

Peis. A truce with poetry, and tell me what you mean.

Cin. Oh give me wings, that bathing in the silvery
          sheen
Of clouds, I may catch preludes quivering with the air
And snow-tipped.

---

[1] We have no choice but to accept the explanation of this epithet
given by Athenæus. Cinesias being very slender supported the weakness
of his body by a wand or board of linden-wood. He was not really
' lame,' so the imputation is to be carried to the account of his verses.

Peis.   From the clouds? do men get preludes there?
Cin. The secret of our art is there. Our strains are
    light,
The very substance of the air, and dark as night,
The purple of a cloud, the quivering of a wing:
For such are dithyrambs. But you shall hear me sing.
Peis. Not I, I prithee. No.
Cin.   You shall by Hercules.
    I'll trip it, for you, through the air with ease,
    The forms of winged ones, the ether-specks,
    Far stretching their delicate necks—
Peis. Hoop!
Cin.   And anon would I cut the seas,
    Borne by the breath of the breeze—
Peis. By Jove, I'll stop your breath.
Cin.   My body southward steered,
    The keelless vessel flies;
    Now suddenly to northward veered
    Furrows the harbourless skies.   ·
A charming thing, old man, and daintily delivered.
Peis. But you will not be charmed when you are feather-
    quivered.
       [*Buffets* CINESIAS *in the face with a large wing.*
Cin. And is it thus you treat a master in the song,
Whom to possess the tribes have been contending long?
Peis. And will you stay with us as master of the words
To teach for Leotrophides [1] a quire of birds,
Cecropian tribe?
Cin.   You mock me, but I will not stay
My course for you, through air cleaving my winged way.
                       [*Exit.*

      INFORMER, *without, heard singing.*
Inf.   What birds are these of varied wing,
    Wide-pinioned swallow,
    Possessors of not anything,
    Black and white swallow?

---

[1] Either the point of these lines dismissing Cinesias is lost, or it
seems very slight. Leotrophides was a dithyrambic poet of the same class
as Cinesias.

Peis. This matter is becoming grave and troublesome :
Trilling his ditty too,—here is another come.

Enter INFORMER.

Inf.   Broad-pinioned swallow,
            Black and white swallow !
Peis. His shabby coat suggests that song of his I'm sure :
And *that*—one swallow hardly will suffice to cure.[1]
Inf. Who gives away the wings ?
Peis.   I do : but pray explain,
What your desire.
Inf.   Wings, wings ; so do not ask again.
Peis. To fly straight to Pallene ?[2]
Inf.   No ; I'm summoner
About the islands and Informer.
Peis.   'Save you, Sir,
A happy trade.
Inf.   And scent-suit.   So I want the wings
To expedite the cycle of my journeyings ?
Peis. Will wings in any way enhance your faculties
For making informations ?
Inf.   Not in anywise,
But I should fear no harm from pirates when I fly
In company with cranes, stone-ballasted,[3] but I
With suits.
Peis.   And you do this ? a well-grown able youth,
You worry foreigners with actions ? is this truth ?
Inf. What should I do ? I know not how to dig.
Peis.   There are
Many more ways of living, honester by far
Than process-cobbling.

---

[1] The critic who discovered the point here deserves credit for shrewdness. The informer's coat was too threadbare for even early spring wear ; he must needs, with such a garment, wish for the season when swallows are no longer counted by ones and twos.

[2] It was known to the audience that at Pallene there were games at which new clothes were given as prizes to athletes.

[3] This seems to point at another theory about the stone-carrying cranes. They require the stones, as ballast, to prevent their being driven from their course by currents of wind.

Inf.   Sir, pray spare your homily,
And wing me.

Peis.   Nay; my words the best of wings should be.

Inf. How should words wing a man?

Peis. ,   All men are winged this way.

Inf. All men?

Peis.   Aye, you have often heard some father say,
Standing in barbers' shops, ' Diïtrephes' discourse
Has put wings on my son's desire to have a horse.'
Another, speaking of his son, will say, that ' he
' Is gone into the clouds about this tragedy.'

Inf. And is this being winged by words?

Peis.   Aye, so say I;
By them the mind is lifted up and floats on high.
And so by words of higher tone have I essayed
To make you take a flight and learn an honest trade.

Inf. I will not.

Peis.   Then what will you do?

Inf.   I'll not bring shame
Upon my father's father's calling and his name.
So find and fit me with some wings both swift and light,
A hawk's or falcon's; that I may be off and cite
Some foreigner; and having made the charges here
I may fly back again.

Peis.   Your object then is clear;
He shall be fined before he comes.

Inf.   Exactly so.

Peis. And then, while he is coming here by ship, you go
And execute upon his goods.

Inf.   You've nought to learn.
One should be like a top, for ever on the turn.

Peis. Ah! I can whip a top. By Jupiter these strings
Will make it fly as well as Corcyræan [1] wings.

        [*Whirls a double-thonged whip over* INFORMER'S *head.*

Inf. Ah-ha! you have a whip.

Peis.   You mean a pair of wings,
With which I mean to spin my top until it sings.

                    [*Lashes him.*

-----
[1] The police at Corcyra were armed with notable scourges of double thong.

Inf. Oh! ah!

Peis.   Come, try your wings in flying off: be quick.
Will you not scamper, rogue?   Aye, you shall know a
        trick
Of just administration, tasting something bitter.

                        [*Exit* INFORMER.

But come let us be going.   Gather up the litter.

                [*Exeunt* PEISTHETÆRUS *and Attendants.*

Chorus.   Many things and very strange
            Have I seen within my range.
            There for instance is a·tree
            Very marvellous to see;
            In it is no heart at all,
            Men Cleonymus it call;
            Good for nothing; very fat;
            And a coward for all that:
            In the spring it buds and yields
                Slanders with a heavy crop;
            But unhappily its shields
                At the breath of winter drop.
            Then there is another spot
            Where a gleam of light is not:
            There may even mortals hold
            Communion with heroes old;
            Breakfast with them, and abide
            Any time till eventide.
            Then it is not safe to be
            In a hero's company.
            If one should by evil luck
                Meet Orestes [1] after dark,
            One might find his right side struck,
                And himself left naked stark.

----

[1] An allusion to Orestes the footpad and his operations after dark;
with a reference also to evil influences, such as palsy strokes, upon those
who irreverently passed certain places dedicated to Heroes. *Acharnians,*
l. 1032.

Enter PROMETHEUS, *approaching timidly with his head
covered.*

Prom. Ah! how may I contrive Jove shall not spy me
out?
Hist! where is Peisthetærus?

Enter PEISTHETÆRŪS.

Peis.   What is this about?
Why does he hide his head?
Prom.   Behind me,—in the sky,—
Do you see any God?
Peis.   By Jupiter, not I.
But who are you?
Prom.   What time of day is it with you?
Peis. What time?—A little after noon, if that will do.
But who are you?
Prom.   Ox-loosing time? or more than that?
Peis. This conduct is disgusting, quite.
Prom.   What is Jove at?
Clearing the weather? or does he o'ercloud the skies?
Peis. Confound you.
Prom.   Then I will come out from my disguise.
                    [*Throws off the covering of his head.*
Peis. My dear Prometheus!—
Prom.   Stop, stop: you are to blame.
Peis. What is the matter?
Prom.   Hush! don't call me by my name;
For I shall be destroyed if Jove should see me here.
I'm come to tell you news about the upper sphere:
So take this parasol and hold it over me
While I am speaking, lest the upper Gods should see.
Peis. Ha! ha! 'tis neatly done, with wondrous provi-
dence;
So, getting quickly under, fearlessly commence.
Prom. Now, listen.
Peis.   I am listening.
Prom.   Jupiter's undone.
Peis. Undone? How long since?

Prom.   Since this city was begun.
Since that time men have quite foregone their sacrifices;
No grateful savour of the roasting thighs arises
To our abodes; and we in one unending fast
Keep Thesmophoria.   Some Gods of foreign caste,
Who like Illyrians gibber instead of speaking,
Starved out, have taken arms; and are intent on wreaking
Vengeance on Jupiter and all the other Gods,
Unless he will provide a market where the odds
And ends of offal may be bought.

Peis.   ·What?   Is it true
There are barbaric Gods beyond and over you?

Prom. Barbarian indeed!—Not so, when it is known
That Execestides [1] calls one of them his own.

Peis. And what may be the names of these Divinities?

Prom. Triballi.

Peis.   Tribulation—comes from that one sees.

Prom. No doubt of it.   But this that you should know
is meet:
Ambassadors will soon be here on peace to treat
From Jove and those Triballi; make it on no terms
Except that Jove gives up the sceptre and confirms
The act of restitution by the gift to you
Of Basileia for a wife.

Peis.   No doubt: but who
Is Basileia? [2]

Prom.   An incomparable girl,
Whose business is to deal the bolts for Jove to hurl;
She sees to government, controls the pay and ports,
Provides the market, judges' fees, and public sports.

Peis. Quite his factotum?

Prom.   Yes: have her and you have all.
To let you know this was the object of my call.
For ever well disposed to serve mankind am I.

Peis. You only of the Gods enable us to fry. [3]

---

[1] See l. 4, note (1).
[2] Basileia means both 'Kingly rule' and 'Queen': in this *equivocal sense* it is used here and to the end of the comedy.
[3] By having supplied to men *fire*.

Prom. And, as you know, all Gods I utterly detest.

Peis. Aye, hated of the Gods as hating, 'tis confessed.

Prom. A perfect Timon.   But 'tis time that I should
　　　　run :

Give me the parasol, that Jove may be outdone,

Thinking, if he should see, 'tis only some affair

Of basket-carrying.

Peis. 　　　　　　Aye so, and take the chair.[1]

　　　　　　　　　　　　　　　　　　　　　　　[*Exeunt.*

Chorus.　Where the Shadow-feet [2] reside
　　　　　There have I a lake espied ;
　　　　　Out of its unwashen holes
　　　　　Comes Socrates to draw up souls.
　　　　　Much Pisander longs to see
　　　　　Once again the spirit which he
　　　　　Lost when living : for a lamb he'll
　　　　　Cut the weasand of a camel,
　　　　　And retire as did Ulysses.
　　　　　　To the blood and camel-fat,
　　　　　'Tis a feast he never misses,
　　　　　　Up comes Chærephon the Bat.

Enter NEPTUNE, HERCULES, *and* TRIBALLUS *the Barbarian*
God.

Nep. Fellow ambassadors, survey this city round,

This is HIGH-CUCKOOBURY, whither we are bound.

　　　　　　　[*To* TRIBALLUS, *whose dress, language, and*
　　　　　　　habits are very unbecoming a God and a
　　　　　　　Gentleman.

What are you at ?   One would suppose you did not know

How to put on a mantle !—Over your shoulder,—so ;—

---

[1] In a sacrificial procession a parasol and stool were usually carried
behind the 'basket-bearer.'

[2] This strophe, and that which follows, l. 1605, are continuations of
the narrative of strange sights seen by the Birds. The references to
Socrates and Chærephon are in the spirit of the *Clouds.* The Shadow-
feet are a tribe supposed to live in the hottest parts of Libya ; they walk
on all-fours, and forasmuch as there are no trees to protect them from
the direct heat of the sun, they are favoured by nature with such large
feet, that one of them, held up over the back, provides an agreeable shade
for the whole body.

Not the left shoulder, booby : we shall be disgraced :
Laspodias himself would dress with better taste.
Democracy has brought us to a strange abyss,
When Gods elect for Legate such a clown as this !

Tri. Wo'ot-thee houd thee noise ?

Nep.   Bah ! God so uncouth as you
I never saw.—Come, Hercules, what shall we do ?

Her. You know my mind.   I wish to suffocate the man
Who first conceived against the Gods this walling plan.

Nep. But we have been despatched commissioners to try
For terms of peace.

Her.   So, so ! then hang them twice, say I.

Enter PEISTHETÆRUS (*in his hands birds ready for
cooking*).

Peis. Bring me the cheesegrater, some silphium and
        cheese,
And blow the fire.

Her.   We three Gods this occasion seize
To offer our respects.[1]

Peis. (*not noticing Her.*).   Put in the seasoning.

Her. What meats are these ?

Peis.   Some birds whom they thought right to bring
To justice for sedition.

Her.   Is this then your way
To season them ?

Peis. (*recognising Her.*). Ah ! worthy HERCULES, good
        day.
What brings you here ?

Her.   The Gods, wishing this war to cease,
Have sent us to arrange an honourable peace.

Enter SERVANT *of Peisthetærus.*

Ser. There is no oil, Sir, in the flask.

Peis.   No oil ? that's bad :
For look the birds be basted well : some must be had.

---

[1] It should not be lost upon the unclassical reader, that it is the sight
of the birds made ready for the spit which works this sudden change in
Hercules's sentiments towards Peisthetærus.

Her. We find that we gain no advantage by the war :
And you, if you be friends with us as heretofore,
Will have rain-water in your pools, and all your days
Be halcyon. The terms we are prepared to raise.

Peis. It was not we who did commence the war; but
    ˗ still
We are disposed to hear your overtures; and will,
If you will do but right, accord you terms of ease
For solid peace. The terms which we think just are
    these :—
Let Jupiter give back the sceptre to the Birds ;
We will be pacified. What need of further words ?
And hereupon we ask the Legates in to dine.

Her. (*to the other two Commissioners*).
Well, that is fair. How are your votes ?—I give it mine.

Nep. Half-witted glutton, for your belly's sake alone
Would you deprive your father of his ancient throne ?

Peis. Nay; will not your dominion so much vigour gain
If we, the BIRDS, below resume our former reign ?
At present mortals take advantage of a cloud
And, swearing by your names, stoop down and lie aloud.
But if the BIRDS were your allies, and one should swear,
' By the Raven and by Jove,'—before he was aware,
A Raven on the wing might hear the fellow lie,
And at a blow knock out the perjurer's right eye.

Nep. By Neptune ! I admit it, in that point of view.

Her. And so do I.

Peis. (*to* TRI.)   And what say you ?

Tri.   Nabaisatrew.

Peis. You see that he assents.—But further, I suggest
A case in which we might promote your interest.
Suppose a man has vowed to you some sacrifice,
But when it comes to payment,—says his avarice,—
' The Gods are very patient.'—*That* we will arrange.

Nep. How so ?

Peis. We watch a time when he is counting change,
Or may be, at the bath, and stripped,—down comes a kite
And swoops two-sheeps'-worth, that the God may have his
    right.

Her. On this, the sceptre shall go back with my consent;
That is my vote.

    Nep.   But is TRIBALLUS quite content?

    Her. TRIBALLUS, will you yield yourself to feed the
        crows ? [1]

    Tri. Sunaka baktarikrousa.

    Her.   He will not oppose.

    Nep. Since both of you consent, I also vote to cede.

    Her. The sceptre, Sir, is ceded; we are all agreed.

    Peis. By Jove there is another thing, I recollect.
Juno of course I leave with Jove, but I expect
That BASILEIA shall be yielded for my wife.

                 [NEPTUNE *moves to go away in disgust.*

    Nep. Let us go home. You wish for nothing else but
        strife.

    Peis. 'Tis all the same to me.—Cook, let the sauce be
        sweet.

    Her. My good man, NEPTUNE, what is this? We came
        to treat.
What? Do you mean to let the hope of peace drop through
About a single wench?

    Nep.   What would you have me do?

    Her. What do? Make friends.

    Nep.   You have been cozened all along,
And do not know it, fool. You do yourself a wrong.
See you, if Jupiter should cease to be the king,
And afterwards should die, you would lose everything.
For, being now the heir, in you at once would vest
The whole estate in fee of which he died possessed.

    Peis. Dear, dear! How he bamboozles you! Come
        here to me,
And in a word I will explain how things would be.
Poor rogue, your uncle tricks you; not a single straw
Of all your father's goods would fall to you by law,
For you are base-born.

    Her.   I? I base-born? what d'ye mean?

    Peis. You are, by Jove; your mother was some foreign
        quean.

---

[1] Note, *Peace,* l. 86.

How could Minerva have been heiress if there were
Brothers legitimate?—then, daughters take no share.

Her. But if my father should devise, as he sees fit,
The ' bastard's havings '?

Peis.   That the law would not permit.
Neptune would be the first (though now he fires your mind)
To lay his claim to all your father left behind ;
Alleging he was brother, and legitimate.
Listen to Solon's law about deceased's estate :

> 𝕮𝖍𝖊 𝖇𝖆𝖘𝖙𝖆𝖗𝖉 𝖘𝖍𝖆𝖑𝖑 𝖓𝖔𝖙 𝖍𝖆𝖇𝖊 𝖆 𝖘𝖍𝖆𝖗𝖊
> 𝕴𝖋 𝖙𝖍𝖊𝖗𝖊 𝖇𝖊 𝖙𝖗𝖚𝖊-𝖇𝖔𝖗𝖓 𝖘𝖔𝖓 𝖋𝖔𝖗 𝖍𝖊𝖎𝖗.
> 𝕴𝖋 𝖙𝖍𝖊𝖗𝖊 𝖇𝖊 𝖓𝖔𝖓𝖊, 𝖔𝖗 𝖍𝖊 𝖍𝖆𝖇𝖊 𝖉𝖎𝖊𝖉,
> 𝕮𝖍𝖊 𝖓𝖊𝖝𝖙 𝖔𝖋 𝖐𝖎𝖓 𝖙𝖍𝖊 𝖜𝖍𝖔𝖑𝖊 𝖉𝖎𝖇𝖎𝖉𝖊.

Her. Then I should have no portion of my father's goods?

Peis. Nothing.—Has he inscribed you in the brother-
          hoods ?[1]
Come, tell me that.

Her.   Not he; and much to my surprise.

Peis. Why do you stand with open mouth and glaring
          eyes,
Just like an injured man ? Pooh, pooh! come you to me ;
I'll make you king, and pigeon's milk your food shall be.

Her. I thought before that you were right in what you
          said
About the wench; and I assign to you the maid.

Peis. (to NEPTUNE). And what say you?

Nep.   I go against you on division.

Peis. It lies, then, with TRIBALLUS. [*To* TRI.] What is
          your decision ?

Tri. Oi moind ta burd sud morrid tu ta bonny lass,
Un ha ta gear.

Her.   You mean that the concessions pass ?

Nep. He does not say concede, but chatters like the
          swallows.

Peis. Then, that the swallows have it, manifestly follows.

Nep. Do you two, then, draw up the terms of settlement;
Since good it seems to you, my silence gives assent.

---

[1] An Athenian father, on the third day of the feast of Apaturia, introduced his son to the brotherhood of the tribe to which he belonged.
Hereupon the son's name was enrolled and he was admitted true citizen.

Her. We are agreed in ceding all that you demand;
But go with us to heaven, there to receive the hand
Of BASILEIA with possession of the rest.

Peis. The malefactors were cut off, and will be dressed
Just opportunely for the marriage-feast.

Her.   Shall I
Stay here and cook them while you go into the sky?

Peis. You cook? there spoke the man who loves to serve
        his throat.

No.   Go with us.

Her.   'Twould suit me.

Peis.   Bring a wedding coat.
                                        [*Exeunt.*

Chorus. There in Phanæ dwells a race,
        Clepsydra is near the place,
        Who, such is their clever plan,
        Make the tongue support the man;
        Make it sow for them and reap,
        Tread the grape, and shear the sheep;
        But outlandish all the class is,
        Phillipses and Gorgiases.[1]
        From them has the custom.sprung,
            Which through Attica has grown,
        That in sacred rites the tongue
            Is cut out and set alone.

                    Enter MESSENGER.

Mess. Oh, happy in your fortune past the power of words,
Oh, thrice to be congratulated race of Birds,
Take home to you your king.   He comes as never star
Was like him shining from its golden house afar,
As never shone the sun, far darting fiery rays;
So comes he with his bride, in beauty passing praise.
Jove's winged thunderbolt is quivering in his hand;
And round him, circling to the very outmost band,

---

[1] Aristophanes was shocked that Simonides should have taken money reward for his verses: we see here that he was as much scandalised that Gorgias, and other professors of the art of Rhetoric, should have received fees from the attendants at their lectures. Many of these professors were then foreigners.

There floats a nameless odour.   Oh, the sight is fair,
Where breezes lift the incense-fumes as braids of hair.—
But here he is.   So doth it to the Muse belong
Her holy lips to open with a welcome-song.

Enter PEISTHETÆRUS *in state, with* BASILEIA *and*
Attendants.

Semichorus. Retire ! avoid ! depart ! away !
            Flit round him who comes again
            With Fortune in his train.
        Ah ! what a delicate creature !
        Ah ! what grace in each feature !
        Wed for this city in happy day.
                For fortunes great
                Beyond all thought
                Hath this man brought
                Unto the Birds' estate.
        And therefore fill the skies
                Around the path
                Of him who hath
        The Bride, with bridal melodies.
Semichorus. Once the Fates Olympian Juno led
                Unto the high-throned king,
        Lord of lords, to share his marriage-bed ;
                Then did the welkin ring,
            Ho ! Hymen, Hymenæus.

        Brideman, meet for such a blessed pair,
                The bridegroom and fair bride,
        LOVE, the blooming, golden-winged, was there
                The coursers' reins to guide,
            Ho ! Hymen, Hymenæus.

Peis.   Your hymns and songs delight mine ear ;
        Your welcome fills my heart with cheer.
        Be Jove's own weapons now your theme,
        Earth-shaking thunders and the gleam
                Of lightning's fiery sheen.

Chorus. Gold-glowing flash, oh, shaft of fire,
  Jove's messenger of deathful ire,
  And ye storm-bearers, at whose sound
  This man who wields you shakes the ground,
   Through you he all commands,
   And Jove's own throne-mate stands
    Beside him as his Queen.
  Ho! Hymen, Hymenæus.

Peis. Follow, follow, to the wedding,
  All that wing through field or grove,
  Follow to the land of Jove,
  And to the nuptial bedding.
(*To* BASILEIA). Touch me, blessed one, so slightly,
  Lay thy hand upon my wing,
  Linkèd we will dance and sing,
  For I will lift thee lightly.
Chorus. Pœan, Pœan. Lift the cry,
  Shout the song of victory
  For him who reigneth in the sky.

FROGS.

INTRODUCTION.

IF the reader will glance at the Chronological Table, he will see that the deaths of Euripides and Sophocles, and the production of this comedy, rapidly followed each other.

No sooner was Euripides dead than Aristophanes must have conceived the idea of making merry at his expense at the next dramatic festival. The comedy was completed and the actors prepared for the earliest celebration, Lenæa, that is, by the end of February. This rapidity of conception and execution is the more worthy of notice, because by many, perhaps by the greater number, this comedy will be considered the *chef-d'œuvre* of the author.

It is unfortunate for the translator that there are important parts in this play which present to him unusual difficulties. He has to do his best in rhymed verse to represent humorous criticism on the rhythm of verses of entirely different construction; he has to translate parodies so as to tell their own tale of humour, perhaps to those who know nothing of the characteristic style of the original author. For this part of his work, then, especially, he asks the kind and considerate judgment of the scholar.

The idea of the piece is this. Euripides was dead. Bacchus, the patron of the Drama, regretted him. Who could supply his place on the Athenian stage? The God hits upon an expedient. After the example of Hercules, he determines to make a descent into Hades in order to recover his favourite tragedian. Sophocles died such a very short time before the exhibition of the comedy, that we must be convinced that Bacchus had come to this determination before an event which only gave it the more reason. The references to Sophocles are like insertions made to meet the case of his being in Hades too; but he does not appear as a character.

On his way to Hades Bacchus has to cross the Stygian
Lake; here he falls in with the FROGS, who have given
their name to the piece. They play but a small part in
it: they are, so far as appears, heard only; certainly they
do not appear as a Chorus. The true CHORUS of the play
are the Mystics, or Initiated in the Eleusinian Mysteries,
whom Bacchus falls in with while they are celebrating
their joyous orgies in their own place of eternal light. In
the hymns of graceful fancy with which Aristophanes in
his happiest vein treats this part of his plan, we have
probably represented the style of hymns with which the
Initiated accompanied their annual procession from Athens
to Eleusis. Bacchus, having, after many adventures,
arrived at Pluto's palace, finds Hades in commotion.
A high strife is on hand. Euripides is disputing with
Æschylus the right to occupy the Chair of Dramatic Art
in Hades. The arrival of Bacchus is, then, happily timed.
Where could be found a better judge of dramatic composition? The case between the two is referred to him. The
trial of merits affords substance for the latter half of the
comedy, and ample field for the wit of Aristophanes.

Since the representation of *Birds* Athens had gone
through a sea of troubles. The expedition to Sicily,
which had just then set out with brilliant anticipations of
empire in the Italian seas, had ended in disaster. Alcibiades had become the foulest traitor to his country; war
with Sparta had been rekindled; the Lacedæmonians had
established an effective power at sea, and had leagued with
the hereditary, the natural enemy of the free Greek,
Persia. Our old friend, DEMUS, had quietly succumbed
to an Oligarchy of 400; they, in turn, had become in-
tolerable. Yet Fortune had not quite deserted the city:
at Arginusæ the Athenian fleet inflicted a heavy blow
upon the combined forces of the enemy. But the very
darkest day of Athens had now come. Some of its deep
shadows may be observed on the text of this comedy. The
minds of all were dejected; they knew not whom to trust,
to what quarter to look for hope. Before Æschylus could
arrive to prescribe for the sick Commonwealth, the navy of

Athens was utterly, gratuitously destroyed at Ægos-potami. Lysander laid siege to the city by land and sea; Athens surrendered upon terms of extreme humiliation. So ended the Peloponnesian War, with which so many of these comedies were closely connected.

Frogs carried off the first prize in the contest.

Dramatis Personæ.

BACCHUS.

XANTHIAS, *slave to Bacchus.*

HERCULES.

CORPSE.

CHARON.

THE FROGS *of the Stygian Lake.*

CHORUS *of Eleusinian Mystics.*

ÆACUS.

EURIPIDES.

ÆSCHYLUS.

PLUTO.

Woman, attendant on Proserpine.

First Hostess.

Second Hostess.

SCENE.—BACCHUS *and* XANTHIAS, *on their road to the house of* HERCULES ; XANTHIAS *riding on a donkey, and carrying a bundle;* BACCHUS *on foot, dressed in the saffron-coloured frock and kid boots of a lady, and carrying a club and lion's skin in the fashion of* HERCULES.

Xanthias. My lord, shall I begin the stage-slave's com-
  monplaces
To catch the usual laugh from those expectant faces ?
 Bacchus. Say what you will, except ' I'm galled;' be-
  ware of that;
It tends to stir the bile, as being rather flat.
 Xan. Then something clever ?
 Bacc.   Yes; excepting 'How I ache!'
 Xan. I may say something funny.
 Bacc.   Yes, I only make
Those slight exceptions.
 Xan.   There ! why do I bear a pack
If I am not allowed the liberty to crack
The jokes of which our high authorities make use,
Whenever they can find occasion to produce
A slave upon the stage ?
 Bacc.   And every time I hear
The artifice, I feel I'm older by a year.
So pray forego it.
 Xan.   Then, to my chagrin, the yoke
Must *gall* my neck, and I am disallowed the joke.
 Bacc. Tut ! have not pride and luxury too much of it ?
When I, the son of Barrel, BACCHUS, thus submit
To trudge a-foot, and set this rogue on donkey-back,
Lest he should be fatigued by carrying the pack.
 Xan. But don't I carry it ?
 Bacc.   How so ? you ride, say I.
 Xan. Why, *this* I carry.
 Bacc.   How ?
 Xan.   This weight you can't deny.

Bacc. The weight you say you bear does not the donkey
       bear?

Xan. By Jupiter, not he! it is my single share.

Bacc. How take you it, when what you take the donkey
       takes?

Xan. I won't pretend to say; I know my shoulder *aches.*

Bacc. Come, since you say the donkey's labour does not
       profit,

Get off and carry him: and hear what he says of it.

Xan. Why hadn't I the luck to go and fight at sea? [1]

I would have shown you what it was to order me.

Bacc. Get down, you rogue: For here the door, methinks,
       I win

To which my steps were bound.   (*Knocks at the door.*)

                              Hoi! Slave, I say, within.

HERCULES, *looking out.*

Her. Who's knocking at the door a blow as it had been
A centaur charging? what does this disturbance mean?

Bacc. (*frightened at the angry aspect of* HERCULES).
My lad.

Xan.   What?

Bacc.   Did you not perceive?

Xan.   What sort of fact?

Bacc. How he alarmed me.

Xan.   Aye, he might have thought you cracked.

Her. (*bursting into boisterous laughter at the dress of*
       BACCHUS).

This is too much!—this is—I've bit my lip in half—
I cannot stop it—no—I must have out my laugh.

Bacc. Good Sir, I have to beg your very kind attention.

Her. No, really I must have my laugh; there's no pre-
       vention.

The lady's saffron gown and lion-skin thrown over!

Kid boots and club! what means it? whence came you, my
       rover?

_____

[1] The fatal Sicilian expedition had caused such a drain upon the
strength of Athens, that the Athenians were driven to employ slaves to
make up the complement of their ships. So they fought the battle of
Arginusæ. The slaves engaged in that action were rewarded with their
freedom.

Bacc. It chanced to me that lately on a summer trip
I read Euripides; and, lying on the ship,
Was musing over the *Andromeda* apart,
When suddenly a longing shot into my heart.

Her. How large was it?

Bacc.　　　　　　　Nay, do not quiz me, if you please;
The thing is past a jest; and I am ill at ease.
'Tis such a longing, brother, wasting me away!

Her. It's nature, little fellow?

Bacc.　　　　　　　　　　Ah, I may not say.
But I can riddle you my thought, if you will stoop
To guess it.—You have had a sudden wish for soup?

Her. Soup? bless you; yes, a thousand times.

Bacc.　　　　　　　　　　　More must I tell?

Her. Nay, not about the soup: I understand it well.

Bacc. A longing such as *that* consumes me night and
　　day
To have EURIPIDES: though he has passed away.
Yea, man shall not divert my fixed intent to go
And find him where he is.

Her.　　　　　　What? down in Hell below?

Bacc. Aye, lower; if there is a place.

Her.　　　　　　　　　What is your aim?

Bacc. I want a clever Poet, worthy of the name.
The good we had are dead; those whom we have are
　　naught.

Her. But Iöphon is living?

Bacc.　　　　　　Truly: if we ought
To reckon him among the good?　But thereabout
There lies in my opinion certain ground of doubt.

Her. But if you go so far your longing to appease,
Why not bring back the older poet Sophocles?

Bacc. I'll ring the metal of which Iöphon is made,
And see what he can do without his father's aid.[1]
Besides, that rogue Euripides is just the man
To put his artfulness to use, and help my plan

---

[1] Iöphon was the son of Sophocles. He had produced some tragedies, but it was supposed that he was much indebted to works left unfinished by his father.

By giving Hell the slip : whereas the other one,
An easy fellow always, would not care to run.

Her. But where is Agathon ?

Bacc.   Alas, he has departed.

A genuine poet he.   His friends are broken-hearted.

Her. Poor man, where is he gone ?

Bacc.   To the Banquet of the Blest.

Her. And Xenocles ?

Bacc.   Please Jove to take him—to the rest !

Her. Pythangelus ?

Xan. (*speaking towards the audience aside*).

'Tis very strange that no one takes
Notice of me this while ! and yet my shoulder *aches.*[1]

Her. But you must have a thousand lads whose powers
      of talking
Might give EURIPIDES a length, and beat him, walking !

Bacc. Pooh ! grapes you would not glean : swallows that
            twitter round
The Muses' halls ; art-spoilers ; utterers of sound :
Let them produce a drama, give a Chorus to them,
You need but do it once, you perfectly undo them.
We want a man of mettle, such as can invent
And worthily express a noble sentiment.

Her. Of mettle how ?

Bacc.   One who will risk the true sublime ;
' Æther the dwelling-house of Jove '—' the foot of Time ; '
Or thus : ' To be forsworn the honest mind is loth ;
' But say it is the tongue, and you may break the oath.'[2]

Her. But is this what you like ?

Bacc.   It charms me overmuch.

Her. It is a rascal's rubbish, and you know it such.

Bacc. Enjoy your mind. Leave me without your inter-
            ference.

Her. Why then, 'tis villany ! and that is its appearance.

Bacc. Do you teach me to sup ?

---

[1] Again, it will be seen, Aristophanes puts into the slave's mouth *the*
claptrap of the stage-slave.

[2] These expressions, considered to offend against piety, taste, or common
morality, are drawn, with more or less fairness, from the dramas of Euripides.

Xan. (aside).   You'd think I wasn't here.

Bacc. But to the business which has brought me in this
  gear
After your fashion: 'tis that I may know, if wanted,
The hospitable friends and houses that you haunted
When you went after Cerberus. So explain in detail
The towns, the roads, the havens, hostels, shops of retail,
The stages, fountains, lodgings where you got a bed
Most free from bugs.

 Xan. (aside).   Of me no syllable is said.

Her. Have you the impudence to think of going too?

Bacc. Prithee, no more of that.   I only ask of you
The shortest way to Hell, provided it is not
Extremely cold, nor yet insufferably hot.

Her. Which shall I mention first?—the shortest you can
  go
Is by a beam and rope.

 Bacc.   Hanging you mean? Oh no.

Her. There is another way, in some respects the best—
That through the mortar.

 Bacc.   Hemlock you suggest?

Her. Exactly.

 Bacc.   That is cold; as bad as two Decembers,
And gradually chills one from the lower members.

Her. Then shall I mention that which is both short and
  straight?

Bacc. Do: for my walking powers are very far from great.[1]

Her. Then leisurely go to the Ceramicus—

Bacc.   And?

Her. Ascend the lofty tower—

Bacc.   What to do there?

Her.   Stand;
Look at the torch-race; then, when the spectators say,
' Off with it '—off yourself.

 Bacc.   Where?

Her.   Down.

Bacc.   No, not that way.
The membranes in the brain-case might perchance be rent.

---

[1] Bacchus would be represented on the stage as a corpulent young man.

Her. What will you then?

Bacc.   The way you followed when you went.

Her. That voyage is very tedious : you will find a lake,
Wide and of depth unknown—

Bacc.   And how am I to make
The transit?

Her.   You will see an old man keeping there
A nutshell of a boat : two oboles is his fare.

Bacc. How mighty are two oboles,[1] wheresoe'er one goes !
But how did they get there?

Her.   With Theseus I suppose.
Then serpents, and ten thousand thousand beasts you see,
Fearful to look upon.

Bacc.   Don't try to frighten me ;
I will not be diverted.

Her.   Then a foul morass
Of ever-floating filth.   There welter in a mass
Guest-wrongers, parricides, and perjurers ; with whom
Transcribers of a line of Morsimus [2] have doom.

Bacc. If due were done, they would be brought to that
                same pass
Whoever learned the Pyrrhic of Cinesias.[3]

Her. Thereafter will the breath of pipes salute your ear,
And daylight glorious as our own will reappear :
There will be myrtle-groves ; and in them happy bands
Of men and women, and much clapping of the hands.

Bacc. Who, then, are these?

Her.   Those who have been Initiate.[4]

Xan. (*aside*). And I'm the ass who bear the Mysteries in
                state ! [4]
But I'll no more of it.

---

[1] The scoliast refers these 'two oboles' to the dicasts' fee, so often
mentioned in these comedies.   It appears that at different periods the
fee varied between one and three oboles.   By other authors Charon's fee
is said to have been only *one* obole, which was put into the mouth of the
corpse.

[2] A tragic poet. See *Peace*, l. 607.

[3] A dithyrambic poet, introduced as a character in *Birds*, l. 1305.

[4] In the Mysteries of Eleusis. Aristophanes here describes what were
supposed to be the special privileges of those who in life had been admitted to the Mysteries. People going to Eleusis carried the requisites

Her.   They will impart to you
All that is requisite for you to know and do.
They have their habitation just beside your road,
And close upon the gates of PLUTO's own abode.
So fare you well, my brother.
    Bacc.   Take your wishes back
Redoubled, my good friend.   [*To* XAN.] And you, pick up
    the pack.
    Xan. Before I've put it down?
    Bacc.   And quickly.
    Xan.   Sir, I crave
You'll hire A BODY being carried to its grave.
    Bacc. Suppose I cannot find one?
    Xan.   Then I go.
    Bacc.   Agreed.
Ah! here they bring a Corpse exactly at our need.

Enter bearers carrying a CORPSE.

Heigh, Sir! You dead man! fellow! if I pay you well
Are you disposed to take my luggage down to Hell?
    Corpse. How much is there?
    Bacc. (showing the bundle).   There's this.
    Corpse.   Two drachmas for the load?
    Bacc. By Jove, no! something less.
    Corpse.   On, bearers; on your road.
    Bacc. Good fellow, stay: we—
    Corpse.   No, unless you mean to give
Two drachmas.
    Bacc.   Take nine oboles.[1]
    Corpse.   Nay—I'd rather live
Again!   · [*Bearers carry out* CORPSE.
    Xan. How consequential is the dog! He'll smart,
I hope. Now I will go.
    Bacc.   Said with a noble heart!
So now will we to ship.

———————

for due celebration of the rites on pack-asses; hence 'An ass carrying the
Mysteries' became a proverb to signify A man insensible to the importance
of a business in which he was an instrument.
   [1] A drachma and a half!

Enter CHARON, *in his boat.*

Cha.   Ho-oop! keep her afloat.

Xan. What's this?

Bacc.   It is the lake; and there I see the boat.

Xan. By Neptune, it is CHARON!

Bacc.   CHARON, how d'ye do?
Good morning, CHARON.

Cha.   Who's for *Rest-from-trouble?* who
For *Lethe-land?* for *Donkey's-wool,* a pleasant cruise?
Dogs? Crows? or *Tænarum?*[1]

Bacc.   I am.

Cha.   No time to lose;
Jump in.

Bacc.   But are you really going to the crows?

Cha. Aye, aye, to put you down. Now Sir, get in. Who
        goes?

Bacc. Here, slave, be quick.

Cha.   Your slave? I cannot take him in,
Unless he fought at Arginusæ for his skin.[2]

Xan. It was but my ill-luck. It chanced my eyes were
        sore.

Cha. Then please you find your way by running round
        the shore.

Xan. Where shall I wait?

Cha. Close to the landing-place where you will see
The *Drying-Stone.*

Bacc.   You understand?

Xan.   Yes, perfectly.
(*Aside*) See there it is again! I'm out of luck to-day.
When I was coming out what could have crossed my way?
                                                    [*Exit.*

Cha. (*to* BACC.). Sit to the oar.   [more?
        (*to the ghosts ashore*). Make haste, we're going. Any
(*to* BACC.). You, Sir, what are you at?

---

[1] A southern promontory of Peloponnesus; near it was a cave supposed
to afford an approach to Hades.

[2] The only property an unfortunate slave had and could be supposed
to fight for. This translation is a guess at an obscure original.

Bacc. (*who has seated himself on the oar*). I'm sitting at
the oar,
As you directed.

Cha. Here.—Now, out your arms and back.

Bacc. What, so? (*performing with his arms, without touching the oar.*)

Cha. Don't think to play the fool with me, you sack.
Take to the oar and pull.

Bacc. What? row? I cannot do it;
I'm not a waterman: I never was bred to it.

Cha. No matter, dip: and lovely music will be heard.

Bacc. Of what?

Cha. Of singing frogs and swans.

Bacc. Then give the word.

Cha. Ho-oop, hoop; ho-oop, hoop!

FROGS, *heard from the lake.*

Breke-kekex-coäx-coäx.
Brood of the pool and spring,
Open your mellow throats
And pour your sweetest notes
In harmony to sing
Coäx coäx.
Such is the shout we raise,
When on the pitcher [1] days
Nisæan Bacchus comes,
And draws the revelling throng,
Noisy with wine and song,
Into our marshy homes.
Breke-kekex, coäx coäx.

Bacc. Coäx, coäx. But I begin
To feel the chafing of my skin.

Frogs. Brekekekex, coäx coäx.

Bacc. But what care you what state I'm in?

Frogs. Brekekekex, coäx coäx.

Bacc. Perdition catch your throats with coäx;
Have you no other notes but coäx?

---

[1] See *Acharnians*, l. 880.

Frogs.   Then, meddler, mend thine ear.
   The Muses hold me dear;
   And horned Pan, who draws
   Trilling music from his straws;
   Nor less Apollo deigns
   With grateful smile to pay the pains
   With which for him I tend,
    Down in my watery deeps,
   The reed [1] on which to bend
    The strings he lordly sweeps.
   Brekekekex, coäx coäx.

Bacc.   Blisters now are rising fast,
   And my patience will not last.
   Fond as you are of the strain
   Do not let me hear again
    Brekekex, coäx coäx.

Frogs.   Nay, but the louder we
   Will sing our melody:
   As oft on sunny days
    Into the sedge we spring,
    And reappear to sing
   Our many-diving lays:
   Or, flying sullen thunder
    And darkening skies, we go
    To weave our dance below
   With sinking, rising, over, under,
   Timed in many whirls and doubles
   To the bursting of the bubbles. [2]
   Brekekex, coäx coäx.

Bacc.   I must put a stop to this.
Frogs.   Truly you would do amiss.
Bacc.   I should suffer much the worst
   If in rowing I should burst.
Frogs.   Brekekex, coäx coäx.
Bacc.   Have it then! who cares? not I.
     [*Striking at the frogs with the oar.*

---

[1] The strings of the lyre were in some way bridged over the reed.
[2] Dindorf suggests, with great probability, that in the whole of this lyric Aristophanes is parodying the style of the dithyrambic poets.

Frogs.   Ha, ha ! we will the louder cry ;
             Every day, and all day long
             Stretch our throats to shout our song,
             Brekekex, coäx coäx.
Bacc.   No, you shall not beat me thus.
Frogs.   No, you shall not conquer us.
Bacc. (*striking the water furiously*).   `
             If I cry the whole day long,
             I will drown your coäx song,
             Brekekex, coäx coäx.

                                    [*Frogs are silenced.*
I knew that I should stop you coäxing at last.
    Cha. Ease her now; stop her: you Sir, shove her in ;
           hold fast :
And now get out.   The fare ?
    Bacc.   Two oboles ; here they are.
Ho ! Xanthias.   Where is the man ?
    Xan. (*outside*).   Not very far.
Bacc. Come here.
    Xan. (*entering*). How are you, master ?
    Bacc.   Well, and what did you find there ?
Xan. Darkness and mud.
    Bacc.   Then did you not see anywhere
The parricides and perjurers ?
    Xan.   What ? did not you ?
Bacc. By Neptune not as yet. But ah—yes.—Now I do.
What is our best course think you ?
    Xan.   I say, Push ahead ;
For hereabouts we ought to find, from what he said,
Those dreadful beasts.
    Bacc.   Ha ! ha !—I'll serve the fellow out.
It was his vapouring : to frighten me no doubt.
'Twas jealousy.   He knows my taste for martial sport.
I know my Hercules ; and bouncing is his forte.
I only wish we could with some adventure meet,
A something to be talked of worthy of our feat.
    Xan. Hist ! hist !—I heard a noise.
    Bacc.   Which way ?
    Xan.   Behind.

Bacc.   Eh?—Stay,
Get you behind.

    Xan.   Oh no; it comes the other way.

    Bacc. Then go you to the front.

    Xan.   By Jove, I see him now,—
A monstrous beast!

    Bacc.   What like?

    Xan.   It changes. It's a cow;
Now it's a mule; and now—it is, by Jupiter,
A lovely woman!

    Bacc.   Where? oh let me go to her.

    Xan. 'Tis not a woman now; it is a dog.

    Bacc.   Eh? what?
It is Empusa then.

    Xan.   Its face is fiery hot.

    Bacc. And has a leg of brass?

    Xan.   By Neptune, one at least!

    Bacc. Oh, whither shall I fly?

    Xan.   And where shall I?

    Bacc.   My Priest,
Save me!—that you and I may yet take many a cup
Together.[1]

    Xan.   Hercules! we shall be eaten up.

    Bacc. Don't call on *me*, or speak the name: you'll drive
                me mad.

    Xan. Then BACCHUS I will say.

    Bacc.   No, no: that's quite as bad.

    Xan. At any rate, get on.—But no; stay, master, stay.

    Bacc. What is it?

    Xan.   Reassure yourself: we win the day.
And we in happy time Hegelochus may quote:
'The storm has cleared away, and I behold a—stoat.'[2]
Empusa disappears.

---

[1] This appeal was suddenly made by the Bacchus on the stage to the
'High Priest of Bacchus' sitting in his place of honour among the audience, as being a high functionary at this Bacchic Festival.

[2] Perhaps this couplet should have been omitted altogether in translation. The point lies in the fact that 'calm' and 'stoat,' in the original,
admit a pun.

Bacc.　　　　　　　　You swear?

Xan.　　　　　　　　　　　By Jove, it's true!

Bacc. Swear it again.

Xan.　　　　　　By Jove.

Bacc.　　　　　　　　　Swear it.

Xan.　　　　　　　　　　By Jove, I do.

Bacc. Ah me, how pale I grew to see her!—But this varlet,

For very cowardice, outblushed me into scarlet.

What God brings me to this for any fancied crime?

'Æther, the dwelling-house of Jove,' or 'Foot of Time?' [1]

　　　　　　　　　　[*Distant sound of pipes within.*

Xan. Hist, Sir!

Bacc.　　　　　　What is it?

Xan.　　　　　　　　　Don't you hear?

Bacc.　　　　　　　　　Hear what? and where?

Xan. A sound of piping.

Bacc.　　　　　　　　Aye, I do; and I declare

I feel the breath of torches mystically pleasant.

So let us creep aside, and listen for the present.

Chorus (within). Come, come, Iäcchus.

Xan. Yes, master, it is so; 'tis the Initiated

Are sporting hereabouts, as HERCULES related,

And singing to Iäcchus.

Bacc.　　　　　　　So it seems to me.

Let us be silent and observe what we may see.

Enter CHORUS *singing.*

Come from thy holy seats,
Come from thy deep retreats,
　　Come, come, Iäcchus.
Dancing along the mead,
Come, thine own troop to lead,
　　Come, come, Iäcchus.
Let the fresh myrtle bough,
　　Studded with flowers,
Wave o'er thy crownèd brow.
　　Free mirth is ours.

---

[1] There is much reasonable doubt whether this line is not in its place here spurious. It is a mere repetition or quoting of line 86.

So let thy foot advance,
Bold in the graceful dance.
This holy company,
Gathered for revelry,
Wistfully waits for thee :
    Come, come Iäcchus.   [nice !

Xan. Much-honoured Proserpine, this smell of pork[1] is
Bacc. Pray you be still, and you may ~~chance to~~ get a slice.
Chorus.   Kindle the flaming brands,
Uplift them in thy hands,
    Light ! light ! Iäcchus.
All the field shines afar ;
Thou art our Evening Star,
    Bright, bright, Iäcchus.
Elders, by thee inspired,
    Cast away pain,
Cast away years, and fired
    Dance in thy train.
Be thy bright torch on high
Polestar to every eye ;
While o'er thy dewy lea,
Dancing in company,
Fleetly we follow thee,
    Blessed Iäcchus.

Anapæstic Interlogue.

A reverent silence fits this place ;
    and from our Chorus let him depart
Who is yet untaught in the Mysteries ;
    who has stain of guile on his heart ;
Who has not won from the Muses' secrets
    freedom of thought, and bodily grace ;
Who has not learned from Cratinus the bull-fed[2]
    what is befitting the time and the place ;

---

[1] Young pigs were sacrificed in the celebration of the Mysteries. See *Peace*, l. 313.

[2] The epithet translated 'bull-fed' appears to be in mere humour transferred to Cratinus, from the God of *his* special service, Bacchus or Dionysus. No real explanation is given by the scoliast of the reference to Cratinus. I venture to suspect that the allusion may be to some comedy of Cratinus of which these 'Mysteries' were the chief subject.

Who takes pleasure in scurrilous jesting,
　　　　not regarding the 'whom' and the 'waen;'
Who stays not a strife in the city, but
　　　　is a churl towards his own townsmen;
Who, for his private object, fans their
　　　　factious fury and mutual hate;
Who, for a gift or favour, ministers
　　　　wrong for right as their magistrate;
Sells his ship, or deserts his post, or,
　　　　under colour of trafficking, sends,
Like a Thorycio,[1] thongs, or hemp, or
　　　　pitch to serve the enemies' ends;
He who at the feast of Bacchus,
　　　　having been smartly lashed in a play,
Goes to the Courts, and bringing his action,
　　　　nibbles a hole in the poet's pay:
These, one and all, I forewarn, I forbid, I pro-
　　　　hibit from hearing our mystical song!
And summon all others to lend us their voices,
　　　　and keep this feast the merry night long.

Semichorus. Where the turf invites our feet,
　　　　Where the flowers are rank and sweet,
　　　　　　Brave hearts, advance, advance!
　　　　Stirring foot and merry lip,
　　　　Flinging wanton jest and quip,
　　　　　　Befit the Mystics' dance.
Semichorus. Nay, enough of frolic wit;
　　　　　　Wear the palm who wins in it.
　　　　　　　　Praise ye the Holy Maid:[2]
　　　　　　Lady, Saviour, unto thee,
　　　　　　Rise our strains; for thou wilt be
　　　　　　　　Our never-failing aid.
Chorus.　　And now with holy hymns adorn
　　　　　　Queen Ceres of the golden corn.
Semichorus. Ceres, let thine eye be o'er us,
　　　　　　Lady of the Mysteries!
　　　　　　Look benignly on thy Chorus;
　　　　　　Shield us from our enemies.

---

[1] We have no information about Thorycio.　　　[2] Minerva.

So in mirth and dance and song
We may while the whole day long.

Semichorus. Much to please the laughter-loving,
    Much to please the wiser head,
May I speak : that, all approving,
    Everywhere it may be said,
Worthily our part was done,
Worthily the garland won.

Chorus.   Invoke ye now the lusty God
Who oft with us the dance has trod.

Semichorus. Come, master of the sweetest strain,
    Iäcchus come, to guide our train
      Forth to the Goddess' dwelling; [1]
      And show how, toil-dispelling,
Thy guidance in our festal sport
Beguiles the way, and makes it short.

Come, lover of the dance and song,
    Iäcchus come: to thee belong
      The skirt in frolic tatters,
      And sandal rent.   What matters ?
Protected by thy festal sway,
Unchided we may dance and play.

Come, lover of the song and dance,
    Iäcchus come: looking askance,
      I saw two eyes that twinkled,
      A cheek with laughter wrinkled,
For she looked merrily at me.
Iäcchus, join our company.

Xan. Where is that lass ? for I am much disposed to try
To break a jest and dance with her.

Bacc.   And so am I.
Good people, can you tell me, where does PLUTO dwell ?
For we are just arrived, and never here before.

Chorus. Ye need no farther go, nor ask again ; for know
That happily ye stand before the very door.

---

[1] At Eleusis.   These lyrics probably represent the general character
and songs of the Procession formed at Athens to go to Eleusis for the
celebration of the Mysteries.

Bacc. You sir, pick up the pack.

Xan.   Ideas are to lack!

It is the very thing he said no great while back.

Semichorus. Ye who have the holy sign,
  Ye who share the feast divine,
  Through the flowery grove advance,
  Form the circle, lead the dance.
  I must to the deeper shade,
  Where holy women, wife and maid,
  Worshipping shall spend the night;
  For them I must lift the light.

Semichorus. To our meadows, sprent with flowers,
   With our measured step and sound,
   Gracefully tread ye the ground;
  Ever as the blessed Hours
   Bring the festal season round,
  Onward to our rosy bowers.
  Unto us, and us alone,
   Who, at the divine behest,
   Duteously have shared our best
  In service to our own
   And to the stranger coming guest,[1]
  Is this cheerful sun-light shown.

   [*At the conclusion of their dance the* CHORUS
    retires to the right and left of the orchestra,
    until drawn forward presently by interest
    in the dialogue.

SCENE.—*Before the palace of* PLUTO.

Bacc. Stay: shall I knock?—I did not think of that
  before.

How do the natives here knock at a neighbour's door?

Xan. Pooh! do not hesitate; do it with might and
  main;

You must do everything in Hercules's vein.

Bacc. (*knocking*). Ho! slave! ho!

---

[1] From this we see that the Initiate in the Mysteries of Eleusis were particularly engaged to the duties of charity and hospitality.

ÆACUS, coming out.

Æac.   Who is this?

Bacc.   'Tis HERCULES the puissant.

Æac. Oh, you abominable, shamelessly indecent,
Unutterable blotch! you dare to come to us?
You, Sir! who carried off our good dog Cerberus,
Twisting the poor thing's neck, and ran with him away
From my particular charge.   But you are caught to-day.
There is a Stygian rock, black to the very heart,
A blood-distilling cliff, where thou wilt have thy part;
Hounds of Cocytus will around thee chase and yell;
Echidna, with her hundred heads, hungry and fell,
Will rend thy vitals; and thy lungs shall be a prey
To the Tartesian Muræna; rent away
Thy bleeding kidneys shall Tithrasian Gorgons taste,
For whom, to set them on their dainty feast, I haste.

                                                · [*Exit.*

        [BACCHUS, *during this speech, staggers, leans*
                against the wall, and sinks to sitting on
                the ground.

Xan. What is the matter?

Bacc.   Oh—I feel—

Xan.   Pooh, pooh! get up,
Lest anyone should see.

Bacc.   I'm faint—get me a cup—
Oh no, a sponge of water.

Xan.   Was there ever seen
So rank a coward?

Bacc.   Coward? I? whom do you mean?
I asked you for a sponge; what is there in the fact
To make me coward?

Xan.   Nay, it was a manful act.

Bacc. Aye, so I think.   But were you not indeed afraid
To hear his words?

Xan.   Not I; I cared not what he said.

Bacc. Well, since you swagger thus and are so stout of
                heart,
I'll give up HERCULES, and you shall bear the part.
So take the lion's skin, and take the bludgeon too,
And I will take the pack, and be the slave to you.

Xan. Done! if it must be so. You'll see that Herculeo-
Xanthias will not be faint at heart, like you.

Bacc. Like me? oh,
You whipping-post of Melité, you leather-back!
But come, it is a bargain: so. I take the pack.

[XANTHIAS *takes the insignia of* HERCULES.

Enter MAIDSERVANT *of* PROSERPINE.

Maid (addressing XANTHIAS *as* HERCULES).
Dear HERCULES, come in; come in without a word.
Soon as my Goddess-mistress, Proserpine, had heard
That *you* were at the door, she made the oven hot,
Put an ox upon the spit, and pea-soup in the pot;
There's white bread and brown bread, and every sort of cake,
Of which my mistress bids you come in and partake.

Xan. (hesitating). That's very kind indeed.

Maid. Nay, by Apollo! stay.
We never could permit that you should go away.
The birds are on the spit, the fish is dishing up,
The fry is in the pan, the wine is in the cup;
My lady tempers it; so, without more ado,
Come in.

Xan. Most certainly (*moves to go in*).

Bacc. Pooh! you're not going. You?

Xan. (to BACC.) Here, slave, bring on the pack.

Bacc. (solemnly). You do not mean to say
You think to take in earnest what I did in play?
The jest has had its time. Fool HERCULES no more;
Be XANTHIAS, and take the luggage as before.

Xan. What's this? You are not thinking, surely, to recall
The part you gave to me?

Bacc. Eh? thinking? not at all:
I do. Put down the hide.

Xan. (giving up the insignia). The Gods will see me
righted;
I call on them.

Bacc. What Gods? why, is it not benighted
That you, a slave and mortal, should, except in fun,
Suppose that you can pass for Alcmena's mighty son?

Xan. Well, never mind, then : take the things ; but
    haply, yet,
You may want that of me which you will scarcely get.

Chorus. 'Tis a smart fellow's way, when the sea runs high
    And over the deck, to keep a bright eye
    For a berth where he may be always dry,
      A thoroughly sharp old salt :
    He is not a painted figure that sticks
    For ever and ever in the selfsame fix ;
    But he sees it coming, and the time he nicks
      To be off with a spring and a vault.
    So when times are hard, if there be a spot
    Which is downy and snug, to shift one's lot
    Into that quarter is clever, and what
      Can hardly be called a fault.

        [*While the Chorus is singing,* FIRST HOSTESS
          enters and looks steadily at BACCHUS *in*
          the lion's hide.

1st Host. Why, bless me, Plathané ! here, Plathané,
    don't stop ;
Here is the vagabond who came into the shop
And ate the sixteen rolls.

        Enter SECOND HOSTESS, *running.*

2nd Host.   Don't let the rogue escape.
It is the man indeed !

Xan. (*aside to* BACC.)   Somebody's in a scrape !

1st Host. And twenty collops stewed, just taken from
    the kettle,
Each a half-obole worth.

Xan. (*as before*).   Which somebody must settle.

2nd Host. And garlic without end.

Bacc.   Good woman, you are mad,
And don't know what you say.

1st Host.   That really is too bad.
Because you have those boots, then, does it so surprise you
That, when you least expect it, I should recognise you ?

2nd Host. Good truth, there was the pickle—that I
    have not told,
Nor the new cheese he ate ; and after that the mould ;

And when I only asked him to pay me,—the fellow,
He eyed me through and through, and oh ! to hear him
　　　bellow !

Xan. Just what he always does : 'tis really very sad.

2nd Host. And then he drew his sword, I thought that
　　　he was mad.

Xan. Poor thing !

2nd Host.　　　We ran up stairs, as fast as we were able,
But he ran out, taking the napkins from the table.

Xan. And that's a trick of his; but something must be
　　　done.

1st Host. There's Cleon [1] is the Mayor; go, fetch him
　　　for me : run.

2nd Host. And beg, on my account, Hyperbolus to
　　　follow.

We'll make the rascal smart.

1st Host.　　　　　　Fie on your greedy swallow !
What pleasure it would be to knock the grinders out
With which you ate my little stores, you heavy lout.

2nd Host. And I should like to throw him into Felon's
　　　Hole.

1st Host. I'd cut the throat which ate the short-bread
　　　that he stole.

But I will go to Cleon; he will find the thread
And wind the fellow off: there need no more be said.

　　　　　　　　　　　[*Exeunt Women.*

Bacc. I love you, XANTHIAS : yes, hang me but I do.

Xan. Don't speak: I wouldn't stand in HERCULES's shoe.

Bacc. My dearest XANTHIAS—

Xan.　　　　　　Pooh ! pooh ! except in fun,
How can I, slave and mortal, be Alcmena's son ?

Bacc. I know, I know you're angry; justly so: but now—
—Yes, thrash me if you please ; I won't complain, I vow.
Pray take the Club and Hide, and if I ever try
To get them back again, then may my Wife and I,
And may my children too, be hurried to perdition.

---

[1] The reader of *Knights* and *Peace*, especially l. 574 and following, may
reflect with what pleasure Aristophanes found himself in the neighbourhood of the 'tanner'! And *now*, we see, he may speak of him by his
true name.

Xan. I take them back upon your oath and proposition.
                [XANTHIAS *resumes the costume of Hercules.*
Chorus.   Now you have got again
                        The Club and Lion's mane,
You must pluck up your spirit and look very brave:
                · For if you bring a shame   ·
                        On Hercules's name
You will carry the bundle again like a slave.
Xan.   You are quite right, my friend,
                I know, if matters mend,
That he will try to cheat me as he did before.
                I'll look, to take your hint,
                Like a sprig of peppermint,
And at once; for I hear there's a noise at the door.

                Enter ÆACUS and Attendants.

Æac. Take this dog-stealer up: clap handcuffs on the
        thief.
He'll smart for it; be quick.
Bacc. (*aside to* XANTHIAS).   Somebody comes to grief.
        [*Attendants go to seize* XANTHIAS, *who brandishes
            the club.*
Xan. Be hanged; don't come near me.
Æac.   Ho! ho! Sir, you would fight?
Some three of you go in; and do not spare your might.
                [XANTHIAS *knocks down his assailants.*
Bacc. This really is too bad! The fellow, after stealing, ·
Is beating honest men.
Xan.   'Tis very handsome dealing.
Æac. 'Tis not to be endured.
Xan.   Good Sir, by Jove, I swear,
I never stole from you the value of a hair;
Nor ever came before upon this expedition.
But come, Sir, I will make a handsome proposition.
You see that slave of mine: now, put him to the trial:
I take it on my life he'll second my denial.
Æac. How put him to the trial?
Xan.   Bind him and strip his back;
Scourge him with bristle whips; put him upon the rack;

Let him be crushed with bricks, the better if they're hot;
Pour acids up his nose;—but one thing you shall not,—
Do anything besides—yes, scourge him till he's raw,
But not with onion tops, nor yet with barley straw.

Æac. The offer's fair. And if, while I the truth unearth,
I chance to maim your slave, I'll pay you what he's worth.

Xan. Don't speak of such a trifle; take him off and try
     him.

Æac. Nay, I will do it here; while you are standing by
     him,
To hear his words yourself.

           (*To* BACCHUS.) Now drop the pack and strip:
And don't tell any lies while I lay on the whip.

Bacc. What? torture an Immortal? no. Dare not to
     lay
A hand on me : or, blame yourself. ·

Æac.   What's that you say?

Bacc. I am the Immortal, BACCHUS; Jupiter's my
     father :
He is a slave.

Æac. (*to* XANTH.)   You hear?

Xan.   And say, 'tis reason rather
Why you should lay it on : a whipping will reveal it;
For if he is a God, of course he will not feel it.

Bacc. You vagabond! yourself, you say, you are a God :
Why should not you, like me, be tested with the rod?

Xan. The offer's fair, I own. Come, worthy Sir, and try;
Whichever of us two is first to raise a cry,
Or show a sense of whip by flinch, or wink or quaking,
That fellow is no God : there can be no mistaking.

Æac. A noble heart spoke there!—to own it is your
     due :
No flinching from the right.—So, now, strip, both of you.

Xan. But how will you be fair?

Æac.   Without the slightest pother;
I'll give you cut for cut, first one and then the other.

Xan. Unimpeachable the plan! so now, go to the work;
Watch narrowly in me the least desire to shirk.

               [XANTHIAS *offers his back for a blow.* ÆACUS
               strikes.

Æac. I hit you.

Xan.　　　　　　No, by Jove?

Æac.　　　　　　　　　You did not feel it then?
I'll try a cut upon the other fellow.

Bacc. (*sucking a breath while he is hit*).   When?

Æac. I hit you.

Bacc.　　　　　Ah? indeed? how did I stop a sneeze?

Æac. I'm sure I do not know.—Now, you Sir, if you
　　　please

Xan. Be quick (*is hit*)—e-ah-te-tœ!

Æac.　　　　　　　What's that 'e-ah-te-tœ'?
Did you feel anything?

Xan.　　　　　　Oh! not at all. You see
It crossed my thought just as you might have touched my
　　　skin,
When the next sacred Rites to Hercules begin.[1]

Æac. You are a pious man.—So now to him again.

Bacc. Hoa! hoa!

Æac.　　　What's that?

Bacc.　　　　　　I see some horsemen on the plain.

Æac. But tears are in your eyes?

Bacc.　　　　　　　There's onion in the air.

Æac. You do not feel the lash?

Bacc.　　　　　　Pooh! nothing: 'tis a hair!

Æac. Well then, the other one must take his turn about.

Xan. Dear! dear!

Æac.　　　What's that?

Xan. (*putting up his foot*).   A thorn; I wish you'd take
　　　it out.

Æac. Now you;—for which is rogue there really is no
　　　telling.

Bacc. Apollo!—who at Delos, or in Delphian caves art
　　　dwelling.

Xan. He smarted then: you heard him, Sir.

Bacc.　　　　　　　What I? I smart?
I did but quote a verse of Hipponax by heart.

Xan. Try the breadbasket, Sir; that is the place, you'll
　　　find.

---

[1] The explanation given is that the exclamation uttered by Xanthias
was a cry in use at the feast of Hercules in the Attic borough Diomeia.

Æac. We're losing time indeed.

　　　　(*To* Bacchus.[1])　Come, turn your front behind.

Bacc. Neptune !

Xan.　　　　　That touched the nerves !

Bacc.　　　　　Whom the Ægean serves ;

　　　　　　　　Lord of the rocky shore,

　　　　　　　　Lord of the waves that roar.

Æac. By Ceres, I cannot a safe conclusion win

Which of you is the God ; so, both of you come in :

My Lord upon his throne, and Lady Proserpine,

Will find it out at once, being themselves divine.

Bacc. That's true ! I only wish that you had thought of
　　　　that,

Before you welted me with your confounded cat.

　　　　　　　　　　　　　　　　　　　[Exeunt.

PARABASIS.

Chorus.　Muse of the sacred choirs, descend ;

　　　　　Invited by our pleasant song,

　　　　　Here you shall see a mighty throng

　　　　Where clevernesses have no end,

　　　　　More daring each than Cleophon ;[2]

　　　　Whose twice-loquacious lips beat hollow

　　　　The twitter of a Thracian swallow

　　　　　Her spray outlandish sitting on :

　　　　But he vies with the Nightingale

　　　　Piping his melancholy wail,

　　　　　Although the votes had even gone.

---

[1] It should not be lost upon the reader that the mischievous suggestion of Xanthias has disturbed the fair reckoning of Æacus. He, and
Bacchus too, forget that this ' turn ' should have fallen to Xanthias.

[2] Cleophon was the Cleon of his day, a leader of the popular.party.
Some five years earlier he had sufficient influence to defeat a proposal for peace with the Lacedæmonians. In the course of this year,
during the siege of Athens, the aristocratic party effected his overthrow
and death. It does not appear to what circumstances the last lines of the
strophe allude. Equal votes were held to give acquittal of a criminal
charge.

Semichorus. We shall be within the office
               which the sacred Chorus bears,
   If we tender to the City
               good advice on state affairs.
   Unto us, then, good it seems that
               citizens should be relieved
   From disturbing fears and forfeits.
               What though óne has been deceived
   By the arts of Phrynichus,[1] and
               failed in duty once or twice,
   He admits his fault : then, be not
               in forgiving over nice.
   To degrade a citizen must
               surely be a great mistake,
   While the fighting of an action
               on your galleys is to make
   Any slave a full Platæan [2]
               and a master out of hand.
   Not that such a gift of honour
               is a policy ill-planned ;
   Nay, I praise your wisdom in it.
               But when citizens have fought,
   And their fathers, all your battles,
               and are kinsmen too, you ought
   Readily to grant the pardon
               which they heartily desire.
   You are genial in your nature :
               Pray relax this stubborn ire :

---

[1] The scoliasts are very uncertain in determining this Phrynichus ;
but regarding the strength and direction of Aristophanes's political principles, it seems most probable that he refers to Phrynichus the oligarch,
who entered warmly into the revolution of the Four Hundred, and was
assassinated during their term of power. On their subversion Pisander,
Aristarchus, and doubtless many others, were obliged to leave Attica.
Then the subject of this Choric address will be an appeal to the Athenians
to reverse the attainder of so many of that broken party as had not yet
returned to the country, or recovered the rights of citizenship. See
Chron. Table.

[2] After the loss of their city the faithful Platæans were adopted to
the rank and rights of Athenian citizens.

Let us frankly repossess them,
              overlooking little slips,
Who have common blood and country,
              who have fought upon our ships.
Give them back their rights as freemen,
              let them tread high Honour's road.
If we will be proud and stubborn,
              if we lay our rancour's load
On the City in its struggles
              with the angry seas and skies,
Time will come when we shall find that
              our proceedings were not wise.

Chorus.   If I have any skill to scan
              The bearings of a human ape,
              Who will not very long escape,.
           That Cleigenes, the little man,
              The nuisance in our public way,
              Bath-keeping scamp, and rogue in soap,
              Will early find his length of rope.
              He knows what people think and say,
              Therefore he is to quarrel quick;
              And never goes without a stick,
           Lest, drunk, he should be stripped some day.

Semichorus. It has often struck me that the
              men employed about the State,
And the new and ancient coinage
              undergo a common fate.
That, which we have ceased to use, was
              honest metal through and through,
Handsome of the handsomest, and
              ever truest of the true;
Fairly struck from perfect die; and
              ringing with a cheery sound;
Equally with Greek and Stranger
              current all the country round.
This is gone from circulation;
              that which now supplies its place
Is of yesterday's production,
              faulty die and metal base.

Thus among our Citizens, if
        there are any known for worth,
Unimpeachable in honour,
        sterling principle and birth,
In the schools of taste and science
        formed and liberally bred,
These we treat with contumely :
        while the men we use instead
Are a trash of brass, and strangers ;
        ' slave ' is written on each face ;
Rogue-born sons of rogue the father ;
        latest comers to the place ;
Whom, in better times, the City
        barely would have deigned to use,[1]
In a time of plague or blasting,
        when a demon claimed his dues.
Foolish people, change your fashion,
        use again the better mint.
If they right the city vessel,
        there will be a credit in't.
If we come to misadventure,
        whatsoever that may be,
Men of sense will have to say, we
        hung upon a worthy tree.

---

[1] Evidently as propitiatory human victims.

Enter XANTHIAS *and* ÆACUS [1] *in conversation.*

Æac. By Jove, a noble-minded fellow, I should think,
Your master is.
    Xan.   Aye, noble truly; he can drink.
    Æac. Nay, but I mean 'twas noble in him, when you said
You were *his* Master, that he did not break your head.
    Xan. He dared not.
    Æac.   You can do that servant's duty well,
Which always gives me more delight than I can tell.
    Xan. Delight? I miss your meaning.
    Æac.   When I get my fling
Of backbiting my master, I feel like a king.
    Xan. But what when on your back a thrashing has been
           lavished,
And you go out of doors and mutter?
    Æac.   I am ravished!
    Xan. If you have meddled, what?
    Æac.   I cannot find the word!
    Xan. What, eavesdropping and telling neighbours what
           you heard?
    Æac. I'm frantic!
    Xan.   Let me have your hand; give me a kiss,
And let me kiss you too. But tell me what is this?
By Jove (who is our fellow-slave), explain to me
What all this noise within and quarrelling can be?
    Æac. 'Tis ÆSCHYLUS's wrangle with EURIPIDES.
    Xan. Indeed!
    Æac.   A mighty suit with pleas and counterpleas
Is moved among the dead with party strife and railing.
    Xan. But what about?

---

[1] Some MSS. read 'A slave of Æacus,' which certainly would better
accord with the tenor of the dialogue. But here, as generally elsewhere,
the text of Bekker is followed as an authority. If Aristophanes had
given the part really to a slave, there seems no reason why he should
not have assigned it to a slave 'of Pluto.'

Æac.   We have a custom here prevailing,
Touching the higher arts, that, for the time, the man,
Who in his craft has proved the master artisan,
Should in the public hall enjoy a daily mess,
And have a seat of honour next to PLUTO.

Xan.   —Yes—

Æac. Until a greater artist in his proper line
Should come; who then of course would have the right to
          dine.

Xan. But why in such a strife should ÆSCHYLUS take
          part?

Æac. Because he had the seat assigned to Tragic Art.

Xan. Who has it now?

Æac.   No sooner had EURIPIDES
Come down than with his art he set about to please
The men who break into our houses, steal our coats,
Cut now a purse, or, changeably, their fathers' throats;
Of whom hell has great store.   The villains of this sort,
Charmed with his shifts and quirks, and keenness in
          retort,
Declared he was the master man.   Whereat puffed up,
He claimed the seat where ÆSCHYLUS was set to sup.

Xan. Was he not stoned?

Æac.   Oh, not at all.   The people cried,
Demanding that the right to mastership be tried.

Xan. The rascals!

Æac.   Yes: they filled the heaven with their cries.

Xan. But surely ÆSCHYLUS was not without allies?

Æac. The better sort are fewer:
(*with a motion towards the Audience*) just as in this place.

Xan. But how does PLUTO mean to manage in the
          case?

Æac. He means to make a match between them even
          now,
And bring the art of each to proof.

Xan.   But tell me,—how
It happens SOPHOCLES has never claimed the seat?

Æac. Not he!—But when he came right glad he was to
          meet   [face;
His former friend; and shook his hand, and kissed his
And yielded willingly to ÆSCHYLUS the place.

But now, for so I heard CLEIDEMIDES aver,
He means to make himself a bye-competitor :
If Æschylus should win he leaves the place alone ;
But with Euripides he will contest the throne.

Xan. And will this be?

Æac. The conflict is immediate.
Frightful to think of! Muse-work will be tried by weight.

Xan. What? will they put a tragedy upon the scales?

Æac. Aye, bring the standards ; see where an expression
fails ;
Mete words by cubits ; bring the substance to degrees,
Diameters and angles. For Euripides
Requires that verse by verse they shall be scrutinised.

Xan. If Æschylus is not indignant—I'm surprised.

Æac. He lowers his head just like a bull about to toss.

Xan. But who is to be judge?

Æac. There they were at a loss ;
For fit men were so scarce that they could think of none :
And Æschylus and Athens hardly were at one.

Xan. He thought, belike, the tribe of thief abounded
there.

Æac. At any rate he thought that the Athenians were
Slight judges of a poet. So, it is committed
Into your master's hands, as eminently fitted.
But let us in. For, when a master has a trouble,
The servant's back will often have to carry double.

[*Exeunt.*

Chorus.[1]

Indignation indeed in the heart of the Thunderer will boil,
Soon as he catches a sight of his agile and voluble rival
Whetting his tusks : and his eyes in their terrible mad-
ness,
Roll about incessantly.

---

[1] The translator, in the instance of this Chorus only, has endeavoured without rhyme to imitate the metre and rhythm of the original, where every syllable corresponds through the four stanzas. In the original at least, it will be recognised as an admirable preface to the critical examination of the style of the two poets.

Then will towering phrases in eagerness rush to the
 battle :
Quibbles will break at the axle, contrivances fly into splin-
 ters,
  In the repelling the high-riding words of the hero,
    Sounding-phrasi-tectural.
Bristling up on his neck all the shaggy endowment of
 nature,
Knitting his terrible brows, he will gather to launch with
 a bellow
  Contabulations of syllables, torn from the text-block
    With a giant's energy.
Smooth-Tongue comes to the battle, the mouth-working
 tester of verses,
Quietly splits an expression, and shaking the envious
 bridles,
  Into a nothing reduces the words which have tried the
    Lungs of his antagonist.

Enter PLUTO, BACCHUS, ÆSCHYLUS, EURIPIDES.

Eur. Urge me no more. The seat by right, I say, is
   mine :
I am the better Artist; and he should resign.
 Bacc. Why are you silent, ÆSCHYLUS ? you surely hear.
 Eur. He's ever to begin with silent and austere ;
In all his tragedies he does it, for sensation.
 Bacc. Good Sir; do not begin with too much exultation.
 Eur. I know the man and have considered him of old,
Uncouth in his conceptions, arrogantly bold,
Undoored, unbitted, of his lips incontinent,
A rambler in discourse, much-fustianiloquent.
 Æsch. Child of the greenfield-goddess, beggar-maker,
   patcher ;
And dare you this to me, you floating-chitcat-catcher ?
But yet you shall repent.
 Bacc.   Stay, ÆSCHYLUS, do not,
I beg you, let your wrath become so very hot.
 Æsch. Nay, check me not, until I bring to proper shame,
With all his consequence, this poet of the lame.

Bacc. Be quick, my lad, a lamb;—bring out a lamb
    that's black;[1]
A tempest is upon us, and the skies will crack.
Æsch. Oh thou who string'st together Cretan monodies,
And introducest to the Art incestuous ties,—
Bacc. Much-honoured ÆSCHYLUS, pray moderate thy
    course;
Restrain thyself. Thou, surely, wilt not bide the force
Of such a pitiless hailstorm, poor EURIPIDES!
Withdraw thee to some shelter for thy better ease;
Lest by some angry word your brain-pan should be broken,
And from the fracture *Telephus* be spilt—unspoken.
Restrain that vehemence to which you are addicted,
And gently, ÆSCHYLUS, convict and be convicted.
It is not fitting that two Poets vent their ire
Like baker-wives: but *you* roar like an oak on fire.
Eur. For me, I am prepared to do just as he likes.
I shall not hesitate at striking if he strikes.
The lines, the rhythm, the sinews of my plays I wager,
The *Peleus*, or the *Æolus*, or *Meleager*;
Nay, I will not decline if he choose *Telephus*.
Bacc. Explain how you intend to fight it, ÆSCHYLUS.
Æsch. 'Twas not my wish at all to fight it here below.
The trial is not made on even terms.
Bacc.   How so?
Æsch. Like his with him, my poems did not die with me;
So he may read. But as you wish, so let it be.
Bacc. Fetch me some incense here, and fire, that, as 'tis
    fit,
I may devoutly pray, before this strife of wit,
For power to judge the cause with critical acūmen.
Meantime in proper strain invoke the Muses, you men.

Chorus. Ye Nine pure Maids of Jove, whose ken
Pierces the shrewd and subtle minds of men,

---

[1] Black sheep were sacrificed to the Infernal Gods and to Tempest.
    Sic fatus, meritos aris mactavit honores . . .
    Nigram hiemi pecudem, Zephyris felicibus albam.
                                        Æn. III. 118-120.

That strike new thoughts, when, racking the invention
To find new falls, [1] they meet in fierce contention,
  Come, Muses; and presiding sit:
  Watch ye the force of rival wit;
  And give them words; that neither fail
  When verse-dust may incline the scale.
   The contest is engaged,
  And this great wit-war must be waged.

Bacc. Now I allow to both a fitting space of leisure
To make your several prayers before ye quote a measure.

Æsch. Ceres, who ever cherishedst this mind of mine,
Make thou me worthy of thy mysteries divine.

Bacc. (to EURIPIDES.) Now you, Sir, put your incense
  on the altar.

Eur.   Nay:
For they are other Gods than these to whom I pray.

Bacc. Gods of your own perhaps, new minted? [2]

Eur.   Possibly.

Bacc. Pray to your private Gods, whoever they may be.

Eur. Æther, who dost to me the food of life dispense,
Tongue's Versatility, and Shrewd Intelligence,
Nostrils that snuff all essences too fine for sight,
Grant me a hold on words, and strong refuting might.

Chorus. Let us too have our station
  To view the strife; where wits so keen
  Will fence with words in dainty modulation.
  For passions stirred and tongue unsparing
   Leave one no room to choose between
  Two poets of unquestioned daring.
   One will produce, as ever,
   A something very clever
    And exquisitely neat:
   Him will the other shake
   With words of weight to make
    Discomfiture complete.

---

[1] Devices for throwing an antagonist. Language borrowed from the wrestling-ground.

[2] Aristophanes always treats Euripides as a disciple of Socrates, the Socrates of the comedy *Clouds*. It was now eighteen years since that picture was exhibited; we may understand from this and some other like touches that Aristophanes deliberately persisted in the view there given of the character and doctrine of Socrates.

Bacc. Now, forth to the encounter spring :
          and looking to your credit,
See that you say a clever thing,
       · and no one else has said it.
Eur. Hereafter I will manifest
          what I am, as a Poet :
That *he* is but a cheat at best,
          I say and I will show it,
When he brings foolish persons in
          to mock the poor spectator
(A habit caught from taking Phryn-
          ichus[1] for educator).
A figure you will sometimes see,
          wrapped in a veil that flutters,
Achilles or a Niobe ;
          but not a word it utters !
A mere excuse, a gross abuse,
          not tragedy at all, sir.
Bacc. By Jove, it's true ! I grant it you.
Eur.   A fault not rare nor small, sir.
Meanwhile the Chorus had to sing
          three melodies, in fact, or
Some four, in an unbroken string ;
          but not a word the actor !
Bacc. That silence used to win my praise ;
          I was not less delighted
Than with the speakers nowadays.
Eur.   Because you were benighted.
Bacc. And so say I.   But tell me why
          he did it ?
Eur.   For sensation.
To keep the hapless sitters by
          in constant expectation,

---

[1] There can be no question that *this* Phrynichus is the successor of
Thespis and predecessor of Æschylus as tragic dramatist. I presume
that it is understood that the Attic Drama was founded upon the Chorus.
Gradually only would other characters and plot absorb the chief interest of
the drama. The mere want of qualified actors would for some time limit
the invention of the poet. The use of *mute* persons, or characters nearly
mute, by Æschylus and by Phrynichus would doubtless be offensive to
those whose taste was already formed upon an improved art.

Till Niobe should speak! meanwhile,
   the drama was proceeding.
Bacc. Oh, fool! to let him so beguile
   my ignorance unheeding!
Pray, pray, compose yourself: what need
   to be so agitated?
Eur. Because I hit him home; indeed
   I may be too elated.
Thus, having fooled us, when at last
   his play is in the middle,
Come twelve huge words of pure bombast,
   to all a perfect riddle,
High-crested, beetle-browed, and tall,
   to fill us all with fear, sir.

Æsch. Oh! oh!—
Bacc.   Be quiet.
Eur.   Nonsense all.
Bacc. (*to* ÆSCHYLUS). Don't grind your teeth, my dear sir.
Eur. Scamanders, words like dizzy cliffs,
   abysmal excavations,
Or brazen-taloned eagle-griffs,
   their broad shield's decorations.
'Twas not an easy work to set
   oneself to find a meaning.
Bacc. True, true: I never can forget
   the fever I have been in,
Tossing about my bed, because
   my mind would still be seeking
What sort of bird the 'horse-cock'[1] was,
   of which I heard him speaking.
Æsch. You blockhead! 'twas a figure-head,
   such as a captain fixes
For mark upon his ship.—
Bacc.   Instead,
   I thought it was Eryxis.[2]

---

[1] The word of which this is etymologically a translation was used by Æschylus. Its meaning was not very obvious in Aristophanes's day, or we should not find it quizzed by him here and elsewhere. It seems likely that the word 'horse' was used adjectively, in the sense of 'huge.'

[2] To the audience Eryxis was known, and probably the reason why Bacchus fell into the error of thinking that *he* was the 'horse-cock.' I am afraid that we must be content to remain in ignorance.

Eur. A cock in Tragedy at all
         is highly indecorous.
Æsch. You infidel, what shall I call
         what you have set before us?
Eur. Not 'horsecocks' nor 'goatstags' by Jove,
         the creatures he has made his;
Like those that rove through field and grove
         in needlework by ladies.
But when from you to me the art
         came down in due succession,
Puffed and disfigured in each part
         with tumours of expression,
At once I used emollients,
         and, to relieve the burden,
Threw in some light divertisements,
         with here and there a word in;
Beet-poultices I then applied,
         where swellings showed it needing,
And juice of little speeches tried,
         strained through my former reading;
Last, monodies I gave for fare,
         Cephisophon [1] infusing,
Mixing the articles with care,
         not trifles lightly using.
The Prologist was made to tell
         the drama's first suggestion,
Its origin and—
Bacc.   It was well
         your own [2] was not in question.
Eur. The story's course no dumb show broke,
         for mutes—I would not stand them;
The slave as well as master spoke,
         the master, maid, and grandame.
Æsch. And did you not deserve to die
         for outrage so un-Attic?

---

[1] The slave and familiar of Euripides, supposed to assist him in composition. See *Acharnians*, l. 331.

[2] Again the invidious reference to the mother of Euripides. See *Acharnians*, l. 405, and many other places.

Eur. That, by Apollo, did not I ;
                'twas truly democratic !
Bacc. Nay, do not tell us your intent,
                to justify the action ;
    For this is a divertisement
                that gives no satisfaction.
Eur. From me spectators caught a store
                of points-for an oration.
Bacc. I would that you had burst before
                you gave that education.
Eur. I introduced the nicest laws
                and measures of expression ;
    To seize a thought, to weigh a cause,
                to estimate profession,
    To look about, to cast a doubt,
                and be somewhat suspicious.
Bacc. I grant your claim, and to your shame ;
                for what is this but vicious ?
Eur. The ways and thoughts of every day,
                before your eyes presented,
    Challenged your judgment on the play,
                for well or ill invented.
    I never tried the hearer's mind
                to dazzle or astony
    With Cycnuses, or Memnon-kind,
                or ' bell-begarnished-pony ' ;
    But, dissipating such pretence,
    I made the art speak common sense ;
    And those who came to hear were taught
    To shape an argument or thought ;
    And what they had to do and tell,
    To do it and to say it well.
    The master of a house would find
    The use of an enquiring mind,
    When saying, ' What have you been at ? '
    ' Where's this ? ' and ' Who has taken that ? '
Bacc. Aye ; now, each smart Athenian,
    On going home, says to his man,
    ' Where is the pot ? ' ' Was it the cat
    Ate the fore-quarter of the sprat ? '

' Alas ! the dish I bought last year
Is broken.'   ' It is very clear
Some one has touched the olives ;—who ?—
And yesterday's cooked garlic, too.'
Whereas before, with open mouths,
They sat as mute as Mammacouths !
Chorus. ' Thou seest this, illustrious Achilles.' [1]
How wilt thou answer him ?   But, prithee, learn
    To rein thy temper, lest the fillies
    Bear thee beyond the olive [2] turn.
    Though grievous be the accusation,
    Yet answer not with irritation.
    Close-reef thy sails : so shalt thou keep
    Thy boat the better in thy hand :
    But when the tempest falls asleep,
And light winds follow thee, let them command.
First of the Greeks to build the lofty verse and show
What Tragedy might be, now let thy fountain flow.
Æsch. It angers me to answer him ; and I am vexed
At such a chance : but, lest he say I am perplexed,
Answer me this : How should a Poet earn men's praise ?
 Eur. By wisdom and instruction that shall tend to raise
The tone of public morals.
 Æsch.   Be it so.   If you
Have not this done, but have converted to a crew
Of reprobates a people that was great and high,
Tell me, what penalty is due to you ?
 Bacc.   To die.
Do not ask him.
 Æsch.   What were the men I left behind ?
A six-foot race ; upright in carriage as in mind :
Not skulking idlers, talkers in the market-place ;
Not tricksters by profession, as is now the case ;
But men whose hearts were on a spear, a blow well
  struck,
A handsome helmet, greaves, and seven-bull-hided pluck.

---

[1] This line is from a lost drama of Æschylus, *The Myrmidons*.
[2] An olive tree, or clump of olives, marked the point of turning in the chariot-race-course. The course lay within the olives.

Bacc. The mischief! he will kill me with this helmet-
     trade.

Eur. But tell me how your men of this brave mould were
     made?

Bacc. Nay, ÆSCHYLUS, no haughty airs: say, how 'twas
     done.

Æsch. I made a drama breathing martial life.

Eur.   .   Which one?

Æsch. *Seven against Thebes;* for everyone who saw it
     burned
With zeal for war.

Bacc.   There you did ill, and richly earned
A whipping; for you made the Thebans better men.

Æsch. You might have trained yourselves: but you de-
     clined it then.
Then in my *Persians,* gracing glorious actions, I
Spurred the desire to work and win the mastery.

Bacc. That pleased me, when, about Darius' death, the
     Chorus
Cried 'ah-i-ah,' and beat their hands, like this, before us.

Æsch. Such is the Poet's business. See, what service
     they,
The nobler, to their fellows rendered in their day.
Orpheus instructed us in holy mysteries,
And forbade bloodshedding. Musæus made us wise
To heal distempers and to learn the words of God;
The tillage of the soil was taught by Hesiod:
And whence his high renown had Homer the divine?
But that he taught to form the glorious battle-line,
The points of soldiership, and weapons' seemly trim.

Bacc. Not Pantacles the awkward! Homer failed with
     him;
Who, lately leading a procession, to our laughter,
Put on his casque and tried to tie the crest on after.

Æsch. Nay, but the valiant men are many he has
     taught.
Not least, our Lamachus. Thence I myself have sought
The many types of virtue which I have expressed:
Patroclus, lion-hearted Teucer, and the rest,

If haply I might move some virtuous citizen
To train himself unto the measure of these men.
Phædras and Sthenobæas were not of my fashion !
Nay, never did I shape a woman slave of passion.[1]

Eur. True : Venus had no part in thee !

Æsch.   Might she have none !
She had in thee and thine ; as thou didst find, undone.[2]

Bacc. By Jupiter, that's true : for characters you
  feigned
For others' wives to bear, your own full well sustained.

Eur. How say you, wretch, my Sthenobæas hurt the
  state ?

Æsch. As vice its likeness vice ever does propagate.

Eur. But did my *Phædra* sin against the common
  tale ?

Æsch. It did not.   But the Poet ought to throw a veil
Over the evil : not parade it.   Children's ears
We trust to tutors, Poets train the riper years.
And Poets should but speak what useful is and good.

Eur. And when they make men speak what should be
  understood,
Should they express themselves in mountain-altitude ?
Call you that useful ?

Æsch.   Must I tell a wit so rude,
That ample thoughts and great conceptions justly breed
Proportionate expression ?   Demigods must need
Use a more large discourse than ours ; as they invest
Their forms in statelier robes, appropriately dressed,
At my suggestion.   You have marred that order.

Eur.   How ?

Æsch. To move the souls of men to wholesome pity,
  now
You dress a prince in rags.

Eur.   What harm can thence arise ?

Æsch. The dignity of place is lowered in men's eyes.

---

[1] It is noted that this boast put into the mouth of Æschylus is not jus-
tified by fact.   Clytemnestra is such, in *Agamemnon*.

[2] Euripides at least did not, like Molière, make merry with adultery ;
but if he did anything to taint public morals, his wife, it is said, like
Molière's, requited the fault upon him.

Your man of wealth avoids the service of the city;
And, showing poverty in dress, invites your pity.[1]

Bacc. Aye, but the softest wool is had for underlining,
And on the best of fish you'll see that he means dining.

Æsch. Through *him* it is the rising generation courts
Praises for chattering, and flies athletic sports.
The sort of men that used with will to ply the oar
Now answer to their captains, and obey no more.
In my time such a kind of rascal did not know
Another form of words than 'soup' and 'ho-e-yo!'

> To him a thousand ills are owing;
> Through him the place is overflowing
> With law-clerks making out decrees,
> Indictments, processes and pleas;
> With hustings-wags and mountebanks,
> To cheat and trick the people's thanks:
> Till, out of all condition, none
> Are able with a lamp to run.

Bacc. By Jove, no: at Panathenæa
> I laughed till I was faint to see a
> Fellow running almost double,
> White, hindmost, corpulent, in trouble:
> The mob within the gate that stands
> Received him with their open hands;
> Oh! but his naked ribs and back
> Sounded with many a hearty smack;
> > Till, blowing out his lamp,
> In dudgeon did the rogue decamp.

Chorus. This is no light affair, and vigorously pressed.
> Where one so stiffly holds his cause,
> And one from falls new vantage draws,
> It is not easy to divine which has the best.

---

[1] When the richer citizens are marked to bear extraordinary public burdens, many will try to dissemble their wealth. Men so disposed would hardly wait for the sanction of Euripides's heroes. In every case where the point of a reflection depends upon the name of an article of clothing, it becomes an insurmountable difficulty to a translator to render the idea simply. Such is the case with the word χιτών in the next line. It must mean a garment next the skin and not seen. The dissembling rich man would wear that of the finest texture.

But shift your ground : recruit your forces :
For artifice is fertile in design.
    If ye have any such resources,
    Speak from your stores of new or old;
    Some unsuspected art unfold
And something venture on that clever is and fine.

But if ye have a fear lest among these that sit
    Spectators, there be lack of sense
    To appreciate your finer fence ;
Lay such misgiving by, there is no ground for it :
    For old campaigners are they all ;
And each one has his Book of Art, and knows the
        Rules ;
    Besides a mother-wit not small
    And keenly sharpened for this fray.
    So give your wit its freest play,
With no suspicion that your audience are fools.

Eur. Now take his Prologues. There the Tragedy begins:
There first will I reprove your clever Poet's sins.
In giving out the facts he is not clear at all.
Bacc. Which will you have of him ?
Eur.   I will have several :
One from the *Oresteia* I will first discuss.
Bacc. Hold every man his tongue. Repeat it, ÆSCHYLUS.
Æsch. ' Hermes of Earth, who watchest with a friendly
        eye
My Father's realm, be thou my guardian and ally :
Here to this land I come and have returned once more.'
Bacc. Find you a fault in that?
Eur.   Aye, more than half a score.
Bacc. But all the lines together are no more than three.
Eur. But twenty faults in every one of them I see.
Bacc. Be counselled, ÆSCHYLUS, and hold your tongue ;
        each verse
Over the three will only make the matter worse.
Æsch. I hold my tongue for him ?
Bacc.   If you let me advise.
Eur. At once there's fault enough in that to fill the
        skies.

Æsch. (*to* BACC.)   You are mistaken, see.

Bacc.   'Tis no affair of mine.

Æsch. Pray where am I in fault?

Eur.   Again recite the line.

Æsch. ' Hermes of Earth, who watchest with a friendly
   eye
My Father's realm.'—

Eur.   And *this* Orestes says hard by
The tomb of his dead father?

Æsch.   That I don't deny.

Eur. And Hermes was then watching with that friendly
   eye,
And aiding, it may be with fraud, his father's wife,
When she by force despoiled her husband of his life?

Bacc. Not of *that* Hermes spoke he, but of ' Good-at-
   need '
Hermes of Earth.[1]   And that is clear if you would heed;
'Twas of his father he had this official care.

Eur. Oh? ' of his father '? he took to it as the heir?
This Hermes of the Earth! the fault is so much bigger.

Bacc. Then in his father's right, he must have been
   grave-digger.

Æsch. BACCHUS, the wine you drink does not smell
   pleasantly.

Bacc. Continue now.

Æsch.   ' Be thou my guardian and ally:
Here to this land I come and have returned once more.'

Eur. Your clever Æschylus repeats what he said just
   before.

Bacc. Repeats? how?

Eur.   Note the word: I'll make you understand.
He says ' I have returned ' and ' I come to '—this land:
They are the same.

Bacc.   By Jove, as though a man had said,
Lend me a *bucket*, or a *pail* will do instead !

Æsch. 'Tis not the same, you chatterbox, and I maintain,
'Tis the best verse of all.

Bacc.   How so? I pray; explain.

---

[1] For the curious variety of the attributives of Mercury, and the uses
they are comically turned to, see the last scene in the comedy *Plutus.*

Æsch. A man who wills may 'come;' but exiles driven
     out
Come and return unto the land once more.
   Bacc.   No doubt.
EURIPIDES, what say you?
   Eur.   Driven forth to roam,
Orestes did not so return back to his home,
But came back privily.
   Bacc.   By Mercury, 'twas so;
And shrewdly said!—But what you mean I hardly know.
   Eur. Recite another line.
   Bacc.   Aye, ÆSCHYLUS, recite.
And you, Sir, keep an eye to bring the fault to light.
   Æsch. ' From this sepulchral mound, Father, I summon
     thee
To hear and listen.'—
   Eur.   There! again tautology.
' To hear ' and ' listen ' are synonymous it's clear.
   Bacc. But pray observe, you rogue, *whom* he addresses
     here;
When one desires attention from the Dead to gain
One has to speak three times :—and often then in vain.
   Æsch. But how do *you* make Introductions?
   Eur.   You shall know.
And if you find tautologies, or you can show
That I have stuffed in matter in the tale's despite,
Spit on me and my work.
   Bacc.   So then do you recite.
For I have nothing else to do but sit and hear
The excellences of your Prologues made appear.
   Eur. ' At first was Œdipus a fortune-favoured man.'
   Æsch. Not so : his evil fate his very life foreran;
Being his father's slayer, as ere birth predicted.
   Eur. ' Then of all mortals he became the most afflicted.'
   Æsch. Not so : There was no change. Beneath an
     angry sky
Immediately on birth was he exposed to die,
Lest his own father he should yet survive to kill:
With swollen feet [1] his evil fortune to fulfil

---

[1] The name ' Œdipus ' is derived from words which express this.

He came to Polybus: then, still in early life,
He took a woman far advanced in years to wife,
And that his mother! After which with his own hand
He plucked his eyes out.

Bacc.   Still, if he had held command
With Erasinides, his fortune might excel.[1]

Eur. You trifle, Sir. I say that I write Prologues well.

Æsch. But come, I will not crush each verse; but I will
        spoil
Your Prologues simply with—a little flask of oil.

Eur. A little flask of oil you say?

Æsch.   Yes: only one.
As you compose, the thing may easily be done.
I'll show you with a Flask, or Purse, or Little Skin.

Eur. You'll show me? will you?

Æsch.   Yes.

Bacc.   EURIPIDES, begin.

Eur. ' Ægyptus, as tradition bears the general tale,
With fifty sons aboard a fleet of twenty sail,
Touching at Argos—'

Æsch.   —lost a little flask of oil!

Eur. What's this? Rebuke him, Sir.

Bacc.   I do not want a broil.
Recite another Prologue. See what he can find.

Eur. 'Bacchus, who oft with thyrsus, vine and ivy
        twined,
And wrapped in kid-skins on Parnassus treads the soil,
With light foot dancing—'

Æsch.   —lost a little flask of oil!

Bacc. Dear, dear! the little flask again; and we are hit!

Eur. Pooh, pooh! I'll find a Prologue where it will not fit.
' The world knows not the man in all things fortunate.
For either rich in blood he falls to poor estate,
Or, humbly sprung, has '

Æsch.   —lost a little flask of oil!

Bacc. EURIPIDES!

---

[1] The remarkable good fortune of Erasinides was manifested in this.
He was one of the six victorious commanders at Arginusæ, who were
put to death on their return to Athens for not having remained to gather
and bury those who had fallen in the action.

Eur.   Aye, what?

Bacc.   I think you must recoil:
This flask—

Eur.   I'll crack it soon.

Bacc.   Good: but beware its powers.

Eur. 'Cadmus, Agenor's son, of Sidon's princely towers,
Leaving the city—'

Æsch.   —lost a little flask of oil!

Bacc. Nay, buy it: buy it, man; for fear that it should
            spoil
Our Prologue altogether.

Eur.   Not at any price!
What? buy of him?

Bacc.   You will, if you will take advice.

Eur. No, no, I've many Prologues yet will sorely task
His ingenuity to baffle with his flask.
'Pelops the Tantalan, coming to Pisan soil
With rapid horses—'

Æsch.   —lost a little flask of oil!

Bacc. There, there! You see he fastened on the flask
            again.
(*to* ÆSCH.) Good fellow, sell the thing! to save us further
            pain.
You'll get the article, a good one, for a penny.

Eur. Not yet by Jove: my Prologues still are very many.
'Œneus at harvest—'

Æsch.   —lost a little flask of—

Eur.   Nay;
Let me at least complete the lines, I pray.
Œneus at harvest, having won rich grain with toil,
While sacrificing—'

Æsch.   —lost a little flask of oil!

Bacc. What? sacrificing too? Who stole it?

Eur.   Stay, my friend,
Just this; and let him tack his flasket to the end.
'Zeus, if the common breath of history be true.'

    Bacc. Pooh, pooh! he'll say he lost the flask,[1] and ruin
            you.

---

[1] Of course this criticism by the 'flask' is merely whimsical. At the
most it indicates a slight mannerism in Euripides. In the first sentence

It sticks upon your Prologues just as styes on eyes.
But are there not his Melodies to criticise?

Eur. Aye, I will turn to them, and show you in a trice,
That all his Melodies have one persistent vice.

Chorus.   What is going to happen next?
            Truly I am quite perplexed,
            Thinking what he will or can
            Say, to reprehend a man
            Unto whom the nation owes
            All the choicest songs it knows.
                 Yes, I am amazed to think
            What impeachment he will bring
            On the very Tragic King.
                 And I cannot choose but shrink.

Eur. Oh! wondrous Melodies! reducible to one!
I'll amputate his limbs:[1] it will be quickly done.

Bacc. And I will score and keep account of what you do.
            [*An air is played upon a pipe to accompany*
            EURIPIDES.

Eur. (*singing*). Pthiotian Achilles! why, hearing the
            fury of slaughter,
Toil-allaying dost thou not bring us assistance?[2]
Hermes our forefather we honour that dwell by the water;
Toil-allaying dost thou not bring us assistance?

Bacc. Ha! Æschylus, there are two 'toils' for you!

Eur.   Achæan chief of wide command,
            Son of Atreus, understand,[3]
Toil-allaying dost thou not bring us assistance?

---

of a narrative he, at least occasionally, fell into a certain rhythmical period,
which allowed the Iambic verse to be finished by the two (original)
words of nonsense, supplied by Æschylus.

[1] Euripides seems invited to this operation in particular because one
word in the original expresses both 'limbs' and 'songs,' μέλη.

[2] These two lines are quoted from a lost play of Æschylus, *The Myrmidons.* The other lines here and below are patched together without
meaning; but, as it seems, to illustrate to the ear of the Greek audience
the charge of sameness of rhythm. So far it is a fair return for the
'flask.' But it is not the purpose of Aristophanes to let Euripides make
a real hit.

[3] I would fain follow some scholar who would satisfactorily settle the
text of these two lines by making them *one*, and that, such that it should
have the same rhythm as the other lines objected to by Euripides.

Bacc. See, Æschylus, a third ' toil ' to the two.

Eur. Silence! Forth from the shrine of Artemis are
they advancing.

Toil-allaying wilt thou not bring us assistance?

May I not tell of men their power by justice enhancing.

Toil-allaying wilt thou not bring us assistance?

Bacc. King Jupiter! I must after such ' toils ' as those
Betake me to the bath for washing and repose.

Eur. Nay, prithee, not till you have heard a single strain,
Of lyric measure.

Bacc.   So we have not ' toil ' again.

Eur.   When as Achæa's twin-throned power,
          With flatto-thratto-flatto-thrat,
     Despatches Sphinx in evil hour,
          With flatto-thratto-flatto-thrat.
     With armed hand a bird to stoop,
          With flatto-thratto-flatto-thrat.
     Meeting the dogs through air that swoop
          With flatto-thratto-flatto-thrat.
     To Ajax as they cower
          With flatto-thratto-flatto-thrat.

Bacc. What is this ' flatto-thrat ' ? Is it a Persian song ?
Or bucket in a well upon a leathern thong ?

Æsch. Nay but from a fair plot, unto a plot as fair,
Did I transfer the melody,[1] that none should dare
To say that on the Muses' mead I sought my store
Where Phrynichus [2] had culled the choicest flowers before.
But *he*—he picks his measures up from ballads, glees,
Street pipers, catches, dirges, dances,—what you please.

-----

[1] This is understood to signify, that Æschylus found the rhythm in use
in old lyric poetry and transferred it to Tragedy: but, in connection with the
question of Bacchus, it seems to include the very comical refrain itself.
It must be confessed that the words assigned to Bacchus are here rather
a gloss than a translation. He asks, 'Is it from Marathon?' Because, says
the scoliast, a great deal of the herb 'Phleos' grows there, or, because
Æschylus fought there. Nor is the next line much clearer; but it appears
to suggest that the sound or rhythm was like that made by a leather
strap upon a wheel.

[2] This is yet another Phrynichus, the lyric poet referred to in *Birds*,
l. 719.

The thing will show itself.   Bring me a lyre : but, nay,
What need of lyre ? find me the wench that used to play
Her tunes upon two sherds.   Muse of Euripides,
Advance ; for thou art fit to time such airs as these.

[He sings : accompanied by the rattle of castanets.

Halcyons, who by the waves of the ocean
Ever in motion,
Are singing,   ·.
And flinging
From wings with plumage soft and bright
Sparkling drops of dewy light.
And spiders, who with slender joints
Hang at all points
Over our heads
Delicate threads,
Frame-stretched webs, as one that plies
Shuttle, singing as it flies.
Or where pipe-loving dolphin chases
By azure prows, weird words and races,
Gleam of the grape a-blossoming,
Care-soothing tendril of the vine,
Oh fling ! oh fling
Thine arms about me, child of mine !
See you this foot ?

Bacc.   I do.
Æsch.   Nay, look ye to't.
Bacc.   I do.
Æsch.   And you, that write such stuff as this,
Presume to take my lines amiss ?
But suffer me awhile, for I should like to show
The style in which he makes his Monodies to flow.

Black darkness of the night,
What wretched dream is this thou sendest me,
Out of thy invisible,
Soul soulless, minister of hell,
Raven night's child, and terrible to see,
In corpse clothes dight,
With murder, murder in its looks,
And nails like hooks ?

But maidens, strike a light;
In vases fetch the dew of stream;
Set it to heat, that I aright
May purge away this morning dream.
Ho! demon of the flood! my soul divines!
Ho, housemates, see these wondrous signs!
My cock! yes, I see,
That thief, that Glycé, ·
Has stolen it, and disappeared.
Ho, Mania,⨍ seize upon the jade:
Nymphs, daughters of the hills, to aid!
While I, who nothing feared,
My proper business minding
Was winding, winding, winding
A ball of yarn to sell
As soon as evening fell.
But he, he sprung, as ever he springs,
Into the air on lightest wings;
But he left to me, he left to me
Troubles, fears, tears, tears,
Which I shed incessantly.
Ida's children, men of Crete,
Seize your bows and stir your feet,
Haste, cut off the thief's retreat.
Virgin Dictynna, Artemis the fair,
Come with thy little hounds and beat the lair!
And thou, Jove's daughter, Hecate, to stand,
A fiery lamp in each extended hand,
To light me while I search each nook,
Where Glycé hides the prey she took.[2]

Bacc. Enough of this.

Æsch.   For me! I only wish to bring
This fellow to the scales: that is the only thing

---

[1] The name of a female slave.
[2] Amid the rapid changes of this Euripidean ballad it may escape the
reader that it is narrative. The singer of it is warned by an uncomforta-
ble dream of an impending misfortune. The event declares the meaning
of the dream. Glycé steals her noble cock. First the household slaves, .
and afterwards the police, are called upon to follow the thief and recover
the bird. The rest is given by way of illustrating how Euripides would
poetically tell and ornament an event of every-day life.

To put it to the test, which of us is the Poet:
The weight of our respective words will clearly show it.

Bacc. So be it: I am ready. Bring them if you please,
If I must try a poet's talents like a cheese.

Chorus.   These clever folks go far to find !
>   For surely never was there heard
>   So strange a fancy and absurd
>   From any ordinary mind.
>   I do declare if such a one
>   Had broached to me the odd idea
>   I should have taken him to be a
>   Wag or simpleton !

[*A large pair of scales is brought on the stage.*

Bacc. Now stand you at the scales, each at his basin.

Eur. and Æsch.   So ?

Bacc. And holding on, each say a verse : and don't let go
Till I say 'Cuckoo.'

Eur. and Æsch.   We are holding.

Bacc.   Turn your face in,
And each one quote his verse, speaking into his basin.

Eur. 'I would the Argo ship had never winged its way.'

Æsch. 'River Spercheius! Pastures where the oxen
      stray.'

Bacc. Cuckoo! Let go. EURIPIDES, the side that he's
      on
Goes much the farthest down.

Eur.   But what can be the reason ?

Bacc. He put a 'River.' Moisture is a heavy thing :
Wool-sellers know that well.   But you put in a 'wing.'

Eur. Well let him speak again and put another in.

Bacc. Hold on again.

Æsch.   I do.

Eur.   And so do I.

Bacc.   Begin.

Eur. 'The voice of Reason is Persuasion's only shrine.'

Æsch. 'Death is the only God who will a bribe decline.'

Bacc. Let go, let go. Ah, see, his basin downmost goes ;
And why ? he put in 'Death,'—the heaviest of woes.

Eur. But I put in 'Persuasion,'—word of excellence.

Bacc. Persuasion is but light, not ballasted by Sense.

But look for something else of good substantial weight,
That may draw down your scale.

Eur.   What have I that is great?

Bacc. 'Achilles made his cast, two aces and a four.'[1]
Say on, for there remains but this one weighing more.

Eur. 'An ironweighted club he heaved above his head.'

Æsch. 'Car upon car confounded lay, and dead on dead.'

Bacc. Oh, there again he has outwitted you!

Eur.   How so?

Bacc. As if two cars were not enough alone! to throw
Two bodies, for a make-weight, is enough to tax
A hundred of the best Egyptian porters' backs.

Æsch. A fig for verses in the scale! Let him get on,
Himself, his wife, his children and Cephisophon,
Yes, and his books [2] to boot: to me it matters not.
Two lines of mine shall be enough to match the lot.

Bacc. The men are both of them my friends : I love them
          both :
I cannot make a choice between them, and am loth
With either to incur the risk of enmity.
One I think clever and the other pleases me.[3]

Pluto. But think, Sir, that the object of your expedition
Will be frustrate unless you come to a decision.

Bacc. What if I judge?

Pluto.   Then take the one you choose and go;
That not in vain you may have come to us below.

Bacc. (*to* PLUTO). I thank you.

---

[1] It seems uncertain whence this line is quoted; but probably from
Euripides : nor is the application clear. One scoliast on the passage
tells us that dicers said '2, 4, 3, 5.' It is understood to mean at any
rate, on the part of Bacchus, that Æschylus had been victorious in the
two casts.

[2] That Aristophanes harboured a strong suspicion and hatred of
learning, apart from the cultivation of taste, and in the modern sense of
science, has been suggested in the Introduction to *Clouds*. I apprehend
that it is to such 'books' he here refers.

[3] It is rather amusing to find that the ancient commentators are not
agreed in apportioning to the several Poets this critical appraisement
of them : but the word cleverness (σοφία) is so constantly used by Aristophanes with a sneer, that the epithet must surely belong to Euripides.

(*To* Æsch. *and* Eur.)   Let me now inform you why I
                                         came.

It was to find a Poet.

   Eus.   Wherefore? with what aim?

   Bacc. To aid the City; that, redeemed from low estate,
It might its Choric feasts with leisure celebrate.
I will take back with me whichever of you two
Will give the City wisest counsel what to do.
Now tell me what you think of Alcibiades?
'Tis a moot point on which the City disagrees.

   Eur. But what thinks it of him?

   Bacc.   According to the vein:
Regrets him, hates him, wishes he were back again.
Now, touching him, I pray, your sentiments reveal.

   Eur. I hate the citizen who for his country's weal
Is slow to move, but quick to do it mighty hurt;
To serve the State unapt, but for himself expert.

   Bacc. Well said, by Neptune! Now, do you give us your
                                         help.

   Æsch. 'Tis hazard in the State to breed the Lion's whelp;
But wise to suffer him, if you have perilled it.

   Bacc. I can't decide between them: one has so much
                                         wit,
The other clearness. Yet once more. The State, one
                                         knows,
Is sick: what for its healing would you each propose?

   Eur. I know and I could say.

   Bacc.   Speak then.

   Eur.   That we distrust
Our trust; and hold our present fancies in disgust.

   Bacc. How so? Consider me a rather stupid hearer;
And speak less learnedly, I pray, and somewhat clearer.

   Eur. When we distrust our present leaders, and employ
Those whom we trust not now, the City shall have joy.
When, doing as we do, our state is getting worse,
How shall we not do well if we do the reverse?

   Bacc. Well said, my Palamedes, shrewdest of the witty!
But what say you?

   Æsch.   I'd know what sort of men the City
Employs about its service: Are they of her best?

Bacc. How so? it hates all such.

Æsch.   Then does it love the rest?

Bacc. I say not that.   But, when the good have been
    rejected,
The rogues remain the only men to be elected.

Æsch. How can a city hope to be at any ease,
Whom broad-cloths do not suit, and flannels do not
    please?

Bacc. Pray you, suggest some means by which the City still
May thrive again.

Æsch.   Not here.   When I am there, I will.

Bacc. Nay, nay: but from below send up a cheerful hope.

Æsch. When they shall treat the land of those with whom
    they cope
As their own property, and yield their own to be
A pleasaunce at discretion of the enemy.
When Ships are Income: and what now they Income call
Seems thriftlessness.[1]

Bacc.   Well!—but the Dicast gets it all.

Pluto. Now judge.

Bacc.   I will decide; and I will take the one
In whom my soul delights.

Eur.   Remember what you've done,
And take me home.   You swore by all the Gods to us.

Bacc. The tongue it was that swore, but—I choose ÆS-
    CHYLUS.[2]

Eur. Most infamous of men, what have you done?

Bacc.   What? I?
Adjudged the palm to ÆSCHYLUS.   Who should ask why?

Eur. Having disgraced yourself, you look me in the face?

Bacc. If bystanders approve, what is there in disgrace?[3]

---

[1] To explain these lines would be to enter on an essay on the policy of
Athens.   But the substance of the advice put into the mouth of Æschylus seems to be that which Pericles had given so many years before;
namely, to prosecute the war vigorously and trust to the domain of the sea.
This is very different from the policy advocated in the *Acharnians* and
Peace.   The reference to the public revenue means that it was very
ill spent in paying fees to idle citizens to play Dicasts in the courts.

[2] In allusion to the notable line of Euripides, *Hippolytus*, l. 612:—

    'The tongue it was that swore, the mind remains unsworn.'

[3] A parody on a line of Euripides, as are ll. 1385-6-7.

Eur. Wretch, will you leave me dead?

Bacc.   Eh? dead? Who knows if death
Be but a truer life?   Who knows if drawing breath
Be but a sort of supping?   Sleep itself may be
A blanket!

Pluto.   Now, this finished, come you in with me.

Bacc. Why so?

Pluto.   That I may offer you some slight collation
Before you go.

Bacc.   Well said; it meets my inclination.

Chorus.   Happy the man whose intellect
　　　　Is such as to command respect.
　　　　The man is going home to see
　　　　His friends and kindred, and to be
　　　　A blessing to his neighbourhood;
　　　　And all because his sense was good.
　　　　A happy thing, one therefore sees,
　　　　Not to sit under Socrates,
　　　　Learning to prattle and to part
　　　　With all that's great in taste and art.
　　　　To make a great display of force
　　　　About a trifle, and discourse
　　　　According to a solemn rule,
　　　　Is the employment of a fool.

Pluto. Go, with my felicitation,
　　ÆSCHYLUS.   With counsels wise
　　　Seek our citizens' salvation,
　　And the many fools chastise.
　　This (*giving a halter*) to Cleophon [1] from me;
　　And these (*halters*), the tribute-farmers' fee,
　　To Myrmex and Nicomachus:
　　This, also, to Archenomus.
　　Bid them, at an early day,
　　Come to me without delay;
　　　And let them know,
　　If they are not very quick,
　　I will come, and with a kick
　　　Send them below.

---

[1] See note, l. 615.

Æsch. I will do so.   If you please,
Give my seat to Sophocles ;
He is next to me in skill,
And is equal to fulfil
All the duties of the station
Till my coming back again :
If I ever have occasion
To revisit your domain.
Do not let that arrant knave,
Lying coxcomb, fooling slave—
Do not let him for a minute,
Not against his will, sit in it.

Pluto. Forward, with your torches burning,
Lead the Poet, home returning ;
Lead, and high your voices raise,
Singing his own, his glorious lays.

PLUTUS.

INTRODUCTION.

ONE can hardly presume in the present day that many readers will have been arrested by Paper 464 of 'The Spectator,' and thence have been stimulated by Addison himself to make further acquaintance with, what he describes as, 'a very pretty Allegory, which is wrought into a play by Aristophanes the Greek comedian.'—*Plutus* is that play. Those who before or after reading a translation desire to see an outline of the drama drawn by Addison himself, may find it there.

The comedy differs much in structure and character from the others, bearing marks of the changed circumstances under which it was produced. Three years before the *Frogs*, Aristophanes had produced a comedy·with this title, *Plutus*. But that which we have here, called the *Second Plutus*, was not brought out till twenty years later. In the meantime the political temperament of the Athenians had cooled down. The comedians, and no wonder, were not allowed to bring eminent living citizens upon the stage by name and character. The composition of Comedy necessarily was modified, and the New Comedy was developed; the comedy of plot and character derived only from private life. There was, however, an intermediate period: to this the *Second Plutus* belongs. The dramatis personæ here are ordinary Athenian citizens, but in contact with such mythical persons as Plutus and Mercury. While these, as well as Jupiter, still were acknowledged as Deities, they can hardly be considered as characters for 'allegory.' Be that, however, as it may be judged, the moral of the drama is scarcely, what Addison suggests, 'A Satire on the Rich,' or on the vices of the rich: it is rather the elementary lesson in Political

Economy, that the unequal, but not absolutely arbitrary, distribution of riches and poverty serves the common interest of society.

How far the *Second Plutus* was a rehabilitation of the *First*, we cannot say. In the earlier play, doubtless, the usual part was assigned to the Chorus. That which the Chorus then sung would now be out of date. If new lyric compositions were supplied to the substance of the older comedy, they have not come down to us. The Chorus still remains in name, but its life and poetry are gone. The pauses or changes in the action of the drama are no longer sustained by snatches of song or extravaganzas of humour. Their omission in this comedy has, we may say, left deep scars upon it. As however, the piece shows at least rudiments of regular division into five acts, these notes have been superscribed in the translation, by way of indicating to the reader's eye and mind a pause or change in the action.

It is said that the comedy was produced in order that Aristophanes might introduce his son Araros as an actor on the Athenian stage. Subsequently Araros introduced other comedies of his father's, and of his own.

Dramatis Personæ.

PLUTUS, *the God of Riches.*

CHREMYLUS, *a poor Yeoman of Attica.*

CARION, *Slave of Chremylus.*

BLEPSIDEMUS, *Citizen of Athens.*

POVERTY.

WIFE *of Chremylus.*

JUSTMAN.

AN INFORMER.

MERCURY.

The PRIEST *of* JUPITER.

CHORUS *of Attic Yeomen, neighbours of Chremylus.*

ACT I.

SCENE.—*On the road from Delphi, near Athens.*

Enter PLUTUS, *squalidly clothed, as a blind old man;* CHRE-
MYLUS *and* CARION, *with laurel chaplets, follow.*

Carion. It vexes one to think, a man may be a slave
And have a fool for master. Look ye, if the knave
Should happen, as may be, to speak a word of sense
His master does not see,—what is his recompense?
Curses and kicks.—So He that orders the world wills it:
The body's purchaser, and not the soul that fills it
Is Body's master. Be it so.—But, for myself, I
Am most indignant with this God that lives at Delphi,
And from his golden ·tripod mutters prophecies :
In medicine too he has a name for being wise.
Yet here—he sends my master bilious, cross and yellow,
Still dodging at the haunches of a blind old fellow,
Against all common sense. We, that have eyes to see,
Should lead the blind; but now, for so he makes me, we,
Stark idiots, are doing nothing else but hunt
A man, who for an answer will not even grunt.
I'll speak.—So, Sir, unless you wish to come to trouble,
Say frankly, why we are by this old dotard led?
You will not thrash me with the chaplet [1] on my head.
   Chremylus. By Jove, but I will knock it off, and give you
        double,
If you are saucy.
   Car.   Nonsense! I insist on knowing
Who yonder fellow is? and where on earth we're going?
And this demand I make with very good intent
For you at least.
   Chrem.   I know your words are kindly meant;
So I will tell you; for you are in my belief
Of all my slaves the faithfullest—and greatest thief.

---

[1] The chaplet with which he had gone with Chremylus to consult
Apollo at Delphi.

Though honest I have been, and paid the Gods their due,
Yet have I never thriven, and am poor.
    Car.   That's true.
    Chrem. While men that steal and cheat and lie without
        remorse,
The rogues of every grain, were growing rich.
    Car.   Of course.
    Chrem. So came I to the God to satisfy a doubt.
My term of wretched years is now well-nigh shot out;
I care not for myself; but for my only son
I asked the God's advice the best thing to be done.
Would it secure for him the hope of better days
If he should change the course of my old-fashioned ways?
And should I now begin to educate the lad
To be a rogue, a cheat, an everything that's bad?
    Car. And from his laurelled tripod, pray, what said
        Apollo?
    Chrem. I'll tell you : very clearly he told me to follow
The first man that I met; and not to let him rest
Until I got him home, and had him for my guest.
    Car. Whom did you meet with first?
    Chrem.   That man.
    Car.   Then, you must see
The meaning of the God is clear as it can be.
He tells you, stupid man, that your son's education
Should be conducted on the fashion of the nation.
    Chrem. How judge you that?
    Car.   Bless me, one really would suppose
A blind man could not miss a thing before his nose!
The proper education for success to-day
Is roguery of course; it is the common way.
    Chrem. I do not think the words admit of such a turn;
There's more in it than that. If we could only learn
Who this man is? and what his business with us here?
What we should understand might certainly appear.
    Car. (*to* PLUTUS). Hulloh! Sir, who are you? Be quick
        and say before I
Take other measures with you: don't make a long story.
    Plut. Be hanged to you, I say.
    Car.   There, Sir; you hear his name!

Chrem. He spoke to you, not me : but you are much to
>blame
For asking him so rudely. (*to* PLUTUS) Speak to me, I
>pray,
I am an honest man.

   Plut.   Be hanged to you, I say.

   Car. There ;—take the man and omen ; make the most
>of it. '

   Chrem. (*to* PLUT.) By Ceres, you shall not so easily be
>quit.

   Car. Tell me your name, or I will kill you on the spot.

   Plut. Good fellows, go away ; and leave me.

   Chrem.   We will not.

   Car. There's nothing to be said for bettering my plan ;
I'll make a wretched end of this most wretched man.
I'll take him to a cliff, and there I'll let him go ;
He's sure to break his neck.

   Chrem. (*both seizing* PLUT.) Yes, off with him !

   Plut.   No, no.

   Chrem. Then will you tell us who you are ?

   Plut.   And if I do it,
I'm sure you will not let me go, and I shall rue it.

   Chrem. Nay, by the Gods, we will, if such your wish
>should be.

   Plut. Take off your hands at once.

   Chrem.   Well, there, Sir, you are free.

   Plut. Then listen : for perforce it seems that I must
>yield,
And tell the fact which I was bent to keep concealed.
Know then that I am—PLUTUS.

   Chrem.   And you wished to go,
You rogue, you villain, you ! and not to let us know ?

   Car. You PLUTUS, God of Wealth ? in such a filthy
>suit ?

   Chrem. Apollo ! Gods and Demons ! Jupiter to boot !
What did you say ? Eh, really, are you PLUTUS ?

   Plut.   Yes.

   Chrem. The very ?

   Plut.   Yes, the very.

   Chrem.   Why in such a dress ?
So dirty !

Plut.   I have been housed with a man of pelf,
Who never in his life was known to wash himself;
You know him,—Patrocles.

Chrem.   ˙   That was a wretched fate:
How happened it?

Plut.   'Twas Jove, that brought me to this state,
In jealousy of men.   For, when I was a youth,
I said that I would favour Honesty and Truth,
And never enter houses where I could not find
Good character within.   On this he struck me blind;
That, groping in the dark, I might no more discern
Between the bad and good.   So does his rancour burn.

Chrem. And yet no sort of men pay Jupiter his due
Except the good and honest.

Plut.   That is very true.

Chrem. Come; if you had your eyesight as you had
                    before,
Would you avoid all wicked people?

Plut.   Ever more.

Chrem. And go to honest folk?

Plut.   Aye, with a willing mind;
The more because 'tis long since I have seen the kind.

Chrem. Truth, nor have I—with all my eyes.

Plut.   Now let me go;
I've done my part, and all you wished of me you know.

Chrem. By Jove, that only gives us reason more to hold
                    you!

Plut. There now! you're bringing on me trouble as I
                    told you.

Chrem. Pray be persuaded not to leave me in the lurch;
I am a worthy man.   I give you leave to search,
You will not find a better all the country round;
Indeed I'm sure there is no other to be found.

Plut. Just what they always say,—the poor, I mean;
                    but when
They once have got me fast, and come out wealthy men,
Their wickedness is such, you'd think that they were mad.

Chrem. It is so! yes, it is.   But all are not so bad.

Plut. Just one and all alike.

Car.   That speech shall cost you dear!

Chrem. But only listen, Sir; be good enough to hear

How much it is to your advantage to remain.
I hope it, yes, I hope the boon of God to gain;
I hope to be the means of your recovering
The blessing of your eyes.

Plut.   Don't think of such a thing ;
I would not see again.

Chrem.   You would not !

Car.   The man said it,
And shows a despicable nature beyond credit.

Plut. If Jove should come to know these wretched fel-
          lows' schemes,
He'd grind me.

Chrem.   That he does already, as it seems,
Who sends you out in darkness through the world to
    blunder.

Plut. Perhaps so : but I stand in great fear of his
    thunder.

Chrem. Afraid ! you basest deity ! why, what on earth
Do you suppose that Jove and all his power were worth,
If you could see again ?   I tell you that they are things
That need not be to you the value of three farthings !

Plut. Hush, hush ! you wicked man.

Chrem.   Content you ; I will show you,
Jupiter is a God who ought to rank below you.

Plut. You'll show me that ?

Chrem.   I will.   What makes the other Gods
Look up to Jupiter and tremble at his nods?

Car. ' His money '—say ; for he has so much more to
    spend.

Chrem. Now tell me who it is that gives him that ?

Car. (*pointing to* PLUTUS).   Our friend.

Chrem. Why do men sacrifice ? for *his* sake, is it not ?

Car. Yes ; and, by Jove, they pray for riches on the
    spot.

Chrem. 'Tis money all ! and PLUTUS can at any hour
Alter the disposition of this mighty power.

Plut. How so ?

Chrem.   Because there's not a mortal who would bring
A bullock to the altar, cake, or anything
Against your will.

E E

Plut.   How so?

Chrem.   Eh? how?—he could not buy it,
If wanting money, and your kindness to supply it.
So, if he's troublesome, you might in my opinion
Alone annihilate all Jupiter's dominion.

  Plut. For my sake is he worshipped?

  Chrem.   Yes; and more, I swear,
There's nothing that is splendid, elegant, or fair,
So reckoned among men, but what they owe to you, Sir:
Wealth is the universal master and producer.
For you are carried on all arts that one can mention;
You set all men to work and stimulate invention.
For you a man will sit the whole day cutting leather.

  Car. One forges brass, another hammers boards together.

  Chrem. In fashioning of gold one fellow is expert.

  Car. One robs his neighbour's house, another steals his shirt.

  Chrem. One is a fuller.

  Car.   And another washes fells,

  Chrem. This one tans hides for you.

  Car.   And that one onions sells.

  Plut. And all this is for me? to think I did not know it!

  Car. If great men have long hair—'tis he who lets them grow it.

  Chrem. And does not he supply the council hall with votes?

  Car. Of course he does, and finds the crews that man our boats.

  Chrem. And does he not at Corinth keep the foreign troops?   [droops?

  Car. And is it not through him that Pamphilus still

  Chrem. To him the public owe Philepsius' descriptions?

  Car. And are indebted for alliance with Egyptians.

  Chrem. And Lais for his sake receives Philonides.

  Car. Timotheus's tower—[1]

---

[1] I would not venture to be positive in giving explanations of all the personal allusions which here follow. It is sufficient that more or less

Chrem.   May crush you if it please !
The sum and substance is,—whatever people do,
For evil or for good, it all is done for you.

Car. At any rate in war, no matter which is strongest,
They win, who by his aid, can hold the game the longest.

Plut. And can I do so much, I that am only one ?

Chrem. The story of your power is barely yet begun :
Your power is infinite : a man may have too much
Of everything besides that's reckoned pleasant; such
As love.

Car.   Bread.

Chrem.   Music.

Car.   Sweetmeats.

Chrem.   Honour.

Car.   Toasted cheese.

Chrem. Prize-winning.

Car.   Figs.

Chrem.   Ambition.

Car.   Dough-nuts.

Chrem.   Office.

Car.   Peas.[1]

Chrem. But man was never known to have too much of
        you !   [do ?
Give him a round three thousand down,—what will he
Wish that it was but four ! Well, give him that,—and
        then ?
Forsooth he'd rather die than live with less than ten !

Plut. Your views are well expressed, and quite correct,
        no doubt,
But yet I have a fear—

---

they are dependent on the influence of Wealth. Men of fortune and
fashion wore their hair long; as a sort of indirect property tax, wealthy
citizens equipped the State's ships; the troops at Corinth were mer-
cenaries; the Athenians would not incur the cost of an expedition to
relieve their general Pamphilus, blockaded by the Lacedæmonians;
Philepsius bored his guests with long stories. The point about the
Egyptian alliance is very obscure, and the explanation too long to give
here. Lais may be supposed to have found the presents of Philonides
more agreeable than his person. Timotheus's Tower was probably a
Timotheus's ' Folly.'

[1] The translator admits that under stress of rhyme he has taken some
liberty with the names of Carion's delicacies.

Chrem.   Pray, what is that about?

Plut. Although my right to power is clear to under-
      stand,

I fear that I shall never get it into hand.

Chrem. By Jupiter, that's true which people often say,

'There's nothing half so full of fears as riches.' [1]

Plut.   Nay,

That is the libel of some disappointed thief,

Who entering a house, and finding to his grief

The locks and bolts too strong, has come away in dud-
      geon

And called a prudent man a cowardly curmudgeon.

Chrem. Then never mind your fears, do only as I bid,

And you shall see as well as ever Lynceus did.

Plut. But how can you, a mortal, do so great a thing?

Chrem. Apollo's words to me were most encouraging.

Plut. Does he know anything about this business?

Chrem.   Yes.

Plut. Beware.

Chrem.   I pray you, Sir, don't fear for our success.

Assure yourself of this, that I would rather die

Than fail to carry out the plan.

Car.   And so would I.

Chrem. We shall have many friends to back our cause
      with zeal,

Good fellows that have more of honesty than meal.

Plut. Allies of little substance!

Chrem.   'Tis a failing which

Will very soon be mended, if we make them rich.

But go you, slave.

Car.   What for?

Chrem.   To get our friends together:

You'll find them at their farms (and grumbling at the
      weather

Or at the price of wheat), that each may have his share

Of Plutus since we have him; that is only fair.

---

[1] To catch the full point of the author here, one must have a varied
reading of this line; thus,

      'There's nothing half so full of fears as Plutus '—Nay,

In the original both the ideas are conveyed by the same word.

Car. I'm off: but who will take this dainty piece of
    fat?[1]
Call some one from the house.
   Chrem.   Leave me to care for that;
And run, I say.   [*Exit* CARION.
           Now you, most sovereign God of Riches,
Vouchsafe to cross the threshold of my cottage, which is
The house that you propose to fill with wealth to-day
Acquired by righteous means,—or in some other way.
   Plut. Nay, but I hate to go to any house that's
    strange:
I never yet have got advantage from the change.
If in a miser's house by hap I should be found,
He digs a hole at once and puts me underground;
Then when a neighbour comes some trifling sum to borrow,
Oh no! my host has never seen me to his sorrow!
If then some witless spendthrift I should chance to visit,
He does not bury me, but, how much better is it?
I'm feasted on and fleeced, I'm drabbed and diced away,
And bundled bareback out of doors some early day.
   Chrem. You have not found the man who guides himself
    between
The two extremes; but that is just what I have been.
I have a turn for saving, no man likes it more;
But when occasion calls I can dispense the store.
But come into the house or nothing will be done:
And you must see my wife, and know my only son,
Whom I love very much,—next after you.
   Plut.   No doubt.
   Chrem. That is the truth for you! and why not speak it
    out?
               [*Exeunt* PLUTUS *and* CHREMYLUS.

---

[1] The slave Carion was bringing home a piece of the animal sacrificed
to Apollo at Delphi.

ACT II.

SCENE.—*Near the house of* CHREMYLUS.

Enter CARION *leading* THE CHORUS, *stepping to dance music.*

Car. Men who have eaten many a time
    leek porridge with my master,
 Good neighbours and good workmen too,
    pray move a little faster ;
 Indeed you must knock up the dust,
    nor grudge a little labour.
 So pray be quick, 'tis just the nick
    to serve a worthy neighbour.

Chorus. You blockhead, don't you see that we
    make all the haste we can ?
 What more can be expected from
    an old and broken man ?
 You think it fun to make me run
    without the information
 Why CHREMYLUS has sent for us,
    and what his expectation ?

Car. Did I not tell you long ago ?
    —but you are hard of hearing—
 He fancies you would like to know
    how much the times are clearing,
 And gladly you would bid adieu
    to all your former labours.

Chorus. But is there ground on which to found
    this notion of our neighbour's ?

Car. It is an ancient gentleman
    he has in his possession,
 Bald, wrinkled, wretched, toothless, bent,
    filthy beyond expression,
 And powers divine, there is a sign
    by which I think him—Jew !

Chorus. Oh words of gold too quickly told,
　　　　　　the flattering tale renew ;
　　　　It makes one wink only to think
　　　　　　the heap that he has got !
Car.　　Old age's failings, aches and ailings,
　　　　　　—yes, he has the lot.
Chorus. You rascal, do you think, if you
　　　　　　should play us any trick,
　　　　You will get off without your pay ?
　　　　　　No, if I have a stick.
Car.　　Do you suppose I'm one of those
　　　　　　who are so very clever
　　　　That they must always poke their joke,
　　　　　　and speak in earnest never ?
Chorus. A rogue in earnest—that it is !
　　　　　　I know your shins are crying
　　　　All for the fetters and the stocks,
　　　　　　where they are used to lying.
Car.　　To play the judge in coffin-court [1]
　　　　　　I know you have the ticket ;
　　　　And Charon stands with cheque in hand
　　　　　　to pass you through the wicket.
Chorus. Now you be hung, you limber tongue,
　　　　　　you thorough gallows-bird ;
　　　　'Tis very cool to play the fool,
　　　　　　while we have never heard
　　　　The reason why my friends and I
　　　　　　are sent for by your master,
　　　　Though in our way to lose a day
　　　　　　may prove a sore disaster.

---

[1] The Dicasts or judges for the ten law courts at Athens were taken by lot from their tribes. Each lot had on it one of the first ten letters of the alphabet. The letter indicated the Court where the holder of the ticket was to sit for the day. On the presentation of his ticket the Dicast received some countercheck from the proper officer, which entitled him to draw his fee of three oboles. An allusion has been made to this in a previous passage, where Plutus is said to supply votes to the Council ; and another allusion is made later, where the Chorus say they are accustomed to bear being hustled all day in the Assemblies for this paltry sum.

Yet, notwithstanding that, we ran
with all our zeal and muscle,
And trampled flat a pretty plat
of garlic in our bustle.

Car.   Good honest men, I'll tell you then,
—my master has got PLUTUS,
The God himself, who with his pelf
is well disposed to suit us.

Chorus. Shall we be rich!

Car.   Of course you will ;
dismiss all idle fears ;
You'll be as rich as Midases,
unless you lack the ears.

Chorus. If that is true—Ri-too-ral-loo !
Away with melancholy :
Eh ! dash my wig ! I'll dance a jig :
I never felt so jolly !

Car.   Good masters, now a truce to fun :
There's work on hand that must be done,
And I will join you in it.
But first —behind my master's back,
I'll just run in and get a snack—
I shan't be gone a minute.

[*Exit* CARION.

Enter CHREMYLUS, *greeting the Chorus.*

Chrem. To wish you a 'Good Morning,' neighbours, is a
phrase
Quite out of date and keeping with our polished days :
But I salute you all !   The zeal demands my thanks,
Which brings you at my call with full and ready ranks,
Prepared in all respects to countenance a friend,
And for the God's protection willing help to lend.

Chorus. Fear not for that, fear not : I warrant you should
see
No fiercer look in Mars than you shall see in me.
A pretty thing, if we to draw three oboles' pay
Should let ourselves in court be hustled every day,
And then should lightly let the very God of Gold
By any man alive be ravished from our hold.

Chrem. But here comes BLEPSIDEMUS; by his haste and
  air
'Tis evident he has got wind of the affair.

Enter BLEPSIDEMUS.

Bleps. Eh! CHREMYLUS, what's this? Why how on earth
  have you
So suddenly got rich? I don't believe it's true.
And yet, by Hercules, there cannot be a doubt,
In all the barbers' shops the story is about
That CHREMYLUS has come to be a wealthy man:
And further, that he sends (believe the tale who can)
For friends to share his fortune!—I can only say
That's very strange indeed, and not our country way.
  Chrem. I will not hide the fact, not I, by all the Powers,
My fortune is improved in four-and-twenty hours.
And, BLEPSIDEMUS, since I take you for my friend,
If you are so disposed, your fortune too shall mend.
  Bleps. But are you, as they say, in truth become so rich?
  Chrem. I shall be, please the God!—There's just a little
  hitch:
It's nothing: but a—something which must intervene—
  Bleps. And what is that?
  Chrem.   Eh?
  Bleps.   Pooh, pooh! tell me what you mean.
  Chrem. If we succeed our fortune will be made for ever;
But we are ruined if we fail in our endeavour.
  Bleps. Ho, ho! There's contraband aboard—it's pretty
  clear!
I cannot say I like the look of things: when fear
Comes at the heels of growing suddenly so wealthy,
It marks a man whose dealings scarcely can be healthy!
  Chrem. Be healthy! how?
  Bleps.   We know there's gold and silver stored
At Delphi—and you may have stolen from the hoard.
Yes, yes! you may regret it now—
  Chrem.   Phœbus forbid!
By Jupiter, I swear such thing I never did.
  Bleps. Pooh! hold your tongue, my man, the thing is
  clear enough.

Chrem. Don't entertain so foul a thought about me.

Bleps.   Stuff!
How sad! there is not one but is at heart a knave;
And Lucre soon or late makes every man its slave.

    Chrem. By Ceres, BLEPSIDEMUS, I must think you crazy.

    Bleps. How fallen from the higher tone of other days he!

    Chrem. Your liver, I should think, is in a sorry state.

    Bleps. His eyes betray it too! See how they vacillate.
'Tis something very bad—yes, that is my belief.

    Chrem. I know your note, my crow: that you would
          have me thief,
And go in for your share.

    Bleps.   .   I for a share! in what?

    Chrem. You need not think it is: I tell you it is not—

    Bleps. You did not steal—you robbed; that is what you
          would say!

    Chrem. I say you're mad.

    Bleps.   Or—yes, you only took away!

    Chrem. Not I.

    Bleps.   Oh, Hercules! 'tis past me then to guess
How you are to be had: in short, you'll not confess.

    Chrem. You charge me without knowing what I have
          to do.

    Bleps. Good Sir, a trifling cost will carry the thing
          through,
Before the city gets an inkling of the matter:
Some coins were well bestowed to stop the fellows' chatter.

    Chrem. Oh yes, I understand,—quite as a friend you'd
          cozen;
Just lay me out three pounds, and chárge them as a dozen!

    Bleps. Methinks,—behind the bar I see a figure stand
Imploring mercy with an olive-branch in hand;
Beside him are his wife and children all untidy,
Like Pamphilus's picture of the Heraclidæ.[1]

---

[1] The Heraclidæ, driven from country to country by the persecutions of
Eurystheus, came to Athens, and sat as suppliants at the altar of Zeus.
Pamphilus's picture was in the Pœcile or 'Painted Chamber.' The
treatment of the scene no doubt suggests the visionary fears of Blepsidemus for his friend Chremylus.

Chrem. Out, out you lunatic! I don't intend that any
But decent sober people should receive a penny
Of what I have. I'll make the honest fellows fat.

Bleps. And have you stolen then as much as comes to
that?

Chrem. You'll do for me!

Bleps.   I think you'll be your own undoing.

Chrem. I have got PLUTUS, stupid. That is not like ruin!

Bleps. PLUTUS: what sort of one?

Chrem.   The God.

Bleps.   And where is he?

Chrem. Within.

Bleps.   Where?

Chrem.   At my house.

Bleps.   ˙   At yours?

Chrem.   Yes.

Bleps.   Don't tell me!
PLUTUS with you?

Chrem.   I swear it.

Bleps.   Yes, but is it true?

Chrem. Yes.

Bleps.   By your hearth?

Chrem.   By Neptune!

Bleps.   Of the sea—mean you?

Chrem. If there's another, Yes. By him and his concern!

Bleps. But you will send him on to us your friends in turn?

Chrem. It is not ripe for that.

Bleps.   You mean that you will not?
Not let us have a share?

Chrem.   By Jove, we first must—

Bleps.   What?

Chrem. Must give him eyes to see.

Bleps.   Eh! eyes? to whom? explain.

Chrem. To PLUTUS we must give the power of sight again.

Bleps. Then is he really blind?

Chrem.   By heaven, he cannot see.

Bleps. Then that accounts for it, he never came to me.

Chrem. Aye, but he will I promise, by the Gods' permission.

Bleps. Then must we not at once get in a good physician?

Chrem. Physician there is none in all the city; skill,
And will to pay for it, stand equally at ' nil.'

Bleps. Consider.

Chrem.   There is none.

Bleps.   True, that must be confessed.

Chrem. By Jove, my first intention still I think the best:
Which is, to lay him down at night within the shrine
Of Æsculapius.

Bleps.   A capital design :
So up and go at once; delay may spoil the brewing.

Chrem. I'm going.

Bleps.   Then be quick.

Chrem.   The very thing I'm doing.

Enter POVERTY, *a gaunt woman in dirt and rags.*

Pov. You wretched mannikin! you who have dared to
                plan
A deed of infamy, abhorred of God and man.
Stop, stop! why are you flying, wretches?

Bleps.   Hercules!

Pov. Yes, with a villain's death I'll pay your villanies.
For you have ventured on a deed beyond endurance,
Which never man had yet, or even God, assurance
To think of enterprising.   You are lost and gone!

Chrem. Whom do you call yourself, with look so pale
                and wan?

Bleps. I think she is a Fury—come out from the play-
                house;
She has a tragic air, as though she meant to slay us.

Chrem. She hasn't got her torch.

Bleps. (*offers to attack her*). A fault my fist shall tell her.

Pov. Whom think ye that I am?

Chrem.   A tripe-and-onion-seller,
Or costermongeress; for no one else, I know,
Would have abused two unoffending people so.

Pov. Indeed! ye who for me have foulest mischief
                planned!
And even now would banish me from off the land.

Chrem. The pit without a bottom [1]—would not that remain?

But who and what you are will you at once explain?

Pov. Me you would banish! me! Indeed it was your thought;

But I will make you pay the penalty you ought.

Bleps. It is the barmaid—yes! I recognise the treasure

Who always cheats me with a half-pint of short measure.

Pov. I am your ancient house-mate: I am POVERTY.

Bleps. Oh, King Apollo! Gods! oh, whither may one flee?

　　　　　　　　[BLEPSIDEMUS *is going to run off:* CHREMY-
　　　　　　　　　　LUS *lays his hand upon him to stop him.*

Chrem. What are you doing, fellow? Coward-hearted beast,

Why not remain?

Bleps.　　　　　·　　　　I don't desire it in the least.

Chrem. Two men fly from a woman! What's your manhood worth?

Bleps. 'Tis POVERTY, you fool, the greatest curse on earth.

Chrem. Stop, I beseech you, stop.

Bleps.　　　　　　　　　　By Jove, that will I not.

Chrem. I tell you it would be the very foulest blot,

If, terrified by her, we two should run away

And leave the God behind. No: fight it out and stay.

Bleps. What arms could we oppose? Before the sword was drawn,

Or corslet buckled on, she'd put them into pawn.

Chrem. Assure yourself the God will rout her without blows,

And for a trophy hang her out to scare the crows.[2]

Pov. Offscourings! do ye dare to mutter to my face,

Caught in the very act of plotting my disgrace?

---

[1] The 'barathron,' a deep hole into which malefactors were thrown at Athens. Allusion is again made to this horrible place at the end of the play by Mercury. *Clouds,* l. 1396.

[2] There is here a little variation from the idea of the original, which is untranslatable as involving a small pun.

Chrem. Pray, why should you come here, abominable hag,
To rail at us, who never damaged you a rag?

Pov. You think it, by the Gods, no damage done to me
That you are going to make the God of Riches see?

Chrem. How would it injure you, if we propose the good
Of every man alive?

Pov.   If that intention stood,
Pray how should you propose to manage it?

Chrem.   The piece
We should begin with is—to turn you out of Greece.

Pov. To turn me out! indeed! And do you think you
        can
Contrive a greater wrong and injury to man
Than do as you propose?

Chrem.   There's one thing I could mention;
To set about it, but—to drop the good intention.

Pov. That is a point on which my wish is to supply you
With somewhat sounder views. What, if I satisfy you
That every good you have you owe to me alone,
Including life itself! If that's not clearly shown,
I freely give you leave to do as you are bent.

Chrem. You slut, how dare you utter such a sentiment?

Pov. With confidence and ease. I'll prove that you
        would make,
If you will only learn, a very great mistake,
If you should make the righteous very well to do.

Chrem. Ho! cudgels to my aid! joint-twisters, where
        are you?

Pov. Do not disturb yourself. Your noise is out of
        season,
At least, till you have heard a word or two of reason.

Chrem. Who can endure with any sort of patience
To listen to such stuff?

Pov.   A man of common sense.

Chrem. Then let us settle what the penalty shall be,
If you are cast.

Pov.   What you think proper.

Chrem.   We agree.

Pov. If you should lose your case, you will endure the
        same.

Bleps. Think you that twenty deaths will be enough to
　　name?
Chrem. No whit too much for her; but as for me and you
'Tis somewhat overdone; we need no more than two.
Pov. Be quick about it then, and set about to die;
For what I have to say admits of no reply.

　　　[*Actors arrange themselves as for an Athenian Court of
　　　Justice. The* CHORUS *as judges.* CHREMYLUS *and*
　　　BLEPSIDEMUS *as prosecutors.* POVERTY *defendant.*

Chorus. Something that's clever, and nothing soft, you
　　must
　　　find in your wits to this woman to say;
　　Rapping out reasons, and capping her arguments,
　　　if you hope to carry the day.
Chrem. This at the least, I suppose, to begin with,
　　nobody will be found to deny,
　That it should ever be well with the righteous,
　　and that the wicked in sorrow should lie.
There is a fault in the world about this, which
　　we have discovered a plan to correct,
Nobly designed, and such that, from using it,
　　nothing but good is it fair to expect.
Look you; if PLUTUS recovers his sight and
　　wanders no more in error and blind,
Will he not go to the honest, and only
　　stick to the excellent men he will find?
While he will fly from the evil and impious.
　　How can it happen otherwise, then,
But that the world will be furnished alone with
　　wealthy, and sober, and worshipful men?
Who can devise a more feasible scheme for
　　bringing the world to an excellent state?
Bleps. Nobody!—trust me; and as to this woman,
　　why should we trouble ourselves with her prate?
Chrem. As the world goes, one really would think it
　　crazy, or by some ill spirit possessed.
Here is a rogue, who is rolling in riches
　　robbed from his fellows to feather his nest;

There are the honest, who never know fortune,
    never from hunger or scantiness free,
All through a life of toil unending,
    desperate POVERTY, stable with thee.
This I aver without fear of a question,
    PLUTUS can never be doing amiss,
If he should use the renewal of sight for
    curing the world of disorder like this.

Pov. Elderly dotards! drivellers! never were
    men so easily proved to be mad!
Only allow you to tinker the world, and
    you would make it thoroughly bad.
PLUTUS will see, and divide himself equally;
    Science and Art will fall into decay.
Who will be smith? or shipwright? or shoemaker?
    who will tan leather? or puddle in clay?
Who will look after the ploughing and reaping?
    washing of linen? or setting a stitch?
Who is to care for laborious arts, when
    all may be idle as all will be rich?

Chrem. Truce to your list! and the nonsense you're talk-
    ing!
    all that we want our slaves will supply.

Pov. Aye!—but who will supply you the article slaves?

Chrem. Slaves!—have we not money to buy?

Pov. Who is to sell them, when money's an article
    not in demand?

Chrem.   Some lucre-led hound,
Merchant in man-flesh from Thessaly coming;
    where as we know man-stealers abound.

Pov. Softly! but, as you order the world, there
    never will be a man-stealer at all:
Who that is rich will encounter the risks that
    must to the share of the kidnapper fall?
Driven each man for himself to dig and
    labour, your world will certainly be
Very much fuller than now of trouble.

Chrem. Fall it, prophet of evil, on thee!

Pov. Never will you go to sleep on a bed; for
    beds, of course, will never be made:

Never put foot on a handsome carpet;
    will a rich man be a weaver by trade?
Never with perfumed spirit or essence
    charm the nose of your beautiful bride;
Never delight her eye with a satin
    cut to the fashion, and charmingly dyed.
What is the value of silver and gold if
    you are at fault for such matters as these?
Under my reign if you require a
    thing of the kind, you have it with ease:
I, like a sharp tyrannical mistress,
    ever sit by the artificer's side,
· Threatening death, or making him work for a
    call from within that will not be denied.
Chrem. You to pretend to be our benefactress!
    Truly you give us—blains on our toes,
Hungering children, withered old women,
    fleas in numbers that nobody knows,
Armies of gnats to slaughter our sleep, ever
    trumpeting, while they encircle one's head,
'Sleeper, awake! you may waken to hunger,
    nevertheless, you must get out of bed.'
Bed, did I say?—'tis a mattress of rushes, your
    cover a moth-eaten matting of flags;
Under your head you may have a great stone, and
    wear for a coat a mere bundle of rags.
Add to these treasures the stalks of a mallow,
    succulent food when one cannot get bread;
Dishes of peas in their season—oh, no! old
    tops of the turnip will serve one instead.
Is it a stool, or a basin you wish for?
    Jars that are broken [1] will serve you; and then
What would you ask more?—These are the treasures,
    POVERTY, you have presented to men.
Pov. You are describing the fare of a beggar: while
    I by my labour my livelihood win.
Chrem. Say we not well that POVERTY is but
    naked BEGGARY's sister and twin?

---

[1] Large earthenware jars for wine.

F F

Pov. Yes, you say it, and much beside, that
    anyone may believe if he can.
That which you speak of is not my life, nor
    will be the fare of a labouring man.
Poor, not a beggar, he wants not and wastes not; has
    bread for his eating, and clothes for his back;
All day cheerfully sticking to work he has
    nothing superfluous, nothing to lack.

Chrem. Happy indeed, is the man you describe, and
    blessed, by Ceres, the life he has led!
All through his days he has laboured and stinted, yet
    leaves not enough to bury him, dead.

Pov. Try to be funny when reasoning fails you!
    Do you not know that the men of my breed
Are, as to figure and mind, much better than
    any who spring from PLUTUS's seed.
His are the men with the ' fair round belly,' the
    fat on their ankles, and gout in the toes;
Mine are the slender, the lithesome, and lively,
    wasps in the waist, and wasps to their foes.

Chrem. Elegant, terrible wasps if you please, all
    carefully starved to the requisite shape.

Pov. Now look at character : there I will have you
    beyond all hope of reply or escape :
Mine you will note for their habits of order;
    his for their insolence, license, and pride.

Chrem. Burglars and thieves are an orderly sort!

Bleps. Concealment being a duty,—they hide.

Pov. Everywhere look at the Friends of the People, the
    favourite leaders of public opinion;
While they are poor, how honest and just are their
    views about popular rights and dominion:
Let them, however, but get into office;
    let them get fat on the spoils of the town,
Straight they will turn into rogues, and will talk of the
    duty of putting the Populace down.

Chrem. There you have spoken the truth no doubt;
    though
    jealousy prompts you to say it : but, pray,
Be not conceited upon it or think that
    we will allow you to lengthen your stay.

After your shameful endeavour to talk us
    into a thesis so wild and absurd,—
Poverty better than Riches : impossible !

Pov.   Yet you could answer me never a word ;
    Nothing to purpose ; all empty vapouring.

Chrem. Why does everyone fly from your face ?
    Answer me that.

Pov.   Because I improve them.
    Children will show you a parallel case :
Do they not fly from the face of their fathers,
    Be they never so loving and wise ?
So very rare is that soundest wisdom
    which discerns where our interest lies.

Chrem. Jupiter, next you will say, is a fool, who,
    not knowing well what riches are worth,
Chooses this mischievous Wealth—

Bleps.   and packs off
    POVERTY down to us upon earth.

Pov. Oh, but the eyes of your mind are glued by
    ancient rheum and primitive dirt !
Jupiter's poor. And that I will show you by
    process of reasoning lucid and curt.
If he were rich, how could it have happened that
    when he set up the Olympian course,
Duly to which in quinquennial periods
    Greeks from all quarters assemble in force,
He should have offered the winner no more than a
    spray of wild olive to set on his hair ?
Nothing but gold would have met the occasion,
    if, as you fancy, he had it to spare.

Chrem. Rather it shows him as valuing gold, and
    holding his own with remarkable thrift :
Nothing is lost from his store, while conquerors
    go away proud with a trumpery gift.

Pov. That's a reproach far greater than any that
    poverty ever entailed of itself ;
Being so wealthy, as you maintain, but a
    mean and pitiful lover of pelf.

Chrem. Off to destruction ! thou foulest of creatures, with
    Jupiter's wild olive crown on thy head.

Pov. Fie on your impudence! beaten in argument,
  you that have dared to gainsay what I said,
 —All that is pleasant and good in your life, is
  POVERTY's earning and POVERTY's gift.
Chrem. Hecate knows and will say if it's better, to
  have an abundance, or live by a shift,
If it be true, as she says, that the wealthy
  send her each month a supper[1] to eat,
But that the poor waylay the servers, and
  snatch it before it is set in the street.

   Perdition catch thee! hence! away!
  No whisper more! I tell thee, none!
   Win my reason as you may,
  No! I never will be won.
Pov. Hear it, Argos! noble city,
   Hear the things that they have said.[2]
Chrem. Have you not a friend to pity?
   Call in Pauson[3] to your aid.
Pov. Heavy, heavy, are my woes!
Chrem. Hussey, off! to feed the crows.
Pov. Earth, where go I?
Chrem.   To the rack.
  Do not trifle with delay.
Pov. You will surely fetch me back.
Chrem. Then return: but now away.
        [*Exit* POVERTY.
  I profess that I prefer
  Wealth for me, and grief for her.
Bleps. I too have decided wishes
   For an easy kind of life,
  Living upon dainty dishes
   With my children and my wife:

---

[1] At the new moons the rich sent into the streets a supper for Hecate: it was commonly disposed of as here described, hence 'Hecate's supper' came proverbially to mean pretty much the same as 'dining with Duke Humphrey.'

[2] Burlesque references to passages of Euripides.

[3] A painter and very poor, as such here and elsewhere made a butt by Aristophanes. Pope would have assigned some bookseller's hack as the 'trencher-fellow' of Poverty.

Coming daily from the bath
Clean and comfortably fat,
Working men that cross my path
I will snap my fingers at.

Chrem. Now that the jade is gone, 'tis time the God
were led
To Æsculapius's shrine and put to bed.

Bleps. Let there be no delay, for fear that anyone
Should hinder us again, before the thing is done.

Chrem. (*calling to the slave in the house*).
Ho! CARION, my lad, lead PLUTUS carefully,
Bring on the beds and stores for night, and follow me.

[*Exeunt.*

ACT III.

Enter CARION *to* CHORUS.

Car. Good men, who on a crust, and that one of the
  least,
Have often kept Theseia![1] your luck is increased:
Good days indeed are come to you and all the rest,
The morals of whose lives will bear a searching test.

  Cho. Eh! what have you to say, your own most worthy
    friend?
Your salutation seems good tidings to portend.

  Car. My master's business has succeeded to his mind,
Or rather PLUTUS'S; instead of being blind,
His sight is perfect with a pair of brilliant eyes.
Æsculapius has proved a doctor good and wise.

  Cho.   Charming tidings! I must shout.
  Car.   If you wish it, sing it out.
  Cho.   Light of Science, bright for us,
        Thou hast many sons of fame,
        Worthy of their father's name;
      Hail! hail, Æsculapius.

Enter WIFE *of* CHREMYLUS.

  Wife. What is the shouting for? good news? I long to
    learn;
For I have sat indoors waiting for their return.

  Car. Here, mistress, bring us out some wine in double
    haste,
And take a cup yourself; I know it's to your taste:
For such a heap of good I'm bringing home to you.

  Wife. Where is it?
  Car.   Only wait to hear my story through.

---

[1] A feast in honour of Theseus, kept on the 8th of each month: with
the poorer classes an occasion for what would be with us a Sunday's
dinner.

Wife. Be quick about it then.

Car.   Be patient, as I said:
From foot to head you'll have the things.

Wife.   Not at my head?

Car. The good?

Wife.   Aye, not the things.

Car.   —Soon as we reached the place,
Leading the man that *was* in most afflicted case,
But *is*—oh, fortunate and blest beyond the reach
Of competition: him we took down to the beach,
And bathed him there—

Wife.   By Jove, a blessed man was he,
When he, and at his years, stood shivering in the sea.

· *Car.* This done, unto the Temple of the God we came,
And offered there the meal cakes, which by Vulcan's
    flame
Were consecrate: then duly laid we PLUTUS down
Upon a bed; and each of us contrived his own.

Wife. Were there no other suppliants for succour there
        reclined?

Car. Yes, there was Neoclides, seeming to be blind
(In thieving he can distance any man that sees),
And others, representing every disease.
Now, when the reverend priest had put out every light,
And charged us, if disturbed by noises in the night,
To take no notice of them, we lay down in rows.
But I—I could not sleep; disturbing my repose,
I saw a pot of furmity beside the bed
Of an old woman, no great distance from her head.
I had a mind to creep a little nearer, when,
On looking up, I saw that most revered of men,
Our friend the priest, was busy taking figs and cakes
From off the holy table: after that he makes
A circuit of the altars, haply to espy
If anywhere a dough-nut might neglected lie,
Which he might consecrate into a kind of basket.
Seeing the thing was right I had no need to ask it,
So made no more ado, but rose at once to fetch
The pot of furmity.

Wife.   You most abandoned wretch !
Did you not fear the God?
Car.   Indeed I did ; lest he
Should be beforehand with me at the furmity ;
I mean when he should come, just as his priest had said,
To see the patients with the laurel [1] on his head.
Meantime the ancient dame, hearing the noise I made,
To draw the pot away with crafty hand essayed ;
But, hissing like a snake, I seize her with my jaws ;
Whereon her hand again she rapidly withdraws,
And wrapping up her head she lies profoundly still,
While of the furmity of course I take my fill.
Wife. But did not the God come?
Car.   After a while he did ;
When, feeling rather nervous, I confess, I hid
My head beneath the rug. At once he went the round,
Inspecting all the sick who lay upon the ground,
And followed by a slave, who bore, as might be guessed,
A mortar and its pestle, and a little chest.
Wife. Of marble?
Car.   Not the chest!
Wife.   You vagabond, but how
Did you contrive to see it? when, as you allow,
Your head was in the rug.
Car.   I saw it through the stuff;
I take my oath of it, that there were holes enough.
It was for Neoclides he began to make
An ointment for the eyes: for that I saw him take
Three heads of garlic; bruise them; then add squills and
          juice :
When strained with vinegar, the salve was fit for use.
This pretty preparation being then applied
To Neoclides' eyelids, on the inner side,
He smarted, I should think: at any rate he screamed
And rushed away. The God was tickled, as it seemed,
And cried, 'Now sit you still; that salve is for the health
Of liars who pretend to serve the commonwealth.'
Wife. 'Twas clever of the God ; and most considerate,
And shows his interest in the welfare of the State.

---

[1] The head of Æsculapius is so represented on some ancient coins.

Car. Next after this the God entered on PLUTO'S [1] case:
He handled first his head, and then he wiped his face,
Especially his eyes; and Panacæa spread
A sort of crimson veil that covered all the head.
Then the God whistled, when there came out from the
    shrine
A pair of—Oh such snakes! tremendous!
Wife.   Powers divine!
Car. Twisting themselves beneath the veil, it seemed to
    me,
They licked his eyelids; for I well could see
PLUTUS recovered sight, while you might drink a cup
Of wine. I clapped my hands and woke my master up.
The God, as did the snakes, straight vanished out of
    sight.
But we and all the rest got up and spent the night
Congratulating PLUTUS, as you may suppose,
With very cheerful spirits, till the sun arose.
I give the God the greater praise because, beside his
Giving PLUTUS sight, he blinded Neoclides.
   Wife. How mighty is Thy power, most gracious Lord
    and King!
But tell me, where is PLUTUS?
Car.   Coming with a string
Of people at his heels. There's such a how-d'ye-doing,
Shaking of hands, and rushing, crushing and hallooing
Of honest men who've found it hard to live till now:
And then again such scowls and knitting of the brow
By all the men who have won property and station
By lying, robbing, jobbing, bribes, and peculation.
But all the others follow laughing out and cheering,
With crowns upon their heads. And now the crowd is
    nearing,
Hark! you may hear the old shoes tramp it to the dance.
Aye, one and all, old boys, kick up your heels and prance,

---

[1] The waggery of saying Pluto for Plutus is what might have been expected perhaps from anyone who had written in times since the Gods of the Greek mythology have become less than objects of faith. Such a jest put into the mouth of Carion must surely show that all reality of belief in Pluto was already gone in Athens.

And go home when you're tired: for, when you enter in,
You never more shall hear—'There's no meal in the bin.'
  Wife. So love me Hecate! for bringing news so good,
I'd wreathe you with a string of biscuits, that I would!
  Car. Make haste, for here they are.
  Wife.   No; I'll get some supplies
Of sweetmeats, nuts and figs, to throw for PLUTUS' eyes,
As new-come slaves to us, 'tis proper I should greet
      them.[1]
  Car. Now that the men are near, I will go out to meet
      them.   [*Exeunt.*

    Enter PLUTUS, CHREMYLUS, CARION, *and followers.*

  Plut. First I salute the Sun, whom now I see again:
And holy Pallas, mistress of this famous plain:
And all the land of Cecrops, which now entertains me!
To recollect the wrongs which I have suffered pains me!
How was my ignorance imposed upon, when I
Favoured the men I did.   While I, it seems, would fly
The very men that were most worthy of my grace;
By ignorance misled to wrong in either case.
But every one shall know, since I begin again,
How I against my will befriended evil men.
              [*People press on* CHREMYLUS *importunately.*
  Chrem. Be hanged to you! Oh, what a nuisance are the
          friends
That spring up round a man as soon as fortune mends!
They tread upon one's heels, and knock against one's
          shins;
And each one with some petty complaisance begins.
Who did not speak to me?—and then to see the race
Of gaffers to get round me in the market-place!

---

[1] When a newly-purchased slave was brought into the house it was
customary to throw such things at him; the other domestics of the house
scrambled for them.   I have ventured in some measure to develope what
I conceive to be the innuendo of Chremylus's wife: that the new 'eyes'
of Plutus were to enter her service, and to be to her better than an army
of wealth-producing slaves.

> [*Enter* WIFE OF CHREMYLUS, *bringing a bas-*
> *ket of figs, &c., which she offers to throw*
> *at* PLUTUS, *to be scrambled for by the*
> *slaves and others around.*

Wife. Good morning, dearest husband: Sir, the same to
    you;
And you : accept, as is but right, I pray you do,—
Accept these little trifles—
    Plut.   Madam, no such thing :
It is not fit to take ; 'tis rather mine to bring,
On entering a house, now that I have my sight.
    Wife. Pray take the little sweetmeats; 'tis but common
    right.
    Plut. At least within the house: without another
    word :
Don't have a scramble here; the thing would be absurd.
                        [*Exeunt.*

ACT IV.

CARION, *coming out of the house.* CHORUS.

Car. 'Tis very pleasant, friends, to live from day to day in
Every sort of ease and plenty without paying.
The house is full of all that's good to eat or see;
And we—as innocent of earning as can be:
The bin is full of flour, superlatively white;
The jars of fruity wine, a nose's pure delight;
The coffers, boxes, chests, whatever things will hold,
Are full as they can be of silver and of gold;
The well is full of oil; the flasks have nard instead;
And figs fill up the place of lumber overhead;
The pots and pans are brass, that earthen were of late;
The dishes for the fish are turned to silver-plate;
The mousetrap's ivory; and, wonder never ceases,
We servants play at odd-and-even with gold pieces.
My master in the house is sacrificing now,
With a wreath upon his head, a ram, and goat, and sow.
But, truth to say, the smoke so makes my eyelids smart
That for a little while, methought, I would depart.

Enter JUSTMAN, *with a Slave (carrying a
smock-frock).*

Just. Here! this way to the God, boy.

Enter CHREMYLUS, *on the opposite side.*

Chrem.   - Pray, Sir, who are you?
Just. One that was beggared once, but now am well to
         do.
Chrem. One of the Righteous then, it fairly may be
         guessed?
Just. Exactly so.

Chrem.   Then, pray, of what are you in quest?

Just. I come to see the God to whom I am beholden
For rendering my life and prospects truly golden.
'Tis right I should explain that, when my father died,
I had a nice estate, from which I could provide
For all my friends that needed, as I thought was right.

 Chrem. And so your nice estate soon came to nothing?

 Just.   Quite.

 Chrem. And you were beggared?

 Just.   Yes; but I had thought that they,
Whom I had so befriended in their evil day,
If ever I should want it, some return would show me;
But no! They turned aside and did not seem to know
  me.

 Chrem. And laughed at you, no doubt?

 Just.   Especially my dress,
The shabbiness of which completed my distress.

 Chrem. Now it is well enough.

 Just.   That brings me here to-day;
Before the God my just acknowledgment to pay.

 Chrem. But, tell me, why your slave is carrying with
  care
The smock-frock which I see so much the worse for wear?
Does that concern the God?

 Just.   Truly; 'tis my oblation.

 Chrem. Pray, is it that you wore at your Initiation?[1]

 Just. No; but I shivered in it thirteen years on end.

 Chrem. The slippers too?

 Just.   They bore me company to spend
A bitter winter.

 Chrem.   And are they an offering?

 Just. They are.

 Chrem.   The God must thank you for the gifts
  you bring.

---

[1] It was customary to offer to Ceres the garment in which one was
habited at Initiation to the Great Mysteries of Eleusis. The question of
Chremylus may have more point if we suppose that some persons took
care to go to Eleusis in their oldest clothes.

Enter a Common INFORMER.

Inf. I'm utterly undone! alas, my evil fate!
I'm threefold, fourfold, yes, fivefold unfortunate!
I'm twelvefold,—nay it is a hundred-thousand-fold!
So am I drowned in woe that never can be told.

    Chrem. Apollo save us! what can all this be about?

    Inf. I have endured enough to make a man cry out,
Of all my goods and chattels by this God bereft;
Who will be blind again, if there is justice left.

    Just. I guess this is a man fallen to poor estate;
Some faulty piece of coin in die, and sound, and weight!

    Chrem. Then he is rightly served, by Jove, in faring
        thus.

    Inf. Where's he that said he would make wealthy men
        of us,
If he recovered sight? Far from it, there are some
Who by his acts to utter poverty are come.

    Chrem. Pray who has suffered this?

    Inf.   Why, I have.

    Chrem.   Are you, Sir,
A ruined swindler? or a broken housebreaker?

    Inf. You're all the same, by Jove, rogues every one;
        that's flat:
And you have got my goods, I'm positive of that.

    Car. By Ceres, the Informer runs a furious pace!
The fellow's hungry.—

    Inf.   Go, Sir, to the market-place;
I'll break you on the wheel, (it is a rare tongue-looser,)
Till you have told your crimes.

    Car.   I thank you; after you, Sir.

    Just. By Jupiter the Saver, but the God would do
A blessed deed to Greece, to extirpate the crew
Of villanous Informers.

    Inf.   Do you dare to laugh,
While you parade the fact that you have had your half?
Pray where got you that cloak hanging upon your shoulder?
Did I not yesterday see you in something older?

Just. A fig for you ! the ring I wear's an antidote;
'Tis of Eudemus' [1] make ; I bought it for a groat.
Chrem. But not against the bite of the Informer tribe.
Inf. Is not this insolence too great? Ah, ye may jibe ;
But yet ye have not said what ye are doing here :
'Tis not for good to anyone ; that's very clear.
Chrem. By Jove, it's not for yours.
Inf.   I know you two will dine,
I'll take my oath on it, this day on what is mine.
Chrem. You, and your witness too, may do your very
            worst,
And swear it—on an empty stomach till you burst.
Inf. And do ye dare deny ? ye most dishonour-soiled,
The house is full of cutlets, full of roast and boiled !
                              [INFORMER *sniffs.*
Chrem. Do you smell anything ?
Just.   He has a cold, perhaps,
Considering how thin and ragged are his wraps.
Inf. Oh Jupiter, oh Gods ! it is not to be borne
That I so true a patriot should be held to scorn ;
That men like these should dare my honoured name to
            blot—
Chrem. What? Yours an honour'd name ? what ! you
            a patriot ?
Inf. None more.
Chrem.   I'll ask you this ; and answer if you list.
Inf. Answer to what ?
Chrem.   Are you an agriculturist?
Inf. Eh ? do you think me crazy ? Try another guess.
Chrem. A merchant ?
Inf.   'Tis a line which I at times profess.
Chrem. What then ? have you learnt any trade ?
Inf.   By Jove, not I.
Chrem. How do you feed? what do you get your living
            by ?
Inf. I'm active superintendent of the State's affairs,
And private persons'.
Chrem.   How do you discharge your cares ?

---

[1] Known as a maker of charm-rings.

Inf. I am willing to be plaintiff.

Chrem.   That is your honour then !
Meddling with business that belongs to other men.

Inf. And does it not belong to me, you gull, by right
To bear assistance to the State with all my might?

Chrem. And busy-bodying is then a public blessing?

Inf. To bring a man to justice, who is caught transgress-
              ing,
Is to support the laws.

Chrem.   Does not the State depute
That work to magistrates ?

Inf.   But who would prosecute ?

Chrem. Whoever wills.

Inf.   I am that[1] man.   And so you see
The business of the State comes to devolve on me.

Chrem. By Jove, the City has a rogue for its intendant !
You would not do it if you could be independent ?
You would prefer to be an idle man ?

Inf.   What ? lead
The soulless life of sheep ? do nothing else but feed ?

Chrem. You will not then repent, and learn a new em-
              ployment?

Inf. Not if you give me PLUTUS for my free enjoyment !

Chrem. Come ! quick ; strip off your coat.

Car. (to INFORMER).   You sir ! are spoken to.

Chrem. Off with your shoes.

Car.   Attend ! that also is for you.

Inf. Here one of you ; I want a witness to stand by ;
Let anyone who will.   [*Looking towards* CARION.

Car.   No, no.   It is not I.

Inf. I'm stripped in open day, dear ! dear !

                              [CHREM. *and* JUST. *strip him.*

---

[1] The point here depends upon a phrase common at the end of Statutes.
It was the formula giving permission to anyone to prosecute for the
penalty. 'Let him sue whoever is willing.' 'I am just *that* man,'
says the Informer. So, a few lines above, he has said that was his 'calling.'
I am in all cases *willing* to be prosecutor for a penalty. Here it is contrived that Chremylus should use the formula without apparently thinking of the application.

Car. And so you made
A pretty living by the busybody trade?

Inf. You see what he is doing. Bear me witness.

Chrem. Nay.
The fellow, whom you brought for that, has run away.

Inf. Oh! dear! I'm caught alone.

Chrem. Now, would you like to bellow?

Inf. Oh!

Car. Let me have the smock, I'll put it on the fellow.

Just. Nay, nay; 'tis dedicate to PLUTUS long ago.

Car. We cannot to my mind do better than bestow
The clout upon this old acquaintance of the gaoler;
But PLUTUS should appear a credit to his tailor.

Inf. I will withdraw; for one is not a match for three;
But if I find a compeer, cut from the same tree,
I'll make that God of yours, for all he is so strong,
Smartly aware that he has done the City wrong.
He's introducing here a novel institution
Without THE PEOPLE'S leave. I say 'tis Revolution.

[INFORMER *runs off. The others go into the house.*

ACT V.

Enter MERCURY (*after knocking at the door he hides himself*).

Car. (*answering the knock, comes out*). Who's knocking
        at the door? Eh? what? why this is queer!
Did the door knock itself? It seems there's no one here.
   Mer. (*coming forward*). You, CARION, Sir, stop.
   Car.   And was it you, Sir, pray,
Who beat the door just now in such a furious way?
   Mer. By Jove, not I: but that is what I was about
Just when you opened it. Run, fetch your master out;
And then his wife and children, then the slaves and dog;
And after them yourself, and after you the hog.
   Car. Eh? what's this?
   Mer.   Jupiter, you scoundrel, has a wish
To have and knead you up together in a dish,
And pitch you in the Hole.
   Car.   Such messages as those
Are apt to get the tongue slit! Why does he propose
To treat us thus?
   Mer.   Because of the enormous crime
Of which you have been guilty. Ever since the time
When PLUTUS had his sight, no single man has brought
Cake, incense, laurel, victim, anything he ought,
To any of us Gods.
   Car.   By Jove, nor ever will.
You see, in former days you cared for us so ill.
   Mer. I care not for the rest: I won't make that pretence,
But I myself am ruined.
   Car.   Now you're talking sense.
   Mer. The women at the stalls at daybreak used to bring
A wine-cake, honey, figs, or some such dainty thing;[1]
In short, what it was fit for MERCURY to eat,
But now—I lie, for hunger cocking up my feet.

---

[1] As fee-bribes to Mercury, the Tutelary Deity of Cheats.

Car. It serves you right for living idly at their cost,
On dainty things indeed !

Mer.   Woe's me, for I have lost
My fourth-day [1] cake ! shall I not seek for it again ?

Car. Thou seek'st an absent one, and callest out in vain.[2]

Mer. Woe's me, I've lost the ham, on which I loved to
     dine !

Car. Refresh yourself with caper[3]-sauce, the day is fine.

Mer. The chitterlings I had just piping from the pot !

Car. It seems your own are griped a little ! are they not?

Mer. Woe's me, for I have lost the well-concocted cup !

Car. Come, swallow what you've got, and pick your
     bundle up.

Mer. I ever was your friend,—so give a friend a lift.

Car. If anything I can will serve you for a shift.

Mer. Get me a slice of bread, a little roll at least,
With just a cut of meat, a fillet from the feast,
That pleasant sacrifice, now going on within.

Car. What ! bring it out of doors ? but that would be a
     sin !

Mer. When anything was filched, and you were most
     suspected,
I always stood your friend to keep you undetected.

Car. Upon condition that you gained in the affair ;
And so you always had a pasty for your share.

Mer. And you as duly ate it.

Car.   As, of course, I ought.
You would not share the stripes whenever I was caught.

Mer. Don't harbour grudges now ; find me some quiet
     berth.

Car. Then will you leave the Gods and stop with us on
     earth ?

Mer. Life being pleasanter, I readily will stay.

---

[1] The fourth day of the month, dedicated to Mercury.

[2] A burlesque application of a Tragic line representing Hercules seeking Hylas.

[3] That is ' dance.' In the original the idea seems forced in for the sake of a very small pun, on the word signifying ' ham.' As that cannot be represented, perhaps it might have been better to omit the couplet. The ' dance ' signified, however, implies contempt towards the God, as it was an exhibition which would be about equivalent to climbing a greased pole.

Car. And think it well to bear the name of Runaway ?

Mer. One's country is where Fortune is in giving mood.

Car. What service can you render to be worth your food ?

Mer. Make me a turnabout,[1] to stand behind the door.

Car. A turnabout ! but shifts are what we need no more.

Mer. Your President of Trade.

Car.   But we have Wealth itself,
And want no huckster to look after petty pelf.

Mer. Professor of Chicane.

Car.   Chicane ! That cannot be ;
We don't want trickiness, but simple honesty.

Mer. Director of the Roads.

Car.   No question can arise
Which way we ought to go since PLUTUS has his eyes.

Mer. Your Master of the Games. I have you there at
          least ;
'Tis just the thing for Wealth to hold a noble feast,
Where Poetry and Prowess, Wit and Strength shall vie
To win the Critic's ear, and please the manly eye.

Car. I did not think a lot of titles was so good !
'T has given him a shift to get a livelihood.
Thus prudent citizens, however it be done,
Contrive to get their names [2] on more court-lists than one.

Mer. On these terms I may stay ?

Car.   To show what you can do,
Go to the well and wash this tripe ; and quickly too.

                              [*Exit* MERCURY, *with the tripe.*

                    Enter PRIEST *of* JUPITER.

Priest. Where, tell me, may a word with CHREMYLUS be
          had ?

Chrem. (*entering*). What is it, worthy Sir ?

---

[1] Alluding to a figure of Mercury, in some form, set up near house-doors to act against thieves. All the suggestions of Mercury here have a reference to some character in which he was recognised as Tutelary Deity.

[2] The commentators are not clear or agreed how the thing was to be done. But the purpose is sufficiently obvious. The citizen would manage to have his name on more than one tribe-list in order at the ballot to double his chance of being called to serve in court, and thereby earn his three oboles.

Priest.   What is it else but bad?
For ever since this PLUTUS has recovered sight
I, Jove the Saver's priest, am famishing outright.
   Chrem. Gods! how is that?
   Priest.   There's no such thing as sacrifice:
There's no one thinks it worth his while to bring a slice!
   Chrem. How so?
   Priest.   Because they're rich: it was not so before
When they were poor.   Some merchant, got to shore
With cargo safe, would bring us something handsome in;
Or, one who, having been to law, had saved his skin;
Or, one at times would sacrifice and make a feast
To celebrate his birthday, and invite the Priest.
But now there is not one!   There's nothing of the kind!
And so, to say the truth, I'm very much inclined
To let the Saver Jove look to his interest,
And stay with you.
   Chrem.   No doubt, Sir, that will be the best:
The Saver Jove, assure yourself, is well content;
For he is here already.
   Priest.   That is excellent.
   Chrem. And we are on the point of forming a procession,
And putting—pray don't move—PLUTUS in repossession
Of his own proper shrine,[1] unoccupied of late,
The chapel where he keeps the monies of the State.
—Bring torches for the Priest—for you will lead no doubt.
   Priest. Unquestionably, Sir.
   Chrem.   And now call PLUTUS out.
            [*Procession is formed and moves off the stage.*
   Chorus.   Now all are past, and we are last;
               We have no business here.
               So with a song we'll join the throng,
               And follow in the rear.

---

[1] A small chamber behind the Parthenon was used as the Public
Treasury.   It appears that there was there an ancient painting of Plutus
'with eyes and winged.'

LONDON
PRINTED BY SPOTTISWOODE AND CO.
NEW-STREET SQUARE

www.ingramcontent.com/pod-product-compliance
Lightning Source LLC
Chambersburg PA
CBHW022011110726
47901CB00006B/1474